The Audacity of Sara Grayson

a novel

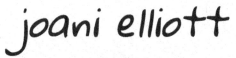

joani elliott

Post Hill PRESS

A POST HILL PRESS BOOK
ISBN: 978-1-63758-406-4
ISBN (eBook): 978-1-64293-783-1

The Audacity of Sara Grayson:
A Novel
© 2021 by Joani Elliott
All Rights Reserved
First Hardcover Edition: May 2021

Post Hill Press
New York • Nashville
posthillpress.com

Published in the United States of America
1 2 3 4 5 6 7 8 9 10

For Mark,

who read every word and always believed.

I could hear my abandoned dreams making a racket in my soul.

Joy Harjo

PART ONE

CHAPTER 1

*Writing is not life, but I think that
sometimes it can be a way back to life.*

STEPHEN KING

She refused to be triggered by breakfast food, so she went straight for the waffles. Real Belgian ones made of yeast dough—not batter. She'd eaten two of them already. Hot, bronzed waffles with Nutella and strawberries and vanilla bean ice cream. There were times to avoid your triggers and times to chew them up slowly and deliberately. Plus, eating was preferable to small talk, not that anyone would want to talk to her. They were here for Ellery, and Ellery was *everywhere*.

Life-size cutouts of Ellery and her family stood proudly next to Belgian flags and clusters of bright red poppies. Since Ellery's family was stationed at the embassy in Brussels, it was an obvious design choice but achingly unoriginal. Elegant black and gold streamers hung loosely across high ceilings. A Neuhaus Chocolatier table crowned the center of the room with pralines, truffles, and dark chocolate medallions stamped with Ellery's portrait. Taps of Belgian beer flowed into frosty mugs with Ellery quotations about gifts and potential and other ridiculous ideas.

It was a smashing tribute to someone who didn't actually exist.

Sara unwrapped an Ellery chocolate and quickly bit her head off. A clean snap is a sign of excellent chocolate, she'd read once. She let it melt slightly in her mouth before she chewed and swallowed. She unwrapped another medallion and bit the heads off several more, leaving a pile of unfinished chocolate torsos on her plate. For 300 bucks an hour, her therapist, Sybil Brown-Baker, might diagnose this as passive-aggressive behavior.

Or was it misplaced anger?

Sybil Brown-Baker sent a pamphlet home last week: "How We Transfer Feelings of Shame and Pain." Sara read it word-for-word and returned it the next day with her editing feedback, all free of charge: bad semi-colons, comma splices, and sentence fragments.

She didn't teach freshman English for nothing.

She just earned next to nothing.

For now.

Her freelance work with Cozy Greeting Cards International was poised to take off. They loved her work and thought she had a real knack for cancer cards, and could she please send more?

A jazz band performed painfully slow Michael Bublé covers while Sara opened another chocolate. Her older sister, Anna-Kath, waved at her from the waffle bar. She chatted happily with a screenwriter Sara had met earlier.

Was this their tenth movie premiere? Or eleventh? Their mom was nowhere to be seen. She was probably still talking to reporters.

At least they were done walking the red carpet, that veritable tripping hazard all lit up with flaming torches. Fans shouted their mother's name, "Cassandra Bond!" like they didn't get out much and shot their arms over crowd barriers with *Ellery Dawson* books for her to sign. Didn't they know they could save $3.99 on the e-book?

Her mother never seemed to mind. She wore Versace in red silk that night, her dark hair tucked loosely in an elegant chignon. Hardly the lonely author in sweatpants, Cassandra Bond looked like a movie star who decided to write a book.

Sara adjusted her strapless, gray formal gown. It was supposed to be emerald green, but they made a mistake when she picked it up and it was too late to change it. The shop ladies assured her that the gray dress held tones of shimmering pink and that she would look absolutely "breathtaking."

She didn't.

Sara delicately scratched the side of her up-do. She had the same dark brown hair as her mother's, but hers was pulled in a French twist of over-priced hair product that smelled like rich, earthy clay. Apparently smelling like coconut was out and smelling like dirt was in.

Someone named Veronica, with glossy lips and a fake facial mole, offered to take Sara's plate. The catering staff at Grauman's Chinese Theatre are passionate about taking people's plates. They also stop and study your face for a moment to determine if you're an interesting part of the film, which means, *Are you an actor?* Sara began making up random roles for herself. She'd raise her eyebrows and whisper, "Gang Boss" or "Python Wrangler" and nod her head knowingly.

Sara took a new plate and ate five more chocolates as she moved through the seafood tables. Her armpits itched from using a dull razor, and she could feel a cold sore stinging on the corner of her lip. She ate some shrimp. *Just be happy for Mom.* It would soon be over and she could sink into a hot bath and finish *Food Truck Wars*. She was wondering if the blackened catfish tacos would beat out the grilled mahi mahi curry when the back of a woman's hand suddenly slammed into Sara's red plastic plate. A shrimp tail shot up in the air and lodged itself down Sara's dress, pre-cisely between her breasts.

She straightened her back, feeling the chill of its exact location as her plate landed with a smack on the gleaming parquet floor. She smoothed her dress and strained to smile like nothing happened while Colin from catering picked up her scattered foil wrappers, chocolate, and shrimp. He piled it back on the plate and stood up to leave when he immediately froze in front of the tall, blonde woman standing next to Sara. Beads of sweat broke out on Colin's forehead as he absently handed the messy plate back to Sara. He had apparently left the planet, and she suddenly saw why.

Char Fox.

Top five of Hollywood's highest paid actors and star of the night's premiere: *Ellery Dawson*.

Sara thought Char looked better as a person than as a piece of chocolate. She wasn't sure that was true about herself. She would probably look better as chocolate. If she were ever made into chocolate. Which was highly unlikely.

Sara laughed it off in a nervous sort of sputter. Bits of cocktail sauce clung to her chest. She looked around for her napkin. Colin was standing on it.

Char pressed a hand to her heart. "I'm so sorry." She handed Sara her own napkin and pointed to the cast-off chocolate on Sara's plate. "I won't take that personally," she said, one eyebrow raised. Then she flashed her gorgeous smile while the piece of cold shrimp stuck between Sara's boobs moved down another quarter inch. Colin still hadn't moved, his mouth slightly agape, saliva beginning to pool in the corners.

Char leaned closer. "I have a dreadful habit of talking with my hands. I think I gave you quite a whack." Her Australian accent had that charming raspy quality that made her voice as famous as her looks. This wasn't the first superstar Sara had ever met, but her back began to sweat and her hands felt clammy.

Char took Sara's plate and handed it back to Colin with a pat on the shoulder. He abruptly gasped for air and stumbled back to the kitchen.

"Charlotte Fox." She reached out her hand. "Did you work with the film?"

Sara shook her hand limply. "Um no. I'm here for my mother, Cassandra Bond." She felt a sting in the corner of her lips. Was that cold sore coming alive?

"Oh my gosh! You're Cassandra's daughter?! She's brilliant. Absolutely brilliant. I read the first *Ellery* book three years ago and called my agent. I said, 'Hal, this is going to make an incredible movie, and I just have to play Ellery.'" She flicked both wrists up gracefully in the air. "And now, here we are."

"That's great. Super great. I'm sure it's a great movie." Did she just say *great* three times? She would have marked that on a student's paper.

Char linked her arm with Sara's, walking them over to a black settee. Sara's feet inexplicably went along. They sat next to a gigantic movie poster with Ellery posed in a dead run, gun-in-hand: *Dangerous Gifts and a World to Save*.

Sara noticed people gathering near both sides of the settee, hoping to get a chance to talk to the star. Char ignored them. She leaned into Sara's shoulder like they were already old friends. She had read that superstars could be very lonely despite all the fame.

"So, what's it like being the daughter of the most famous writer in the world? I mean you probably already know what happens in the final book, right?"

Sara laughed awkwardly, unsure if Char actually expected an answer. "Oh, hard to say, exactly." The shrimp's tail prickled against her skin.

Char reached for Sara's hand and looked at her with pleading eyes. "Just tell me, is my father dead or alive?"

Sara pulled her hand back. "Excuse me?"

"My father…Ellery's father. You know how Book Four ends, with that big explosion outside the Moscow hotel and all that chaos? I know it looks like he was in the blast, but it's so exasperatingly unclear. I can't wait until the final book comes out next year. Maybe you can just give me a teency hint?"

Sara shrugged her shoulders. "Sorry…I…don't really know."

And she didn't really care.

"Are you a writer too?"

Sara shrugged. Her cold sore was stinging, practically growing as they spoke. Her fingers reached for it gingerly.

Char nodded with empathetic eyes. "Cold sore?"

"Huh?"

"I get them all the time. Look, right here." She pointed to her own fading cold sore. "Almost gone." A bald man with an oversized ascot tapped Char's arm and whispered something to her. She waved him off. "I'll be there in a jiffy."

People like Char could get away with using words like jiffy or spiffy. Or teeny-weeny. When you look like that, you can say whatever-the-hell-weird words you want and people just think you're charming. Char opened her black clutch and fiddled with its contents. Sara couldn't help looking. She half-expected there to be a gun inside. Ellery would carry a gun. She was certain that if terrorists stormed the theatre, Char Fox would singlehandedly overpower them while Sara cowered in a bathroom stall texting poorly worded goodbyes. Would she text Mike? No. Of course not. Why would she think that?

She glimpsed a phone, lipstick, a hotel key card.

She felt mildly disappointed.

Char pulled out a tiny blue vial. "Here. My herbalist made this compound for me. It's an absolute gem for cold sores. One dab, three times a day. It'll be gone in a flash. Take this. I've got more at home."

"Um. Thank you." Of course Char Fox had an herbalist.

"Oh, and could you give this to your mum?" She handed Sara a small slip of paper. "My herbalist's number. We talked. I think he can help with her issues."

Sara held the paper. "Her *issues*?"

Char flicked another wrist. "Well you know, loss of appetite, the weight loss. I know she's been *struggling*." She whispered like it was their itty-bitty secret.

"Uh…right." Sara stared at the number with loopy threes and fours. "My mom's fine, really. But thanks for the concern. I should go find her, actually." Sara forced a smile. "Um, break a leg."

Char laughed as Sara walked away.

Did she really just tell Char Fox to break a leg? Does anyone even say that in film? Is that why Char laughed?

Sara walked as quickly as she could in her two-inch heels, her ankle turning only once as she passed the hot frites. She hurried past two busy restrooms to find her favorite one in a back-corner hallway.

She locked herself in a stall, wriggled, and then scrunched her shoulders to loosen the shrimp—which only sent it maddeningly below her breasts, wedging itself against the tight bodice of her dress. She heard the clicking of fast-moving heels.

"Sara, are you in there?" Anna-Kath whispered through the bathroom stall. "I see your feet. Let me in."

Sara huffed. "You didn't have to follow me. I'm fine."

Anna-Kath began laughing so hard she was practically wheezing. "I can't believe you just collided with Char Fox."

"It's not funny. And now I have a piece of shrimp stuck between my boobs."

"Your shrimp or Char's?"

"Does it matter?"

"It does on eBay." Anna-Kath laughed again. She never laughed this much. Sara found it unsettling. Maybe she downed too much Belgian beer?

"You're no help. You can just go back to that ridiculous waffle fest."

Anna-Kath leaned her head back against the stall and sighed. "Best waffles *ever*. You have no idea how good it feels to get a night out. I haven't thought about my kids for an entire hour."

Sara groaned. "Ann?"

"Yeah."

"My zipper's stuck. I can't get it."

"Open the door."

Anna-Kath squeezed in and managed to unzip the top of Sara's dress. "Breathe in." She breathed in. "Lean forward." She leaned forward. Anna-Kath unzipped another inch. "Now grab it."

Sara shimmied her shoulders one last time and pulled the shrimp out. "Yes!" She held it up like a trophy, tossed it in the toilet, and flushed.

"Now suck in." Anna-Kath worked the zipper back up.

Sara sighed with relief as they exited the stall. She studied her reflection as she washed her hands and squinted her eyes at the drab color of her dress. "The gray isn't so bad, right?

"I'm not sure if that actually counts as a color."

Sara rolled her eyes. "It's called 'tickled oyster.' If you step back and squint your eyes, you can see a subtle shimmery pink."

They stepped back, tilted their heads, and tried to see the pink shimmer.

"At least that's what they told me."

Anna-Kath shrugged her shoulders. "Never mind. The gray suits you."

"What's that supposed to mean?"

"Nothing." Anna-Kath smacked her lips and smoothed her blonde hair in the mirror. She handed her lipstick to Sara. "This will help."

Sara exhaled and sat on a red velvet stool, adjusting a few pins in her French twist. Anna-Kath sat down and leaned her head on Sara's shoulder. "You used to love Mum's premieres. The stars, the swag, the reception. What's the deal?"

"I don't know."

Ann smiled gently. Her tone turned softer as she squeezed Sara's arm. "It's time to come back to the living. Find some...ambition again."

Sara stiffened and turned away. "I have a life."

"Really? You teach, you grade papers, you binge-watch reality food shows. And if you were happy doing all that—then great. But you're not."

Sara lifted her chin and folded her arms. "Well then, you'll be happy to know I've accepted a new position."

Ann's eyebrows shot up. "What? You finally got senior lecturer?"

She lifted her chin. "I'm the newest staff writer for Cozy Greeting Cards International."

"Cozies? The ones at all the gas stations?"

"And Costcos."

Ann forced a smile. "Right."

"Hey, don't look at me like that. Cozy Greetings is full of profound, inspirational writing."

"Well…okay then."

Sara narrowed her eyes. "That's all you have to say?"

"Look, you already have a steady teaching job at a respected university. Isn't this kind of a step *back*?"

"Oh, so now my job *is* good enough?"

"I've never questioned the value of your work, only that you lack any enthusiasm for it."

Sara huffed in frustration and mimicked Ann, "'Try something new, Sara. Make a new life for yourself.'" She threw her hands in the air. "That's what I'm trying to do. And I'll keep teaching…until this takes off."

Ann's eyes softened. "Sure. Okay. If that's what you're feeling—"

"It's what I'm *feeling*, okay?" she snapped a little too sharply. She tried to ignore the flash of hurt in Ann's eyes. She twisted her bracelet around. "Sorry."

They both sat quietly for a minute, then Ann handed Sara her compact. "Here, borrow my blush."

ॐ

Sara took her seat next to her mother just before the film started. Cassandra smiled gently at her. Her eyes were still radiant, but her cheeks did look a little hollow.

"You okay, Mum?"

"Just a little tired, love. That's all." Sara leaned her head on her mother's shoulder, feeling herself instantly relax. Cassandra, seated between her two daughters, reached for both of their hands. Sara inhaled deeply, smelling light traces of Evening Rose, her mother's fragrance.

Opulent, red curtains revealed the screen precisely at 8:00 PM, and the director invited Cassandra to join the lead actors and producers onstage for an introduction to the film.

"Does Mum look pale to you?" Ann whispered.

Sara thought about Char's herbalist. "She's probably just tired—all those interviews this week."

She never saw her collapse. She was fumbling through her purse looking for Mentos when the audience gasped, and murmurs of concern rumbled through the theatre. Anna-Kath shot out of her seat, and Sara looked up to see her mother lying on the stage, her head cradled in Char's arm and other cast and crew members surrounding her. Ann stumbled past Sara, practically running to the stage while Sara stood motionless. Her mother's agent, Elaine Chang, grabbed Sara by the arm and rushed her to the stage. Ann was next to their mother now, talking to her, patting her face, trying to help her regain consciousness.

Ann looked at Sara. "It's okay. She's breathing. I think she just passed out."

Cassandra's eyes opened weakly, but she lost consciousness again. Sara knelt down and reached for her hand, her own heart racing.

"It's okay, Mum," said Anna-Kath. "We're right here."

Later at Cedars-Sinai Medical Center, computers monitored Cassandra's heart and oxygen while she received fluids through an IV. Her face was white and her lips a bluish-gray against her red Versace gown.

A daughter sat on each side of her while a nurse with teased '80s bangs adjusted her oxygen.

Cassandra spoke weakly, "When's the doctor coming back?"

"Dr. Ahmed is trying to reach your oncologist. She'll be back soon." The nurse whisked the curtain closed and left.

The air turned thick and suffocating. Anna-Kath looked at Cassandra, her eyes wide with shock. "Mum, your *oncologist*? What's going on?"

Cassandra closed her eyes a moment. She slowly exhaled.

She reached for Ann's hand on one side and Sara's on the other. She squeezed their palms like she had so many times before, trying to infuse them with strength. They had sat like this in their London flat the night their father died. Mum had reached for their little hands around their small Formica table.

And just like that desperate night, twenty-four years ago, she looked at them both and said, "We are going to get through this." It's what Grayson girls did.

Ann reached across the bed for Sara's hand and gripped it firmly. "Get through *what*, Mum?"

Cassandra looked up at the ceiling as she spoke. "I have pancreatic cancer. Stage IV." Her eyes filled with tears. "It's not good."

The words hung heavy in the room. Did her mother say anything else after that? Sara couldn't quite remember. Her vision turned dark and hollow, her brain pulsing loudly against her skull. Medical personnel moved around like actors in a crackly, black-and-white film, sound fading in and out. Something about severe dehydration and returning home to Maryland in a few days.

Sara took her mother's dress back to the hotel with her after Cassandra was admitted into a dreary hospital room for the night.

Sara woke up the next morning to a sliver of LA sunlight peeking through the heavy drapes. Sara sighed in relief. It must have been just a terrible dream. Then she saw her mother's red Versace draped over the armchair and smelled traces of her rose fragrance. She pulled a pillow close to her face and sobbed.

Cassandra died twelve weeks later. It was April, just after the cherry blossoms.

CHAPTER 2

We die. That may be the meaning of life.
But we do language. That may be the measure of our lives.

TONI MORRISON

New York Times: "Beloved Author, Cassandra Bond, Dead at 62"

"Cassandra Bond, whose adrenaline-packed suspense novels sparked a new genre of feminist thrillers, died Wednesday morning at her home in Bethesda, Maryland after a brief fight with pancreatic cancer, reported Thea Marshall, Bond's long-time publicist.

"Ms. Bond's journey as an author began with a tragedy. Left a widow with two young daughters after the untimely death of her husband Jack Grayson, a British educator, Ms. Bond, a former ER nurse, began writing as a way of dealing with the loss. In a 2017 interview with *The Times* she admitted that 'Jack is the one who wanted to be a writer—not me. I loved my career as a nurse and had no intention of ever becoming an author.' According to daughter Anna-Katherine Green: 'Two years after Dad passed away, Mum decided to try her hand at writing and was surprised to find she was actually pretty good at it.'

"What started as a therapeutic exercise turned into one of the most successful literary careers of all-time, with more than 300 million books sold worldwide. Ms. Bond's most recent novel, *Worlds Collide*, is the fourth book in the *Ellery Dawson* series. It sold 15 million copies in the first month and still occupies the number one spot on both the *NYT* and *USA Today* bestseller lists for a record-setting twenty-one weeks. The recent film, *Big Small World,* based on *Ellery Dawson* Book One, earned $450 million at the box office in its opening weekend.

"In all, Ms. Bond wrote eighteen novels, fifteen of which were best sellers. Ten of her novels became blockbuster films. Ms. Bond is survived by her two daughters, Anna-Katherine Grayson Green, Sara Grayson, and two grandchildren."

Washington Post Critic, Steve Krogan
"No one blended the art of the thriller with the art of characterization better than Bond. The literary world has lost a true artist."

Tweet from Karen Siegler, 11th grader at Jordan High School, Sandy, Utah
"I'd never read an entire book until my teacher gave me the first *Ellery Dawson.* I've read every book Bond ever wrote now. I'm not a brave person, but when I read her books I feel brave."

NBC Nightly News
"Makeshift memorials for beloved author Cassandra Bond continue to grow outside Old Spitalfields Market in East London and at Belvedere Castle in Central Park. Both settings feature prominently in Bond's books. Candles, flowers, and donations of books to Cassandra's libraries continue to fill both spaces as mourners grieve the loss of a literary icon."

YouTube Channel *The Riveter*: "Rosie's Reviews"
"Look, everybody knows that Ellery Dawson is the world's greatest female badass and we all know it takes one to create one. So, here's to you, Cassandra Bond. Hoping I can be as strong as you one day." Rose Wade

The Literary Bind
"Someone make it stop! If I see another story about the amazing Cassandra Bond, I'm going to vomit. Give me a break! She's a filthy rich author only famous because of some talented filmmakers. The films sold her books, not her writing."

CNN
"Beloved author Cassandra Bond was laid to rest Sunday at Parklawn Memorial Cemetery in Bethesda, Maryland, after a private service at St. John's Episcopal Church."

Statement from the Bond Family
"On behalf of our entire family, we want to thank you for the outpouring of love for our mother and grandmother. As a family, we celebrate her humanity. Our mum was one of the most generous, loving, and wise women we will ever know. Our lives will never be the same."

LA Times
"Rampant speculation has emerged regarding the much-anticipated conclusion to the *Ellery Dawson* series, Book Five. One source close to the family reports the book is complete yet another source close to her publisher states the manuscript was never finished. Bond's longtime publisher, Iris Books, was unavailable for comment."

✿

MAY

Three weeks after her mother's death, Sara went back to work because she didn't know what else to do. This was step three in Sybil Brown-Baker's master plan called "Finding a New Normal." The flip-flops were not part of that plan. The heel of her shoe broke when it caught between some loose paving stones on the walk to her office. She hobbled back to her car, popped her trunk, and found the neon pink flip-flops in a bag she'd been meaning to give to Goodwill for the past nine months.

Sara tried to ignore the perpetual stomachache she felt since her mother died. She took a deep breath. "New normal."

It was sunny and warm, and students at the University of Maryland were eating, sleeping, or cramming for finals on the beautiful green expanse of the McKeldin Mall.

Sara walked to her office in her navy ankle pants and fitted collar shirt—and pink flip-flops. Maybe she didn't look that bad. Maybe she just looked *artsy*. Like a *free spirit*. For a few minutes she tried to pretend that she was.

It didn't work.

She would never be cool enough to be a free spirit. Sara's straight brown hair was tied back in a neat ponytail. It was all she managed lately, a style that only varied in height.

The flip-flops were unusually noisy. Kind of a flop, then a squish.

"New normal."

Sara was in the faculty kitchen making a cup of tea when Binti walked in.

She hugged Sara. "Welcome back! How are you?"

"I'm here." She shrugged her shoulders, pulling her black cardigan tightly around her. The building was aggressively over-air-conditioned. Sara would need her winter coat by next week.

"Did you get the flowers we left on your desk?"

"I love Gerbera daisies. Thank you." Binti smiled. She tucked a lock of her curly brown hair behind her ear and then poured coffee into her UNC mug. "I can't believe you decided to come back during finals week," she said. "You know your classes are covered. Plus you'll catch a tension headache just walking down the hall."

Sara opened her box of tea. "I need to start planning next semester."

"You hate planning."

"I know." Sara slowly dipped her tea bag up and down in the hot water. She wasn't ready to be back at work, but she didn't want to be at home either. She tried to ignore the incessant smell of reheated spaghetti and stale coffee that plagued the faculty kitchen. An overzealous department secretary named Stephie Frinhauser religiously posted refrigerator signs to warn all faculty that "FOOD WILL BE DISCARDED EVERY FRIDAY, NO EXCEPTIONS" and that "YOUR MOMMA DOES NOT LIVE HERE."

Binti leaned back against the kitchen counter and looked at Sara with concern. "How are you holding up? Really."

Sara shrugged her shoulders, and then she added a bit of sugar to her tea. It was still hard to talk about. Binti seemed to sense her hesitation and changed the subject, chatting about her new "Literature as Film" course. It felt strange, attempting to make normal conversation at work when her own universe felt so altered.

They walked to the faculty workroom so Binti could make copies for her next final exam.

"Hey, nice shoes." She pointed to Sara's flip-flops as they walked. "Kind of beachwear meets ivory tower. I like it."

Sara shook her head. "Don't ask."

Binti prattled on about the latest department news while they passed sleep-deprived students reviewing notes and textbooks with tired eyes.

In the workroom there were new signs from Stephie indicating additional copier and mailbox rules and another that said, "ONLY USE CHAIRS FOR THEIR INTENDED PURPOSE." Binti slapped the sign. "What kind of animals work here? I don't think these signs are doing enough." She grabbed a Sharpie and made new signs: "PLEASE DON'T LICK THE WALLS" and "WARNING: SHARP EDGES. DO NOT EAT THIS SIGN." She plastered them to the wall with Scotch tape. Sara laughed and Binti seemed pleased with her civil disobedience. College campuses were such a hot bed of controversy.

Sara walked to her box and pulled out a stack of department mail, flyers, and newsletters from the past several weeks. She began sorting through her stack between sips of Earl Grey.

"Good news," Binti said, taking a seat across from Sara. "I pulled some strings and I got you a place on the new visual rhetoric committee. This will look great when you apply for senior lecturer next year."

"I don't know if I'll apply again."

"Of course, you will."

"Visual rhetoric isn't exactly my thing."

"And what *is* your *thing*?"

"Why does everyone have to have a *thing*? Maybe some people don't have *a thing*," Sara snapped. She sounded more emotional than she intended.

Binti looked earnest. "Well, maybe Cozy Greeting Cards will be your thing."

Sara pinched the space between her eyebrows. "They rejected my last three projects."

"What?"

"When I couldn't do cancer cards anymore because of…well, you know…then they put me on their anniversary line, but they said my tone wasn't right."

Binti almost choked on her coffee. "Your tone?"

"My manager called it 'despondent snark.'"

Binti pressed her lips tightly together. Clearly, she was trying not to laugh. "I would pay money for those cards."

Sara sighed. "I think they feel sorry for me. They transferred me over to their sister company, Cutie Coupon. Apparently, it's the hottest online coupon site in the world."

"Well, that's *something*."

"Yeah—you'll have to check out my *superb* writing on women's fresh-water pearl necklaces. 'Selling fast at only $39.99.'"

"Look, you'll find the words. In the meantime, just know that you have options. The committee meets tomorrow at Bus Boys and Poets to talk over course content. So, if you want in, come join us."

"I'll think about it."

"Honestly, I'm just glad you're here. I wondered if you would even come back."

"Why wouldn't I come back?"

"Well, you know…"

"Well, what?"

"Well…it's not like you need the money now. Your mom's estate? I mean, I assume, you wouldn't have to work anymore…like ever…if that's what you wanted. I mean you could do anything now, right?"

"My mom never stopped working. Why would I?"

"Sure. Never mind. Forget I said it." Binti walked to the copier and ripped open a new ream of paper.

Sara pulled her laptop out of her bag and tapped her fingers on the table as it started up. "My sister and I are meeting with my mom's attorney right after work today. He said it's about my mom's book. Probably just papers to sign."

"Book Five?"

"I think so."

"*The New Yorker* says they should have a contest to see who gets to write it." Binti added the paper and smacked the tray closed. "Writers would have sixty pages to convince the publisher *they are it*."

"It's already written." Sara typed in her passcode and sipped more tea.

"Really? You've read it?"

"No, but my mother is the most thorough person in the world. There's no way she left it unwritten." The question of Book Five came up when Cassandra was sick. She reassured Sara and Anna-Kath that the book was "already taken care of." It made sense. Cassandra Bond was always ahead of schedule.

Binti leaned back against the copier as it began to print. "It really is impressive—your mom, I mean. Finishing the book, even with the cancer and everything."

Sara blinked away some tears. Binti turned back to the copier, and Sara opened her email. She sighed. Four hundred and two unread emails.

The copier abruptly stopped. Binti pulled the paper tray open and slammed it closed again. "Damn machine."

Sara pointed to the sign that read: "PLEASE DO NOT CURSE OR HIT THE COPIER MACHINES." Binti whacked the machine again. It started working. She looked incredibly satisfied.

Sara closed her laptop. "Take my mind off things. Tell me more about your Lit as Film class."

"Sure! Although, half the final papers happen to be about *Ellery Dawson*'s transition to film." She held up a newly copied exam. "I even have an essay question about it on the test."

Sara covered her face with her hands and groaned.

"Sorry, Sara!" Binti crumpled the paper up and shot it towards the garbage. She missed. It landed next to a sign about cleanliness and cooperation. "Forget about *Ellery Dawson*! Want to hit and curse some copy machines?"

Sara ate four Tums and headed to her office.

❧

Later that afternoon, Sara stopped at the cemetery on the way to the attorney's and placed the vase of Gerbera daisies on her mother's grave. She visited every day. Her grave still looked fresh with specks of dry grass. She reached down to touch the soil, still moist from last night's rain, but warm from the sun. She breathed deeply, seeking a closeness to her mother, longing to feel her near.

As Sara arranged the daisies on her mother's grave, her phone rang. Anna-Kath, out of breath, explained that her daughter Livvy was sick at school. She was leaving to pick her up now and couldn't make the meeting.

"I'm so sorry to do this to you. Maybe we should reschedule." Anna-Kath would still hold Sara's hand in parking lots if she allowed her.

"I can handle this. I'm sure it's more of the usual. Just take care of Livvy, and I'll fill you in." Sara gently patted the damp earth on her mother's grave and walked back to her car.

CHAPTER 3

Writing is like getting married. One should never
commit oneself until one is amazed at one's luck.

IRIS MURDOCH

The law offices of Allman, Peters, and Jenkins filled an entire brown-stone building in downtown Bethesda. The offices, which smelled like cinnamon and eucalyptus, were so overtly elegant, it made Sara want to sit up straight and use good grammar. The mahogany floors were extra shiny when Sara walked in, and she recognized the familiar loop of classical baroque they always played in the lobby.

She hated the place.

McNeil Gallagher, an attorney at the firm, handled Sara's divorce last year. People with two last names were generally smarter than everyone else, and McNeil, who wore wide neckties and tinted his facial hair, did not disappoint. Still, her divorce experience left her hollowed out—not because the divorce was messy, but primarily because it wasn't. Mike was overseas and approached the dissolution of their marriage with a sickening sort of apathy that seemed to hurt more than if he'd fought her with tenacity. The only thing Mike fought for was their dog, Gatsby.

Six years of marriage and Mike only wanted the dog.

McNeil Gallagher made sure that did not happen.

David Allman, Sr., had been a founding partner at the firm and had been Cassandra Bond's attorney, friend, and advisor ever since Cassandra moved across the street from his family twenty years ago. His wife, Sharon, brought over freshly baked apple cake, and since Cassandra needed both apple cake and a good attorney, a friendship was born. Their son, David Jr., took over his father's accounts, including Cassandra Bond's, after David Sr. died one year ago.

Sara and Anna-Kath reviewed most of the will a week after their mother's death. There was nothing particularly surprising. Cassandra, who grew up in a working-class family in Philadelphia, had been profoundly generous to several charitable organizations with multiple trusts designed to fund what Cassandra cared most about, including girls' access to education and micro-loan programs for women. Anna-Kath and Sara shared equally in the remainder of their mother's fortune, including a 50-50 split in future book sales.

Sara waited for David Jr. in his office. At thirteen, she'd moved into his neighborhood just in time to receive a pity invitation to his younger brother's bar mitzvah, which David hand-delivered and shoved into her hand without making eye contact. David was Anna-Kath's age, and the two had gone to senior prom together, although Ann swore she never kissed him.

Sara had.

It was an unfortunate New Year's Eve party in college, and they were both standing next to each other at midnight, and it just sort of happened. The awkward kiss was followed by a stumbling half-hug/pat-on-the-back recovery. Then they went to find their coats—separately.

David had a picture of his current girlfriend, a Canadian named Mia Something-or-Other on his desk. The two of them were riding bikes around some large lake, presumably in Canada. David had been skinny and allergic to exercise for most of his life, but one should never underestimate the power of an exotic Canadian woman.

"Sorry to keep you waiting," David rushed in. He really did look healthier. He still wore his hair too short and his glasses were never sized quite right, but he'd filled out rather nicely in the chest and arms.

David looked around his office. "Where's Anna-Kath?"

"Livvy's sick. I'll fill her in."

"Maybe we should reschedule."

"Come on, David. It's fine. Let's move this along."

"Are you sure?"

"Please."

"Well...okay. Let me just find the right file." He sat down at his desk and opened a drawer. While David flipped through a stack of folders he casually asked, "Do you know much about a Meredith Lamb? She lives in the UK."

"Hmm. Not really." Sara studied another desk photo. David and Mia were sporting oversized backpacks. Mia looked radiant; David looked uncomfortable. Apparently, she was from *Vancouver*, which is so far west, it's practically outside of Canada, or at least like a second cousin once removed.

David found the file he was looking for and placed it in front of him. "Your mother left a small trust for Meredith Lamb and a dependent. Well, actually the trust was established some years ago by my father, entirely separate from your mother's last will. The dependent is an adult now, and the trust included a college fund. Did she mention this to you or Anna-Kath?"

"Doesn't ring a bell, but Mom was very generous."

"No doubt. Maybe she's a relative?"

"My father's parents are dead and buried in England. He has a sister there. Never heard of Meredith Lamb."

"Hmm. Okay." David kept flipping pages in the same file. Sara wondered what he was getting at. She already knew the estate was more like a labyrinth and that the initial review of the will two weeks ago only covered the most pertinent aspects of the estate. In fact, it took a web of legal counsel, including multiple law firms, to support the complicated aspects of Cassandra Bond's small empire.

"I thought we needed to talk about the book. Your secretary made it sound like we couldn't do this over the phone. Is this about Mom's literary trustee?"

He cleared his throat and shuffled his papers. "Well, yes, this is about her work, and it's better face-to-face. I just thought Anna-Kath was coming too."

"I'm a thirty-two-year-old woman, David. I don't need my big sister holding my hand."

"Of course." He took several nervous drinks from a lime green water bottle with a built-in filter. He stretched his neck to one side and then pulled at the collar of his crisp blue shirt. "Yes, well, I'll get to the point." He cleared his throat *again* and wiped his palms on his thighs.

"Spit it out, David. Did my mom fund a trust in Zambia? If it's the girls' school, it's totally legit. Mom researches everything." Sara still slipped from past to present tense when she talked about her mom. That familiar ache pressed against her stomach.

David put his glasses on and took them off again, rubbing the bridge of his nose. "No, this isn't about Zambia." He placed both hands on the desk and took a long, deep breath that felt kind of weird to observe, like maybe Sara was interrupting something and should come back later. He must have learned that in hot yoga with Mia. He showed up really sweaty at Cassandra's after class once. You have to wonder about an attorney who has time for hot yoga.

David was waiting for her now. "Sara, are you with me?"

"Yeah. Sorry! I'm here." She re-tied her ponytail and smoothed it out. She swore she was developing ADD lately. She returned David's attention, willing herself to focus, to make eye contact. Were David's glasses too big or was his face too small?

"So, about Book Five…" David stopped fiddling with his glasses. He clasped his hands together, swallowed hard, and fixed his gaze firmly on Sara.

"Your mom wants you to write Book Five."

Sara laughed.

David didn't.

Sara laughed again. More like a confused sputter.

Then with a quick gasp, the whole amusing absurdity of the joke settled in and Sara laughed fully and deeply. This was actually a very funny joke.

"Aww, David. You know the Graysons too well. You did get my attention, though, with the hands-clasped-together and that scary attorney look—like I'm going to find out my mother is broke."

David laughed nervously. "No, your mother isn't broke. But yes…she did choose you to write the book."

That's when Sara noticed David's sweaty brow and how he wasn't wiping it. Two beads of sweat hung there, practically defying gravity, and David didn't budge.

Sara's stomach dropped to her toes, and disbelief washed over her entire body. "David, you can't be serious. The book's already written. It has to be. Mom's a finisher, a closer. I heard Anna-Kath ask her about *Ellery Dawson*. Mom said it was taken care of. I heard it myself."

David wiped his forehead with the back of his hand and adjusted his glasses. "She was behind on the book. She was working on the outline last year. She was hoping for more time."

Sara's body froze, her eyes wide. Her heart pounded so loudly she could hardly think.

David leaned forward, resting his arms in front of him. "It's her dying wish. She asked me to wait three weeks after her death to tell you. There's a letter for you." He opened a file in front of him and handed Sara a letter on yellow stationery, dotted with white daisies, all sunshiny and bright, like it should contain a birthday greeting instead of some horrifying last wish. Sara's hand shook as she read her mother's words:

> *My Dearest Sara,*
>
> *Audacity. Four fabulous syllables. Remember this was on our favorite words list? A word with superb meaning and long overlooked as a girl's name. So, David has told you the news. Yes, the book is yours. This audacious request is my gift to you. I know what we talked about, but you were meant to tell stories too. You have words, my dear. Write them.*
>
> *Mum*

Sara pulled out her ponytail, threw her head back against the leather office chair, and pressed her hands against her forehead.

The audacity.

The *audacity.*

Sara wasn't exactly a model of emotional stability before she walked into this office. Now her brain felt like it was swelling out of her skull, and the grief clamped around her heart bubbled out of her chest with a rising fury. She shot out of her seat.

"What the hell could she be thinking?!" Sara walked to the window and turned around. She pointed her finger at him. "This is impossible. First of all, there's no way Mom's publisher would ever allow this ridiculous dying wish to go forward. Second, she must have been on drugs when she decided this. She was on heavy pain meds, David. She was drugged, and she was crazy."

"Your mom had an authorship rider on her contract with Iris Books. In the event of your mother's untimely death, the rider stipulated that she had the right to choose the author to finish her series and that she would indicate her choice in her last will and testament, which she did, dated six months ago on November 15th. She was of sound mind."

"My mother made this choice in November? *November*? She wasn't even sick in November!" Sara was shouting now, her face flushed and hot.

David rubbed the back of his neck and discreetly swallowed a few pills.

Sara gasped in understanding. She slumped back against the window, the letter clenched in her hand. "Oh my gosh. *She was sick. Even then.* How long did she know she had cancer, David?"

"I didn't know she was sick then. She's had the rider for years, but she never specified an author until last November. The publisher is legally bound to work with you. They're eagerly awaiting to hear Cassandra's choice of author, and they are understandably *anxious*."

"Oh, you think?" Sara sat back in her chair. Her breathing was short and rapid, and she began to feel lightheaded. This could not be happening. "Mom must have specified an alternate author, besides me, right? I mean she wouldn't pin the future of the *Ellery Dawson* empire entirely on me, right?"

David shook his head, avoiding eye contact. "It's only you." He chewed on his bottom lip, searching for something comforting to say. "I'm sorry. This is obviously overwhelming."

"Overwhelming? My mother sold *15 million* copies of Book Four. Those fifteen million people are waiting for Book Five. They cannot be waiting *for me*." Her voice had turned shaky and high-pitched. She hardly recognized it. She covered her wet face in her hands again.

David walked around the front of his desk and handed Sara a box of tissues in a solid walnut holder with the firm's monogrammed initials. Sara stared at the box with an inordinate amount of disgust. No wonder people hated attorneys. She started pulling tissues out by the fistful in crazed quick movements. She wiped her face. Blew her nose. She pulled out more tissues and stuffed them in her bag. She huffed and stood up.

"Thank you, David. I've got to get back to work now." She folded her mother's letter in half. And then again. And again. And one more time until it resembled a stick of Juicy Fruit gum. She slipped it inside her leather work bag with a pile of tissues.

"Wait," said David. "We have a lot to talk about, and I'm sure you have more questions. Can I get you something to drink?"

"I have to go." She attempted to hold her chin high, to feign confidence. Sara reached past David to gather another fistful of Kleenexes. She finally opened the walnut tissue holder and removed the entire tissue box, placing it securely under her arm like a clutch. "I'll just be going now." She smoothed out her shirt and marched towards the door. Her flip-flops made a squishing sound as she stomped away.

"Look, I know it's a shock. There will be many details to work out, but you have a great deal of support."

"Shock. Yes. Support." It was getting hard to form complete sentences. Sara turned back to face David. The lightheaded feeling was back. "Right then. Or rightio. Isn't that what they say in Dad's country?"

"I don't know."

"That was rhetorical, David." Sara turned to leave.

"Wait. Take this file with you. It's about key stakeholders in the series. Let's talk in the morning, okay? I know this needs to settle in, but there are some things we've got to address. The publisher has been on my back since the funeral, and I have messages from your mother's LA firm regarding her contract with Sony Pictures. Your mom's agent also called and…"

Sara couldn't hear anything else. She felt like she was viewing the world from inside a swimming pool. Everything was blurry and hard to hear. She just needed to get out. Find a place to think.

She found her car and quickly pulled out of the parking garage. She needed to see Anna-Kath. To tell her the horrible thing. She passed the cemetery on her way. Sara hit her brakes and pulled a U-turn. The wheels screeched as she turned hard and fast. She pulled up close to her mother's grave and marched over. Sara snatched the daisies right out of the vase she'd left just an hour ago and stomped back to her car. An onlooker nearby raised her eyebrows in disgust.

Sara looked right at her. "You have no idea," she said and drove away.

CHAPTER 4

*A writer is someone for whom writing is more
difficult than it is for other people.*

THOMAS MANN

Sara arrived at Anna-Kath's home in Potomac fifteen minutes later. She hadn't been this furious since Mike emptied the checking account and left the note about leaving her in order to *Eat, Pray, Love*. He took only one suitcase of clothes and his Waring Pro Double Waffle Maker. She rang the doorbell impatiently until Anna-Kath finally opened the door.

Sara shoved the wet daisies at Ann and marched right past her into the front room without uttering a word. She looked at her mother's dog, Miss Marple, who slept peacefully next to an awful black-and-white fur ottoman Anna-Kath added last week. Interior designers were willing to take greater decorating risks than the general population and it wasn't always a good thing. She circled around and marched right back to Ann, who stood in the same spot holding the flowers, her eyebrows raised in a questioning look.

"Sara, what's going—"

"Did you already know?"

"What?"

Sara exhaled loudly. She snatched the flowers back and headed straight to Ann's backyard.

She dropped the flowers and her bag on the patio table and grabbed the tether ball. She raised her hand high and spiked the ball hard. It narrowly missed her own head as it looped back towards her. She fell on the grass, the ball and tether whipping around the pole.

She heard the sliding glass door open. "Gerald has a punching bag downstairs." Ann sat on a patio chair. Miss Marple came out, too, and sniffed along the fence line.

Sara looked hard at Ann, her lips tight, her eyes narrowed. She said nothing and smacked the ball again and again until she was winded and sweaty.

"You know," said Ann, "anger is one of the stages of grief. It's okay to feel this way." She used her milk of magnesia voice. It was smooth and instantly comforting—if you could stand the taste.

Sara angrily brushed grass off her pants. She walked over to Ann. "Mum really didn't tell you?"

Ann lifted both hands up and shrugged her shoulders. "I honestly don't know what you're talking about."

Sara yanked off her flip-flops and threw them hard across the yard. They only went about five feet, but they startled Miss Marple, who whined a bit and hopped onto Ann's lap for support.

She pointed her finger at the dog. "I bet you knew about this too." Miss Marple looked up at Sara, her eyes full of a sweetness. "Yeah. You *would* take her side."

Sara grabbed her bag and walked back into the house where she sunk into the living room couch, pressing her face against her hands.

Ann followed her and sat down on that awful fur ottoman across from her. Sara felt itchy every time she looked at it.

"Okay. So, what happened with David?" Ann exhaled quickly. "I knew I should have come."

Sara took a deep breath. Her lips and chin quivered. She leaned back against the couch and hugged a pillow to her chest. "Mum wants me to write the book."

"What book?"

Sara looked up at the ceiling, then back at Ann. Her eyes filled with tears. "Mum's. Last. Book." Her chest ached with each uttered syllable.

Ann's eyes grew big. "*Ellery Dawson?*"

Sara groaned and dug her fingers into her own scalp.

"But Mum already wrote it. We asked her. She said it was taken care of."

"Well, she lied. Yeah…turns out Mum's a liar."

"Right. Our Mum?"

"Maybe."

"So, this was all part of her master plan: Birth you, establish trust for thirty-two years, and then *zing*! She gets you at the end?"

Sara sniffed a little. "Maybe."

"Do you know how ridiculous that sounds?"

"Do you know how ridiculous it is for me to write this book?"

"You're a writer!"

"Ann, I write jewelry descriptions for Cutie Coupon."

"But you teach writing—"

"I teach hungover freshmen how to find the periodicals."

"What about your greeting cards?"

"They were chemotherapy humor cards. And I only published fifteen, so do not attempt to make this sound logical."

Ann pressed her hand against her forehead. "I'm making tea." She walked away.

Tea.

Sara sunk back into the sofa, wishing it could swallow her whole. Hot tears flowed against her will, turning muddy with her mascara. She reached for her bag and pulled out more tissues.

Of course, Anna-Kath would make tea. It's exactly what their mother would have done. She wasn't sure if she wanted to throw something or just sit and sob.

When Sara would come home from a terrible day, her mom would hug her tightly, give her a tissue and say, "I'm making tea." Lavender Earl Grey was an afternoon staple. Peppermint tea for a pick-me-up, chamomile to help them sleep, and Cassandra's own happiness blend: St. John's wort and passion flower.

The night their father died, Cassandra made them tea. They were living in their little flat in London's East End. Sara was seven, and Ann was ten. They had just returned from the hospital, and there would be no reason to go back. Cassandra wiped her tears with a dish cloth while she mixed her sadness tea, a blend of green tea and orange peel that tasted like loss even today.

Sara took some deep breaths and gathered her pile of used tissues. She slung her heavy work bag over her shoulder and followed Anna-Kath into her kitchen. She stopped. She looked back at that furry ottoman. It was like a black and white cow—if cows had long shaggy fur and skinny gold legs. Which they do not. Because nature is smarter than that.

She picked it up and moved it to a corner behind the couch. She took a throw from the loveseat and covered the whole thing up.

Much better.

She walked into the kitchen. Ann stood at the counter opening canisters of tea. "Why do you lug that bag everywhere you go?"

"It has what I need, okay?"

Sara began dumping her tissues into Ann's magic trash can that opened automatically with a wave of the hand. "Much more sanitary," Ann said proudly when her husband, Gerald T. Green, brought it home "just because" one afternoon. He was an economist at NASDQ, one of seven people in the known world who actually knew what that stood for. He wore sweater vests and bought Livvy and Jude smart toys like "Inventing with Electronics" and "Hydraulic Robot Kits." The kids were six and seven and considerably smarter than Sara, but they loved her anyway.

Sara went to the sink and splashed cool water on her face. She blotted her face dry with a paper towel and tried to wipe away some of her smeared mascara.

Ann handed her two ibuprofen and a cup of water. She looked at her with gentle eyes. "I'm sorry I wasn't there. I thought it would be more routine stuff with David. Did anything else come up?"

"David asked about some woman named Meredith Lamb. I guess Mum left a trust for her and a college fund for a dependent. Do you know her?"

"Hmm. Sounds vaguely familiar," she said, turning back to making tea, "but I can't place her."

Anna-Kath had their mother's gift for mixing her own tea blends, and it was comforting to watch her mix fragrant dried leaves and roots together in a wooden bowl. Anna-Kath took the kettle off the stove and pulled two cups and saucers out of a glass cabinet.

Sara's breathing slowed while she watched Ann gently scoop her tea blend into the infusers, pouring hot water from the kettle into each cup. "So…Mum really didn't tell you anything?"

"I promise. I thought the book was done too." She finished the tea and brought a plate of shortbread squares to the table with cream and sugar. She handed Sara a cup of tea and sat down with her own.

Sara inhaled the scent of vanilla and peach. Her heart rate finally slowed, but her chest still ached like something heavy was lodged inside. She swirled in some milk and brown sugar, the way her father liked it, and sipped it slowly. She wished this could be a simple afternoon tea where they talked about movies or good books or funny things the kids said.

"Ann, I just don't know what Mum was thinking. I mean, I'm still trying to deal with her death and my own weird, divorced life, and now she throws me into this nightmare."

Ann sighed. "I don't know either. I mean, this series was, like, her ultimate *baby*. She loved it more than any other."

"Mum loved all her books."

Ann shook her head. "No. This was her favorite. Hands down. You know that."

Sara was quiet a moment. "I didn't know that."

"Mum spent more time, more energy, more tears on this one. It's her very best work. And that's not just my opinion." Ann paused. "What... don't you agree?"

Sara took a breath and sipped more tea. "I mean, yeah. I just didn't realize Mum felt that way."

Anna-Kath took a bite of shortbread. "This wouldn't be your first novel."

"Oh *right!*" Sara's voice turned acrid with sarcasm. "My unpublished book that the great Phil Dvornik basically disemboweled."

"It's called criticism, Sara."

"Yeah—I go to my mum's editor for some feedback and I get ten pages—single spaced—of how much he hates my book. I never could find a publisher."

"Your whole life you dreamed of becoming a novelist, and then you didn't even try to get it published. You gave up after Phil's criticism."

"Thanks, Ann. Go right for the heart."

Anna-Kath set down her cup and folded her arms. "Harper Lee said that everyone has at least one book inside of them."

"That doesn't mean they should write it. And by the way, Harper Lee didn't say that. No one knows who said that." Sara threw both hands in the air. "Cite your sources, people!"

Anna-Kath blinked twice at Sara—her classic, dismissive blink.

Sara huffed. "I just don't believe Mum was thinking clearly. I'm barely functioning as a human—and now this?"

Ann suffered from the misconception that older sisters were smarter than younger ones, which Sara refused to believe except when it was convenient. Now was not convenient.

Anna-Kath leaned forward. "Call Phil. You need his help."

Sara choked on her tea and began a fit of excessive coughing, her eyes watering up. "There is no way I'm calling Phil. Having him in Mum's house when she was sick was more than I could handle. Why was he there anyway?"

"Come on. It's obvious how he and Mum felt about each other."

"I refuse to believe Mum could truly love that man. It was a phase. She was confused."

"Phil was good to her. And you hardly spoke two words to him."

"I spoke to him."

"Hello? Good Night? You took great lengths to avoid him."

She narrowed her eyes. Nothing but sheer discipline kept her from shouting, *You're not the boss of me!* She sipped her tea again, silently pleased with her astounding self-control.

Recently retired, Phil Dvornik not only owned Iris Books, but he had been Cassandra's editor for more than twenty years. Sara was well aware that he gave Cassandra her start, and yes, she knew he was the best in the business. But he was old, and he was ornery, and *he didn't like tea.*

Ann placed a hand on Sara's arm. "You need to call him."

"I *need* to go home!" She took her teacup to the sink and rinsed it out vigorously, getting her sleeves wet. She suddenly felt anxious to leave. She did not need this additional pressure about Phil.

"Fine! We don't have to talk about Phil." Ann began unloading the dishwasher, plates and glasses clanking loudly against each other.

Sara picked up her bag and headed towards the front door. Ann slung a dish towel over her shoulder and followed her out. Sara knew Ann couldn't stand having anyone leave angry—even when it wasn't her fault.

Ann's eyes turned gentle. "We'll figure this out, okay?"

Sara didn't believe her but mumbled a half-hearted thanks.

"I think your flip-flops are in the back."

"Keep them."

"Look," Ann said, trying to be helpful, "maybe you start with rereading her books, you know, to get a feel for Mum's flow, her style."

"There are eighteen books, Ann. And I still have a job." Sara knew she was officially becoming *difficult*.

"Just let this settle in, okay? We'll come up with an action plan." Anna-Kath had three passions in her life: Gerald T. Green, her children, and action plans, not necessarily in that order. "And I'm sure Mum's new editor, Lucy, will be a huge help. Maybe you'll never have to talk to Phil."

"Stop trying to make this disaster sound reasonable. You're at least right about Phil. I'll never need to talk to him." Sara could see the frustration in Ann's eyes. Her sister was a problem solver, a solution finder, someone who could negotiate for hostages while deboning a chicken. But Sara didn't want someone to fix this. She wanted someone to make it disappear. *Poof!* Gone. Just like that.

She said goodbye and walked barefoot to her car. She'd go home to Gatsby. Dogs were good with difficult people. Perhaps being difficult was her new normal.

There were worse things to be.

CHAPTER 5

*If you find yourself asking yourself…, 'Am I really a writer? Am
I really an artist?' chances are you are. The counterfeit inno-
vator is wildly self-confident. The real one is scared to death.*

STEVEN PRESSFIELD

Gatsby was a yellow lab who flunked out of the Louisville Companion
Dog School. He had "attention issues in high traffic areas" and "displayed unusual hyperactivity" in grocery stores. Mike and Sara had been
married for three years, and Sara wanted kids and Mike didn't. That's when
they found Gatsby. Sara felt a sort of kinship for dropouts. His coat was
a pale, buttery yellow. He had floppy ears and large, sensitive brown eyes
that spoke three distinct phrases to Sara: 1) I totally get you, 2) Everything
is going to be okay, and 3) We're better off without Mike. The last line was
new, but it clearly appeared in Gatsby's eyes the morning Mike left.

When Sara returned home, Gatsby immediately showered her with
every good thought and affection a dog could muster. She rustled the fur
on his back and rubbed her cheek against his neck before she took two
Xanax and plopped onto her bed.

She lay with Gatsby's head in her lap. Mike would never let Gatsby on
the bed. She flipped through channels. Her favorite food shows had lost

39

their appeal months ago. Food simply didn't look as good to her anymore, and it definitely didn't taste as good. She started some British comedies, but found it was difficult to focus. She took Gatsby for a walk, but she was still mad at her mother and wanted to walk fast and hard while Gatsby meandered, slow and distracted.

Later she tried to sleep, turning her pillow over again and again as her frustration and anger dissolved into a deep and penetrating sadness. She clung to her pillow, feeling so incredibly weak, so utterly irrelevant in the universe. There was a time she would have taken the book on, relished it even.

She called Anna-Kath. "I'm not very brave," she whispered.

"What are you talking about?" Ann sounded groggy.

"I used to be brave. I had dreams. I used to think I could do things. Do you think that's the real reason Mike left? He needed someone more brave?"

"Mike's an idiot. He didn't know what he had. He didn't need more brave, he needed more…*brain*."

"Right. You're right. Of course, you're right."

"It's late. Get some rest. We'll figure this out tomorrow. We'll work out an action plan."

Sara switched off her lamp. Gatsby snored gently on the floor next to her. She stared at the outline of the window in the dark. The streetlight glowed softly around the edges of the blinds.

She switched the lamp back on and knelt in front of her dresser. She opened the bottom drawer. The dried lavender sprigs from her mother's garden still scented the air whenever she opened it. The comfort drawer was her mother's idea after Mike left. It was for both "comfort and possibility," which sounded pretty stupid to Sara at the time, but she went along with it. Anna-Kath made one for herself, too, but she wouldn't tell Sara what was in it.

Sara took out an early edition of *The Tale of Benjamin Bunny* by Beatrix Potter. It belonged to her father. He'd read them all to her. There was a photo of her family when she was seven leaning against a stone wall at Potter's home in England's Lake District, one of their last family outings before her father became too sick to travel. She stood in front of her father, his strong hands resting on each of her shoulders, his face tired but still handsome. They shared the same brown hair and brown eyes. She had so little from him that she always thought of her eyes as a gift he'd chosen just for her. Anna-Kath had blue eyes like their mother.

There was another picture of her and Gatsby, with Mike expertly cropped out; a short story she wrote in high school that won the Princeton Short Story Award; and a manila folder filled with many of her high school and early college fiction awards. Her mother had written on one folder, "The next author in the family!" Her life's path had seemed so clear then. She pulled out a thin, red scarf her mother wore tied in her hair for nearly every photo during her college years at Georgetown. That's where Sara's parents met. Her father, Jack Grayson, was a Brit who loved all things American, who fell for an American who loved all things British. Sara pulled out his leather writing notebook her mom had given to her just last summer after Mike left.

Sara put the items back in her comfort drawer, except for her father's writing notebook. Sara climbed back into bed. She fell asleep clutching the book tightly as if it just might save her.

❧

That night Sara dreamed of a chaotic family party where her mother sat quietly in a corner, like she had a secret but wouldn't tell. When Sara woke up, she kept picturing her mother in the dream. What was she hiding? Sara shot up in bed and grabbed a pad of paper from her nightstand. She scribbled notes about each *Ellery Dawson* book and Googled each of their publication dates, charting out a timeline. She did the same with the *Cobie McClane* books, the series her mother wrote before *Ellery*. All seven of the books in both series followed a clear pattern. She slapped her pen down when finished. "Hah!" she said aloud.

David Allman was completely wrong.

Clearly, her mother had already written the book. She just needed to find it.

According to Cassandra's own schedule, Book Five would have already been in her editor's hands before Cassandra even got sick. She tossed the pad of paper in the air with flourish. Of course, the book was already written.

"Nice try, Mum," she said as she brushed her teeth and poured Gatsby's breakfast at the same time, congratulating herself on her multi-tasking—until she dripped some toothpaste from her mouth onto the kibble.

Sara could see it clearly now: Cassandra facing her illness and realizing she could leverage this to force Sara to write again. Apparently terminal illness can make very nice people prone to all sorts of desperate, passive-aggressive behavior. She figured her mom told David that story about not having finished the book to try and make Sara feel compelled to write the book. There was an element of twisted logic to the whole thing.

Sara actually felt some hope as she showered and got ready for the day. She called in sick for work, feeling a little guilty about missing her second day back, but her mission today was too important: *find the book*.

Sara called Anna-Kath on her way to her mom's.

"I've mapped out Mum's production schedule for *Ellery Dawson*. Despite whatever she told David, I'm sure she already wrote this book. It has to be done. It's probably stashed in a file on Mum's computer or stuck in a drawer or thumb drive—or the cloud."

"Then why would she tell David there's no book?"

"It's obvious she wanted to get me to write, but Mum wouldn't dare leave this all up to me without some kind of back-up plan. You don't leave your most famous literary character in the hands of a daughter who just flunked out as a greeting card writer. I'm heading to Mum's to go through her office."

"It's worth checking out."

Sara could hear clanking dishes and Jude and Livvy singing in the background. "Would you call Mum's editor, Lucy, and ask her for the drafts Mum sent her of Book Five?"

"Sara, we don't even know if there are any drafts."

"Act like we do! Pretend we know what's going on. Would you ask Phil too?"

"Okay. I have to drop the kids off at nine. I can call after I meet with my first client."

Sara felt more energized than she had in weeks. She had faced the horrifying prospect of having to finish the world's most popular series, but now she could sense a promising escape.

Relief felt close at hand.

CHAPTER 6

I put it down on paper and then the ghost does not ache so much.

SANDRA CISNEROS

Cassandra Bond had lived in her Tudor-style home for twenty-one years. Its brick walkway led to an arched front door and continued through a rose-covered, stone trellis on the side. As Sara parked in front, it still felt like Cassandra might be home. If she closed her eyes, she could imagine the cancer never came. She could picture her mom busy writing in her office with Miss Marple at her feet and a full cup of English breakfast beside her. She whisked those thoughts away and turned to Gatsby, who sat happily in the front seat.

"This morning is about purpose. Okay? We have one job to do."

Gatsby put his paws on the window, anxious to get out.

Sara had lived in this home from the time she was eleven until she went away to college at the University of Virginia. Even now it still felt like home. Cassandra had designed the interior to look like an English country cottage, and she had hardly changed anything in twenty years, despite Ann's frequent encouragement to remodel. *Architectural Digest* had done a feature story on her home years ago. If you looked closely, you could see a tiny bit of Sara's elbow in the dining room photograph.

She unlocked the front door and tried to ignore the way Gatsby anxiously looked for her mother. He went straight to her office and then her bedroom. Death was hard for animals too.

She walked into the quiet kitchen. The energy she felt earlier vanished as she smelled traces of her mother's gardenia candle. House plants and succulents still thrived in terra cotta pots and ceramic vases next to a large kitchen window.

Sara felt the familiar grief reshuffling in her heart. She paused to take some deep breaths. She was usually there with Ann.

Her phone buzzed with a text. She was trying a new app for daily affirmations, each one set against peaceful scenic backgrounds. Yesterday's said: "I will not compare myself to strangers on the internet." Today's read: "I am my own superhero." She repeated it aloud, drank a glass of cold water, and forced herself into her mother's office.

Gatsby was already lounging near the overstuffed floral sofa. Sara ran her fingers along her mother's mahogany writing desk, an old Victorian piece from her father's family, which sat in the large bay window. Her father used to write at this very desk. It had barely fit into a corner of her parent's bedroom in their London flat.

She sat down and found her mother's password list she'd given them when she was sick. She started her mother's computer and began her search there. She brought a stack of *Ellery* books to the desk and searched keywords and phrases for Book Five. She looked through additional drives on the computer. Her heart raced as she found several promising docs. Her shoulders sagged. Each one contained only various contracts with stakeholders.

She went to Cassandra's emails. Surely her mother sent drafts to Lucy or to Phil. Keyword searches were difficult. Hundreds of related emails would result, and thousands existed between Cassandra and her literary team.

She logged into Cassandra's personal email and began searching and sorting there. One came up from Sara, dated last August. Her throat tightened.

From: Sara Grayson
To: Cassandra Bond; Anna-Katherine Green
Date: Thursday, August 2, 7:02 AM
Subject: He left

Mum and Ann,

He's gone. We had a fight last night. He told me his start-up failed because I didn't believe in him. He slept in the office. I slept with Gatsby. When I got up, he'd left me a copy of *Eat, Pray, Love* on the futon and this note:

> Sara,
>
> We both know it's time for me to go. I'm going on a journey. Need to find myself. You should too. I took the Subaru. It will be at Dulles, long-term economy. It's been good, but I think we both know it's time to move on.
>
> Best,
> Mike

From: Anna-Katherine Green
To: Sara Grayson; Cassandra Bond
Date: Thursday, August 2, 7:16 AM
Subject: RE: He left

Oh, Sara. I'm so sorry. I'll be right over.

P.S. What the hell? He couldn't call an Uber? The man leaves his wife AND makes her pick up the car at Dulles?

P.P.S. Like he could ever grasp Liz Gilbert.

Her mother was out of town. She wrote back:

From: Cassandra Bond
To: Sara Grayson; Anna-Katherine Green
Date: Thursday, August 2, 8:42 AM
Subject: RE: He left

Oh, darling. Let him go. And don't believe Mike. His start-up failed because he can't tell the difference between his friends and his victims. I'm coming home. I love you.

Sara didn't like to think about that morning nine months ago. She hadn't been happy in her marriage, not for years, but the abrupt departure—with a note and a book—was cold and painful. Their last fight was actually about Cassandra. Mike wanted to borrow more money from her to save his failing start-up for a "revolutionary" new exercise app. Sara said there was no way they were asking her mom for more money. Cassandra had already given them thousands of dollars for the last two start-ups. Sara said it was time to put that GW law degree to work and get a real job with a regular salary. Mike said he had bigger plans, a bigger destiny than being a Washington attorney like his father. She wasn't surprised that he slept on the futon that night. He'd been sleeping there a lot those days.

When Sara found the note and the book the next morning, she could barely breathe. She emailed her mom and Ann. Then she crawled back in bed. She needed them to know, and yet part of her wished they would never get the email so she could stay hidden under her covers and never come out.

Ann walked into Sara's dark townhome an hour later. Ann was an "open-the-blinds-and-let-the-sun-shine-in" kind of person. But not that morning. She let herself in and went straight to the kitchen to make tea and toast while Sara lay in bed. She brought Sara a tray, left the blinds closed, and lay on the bed with Sara while they binge-watched Cupcake Wars. Ann picked up Thai food for dinner. She let Sara talk and cry and made more tea.

The following weeks were dark and slow and empty. Five weeks after Mike left, Sara had a dream that her father had come into town and was staying with her. They were making breakfast, and he was wearing a smart pair of navy flannel pajamas with a gray, pin-striped robe. He looked much older than when he died at thirty-eight. His morning scruff was gray, and his laugh lines were deeply etched around his eyes. Though older, he was as handsome as Sara remembered. He hugged Sara tightly, and she felt enveloped in a deep, nourishing love that filled her soul completely. They ate bagels with marmalade and cream cheese. Dad said he could stay as long as she needed him. She looked around, suddenly aware of her incredibly messy house, and felt a desire to make things nice for her father's visit.

Sara awoke at 6:00 AM the next morning, her eyes wide, a sense of her father's love settled deep inside her heart. She hugged a pillow close to her chest, savoring the dream's warmth. Soon, a new energy flooded her body. She threw on her exercise clothes and her running shoes. She opened every window in her townhome and began scrubbing everything in sight. Sara sensed a new beginning was possible, even if she wasn't sure how. Her mom and Anna-Kath joined her that afternoon helping her box up mountains of Mike's belongings. The next day Sara picked out a new duvet and headboard for their bed. Ann chose new bed pillows and bought fresh flowers for Sara's nightstand.

Sara's home felt refreshed. Better. The ache of loss still hovered like smog, somedays thicker than others. Six years of marriage left so many questions. But there was also a growing sense that perhaps this was a necessary loss, one she should have accepted a long time ago. She would never have had the strength to leave on her own.

"I am purpose," she said again, willing herself to focus on the present task at her mother's. She sifted through papers in file cabinets and went through each desk drawer for hard copies or external drives.

Nothing.

She found a few flash drives, but they contained only drafts of speeches and presentations. Sara worked through lunch, searching files on her mother's laptop and tablet.

Nothing.

She moved to the office closet and pulled nine large file boxes out. She emptied every single one.

Still nothing.

CHAPTER 7

For heaven's sake, publish nothing before you are thirty.

VIRGINIA WOOLF

Three days later:

Text on Fri. May 17, 10:44 AM

Binti

Girl, what's up? You were back at
work and now you've disappeared
again. You're not answering
your phone. You okay?

From: Bethesda Veterinary Clinic
To: Sara Grayson
Date: Friday, May 17, 11:00 AM
Subject: Bark, Bark!

Dear Gatsby,

You missed your head-to-tail physical yesterday.
Please remind your responsible owner, <u>Sara</u>

Grayson, that yearly check-ups for an adult dog
like you are essential to vibrant dog health.

We wuff you!
Dr. Pat

From: Zoey @ Cutie Coupon
To: Sara Grayson
Date: Friday, May 17, 11:15 AM
Subject: Real Talk

Hey Sara,

Suh, what's up? Time for some real talk. Your copy for
the Escape Room sounds like it was written for old
people like my mom. Please rewrite by Fri. If I don't hear
from you today, the account goes to Brylie and you'll
be back on Tahitian pearls. Show me you want this.

Zo
Rec Team Supervisor B
Cutie Coupon LLC

❧

She stood outside the doorway.

She couldn't avoid that room forever.

Gatsby went in and out like it was no big deal.

After three days, she had searched everywhere else and turned up
nothing. Ann had talked to Phil, who said that he'd never seen a draft of

Book Five. Lucy, Mom's editor, was out of the country and hadn't returned any calls.

Sara hadn't stepped foot in her mother's bedroom since she died there twenty-four days ago. She stood in front of the door frame and hesitantly peeked inside. Home health and hospice had cleared out all the medical supplies. Now the housekeeper, who stopped by once a week, had the room looking like it did before Cassandra ever got sick. It was almost harder to see it looking so fresh, so normal, when the very worst had happened right there.

Fifteen minutes.

That's the only time they left her alone those final days. Her kidneys were failing, and doctors said it was only a matter of days. Sara and Anna-Kath didn't leave her side, determined that their mother wouldn't die alone. She grew weaker and weaker. Her skin more pale and gray. She would whisper things occasionally, but she was difficult to understand.

Anna-Kath left briefly that morning to pick up Jude, who was sick, and the hospice nurse had already made her morning rounds. Sara desperately needed a shower. She thought she could do it quickly and be right back. But when that warm water fell on her tired body, she stayed too long. When she got out, she threw on a bathrobe and went straight to her mother's room for a quick check before she got dressed.

She hurried in and then froze the moment she stepped inside the room. Everything felt different. A heavy stillness hung there. She stood at the end of her mother's bed and rested her eyes on her face. Sara pressed her fingers on her lips. She didn't need to take her pulse or check her breathing. Her mother was gone and Sara knew it. Felt it. She walked slowly to her and sat on the bed beside her. She touched her mother's arm, still warm and soft, and lay her drippy, wet head against her mother's shoulder. Then Sara kissed her face and told her she loved her again and again.

She heard Anna-Kath's car pull up. Heard her gasp as she walked into the room.

"No, no, no," Ann said as she rushed to the other side of her bed. "Oh, Mum. I wanted to be here." Anna-Kath cried as she took their mother's hand and held it to her cheek, tears flowing down her face and onto their mother's hand. Cassandra's presence still felt near, comforting, gentle. Ann reached for Sara's hand across their mother's body. They embraced their mother together, feeling the warmth of their embrace one last time.

That was exactly twenty-four days ago. Sara wiped some tears away and slowly stepped inside her mother's bedroom.

Stacks of books still sat on a bed-stand. Mum's yellow afghan draped over her favorite soft reading chair. Gatsby sniffed around Miss Marples's empty dog bed in the corner.

The pink and yellow room held mostly clothes and books and small photos in antique Victorian frames, including their last family portrait. There was a Mary Cassatt painting on one wall, a framed map of London on another. No file boxes. No computer. Nothing that resembled her writing life except the books she loved, scattered in stacks and lining two small bookshelves. She was never reading just one book. Sara wondered how she kept it all straight.

She looked inside each of her mother's dresser drawers and reached inside to feel for any sign of paper or external drives.

She sighed. Nothing but clothes, folded neatly—expectantly. How sad for them.

She pulled out a pair of her mother's thick socks and slipped them onto her bare feet. She opened the last drawer. She looked inside and exhaled slowly.

Her comfort drawer.

She drew Gatsby close to her while she took out Mother's Day cards and artwork from Sara and Anna-Kath when they were children. There was a men's necktie in green and yellow stripes that belonged to their father—

part of the headmaster's uniform he wore to school in London. She found a box of Lindt dark truffles with two pieces left; a necklace with a tiny red heart that looked like gingerbread; a new bottle of Sugar Lemon lotion; and a book of poetry by Elizabeth Barrett Browning. Inside were several love letters her father wrote her mother. Sara had read them all a hundred times before. They were full of lovely British words to describe love that Americans rarely used. Words like *besotted* and *smitten* and *beguiled*. The kind of words that made her feel tingly and happy as a child—and even now. She slipped one of the letters into her back pocket.

In the very bottom corner, wrapped in a blue silk nightgown, sat a well-worn book with the covers ripped off the front and the back. The title and author page were missing. It didn't look terribly old, but it was obviously well-used. Or run over by a bus. It was 423 pages long. She found the title printed on the top left of each page after chapter one began but no author listed on the right page. *Silence in Stepney.* There was a park near their home in the East End with that name. She wondered why the book was in such miserable shape and why her mother would love it enough to keep it in her comfort drawer. She carefully placed each item back in the drawer but kept the book. Maybe Anna-Kath knew more about it.

She walked slowly back to her mother's office. Her phone buzzed with a notification.

> From Daily Dose Affirmations:
>
> Your free trial has ended. Put on your positive pants! Please click here to subscribe to more soul-enriching daily affirmations for only $1.99 a month. Click now!

She turned her phone off and left it in the kitchen. Her head ached from all the searching. Now her heart ached even more. She found it took a great deal of effort to be angry with someone you missed so much, and she was tired of trying.

She walked into the office, stepping over stacks of files, boxes, and papers. She stretched out on the floor. "Come on, Mum," she whispered. "You don't really want me to write this thing. You must have had a back-up. Just show me where it is?"

Gatsby jumped up and raced for the front door at the sound of company. Anna-Kath walked into their mother's office and surveyed the mess with a raised eyebrow. She was still dressed for work: gray trousers and a cropped blue jacket, her wavy blonde hair always on its best behavior. She kicked off her pumps, gingerly stepping around boxes to find a place to sit next to Sara, who remained prostrate on the floor in yesterday's yoga pants and UMD t-shirt.

"I finally talked to Mum's editor," Ann said.

Sara sat up, suddenly alert, hopeful. "You talked to Lucy?'

"No draft."

Sara flopped back on the floor.

"Here's the strange thing. Lucy said Mum was working on another project—that Mum insisted *Ellery Dawson* needed to wait. Iris Books was giving her more time to write the book, with a spring launch date for next year, but Mum wouldn't tell Lucy or Iris Books what the other project was. Once Mum got sick, Lucy backed off. So basically, during the time Mum should have been writing *Ellery Dawson*, she was writing something else, but no one knows what she actually wrote or where it is. Lucy thought *we* would know what she was writing."

"This is bad." Sara clasped her hands tight over her eyes.

"I asked Phil if he knew anything else. He insisted that Mum never wrote Book Five and that they hadn't even talked about *Ellery Dawson* in over a year, which I don't get how that's even possible considering all the time they spent together."

"It wasn't that much time."

"They were inseparable," said Ann.

"You're exaggerating."

"Mum was with Phil in Europe when she came to help you after Mike left."

"No, she wasn't. She was in Maine. By herself." Sara was sure she was in Maine.

Ann shook her head. "It doesn't matter. Anyway, Lucy wants to talk to you as soon as possible. Iris Books just learned that you are the designated writer. I think they had someone else in mind."

"No kidding."

"They want a meeting as soon as possible."

"I know. I have a dozen messages from David Allman and Mum's agent and someone named Jane from Iris Books."

"There's no manuscript, Sara."

Sara pressed her fingers against her eyes. "I know."

"Lucy said the press won't know anything for now, but stakeholders are getting antsy to know where you're going with this book. They want a meeting with you ASAP. They'll come to Washington."

Sara sat up. She took a drink from her water bottle and then lay back down. Anna-Kath stretched out beside her.

They lay in silence for a few minutes.

Sara studied the ceiling. "If you squint your eyes, you can see the outline of a squirrel."

Ann squinted her eyes. "It looks more like a lighthouse."

Sara brought her hands back to rest behind her head. "Maybe you should write it, Ann."

"I'm too nice. The book would be full of beautiful interiors, and nothing bad would happen to anyone."

"Sounds like a bestseller."

Ann sat up and began putting some folders back in a file box. "Do you think Ellery's father is really dead?"

"Who knows? I don't even know if Ellery finds her brother, Charlie."

"Of course she finds him. That's all in Book Two. The big mystery in Book Five is about her father."

"So I've heard."

Ann slowly turned toward Sara.

"So you've *heard*?" She studied Sara's face for a moment. "Well then, you know how sad it is when Charlie steps on the land mine in Book Four."

"Um. Yeah. That was awful."

Ann squished her eyebrows together so tightly they'd become one. "Nobody steps on a land mine in Book Four." She grabbed a couch pillow and threw it at Sara's face. "Oh my gosh, Sara! You haven't read the books?"

Sara grabbed the pillow and smashed it against her face. "I saw the movie," her voice muffled against the pillow.

"You saw the movie?"

"Yeah. With Mom."

"But you haven't read the books."

Sara groaned. "I've been busy."

"For five years?"

Sara shrugged her shoulders, her face still pressed against the pillow.

"I don't understand. You've always read Mum's books. You were her biggest fan. You followed her around like her own little apprentice. How could you *not* read this series—and you're supposed to write the conclusion?"

Ann snatched the pillow away from Sara's face. "What was Mum's last book you read? *Confess.*"

Sara swallowed hard. "*Cobie McClane.*"

"That's four books ago! Did you at least read the whole *Cobie* series?"

"Most."

"What about *Mace Kellers*?"

"Every book. It was my favorite."

"Mine too. Until *Ellery*." Ann threw the pillow back at Sara, who sat up and leaned against the sofa, her arms wrapped tightly around her scrunched-up knees.

"Okay," Ann said. "I'm not going to psychoanalyze you right now, but there is some serious crap you need to work through. You should probably mention this to your therapist."

"Don't blow this out of proportion. And for the record, Sybil Brown-Baker says that I'm functioning extremely well."

Ann huffed. "Last week."

"Well none of this would matter if Mum hadn't thrown me under the bus." She couldn't stop the tears now. She moaned, "Why would she do this to me?"

Ann gave an exasperated sigh and kicked Sara's foot. She didn't respond. Ann kicked her foot again, harder this time.

"Stop kicking me."

Ann kicked her again.

"Stop it."

"Look at me, Sara."

She wouldn't look up.

"I've got two words for you. Will you look at me?"

Sara finally looked up with bleary, swollen eyes.

Ann pointed a finger at her face and said, "*Man up!*"

Sara gave Ann a piercing glare and put her head back on her knees.

"I'm serious." Ann kicked her, and Sara kicked her back.

"'Man up' is a completely sexist remark," Sara said. "Mum hated that phrase."

"Mum knew when it fit and so do you."

She wiped her eyes and scowled at Ann.

"*Man up*, Sara. Do you hear me? You keep acting like this is such a crazy, horrible thing for Mum to do. Look, you're a writing teacher. You've even written a novel. It's not like Mum asked me to do it. Mum isn't stupid you know. Can you actually write this book? Of course you can, but stop acting like you have no choice. You do NOT have to do this. Meet with the publisher. Find out what kind of help they can give and then make your own damn choice."

"You think I can find a way out of this?"

"Either you write this book or you don't, but enough with all the self-pity."

Sara nodded her head slowly. "You're right." A hint of calm began to spread through her chest, a sense that maybe Sara could really, truly say no to this whole thing. It's not like anyone in the universe actually wanted her to write the book. Mum was the only one who had harbored any lingering delusions about Sara becoming a novelist.

Sara stood up and walked over to the window. She stared pensively at her mother's purple clematis that climbed up a white trellis in full bloom. This variety only bloomed in May. It couldn't be forced to bloom any other time, except maybe in a hothouse. Sara felt like she was living her life in a hothouse where people expected her to bloom into some kind of rare orchid, but all she could do was sweat profusely and pop a few ears of corn. She turned back to Ann.

"You're right. Mum would understand. She would get this. She gets me. I'll have the meeting with the publisher, and it's totally fine for me to walk away."

Ann smiled. "Let's call David."

CHAPTER 8

*I am aware that, every time I have a conversation with a
book, I benefit from someone's decision against silence.*

YIYUN LI

Anna-Kath and Sara arrived in Georgetown an hour early for their 7:30 PM meeting with David Allman and a team from Iris Books. Ann was always overcompensating for DC's bad traffic. Now the extra hour made Sara feel jittery about the meeting while they wandered through a specialty grocery store to kill time.

After Ann told her to "man up" and make a decision, Sara had quietly come to the conclusion that she had every right to say no to her mother's dying wish, and that is exactly what she intended to do. But now her stomach crawled with fear about being a total let-down to her family. She would always be the daughter who rejected her mother's dying wis*h*.

"Phil's not coming, right?" Sara asked.

"I told you. Phil still owns Iris Books, but he turned operations over to Jane Harnois two years ago." She smelled a box of tea, shook her head, and put it back. "He won't be there."

"Oh good."

"I don't think Jane's a peach either. You might prefer Phil."

"I doubt that. And who uses that phrase anymore. 'A peach?' Are you a peach?"

"Peaches are in aisle four," said a skinny employee whose bleached bangs covered most of her face.

"Thank you." Ann smiled tightly. She opened another canister of tea. "Ooh...smell this one. The bergamot orange makes all the difference." She held it up to Sara's nose. "Don't you love that?"

Sara sniffed absently and handed it back to Ann. "Mum will understand, right? About the book?"

"It will be *fine*."

The store was getting more crowded, and Sara's anxiety was rising. She felt like she was wearing a sign across her chest that said, "Bad daughter." She just needed to get through her little announcement at the meeting, and then she would experience complete and total relief. The past week would fade away like a bad dream, and she would move forward.

Sara pointed to a bench outside the store. "I'll wait for you out there."

She sat down in the warm evening air. The dogwoods were in bloom, and the purple coneflowers had sprung early. A long line stretched outside Georgetown Cupcakes. Patrons regularly waited over an hour for service. Binti had a close-up on Instagram last week of the Madagascar Vanilla Cupcake with Milk Chocolate Buttercream Frosting.

Sara and Mike had a fight once about the place four years ago. They'd just had dinner at Café Milano to celebrate their second wedding anniversary. They took a walk after dinner and passed Georgetown Cupcakes. They hadn't been there yet and Sara really wanted a cupcake for dessert. Mike refused to stand in line that long.

"Come on. I've heard they're amazing," she coaxed him. Mike was in a sour mood and just wanted ice cream. She tried to barter. "Let's get your ice cream, and you can eat it while we stand in line."

Mike agreed, but while other couples held hands in line or nestled into each other while they waited, Mike downed his ice cream without tasting it and complained about the poor business model of the place. He would redesign everything so valuable customers didn't have to wait in despicable lines like this. He predicted the business would fail by spring, but if he were in charge, he would take that cupcake business to an entirely new level. Weary of Mike's complaints, Sara finally walked away, leaving him standing in line without her. She walked towards the parking garage. Mike, now hesitant to lose their spot in line, called after her to come back and then was furious when he had to give up their place to follow her.

"You are incapable of making reasonable decisions. Thirty minutes for nothing."

"I don't know. You worked out a whole business plan for the place." Sara walked ahead.

"You weren't even listening. I don't know how I'm supposed to get my start-up off the ground when you don't even value my ideas."

She stopped and looked at him. "All we talk about are *your* ideas."

"Oh, you have some ideas you want to talk about? Talk. Go ahead. I'm listening." He folded his arms and glared at her. She said nothing and stewed silently on their drive back to their apartment in Chevy Chase. She'd still never tasted a Georgetown Cupcake.

❧

At 7:30 PM, Sara and Ann walked into Clyde's. The restaurant had that signature scent of buttery garlic mixed with grilled steak and seafood.

"Oh, that smells incredible," said Ann.

Sara thought she might be sick.

A maître d' led them to a private section of the restaurant. A French limestone fireplace burned softly in the back of the room even though it was 75 degrees outside. There was a long table set for twelve and a buffet table to the side filled with fruit, cheese, stuffed mushrooms, crab cakes, and tea sandwiches.

Though it was barely seven-thirty, they were clearly the last to arrive. Everyone was mingling with their drinks in comfortable conversation. Sara grabbed Ann's arm, her knees feeling wobbly.

"Come on," Ann whispered. "It'll be over soon."

David Allman and a couple of his partners greeted them, and Elaine Chang, Cassandra's agent, swooped over and made other introductions. Elaine always wore sleeveless dresses and had these beautiful, sculpted arms that made Sara want to do push-ups. Almost.

Lucy Glenn-Kelly, her mom's editor, smiled and walked over. She had unruly gray hair and frequently made references to one's energy and chakras like everyone naturally believed that sort of thing. She hugged Ann and then Sara. "We're going to make a great team on this book. Oh, here comes Jane." Lucy pointed to a fifty-something woman gliding purposefully towards them.

Jane's hair was cut in one of those attractive, swinging, shoulder-length bobs, although Jane's hair didn't actually swing. Instead it rather held its position mid-air. She wore a crisp, white collared shirt with black pearls and a beige pencil skirt. Her clothes seemed to lack even the tiniest wrinkle. How was that even possible? She took Sara's hand and firmly held it with her other hand as she shook it.

"I'm happy to finally meet you," said Jane in a smooth NPR-newsy voice. "We just couldn't be more thrilled, absolutely thrilled."

She struck Sara as one of those women who drone on about being "thrilled" but never actually appear that way. Jane introduced Sara to the other Iris executives and their attorneys. Sara strained to smile. Within the hour, they would all know she was a quitter—a woman who had no respect for the dying wishes of her own mother.

David invited everyone to sit down so they could start the meeting and excused all restaurant staff to ensure complete privacy. Sara sat next to Ann, with David at the head of the table. Jane sat directly across from her.

David welcomed everyone warmly. Sara was surprised at his ease, his self-confidence. He looked more put-together in his perfectly-cut, gray sports jacket. And were those new glasses? Maybe that Canadian back-packer was really good for him. She reminded herself how wonderful she would feel when this was all over. Unless she passed out first.

Jane cut in. "May I say, on behalf of all of us at Iris, how deeply sorry we are at the loss of your mother. I offer a toast to her memory and her work. Cassandra Bond had the soul of an artiste."

There was audible agreement as everyone lifted their glasses to Cassandra's memory. Sara gripped her glass so tightly she thought it could break.

David quickly got to business. "You've all had the opportunity to review the literary contract between Iris Books and Cassandra Bond, specifically the attached rider. As we begin, I'd like to review the most salient points." Several at the table flipped through a bound copy of the contract as he spoke. Sara opened her copy. She struggled to find the right page. How could she be lost already? She looked at Ann's and finally caught up.

"Cassandra's contract rider stipulates that in the event that she is unable to complete a contracted literary series, Cassandra Bond Grayson, or 'CBG,' maintains the right to choose the author who will complete said series. The new author is bound by previous contractual agreements CBG has made with Iris Books, as I've outlined with Iris Books and their representatives."

"Perhaps," Jane interrupted, "we could hold these details and give Ms. Grayson the floor. I think we'd all be thrilled to hear where she plans to go with this book. Just a little plot summary, perhaps?"

Sara reached for Ann's hand.

"Ms. Grayson has only known about this project for a week," said David. "That's hardly time to provide—"

"I'm sure," said Jane, her eyes fixed on Sara, "that you spent a great deal of time with your mother during her convalescence. Certainly, she talked about the book with you?"

Elaine looked directly at Jane. "Surely, Cassandra had other things on her mind."

"Actually," said David, "we hoped that the *publisher* could provide information about Book Five *for Sara*. Lucy, perhaps you could comment on what you know as Cassandra's editor."

Lucy's eyes darted uncomfortably from Sara to Jane, like she was stuck in a painful custody battle and just wanted everyone to play nicely.

"Well, Cassandra gave me limited plot points for the book. We discussed several different endings, but after she became ill, you know…" Her voice trailed off. She twisted the gold bangles on her wrist as her eyes filled with tears.

"Look," Sara finally spoke, her voice shaky, "let me just make this easier on all of you." She inhaled deeply and tried to remember the words she'd practiced. "While I appreciate my mother's confidence in me as a writer, I think it would be best if I turned this project over to someone else." There. Had she really said it out loud? Her mouth felt chalky and dry.

She felt a hum of response ripple through the group and detected a collective sense of relief from the Iris team. Jane looked visibly more relaxed. The crease in her brow softened. "Well, Ms. Grayson. I'm pleased, I…"

Cassandra's agent, Elaine, interrupted, her biceps flexed as she leaned forward on her arms. "Sara, are you *sure* this is what you want to do?"

David looked concerned. "Yes…your mother was quite convinced *you* should write the book. There was no question in her mind. I can attest to that."

"Look, I appreciate my mother's confidence." Why did her voice sound so timid, so small? She took a sip from her wine glass and tried to sound more assertive. "I am not a novelist, and I think this work deserves a professional. So, Ms. Harnois, I leave this in the hands of Iris Books." She tugged at her shirt collar. *Why is it so hot in here?*

"Legally, the choice of author does fall to Iris, if Ms. Grayson refuses," said an Iris attorney.

"Yes, well, I respectfully…*refuse*." The wave of relief should have hit her by now. Should have washed over her like a lovely Caribbean breeze. She expected to feel free, empowered, unencumbered by her mother's unreasonable dying wishes. Instead, Sara felt terribly uneasy. She took a sip of wine and then wrapped both arms around her stomach.

"Well," said Jane, "I'd just like to say, thank you, Ms. Grayson. I applaud your bold insight into this situation, truly I do."

"Thank you," Sara said weakly. She glanced at Ann, confused. Why did she suddenly feel like she was making the biggest mistake of her life?

"I believe Ms. Grayson's decision shows great character and wisdom," Jane droned on. "Obviously, I'm aware of your little coupon writing venture. Not quite the preparation for writing a renowned bestseller, of course."

"Sara knows what she's doing," Anna-Kath snapped. "She would write a fantastic Book Five."

"Of course, of course," said Jane. "I only want to recognize your sound judgment here. Placing Book Five in the hands of a *non-litterateur* isn't exactly what we'd call common sense. But perhaps Cassandra was not at her best when she made that call—perfectly understandable, of course."

Sara didn't appreciate being insulted by a woman whose hair didn't move. She narrowed her eyes at Jane and sat up a little straighter. "I don't think you're in a position to question my mother's lucidity."

"She was of sound mind, Jane," David confirmed.

"Well, all water under the bridge," Jane said. "Why don't we have Ms. Grayson sign over the authorship rights and we'll move forward. Put all this behind us, right?"

"Cassandra always felt Sara had immense talent," said Elaine, looking straight at Sara.

Sara met her gaze. "She told you that?"

"She said the same to me," said Lucy, ignoring Jane's disapproving eyes. "Cassandra always had tremendous confidence in Sara's gifts."

Elaine turned to Jane. "Cass told me once that Sara had more raw talent than herself and that if she ever decided to get serious with it, her only job would be to get out of her way."

Sara's pulse quickened as whispered conversations erupted in the Iris camp. She felt something new swelling within her.

No. Not new. Maybe just forgotten. She thought of her father's notebook she'd been carrying around in her purse and her mother's note about audacity. Sara looked at Ann who simply smiled at her sister and nodded.

Jane surveyed the room and suddenly looked nervous. She reached for her black pearl necklace and attempted to placate the group. "Perhaps that came out wrong, and really, this isn't about Ms. Grayson's talent, per se. But surely her teaching and her little coupon writing is a bit of a stretch towards the fine art of fiction writing. It's—"

"Let's draw up those papers, shall we?" said an Iris attorney.

Sara felt an energy surge deep within her. "You can find artistry in all forms of writing, Jane." Her voice felt more certain as she spoke.

"Of course. I do apologize," Jane said. "I couldn't agree with you more."

"I don't think you could agree any less." Sara's voice grew in strength.

A crease returned to Jane's brow. She reached for her pearls again. "Well, maybe we should sign those papers now, right?" Her eyes darted to her attorneys.

Sara leaned back in her chair. Her head a little higher. Both feet firmly on the floor. "Those are such lovely pearls, Jane."

Ann looked perplexed at Sara.

"My pearls?" asked Jane.

Sara nodded. She leaned back in her chair and closed her eyes a moment, trying to remember her own words and recited aloud: "Black South Sea cultured pearl necklace, whisks you away on a Tahitian voyage where anything is possible. $39.99 at Cutie Coupon for an escape you will never forget."

Jane gripped her necklace tightly, her face drained of color. "I did *not* purchase these pearls from Cutie Coupon."

David placed a fist over his mouth to cover his smile.

"It's nothing to be ashamed of, Jane. I'm honored that my words convinced you to make such a smart, economical purchase."

"Your words?" Jane forced her hands back to her lap, a small blue vein protruding from her forehead. "Can we get back to the book, please?"

Sara looked at Ann and back at Jane, her heart pounding, but with purpose.

Jane cleared her throat. "Ms. Grayson, I offer an apology. I'm certain your work is quite valuable. Perhaps you could sign those papers now?"

Sara smiled confidently and clasped her hands together. "Thank you…but no."

"No?"

"No. I think I'd like to write that book."

"Surely, you jest."

"Surely. I do not," Sara said, holding Jane's gaze. "The challenge of a little coupon writer like me, finishing a big series like this? Sounds fascinating. You can count me in." Sara glanced quickly at David and Ann. She felt as surprised as they looked, unsure where this surge of confidence was coming from.

Jane glanced quickly at her attorneys, her assistants, perhaps trying to back-track, to retrace her missteps. The Iris camp looked panicky—except Lucy, who smiled to herself as she spread Boursin cheese on her cracker and took a bite.

David stepped in. "I'm sure that Sara can count on everyone at Iris for their full support." Sara lifted her glass of wine to the entire table and took a long swig.

Jane began twisting her necklace, her neck turning red and splotchy.

"Um, look," said Jane. "I think what I said came out wrong. It wasn't that I didn't trust Cassandra or uh…you…I…" Jane's team watched the cracking of their leader with fascination, knowing they should avert their eyes from the wreck but unable to do so.

"Look, Jane," Elaine said, "Cassandra's books turned Phil's little publishing house into one of the biggest little publishing houses in the country. She could have taken *Ellery Dawson* to any of the Big Five, but she didn't. She trusted Iris. Maybe it's time to return that loyalty. If she trusts Sara, so should you."

The room fell quiet.

"Well," David said, "there's more to discuss, but why don't we call it a night?" He turned to Jane. "I'll be in touch with your attorneys. We'll also want to propose a privacy clause so Sara can write without any interference or pressure from the press."

"Fine. But what about the writing deadline?" Jane said. "The book is due on the shelves next spring. Ms. Grayson will never finish in time."

"The rider gives the designated author an additional six months from the current deadline. Page sixteen."

Jane turned to her attorney. "Is that true?"

"Yes. Ms. Grayson technically has until December 15th to complete the manuscript for a summer release date instead of spring."

"What about terms of compensation?" Jane twisted her napkin. "The advance, the percent of sales?" She turned to her attorneys. "Surely we can renegotiate that. Perhaps Ms. Grayson would consider a ghostwriter. Now that would make everyone happy. Right? She can write the book, but have a helper? Who can object to that? A helper?" Her voice climbed in pitch with each sentence.

"The rider stipulates the same conditions and terms," said David. "Why don't we wrap up for the night, and I'll be in touch with your team about the details?"

Jane stood up with a huff. "Well, Sara Grayson, it looks like you have seven months to write the most anticipated book of the decade." She picked up her attaché and smashed her lips in a tight smile. "We'll be in touch."

Jane's entourage exchanged tense pleasantries and exited the meeting. Lucy squeezed Sara's arm as she passed. "I'll call you," she whispered. "We can do this."

Sara nodded quickly.

David, Ann, Sara, and Elaine were left alone. Servers began clearing plates and glasses. Kenny G played gently in the background, like any other normal night with normal dinner at Clyde's where normal people stopped by for steak and seafood.

Sara turned to Ann, her eyes wide. "What just happened?"

David smiled. "I believe that's what my father would call an 'ass-whooping.'"

"I can't believe you just did that," said Ann. "You were brilliant."

Elaine lifted her glass, "Congratulations. I hear you have a book coming out."

Sara's pulse slowed to a jog. She felt the beginning of a headache and threw back the last couple of ounces in her wine glass. "I think I'll go for a walk. Clear my head."

"Where are you going?" Ann asked.

"Georgetown Cupcakes. I want a Madagascar Vanilla with Milk Chocolate Buttercream Frosting. And sprinkles. I don't mind the line." Sara walked out.

CHAPTER 9

I tell my students that the odds of their getting published and of it bringing them financial security, peace of mind, and even joy are probably not that great. Ruin, hysteria, bad skin, unsightly tics, ugly financial problems, maybe; but probably not peace of mind. I tell them that I think they ought to write anyway.

ANNE LAMOTT

The next morning, Sara stumbled out of her bed, practically tripping over Gatsby in search of something for her throbbing headache. She downed two ibuprofen and splashed water on her face, willing her eyes to fully open. She looked at herself in the mirror. Puffy bags hung under her brown eyes and creases from her pillow were carved into one side of her face.

She groaned out loud. "What have I done?"

She went back to her bedroom and sat on the edge of her bed like she was sitting too close to a growing sinkhole that could swallow her up any minute. She watched a sinkhole devour part of a hotel on CNN just last week. And just last year, a sinkhole opened up on this guy's home in Tennessee while he was sleeping, and they never even found his body. The dog was okay though.

She stared unmoving at the floor. She knelt down next to Gatsby. "I'm in so much trouble," she whispered. Gatsby wasn't in the mood to listen. He was anxious to get out and nudged her to stand up. She took him to the small backyard of her townhome, her mind racing through the events of last night.

Could she really write this book?

She had to try. And the truth was that Sara felt something return to her last night. It may have been only a seedling of confidence, but she refused to let it go.

A box of Georgetown cupcakes sat on her kitchen counter. She'd bought three boxes. She wasn't sure why. She ate the Chocolate Coconut for breakfast. It was the first food she could actually taste in months. She ate another. Did coconut count as a fruit or a vegetable?

She hugged Gatsby. "Where do I even begin?"

From: Zoey @ Cutie Coupon
To: Sara Grayson
Date: Friday, May 24, 9:45 AM
Subject: More Real Talk

Sara,

Received your resignation. Keepin it real: I know you were struggling with your coupon assignments, but let me give you some helpful advice from Gen Z: it doesn't pay to walk away, especially at your age. I didn't become a level two supervisor after only two weeks because my uncle owns this place. I earned this leadership position because I understand what it means to get value to the common people. It's a tough market out there, and if you can't take the heat, you're going to be filling French fry cartons at Sonic while you're still living with Mom and Dad. (Yes, I live with my parents, but I'm twenty-one, and I'm moving in with Roger very soon.)

Cutie Coupon is on fire, and I'm sorry it got too hot for you.

Good luck.

Zo
Rec Team Supervisor B
Cutie Coupon LLC

From: Tessa Talbert
To: Sara Grayson
Date: Friday, May 24, 1:20 PM
Subject: Letter of Resignation

Dear Sara,

Thanks for stopping by. I understand your need to step away for personal reasons. I spoke to the department chair and unfortunately, we won't be able to hold your lectureship while you're on leave. You are certainly welcome to re-apply, but I can't promise that we'll have classes for you to teach upon your return.

I extend my condolences once again on the loss of your mother. Perhaps you'll find some time to write during your leave. It can be such a healing balm.

Wishing you all the best,
Tessa
Director of Academic Writing
University of Maryland, College Park

Text on Fri. May 24, 2:18 PM

Binti
Thanks for telling me everything
at lunch. Still kind of in shock.
As my man Vonnegut would
say, "The excrement has hit
the fan." Won't breathe a word
of it. I'm right here for you.

From: Lucy Glenn-Kelly
To: Sara Grayson
Date: Friday, May 24, 3:01 PM
Subject: Next Steps

Thanks for your email, dear. Lea and I will be in
DC next week to visit our son. I can meet with you
then. I'm sensing a developing state of panic in you.
Take some deep breaths. Remember that ideas
exist all around us. They are simply looking for a
willing partner. Open yourself up to the universe.

Namaste,
Lucy
Senior Editor, Iris Books

Texts on Fri. May 24, 3:31 PM

Sara
What does it mean to open yourself
up to the universe? I don't feel very
well. The cupcakes didn't help.

Ann
How many did you eat?

> **Sara**
> Never mind. I just threw up. I
> don't think the universe cares.

Ann
Are you okay? We're on our way
to Deep Creek. It's Memorial Day
weekend. Did you remember that?
Call you when we get there.

Text on Fri. May 24, 6:42 PM

Ann
Made it to Deep Creek. Sara,
why aren't you picking up?
Sara? Are you okay?

❧

She left the last box of cupcakes on her neighbor's doorstep and drove straight to her mother's home. There was no time to think about the lonely house. She grabbed an empty box and walked directly to Cassandra's office, still a mess from Sara's hunt to find the book she'd just agreed to write. All four *Ellery Dawson* books were displayed on Cassandra's writing desk next to five volumes of the *Mace Kellers* series. She swept all nine volumes into the box and hit the closet next.

Sara found CDs marked with interviews her mother had done with media outlets, conferences, and book festivals. Binti thought these would help Sara with her writing process. "Get inside your mom's head!" Ann already sent her links to online lectures including graduation speeches and two TED talks.

Sara packed the boxes in her car and drove straight home.

Stouffer's chicken enchiladas cooked in her microwave as Sara brought out a box of her old fiction writing books. She stacked them on the coffee table in her small living room next to a thick yellow legal pad and her laptop. She changed into her softest UVA sweatshirt, yoga pants, and another pair of her mother's socks and got comfortable in the turquoise reading chair Mike bought her for her birthday two years ago. He claimed he picked it out himself, but she knew it was really Ann. She loved her turq chair anyway. On a few good nights, she and Mike had cuddled closely in the oversized chair to watch his favorite business reports on CNBC. Mike couldn't sit still for very long. He'd eventually finish the report standing up behind their black leather sofa, arms folded.

The microwave dinged, and Sara brought her enchiladas back to her chair. Steaming hot, the edge of the carton looked brown and over-cooked. It didn't matter. Except for the cupcakes, everything tasted the same these days.

Sara jotted notes on a legal pad in between bites of drippy tortillas, the edges hard to chew. She sketched out a brief framework for her writing time as she finished her dinner, settled back, and opened up Book One, *Ellery Dawson: Big Small World.*

CHAPTER 10

*Every moment happens twice: inside and
outside, and they are two different histories.*

ZADIE SMITH

It was Memorial Day evening, and Sara had finally finished reading Book Four. She didn't move from her turq chair for a full hour. She pressed the book close to her chest. She remembered a springtime trip to New York with her mother when she was fourteen. They sat on a bench in Central Park near Bethesda Fountain. A woman played Bach on a harp nearby while they shared a bag of roasted cinnamon almonds.

"Have you ever heard of a social theory called 'Six Degrees of Separation?'" asked Cassandra.

"Nope."

"It's basically the idea that most people on earth can find a connection to anyone else on the planet by no fewer than six relationships. For example, a connection could be traced from a fisherman in Cambodia to…that woman playing the harp to…the president of the United States."

"You mean like they're related—by blood?"

"No. Just common social threads. Like how people know each other. Degrees of separation can reveal how one person is connected to another person—like links in a chain."

"Hmm." Sara was intrigued. "So that person who sold me my hot dog in front of the Met could be the best friend of my science teacher, Mr. Golding."

"Right…And maybe Mr. Golding's father was a teacher in Des Moines and he taught a girl named…?"

"Katya." She liked making up stories with her mom. "Katya's Hungarian cousin had an affair with a KGB operative who was the brother of Vladimir Putin."

"Nicely done, Sara. You just discovered your own connection to Vladimir Putin by six degrees. We should probably have him over for Thanksgiving."

"I'm fine with Putin, just not my science teacher."

They laughed.

Cassandra added, "Sometimes the separation is just a degree or two. We stumble onto those more frequently. They're easier to figure out and kind of fun. Sometimes when I'm people-watching, someone will pass by and I'll think, I wonder how we're connected and by how many links? The man who is pedaling that rickshaw could be the brother of Ronnie Stoltz, my sixth grade crush."

"Or maybe that is Ronnie Stoltz!"

They both cracked up.

Cassandra sighed. "I often wonder what it would be like if someone had the power to figure out those links. What if they could instantly connect me and the driver and identify the links that separate us? Wouldn't that be interesting? I mean, we do share this world with six billion people. Wouldn't it be fascinating to know how we're all linked together? And what if that person could also sense the degree of *emotional* connection?"

"Okay. Interesting, but it seems like a bummer of a 'super power.' I mean, what good could a person actually do with it, other than know interesting tidbits about people? Sounds like knowing a whole lot about nothin'."

"But that's where you're wrong. What if a bank has just been robbed and that gifted person can tell the FBI how the suspect in custody is connected to both the bank manager *and* a mob boss?"

Sara's eyes widened. "Oh, yeah. I never thought of that. Like if there was a terrorist attack, that person could figure out the connections of the terrorists, right? Or if there was a mole in the CIA, then the person with the gifts could, like, connect him to the bad guys."

"See, Sara. You're already thinking like a novelist. I may use that idea. Or *you* should."

Sara giggled. Cassandra offered her the last almond. "I think the knowledge of someone's social map could be more than just interesting. It could be powerful…maybe even dangerous."

Sara shrugged. "It's complicated, though. You'd need a simpler way to explain it. And how would your character develop the gift—would it start small, like when they're a kid? Are they like Peter Parker, testing it all out, you know?"

"Who knows? I've wondered if the person would visualize the links or just sense certain feelings. Would they hear voices? And how would they process that information?"

"Would they get better at it as they go?"

Cassandra laughed and squeezed her hand. "I have no idea—*yet.*"

જી

Sara savored the memory as she held *Ellery Dawson* close. These books answered all those questions. Her mother gave Ellery those powers and called it "social mapping," and it was no small gift, helping Ellery to become a powerful CIA operative. She sighed deeply, setting the last book down in front of her.

She remembered the look in Char Fox's eyes at the premiere when she grabbed Sara's hands and begged her to reveal what happened to Ellery's father in Book Five. She slumped back into her chair with the sober realization that all those answers were actually up to her now.

The doorbell rang, and Gatsby barked excitedly. Ann walked in, looking sun-kissed from her weekend at Deep Creek.

She carried a large brown bag from Whole Foods and stopped in front of Sara. "You okay? You look like a zombie."

"I just finished Book Four."

"Ahhh." Ann waved a hand in front of Sara's glazed eyes. "Come on. You need to eat."

Sara's body felt stiff as she followed Ann to the kitchen. Ann started unpacking plastic containers filled with fresh fruit and vegetables all cut up and ready to eat.

"Here, put these in the fridge," Ann told Sara.

"What's all this stuff?"

"You think I don't know you?" Anna-Kath lifted the lid on the kitchen garbage and pointed at the empty frozen food cartons and pink cupcake boxes. "Just as I thought," she said. "And it smells." She pulled out the garbage liner, tied it off, and handed it to Sara.

"Hey. I was about to take that out. And by the way, there are no preservatives in those frozen meals. They're actually good for you."

"Well, I brought some fresh stuff to go along with your little frozen food festival. It's all cut-up, easy-peasy."

Sara stretched her neck to one side. "You worry too much about me, but thanks anyway." She kissed Ann on the cheek and then pushed the bag of garbage out of the way with her foot.

The two went outside to sit on the patio swing. It was warm and humid outside. Sara ate some fresh mango out of a carton "packed fresh by Nancy," and Ann drank iced tea.

"So, what's next for you?" Ann asked.

"I meet with Lucy, Mum's editor, on Friday. She's in town this week, and we're going to expand the outline. Plus, she's going to compile everything she and Mum discussed about Book Five."

"Sounds like a plan."

Sara took a sip from Ann's glass. "You're right about the series. It's Mum's best work. Hands down."

Ann smiled and held the cold glass against her shoulder. "What did I tell you?"

"So, I need to get a list of possible scenes to start. Lucy likes to approach novel development like a screenplay. You start with all the moments you can visualize and then organize it with all the key plot points."

"I like that approach." Anna-Kath popped some mango in her mouth from Sara's carton. Sara handed her the bowl. The swing rocked back and forth.

"Ann, what do I do with Ellery's father? There's that moment at the end of Book Four when she secretly meets him in the alley by the safe house. He's already suspected of espionage, and he gives her that look and says, 'Elle, there's always more to the story.'"

Ann threw her head back. "Oh—that kills me."

"Then he says he'll always love her, and he disappears into the night! Then there's the big explosion outside the Moscow hotel a week later, and it seems like he's dead, but you're not one hundred percent sure."

Ann held a fist to her chest. "Yeah. That scene gets me every time."

"But now I have to figure it all out. *Me.* I decide."

Ann exhaled slowly.

Sara pressed her feet down to stop the swing. She turned to face Ann directly. "Do you think Peter Dawson is a traitor? I mean, the evidence suggests he is, but he's the one who helped Ellery develop her gifts, and he's this amazing father and patriot...he can't possibly be this horrible traitor, can he? There has to be an explanation."

"You know people aren't completely good or completely bad, Sara. They're complicated. You can be a good father and do lousy things. I wouldn't trust Peter Dawson, in spite of the good he's done. And you can't make everything work out perfectly in the book. This isn't an episode of *Full House*."

Sara leaned back in the swing again. "You're right. Well, any suggestions about handling all the conflict between Ellery and her husband, besides marrying Brooks myself?"

Ann gave the swing another push with her feet. She chuckled. "I didn't think marriage was on your mind." She handed the carton back to Sara.

"Well, it would help if I had Ellery's gifts. She would have run away from Mike the moment she met him." Sara closed her eyes a moment. "What if I don't see the red flags next time around? What if I make the same mistakes all over again? I wasn't that smart."

Ann leaned her head against Sara's. "The rear view always looks different, doesn't it?"

Sara nodded and wiped quickly at her eyes. She speared another mango piece and smiled, pointing her fork at Ann. "I know! I'll pull Ellery out of the CIA and make her the world's greatest gossip columnist. Can you imagine? Who would be better?"

Ann laughed and lifted her glass. "To Sara Grayson, now playing God." Sara's phone buzzed with a text. It was from Lucy. She read aloud, "Can you meet tomorrow instead of Friday? Complications to discuss." Sara shook her head. "This can't be good."

Anna-Kath patted Sara's knee. "I'm sure it's fine. Lucy will get you through this."

Sara put the carton of fruit down. She'd lost her appetite.

CHAPTER 11

Every morning I jump out of bed and step on a landmine.
The landmine is me. After the explosion, I spend
the rest of the day putting the pieces together.

RAY BRADBURY

Sara met Lucy at Cassandra's favorite café in downtown Bethesda across from a Barnes and Noble with a large window display of *Ellery Dawson*. Sara glanced briefly at Ellery as she sat at a patio table. Char Fox looked ominous in the movie poster, her classic "don't-mess-with-me-eyes" looking down on patrons. Sara switched to another chair where she couldn't see her.

Lucy swept in late, looking like she'd purchased her outfit at an airport gift shop in New Delhi. She wore layers of long, thin jewelry and stacks of bracelets paired with a brightly colored skirt and tank top.

She sat down, a little nervous and out of breath.

"Are you okay? Your text had me worried." Sara asked.

"Well, why don't we go ahead and order, and I'll explain everything."

"Everything?" Something didn't feel right.

Lucy seemed jittery as she ordered a chamomile tea and a vegetarian sandwich with avocado. Sara ordered the same.

"So…what's going on?"

Lucy looked around the café nervously. She saw the poster of Ellery and rolled her eyes, "Good heavens, that woman is everywhere." She turned her chair away from Ellery and pulled out a large envelope. "Things have become a little *tricky.*"

"Tricky?"

Lucy opened a bottle of lavender oil in front of her and inhaled slowly. Sara sighed.

Lucy placed a hand over hers. "Jane Harnois is assigning you to a new editor. In fact, she's asked me to have no further discussions with you regarding *Ellery Dawson*. She'll be contacting you soon about all this, but I needed to talk to you myself."

Sara could hardly breathe. She must have heard her wrong. "You're joking, right?"

Lucy shook her head. Her lower lip quivered.

"His name's Benedict Keecher—"

"Keecher?"

"Keecher. He's new. I don't know him well."

"This makes no sense. You edited the last two *Ellery* books. Why would Jane reassign me? My success is her success—right? I mean, I know we didn't exactly hit it off, but Iris would still want me to get this right."

"Sara, I don't get the feeling that Jane sees it that way. Hmm. How do I say this?" She clasped her hands together, her bracelets making a jingle. "Jane believes you are a threat to the *Ellery* franchise. She's bound by contract to let you *try* to write this book, but don't think for a minute that she wants you to succeed."

"I don't understand. If I succeed then Iris does too."

"Don't tell anyone I said this, but," Lucy glanced behind her and then whispered, "she's hoping you'll give up. You know, quit before the deadline so she's free to choose the author she wants."

Sara pressed her fingers into her forehead, certain one of those danger-ous sinkholes was forming right now below the café.

Lucy's face sagged.

Sara shook her head. "I can't write this book without you."

Lucy grasped her arm. "I'm so sorry. I've hashed this out with Jane, but honestly, there's nothing more I can do." She lowered her voice again. "All of her chakras are closed."

She slid the envelope towards Sara. "Here's everything I remember discussing about Book Five. I even had my wife, Lea, write down every-thing she recalls from Cassandra's visits." Lucy twisted her necklaces. "And please don't tell Jane we've talked."

"Of course, but what do I do next? How do I move forward without support from Iris?"

Lucy squeezed Sara's hands so tightly they hurt. "Phil Dvornik. You know he edited the first two *Ellery* books, plus a dozen of your mom's other books. He knows *Ellery Dawson* better than anyone."

Sara pulled her hands away. "Phil's probably behind this. He's the one who hired Jane."

"Phil hasn't stepped foot inside Iris Books for months. He was dev-astated about your mother's diagnosis, and I know he hasn't handled her passing very well. As you know, they were very close."

"Well, he wasn't close to me. Why would he help?"

"Considering his history with your mother, I think he would. And even though he retired two years ago, he kept his position on the board of directors."

Sara pressed her fingers into her scalp. "You don't know what you're asking. Phil thinks I'm a terrible writer."

"We all know Phil's a little rough around the edges."

"He makes Gordon Ramsey look like Savannah Guthrie."

Lucy looked wistful. "He's changed a lot. You know the only reason I became your mom's editor is because Phil adored your mother."

"What does that have to do with anything?"

Lucy sighed patiently. "Your mother and Phil were brilliant together—the ultimate writer/editor team. It's the kind of synergy every editor wants with a writer, but it did create some tension for them that impacted their personal relationship. So, two years ago Phil chose Cassandra, the woman, over Cassandra, the author, and retired from Iris. That's when he put Jane in charge, and I became Cassandra's editor." Lucy laughed lightly. Her eyes softened. "The great Phil Dvornik finally loved someone more than Iris Books. No one could have predicted that."

Sara narrowed her eyes at Lucy, wondering how an intelligent person like her could get her facts so distorted. This was not how she would have described their relationship *at all*. Okay, everyone knew Phil and her mother had a relationship ten years ago. Blah, blah blah. But it didn't last. They broke up shortly after Phil destroyed Sara's first book. Her mother left Iris within the year, finding it impossible to work with him anymore.

Sure, they started spending time together again when Cassandra came back to Iris Books with *Ellery Dawson* four years ago, but *please*. This was no great love story. Didn't anyone cross-check their sources anymore?

"Phil is the very best resource you have, dear."

Sara wanted to cry right then and there, but she didn't want Lucy feeling more sorry for her than she already did. It wasn't Lucy's fault she worked for an unbalanced woman who used too much hair product.

"I'll think about working with him, okay?"

"You will?" Lucy's eyes brightened.

Not on your life, Sara thought, but couldn't say. She would just have to find other help. And maybe her new editor would actually be good.

Sara took a deep breath. "I'll work it out," she assured Lucy. She patted her hand. "It will be okay. Really."

Lucy seemed placated. She shared some inexplicable Hindu proverb about birds and a pond while a server boxed up her vegetarian sandwich to go. Her necklaces brushed up against Sara's face as she leaned over to hug her goodbye.

Sara sat alone at the table. She picked the red onions off her sandwich. She tried a few bites and put it back down. Where was the avocado? She ordered avocado.

She opened the envelope. There were only five pages. How could there be only five pages? It was bad enough that Sara's mother was asking the impossible from the underworld—couldn't she have left her more than a few breadcrumbs? She got up to leave and saw that damn *Ellery* poster again from the display window across the street.

Sara marched into Barnes and Noble and went straight to an open cashier. His nametag said Jeremy P. He was sunburned and had acne and would probably write a paper in her class on how obsessive gaming had no ill effects on a person's social life.

"How much for that *Ellery Dawson* poster in the window?"

"Sorry, ma'am. Our posters are not for sale."

"Of course, it's for sale. Everything is for sale."

"Umm. It's really not." He scratched behind his ear and readjusted his name tag on his polo shirt. "Umm, my manager, Ramona, she'll be back in fifteen minutes. You could talk to her."

"No need to bring in Ramona," Sara said sweetly. "How much just to take it down? It's so big, and it's really bothering a lot of people. And did you know that Char Fox has a problem with cold sores?"

"Who's Char Fox?"

She leaned across the counter. "Jeremy P., you need to get out more."

"Huh?"

Sara pulled out her wallet. "How much? One hundred dollars? Two hundred?" Sara lowered her voice to a whisper. "I'll give it to you, under the table." She winked. "You could just make it fall down, like it was an accident, right?"

A friendly voice interrupted the transaction. "Sara? I thought that was you. How's it going?" She turned around to see David Allman approach her. He wore his usual dark business suit and held *The Ultimate Beginner's Guide to Recreational Kayaking*.

She shot David a brisk hand wave and quickly turned back to Jeremy, who was eyeing the money. She slid the money to him fast. To her great satisfaction, Jeremy slipped the money out of the way with a quick nod. Maybe that kid was going to be okay.

She turned around. "Hi David. Oh look, Jeremy P. is open. Uh, he was just helping me out, right, Jeremy?"

David paid for his book, and then they stopped to talk outside the bookstore.

"Are you okay?" David asked. "You seem a little flustered."

"Actually, I'm not okay. Lucy Glenn-Kelly just told me that Jane Harnois reassigned me to some crapshoot editor named Benedict Keecher? That's not even a name. He sounds like a...like a house elf."

"Jane changed editors? What's her explanation?"

"Nothing—other than an effort to get me to quit. Can she switch editors like this—legally?"

"I'll review the contract terms and get back to you."

Sara shook her head. "So, what do I do now?"

"Well, show her what you've got."

"Show her what I've got? Lucy was supposed to help me outline this whole thing."

"Well, think what your mom would do and then get to work."

"Don't you know any Hindu proverbs? I respond better to Hindu proverbs than to practical advice."

"Um. Willpower knows no obstacles?"

Sara raised her eyebrows.

David shrugged his shoulders. "Hey, remember that old whiteboard your mom used to storyboard her first books? Maybe it's time to pull that out. I remember she used colored cards and markers and moved them around on the board as she played with her plot."

"You're my attorney and you're giving me writing advice? What, are you like John Grisham?"

"Just a thought."

Suddenly, a loud crash in the window display made them jump. The oversized *Ellery Dawson* poster was in a heap on the floor. Jeremy stood in the window and flashed her an awkward thumbs up sign that didn't escape David.

"What was that about?"

Sara smiled. Seeing that poster come down made her feel practically giddy.

"Sara…did you—?"

"The whiteboard's a great idea, David. Gotta go. Good talk."

Sara hurried across the street to the parking garage.

Where was that whiteboard?

CHAPTER 12

Writing is something you do alone. It's a profession
for introverts who want to tell you a story but don't
want to make eye contact while doing it.

JOHN GREEN

From: Jane Harnois
To: Sara Grayson
Date: Tuesday, May 28, 3:32 PM
Subject: Exciting News from Iris!

Dear Ms. Grayson,

I'm thrilled to assign Mr. Benedict Keecher as your new editor. Mr. Keecher has been at Iris for five years now and will bring a new set of eyes to the *Ellery Dawson* series. Of course, your success is our success, and you can trust that Iris Books will help you write the very best book you can in spite of your present limitations.

Sincerely,
Jane H. Harnois
President, Iris Book Publishing

From: Sara Grayson
To: David Allman
Date: Tuesday, May 28, 5:07 PM
Subject: FW: Exciting News from Iris!

David,

I just forwarded you an email from Jane. Ugh!

Are you sure she's not in violation of the contract rider?

I bet she irons her jeans. If she owns any jeans. I
bet she has a clear plastic cover on her sofa.

Sara

From: David Allman
To: Sara Grayson
Date: Tuesday, May 28, 8:00 PM
Subject: RE: Exciting News from Iris!

Sara,

The contract rider states that the new author is
entitled to all the same levels of editorial support that
Cassandra received. From a legal standpoint, Jane is
within her rights to reassign editors. I'll argue that
this is not the same level of support and put pressure
on Jane to reinstate Lucy, but this may take time. My
advice is to work with the new editor for now. See
if he'll come to DC for a meeting to get started.

How's the writing? Did you find the whiteboard?

David

P.S. Definitely irons her jeans.

From: Sara Grayson
To: David Allman
Date: Wednesday, May 29, 10:04 AM
Subject: RE: Exciting News from Iris!

David,

Thanks for following up with Jane. Please take her kayaking over Great Falls with you and Mia.

I've started storyboarding mom's key plot points on the whiteboard. You can tell Ms. Fancy Pants Harnois that the book is coming along in SPLENDID fashion.

Sara

From: Sara Grayson
To: Binti Juma
Date: Thursday, May 30, 4:36 PM
Subject: Bad!

Binti,

This book is going nowhere! There's an oversized whiteboard taking up half my living room. I'm trying to storyboard the key plot points, but nothing fits. My head hurts and my living room clock is ticking, like really loud.

Well it was. I just stuffed it in my neighbor's garbage.

Sara

From: Binti Juma
To: Sara Grayson
Date: Thursday, May 30, 7:18 PM
Subject: Bad No More!

Sara,

You're in luck! I had my students complete a writing exercise: What should happen in *Ellery Dawson* Book Five? Granted, there were a handful that didn't know the books, but overall we've got some great stuff here. Read what I've attached, and we'll meet tomorrow. Disregard the paper that ties Ellery's father to Michael Jackson's death. I wouldn't go that direction.

Binti

From: Benedict Keecher
To: Sara Grayson
Date: Friday, May 31, 6:10 AM
Subject: Greetings

Dear Ms. Grayson,

Allow me to introduce myself. I'm Benedict Keecher, and I've been assigned as your editor for the final volume of *Ellery Dawson*. Admittedly, the assignment came as a surprise since I've mostly edited historical nonfiction. I'm practically an expert now on the War of 1812 and Grover Cleveland. The latest book I edited about the Erie Canal has been called "utterly riveting" and "an unsung joy." I can assure you I'm ready to jump in and assist you now on every level. I'm sorry I'm unable to meet with you in

Washington. I'm afraid I have a severe allergy condition and cannot travel in enclosed spaces for more than an hour. Let's video conference at your convenience next week.

Benedict Keecher, Associate Editor
Iris Book Publishing

From: Sara Grayson
To: Anna-Katherine Green
Date: Friday, May 31, 9:00 AM
Subject: I'm fine!

Anna-Kath,

Got your link to *Prevention Magazine's* "Healthy Frozen Entrees" and have already picked some up. Yes, I know it would be good to see Sybil Brown Baker, but I'm pressed for time, okay? A solid draft of this book is due in exactly 7.25 months. That's 29 weeks!

Sara

From: Sara Grayson
To: Binti Juma
Date: Saturday, June 1, 1:28 PM
Subject: 29 Freakin Weeks!

Binti,

Holy crap! I only have 29 weeks! Somehow 7.25 months sounded so much better. I started hyperventilating in the frozen food section at Safeway this afternoon and had to stick my head in one of the freezer cases to calm down, and then all the glass doors were fogged over, and I had to help a teetering old woman, who looked like the Queen Mum, reach her multi-grain waffles.

Sara

To: Sara Grayson
From: Safeway
Date: Sunday, June 2, 9:22 AM
Subject: WELCOME TO SAFEWAY
HOME DELIVERY SERVICE!

Sara Grayson,

We have received your order of 45 frozen entrees. Your delivery time will be Monday, June 3rd at 4:30 PM. Thank you for allowing us to be your neighborhood grocer.

Doug Goshen
Bethesda Safeway

From: Sara Grayson
To: Binti Juma
Date: Monday, June 3, 11:01 AM
Subject: Lifesaver

Binti,

Thanks for coming over last night. You're right. I was probably trying to outline too much. Maybe I do need more of an organic process. Whiteboard is gone. I need to center myself each day, like you said, and just let the ideas flow. This way I can *feel* my way to the characters.

Sara

To: David Allman
From: Sara Grayson
Date: Tuesday, June 4, 10:15 AM
Subject: Do Something!

David,

This morning I video-conferenced with my new editor, Benedict Keecher. The man's bookshelf held Civil War bayonets and a Spanish-American War pistol, which he talked about for fifteen minutes before we got to my outline. And the man looks ill, I tell you. He's ghostly pale and had a plaid blanket wrapped around his shoulders like he'd just arrived via Ellis Island in the winter. I wonder if they can't fire him because he only has months to live.

Also, he complained that Ellery Dawson's never killed anyone with her bare hands and that I needed to work that in ASAP. He sent me links for some suggested methods.

Do something!

Sara

Texts on Wednesday, June 5, 8:28 PM

Sara

Forget everything I said. It's bad.
Printed the first two chapters so I could
mark it by hand. Pulled out the paper
shredder Mike got me for Valentine's
Day and shredded everything—
including an old stack of student papers
just because it felt good. Starting over.

Binti

This is normal author stuff.
Keep writing. Remember, every
sentence you cut leads you
to a sentence you'll keep.

Sara

Whatever.

From: David Allman
To: Sara Grayson
Date: Thursday, June 6, 9:08 AM
Subject: Jane's Response

Sara,

Jane assures me that Benedict Keecher is not dying.
He has an allergy problem. She says he will provide
you with all the support you need to write this book.
Let me be clear: Jane is not on your side. Please
forward any written interactions directly to me.

David

Texts on Monday, June 10, 1:43 PM

Sara
I finished chapters 1-3. It's
something at least.

Binti
Oh yeah! You've got this!

Texts on June 11, 6:32 AM

Sara
Just shredded chapters 1-3.

Binti
Stop the bloodshed. Move on.

From: Gibbs Cartwright, *NYT*
To: Sara Grayson
Date: Tuesday, June 11, 4:24 PM
Subject: NYT feature story

Dear Ms. Grayson,

I'm a journalist with the *New York Times.* I'm
writing a feature article about your mother's
legacy and would like to meet with you regarding
a 1997 lawsuit in which your mother was accused
of plagiarism. As you know, the case was settled
quietly. Some new details of the case have
emerged, and I would like to get your comment.

Gibbs Cartwright
The New York Times

From: Sara Grayson
To: Gibbs Cartwright, *NYT*
Date: Tuesday, June 11, 4:45 pm
Subject: RE: NYT feature story

Mr. Cartwright,

The lawsuit is old news. It was settled quickly and quietly because it was entirely without merit. Interview requests go through my mother's publicity agent, Thea Marshall, cc'ed here.

Sara Grayson

From: Gibbs Cartwright, *NYT*
To: Sara Grayson
Date: Tuesday, June 11, 4:52 PM
Subject: RE: NYT feature story

Aren't you the least bit curious? A reliable source reports your mother settled for an obscene amount of cash. Her incredible rise from ER nurse to bestselling author did happen rather suddenly. Happy to travel to Washington to discuss.

Gibbs

Text on Tuesday, June 11, 7:30 PM

Thea Marshal
I received the emails you forwarded to me from Gibbs Cartwright. He's baiting you. I'll handle it. I highly

doubt there's anything new. In the
future, use the email template I
gave you for interview requests.

Texts on Wednesday, June 12, 9:13 AM

Ann
You haven't answered my texts in
two days. I'm coming over tonight.

> **Sara**
> Fine. Will you bring your paper
> shredder? Mine is busted.

CHAPTER 13

I thought, 'Nobody wants this book, and I'm an idiot for having worked on it so hard.' But to succeed in writing, you must be willing to look stupid for a long time.

MIN JIN LEE

Sara stood in front of the microwave watching the cardboard tray of Dion's Organic Turkey Vegetable Lasagna rotate round and round. She brought it to the living room, where she had resurrected the whiteboard. She rearranged Post-it notes on the board in between bites of something that shouldn't really be called lasagna. She could only eat half of it. She set it on the coffee table, strewn with dry erase markers and empty barbecue chip wrappers.

She lay on the floor studying the dust on her ceiling fan when Gatsby jumped up and barked at the front door. Anna-Kath walked in and stood towering over Sara, holding a pot of something that smelled fresh, never frozen. Piles of crumpled Post-its littered the living room floor. Sara's shredder overflowed with paper, and the recycling can tipped over, spilling additional paper shavings. Gatsby was sniffing and then scratching through a mound of former chapters.

Ann surveyed the room and took a deep breath. She gave a wide, forced smile. "Okay, well, you've obviously been writing *something*." She kicked Sara's leg. "Come on. Let's eat."

The two sat in Sara's kitchen while Ann served up two bowls of her own white bean, chicken, and lentil soup. Ann cut her a thick piece of whole wheat bread and handed it to her. "You don't look good."

Sara shrugged her shoulders.

"Where are you at?"

"I have an outline, and I had the first three chapters."

"Had?"

"I just shredded them. Again."

"Are they still on your computer?"

"Yes."

"I want to read them."

"Fine." Sara brought Ann her laptop and clicked on the last draft.

Ann rinsed their dishes. "Why don't you go take a shower while I read, okay?"

"I'm fine."

"No. *Please* go take a shower. And put that UVA sweatshirt in the laundry room. I'll throw a load in."

"It's not that bad."

"It's that bad. Take a shower. We'll talk."

An hour later the two walked with Gatsby in Rock Creek Park. They followed a winding path, lined with maple and birch trees.

Ann was unusually quiet. This was never a good sign.

"Well...can you see why I shredded it?"

"It's not bad."

"That's not exactly good." They walked around some geese that Gatsby wanted to chase.

"Well, there are good lines. And I like the dialogue between Ellery and her husband." Ann sighed. "I don't know. Something's not clicking. The suspense feels kind of forced, like it's not natural. And would Ellery really go off on her daughter like that?"

"She's not perfect."

"Okay. Fair enough. But Ellery's father? I just don't think his betrayal can be wrapped up so cleanly right at the beginning. Was that in the notes from Lucy?"

"Lucy's not writing the book." Sara walked ahead.

Ann quickened her pace, trying to drag Gatsby along beside her. "Some of it just doesn't quite sound like you."

Sara stopped and turned to face Ann. She cocked her hip to one side. "Like me? Or like me trying to sound like Mum? Or like me trying to sound like Ellery who sort of sounds like Mum, but who actually sounds like Char Fox?"

"Huh?"

Sara sat down on a bench near a magnolia tree. Ann sat next to her, biting the bottom corner of her lip. "Sara, it's good. I'm just saying maybe there's some scenes that don't ring…emotionally true."

Sara exhaled loudly and pressed her fingers against her forehead. "Can we please talk about something else? Anything else?"

Ann rustled the fur on Gatsby's neck. "Well, okay. I did get an interesting interview request from the *Times*."

"Oh, that? Me too. I found it irritating, actually. That lawsuit is such old news."

"Well, here's the thing—"

"Wait, you didn't actually talk to that reporter, did you?"

"No. I forwarded it to Thea, but I was curious and did a little research about the case. Remember Meredith Lamb, that woman David Allman asked you about? You know how Mum set up a trust for her and a college fund for her dependent?"

"Um. Couldn't we talk about a TV show? You and Gerald T. Green do watch TV together, right?"

"Of course. We just watched a documentary on the building of the Erie Canal. Based on that best-selling book. It was fascinating, actually—"

"Meredith is fine. Go ahead."

Ann pulled her shoe up to the bench and tightened her laces. "Well, Meredith Lamb was the *plaintiff* in the lawsuit. Can you believe it? She's the one who sued Mum twenty-two years ago! Apparently, it was one year after Mum published her first book—right after it skyrocketed—and was about to publish her second when Meredith filed suit *claiming* that Mum plagiarized her. Crazy, right?"

Sara glanced at her phone. Binti still hadn't responded to her last text. "Uh, right."

"Anyway, she claimed Mum's first book had several chapters nearly identical to one of her manuscripts and that the premise of Cache Carter was her creation, not Mum's. Apparently, Mum settled the whole thing privately in just a few months and kept it mostly out of the press."

Sara glanced at her phone again. She had a Safeway delivery the following morning.

"Sara, you with me?"

"Oh yeah. Umm. That's interesting."

"Interesting? This is *bizarre*. Why would Mum leave money to a woman—a trust, no less—to someone who sued her twenty-two years ago? And someone she'd already settled with for an 'obscene amount of cash'? I wonder how much the settlement actually was. Did David ever mention how much was in the trust?"

Sara stared across the trail, her eyes empty.

"Come on, Sara. You're the one who wanted to talk about something else."

Sara sighed. "Sorry. I know this is all interesting, but I just can't think about this Meredith thing right now. David probably knows more. I have a hard time thinking about anything but this blasted book."

"You'll get there."

"How? They took Lucy from me and gave me this Benedict guy who's hiding a terminal illness. I've plotted and replotted the story. David suggested I hire my own editor, but if I do, word could leak to the press that I'm the one writing this book, and if that happens, it's all over for me. Binti's been helping, but she has a full-time job, and I just…I just can't see this coming together. Some days I just want to quit so badly, but every time I think of quitting, I see Jane Harnois's evil eyes staring me down like she's ready to draw a chalk print of my body."

"So, what are you going to do?"

"I don't know."

"I think you do know."

Sara sat up straight. "Don't say it."

"Sara…"

"Don't say it."

"Sara, look at me. You have to go to Phil. Now. This weekend. Go to New York. You're not going to get through this without him."

"What makes you think Phil would help me?"

Ann threw her hands up in the air. "Phil has never had a problem with you. You have the problem with him."

Sara wiped her eyes with her purple exercise shirt ($41.99 with Cutie Coupon).

"What if I just called him for you and just kind of floated the idea?"

Sara's body went rigid. "Absolutely not! Look, I'm starting fresh again tonight. And I have some…new ideas."

"Really?"

"No. But I will."

"Sara, it's been three weeks and you aren't happy with any of your work." Ann scrolled quickly through her phone and flashed Phil's contact info, complete with his horrible, ornery face. She sat up straight. "I'm calling him right now."

"Don't you dare!"

Ann lifted it high, and Sara lunged for it, falling on top of Ann.

"Get off me!" They both rolled off the side of the bench, Ann tucking her knees into her chest to push Sara back. Gatsby watched a moment, and went back to sniffing goose poop.

"I'm just trying to help you." Ann wriggled away. "And you're embarrassing me."

Sara lunged for her again. "Hand me the phone."

Ann scooted backwards on the grass, breathing hard, her face red. She looked defiantly at Sara and shoved the phone down her bra.

"Hey, it's the Grayson girls," said a familiar voice.

They looked up to see David Allman staring quizzically at them. His girlfriend Mia jogged in place, her face dewy and bright. Her hair was darker than Sara's and twisted in two short braids. She smiled, and Sara was pretty sure she'd seen someone like her in one or more teeth whitening ads on the Metro.

Anna-Kath quickly stood up and tried to smooth her messed up hair. A dry leaf clung to her shoulder. Sara stayed seated on the grass. Specks of grass and soil clung to her kneecaps. She was too tired to care. It was only David.

"Hi, David. So nice to see you," said Anna-Kath. "Sara and I were, you know, just…um…joking around."

Sara rolled her eyes. She tried to bite off a hang nail.

"You remember Mia," David gestured towards her.

"Lovely to see you again." Anna-Kath shook her hand and then gave Sara a quick pointed stare that meant stand the hell up.

Sara looked up sweetly and said, "Hello, Mia. David." She shot a quick glare at Ann and stayed put, pulling her legs around to sit cross-legged.

"Oh, I love that stretch after I run," said Mia, pulling her arm up over her head to stretch her shoulder.

"Oh, definitely," said Sara.

Suddenly, the muffled, raspy voice of Phil Dvornik spoke up and out through Anna-Kath's chest. "Hey, you've reached Phil. You know what to do."

Sara suddenly lunged for Ann, reaching a hand down the front of her shirt and snatching her phone out before Ann could stop her. Sara began hitting the "end call" button like she was stabbing the phone to death with her finger. Then she looked sweetly at Ann, gently offering the phone back to her. "Thanks, Ann."

Sara looked at Mia and David and shrugged her shoulders with a smile. "Those telemarketers."

David squinted his eyes, "Wait, was that...?"

"Oh, I used to keep my cell phone in my bra too," said Mia, "but now I've got these running capris from Lululemon with the side pocket. Total game changer. I must have bought twelve pairs."

"That must be very nice for you," said Sara.

"Well, we better keep pace," said Mia, tapping her orange smart watch that matched her orange running shoes.

"Of course," said Ann.

"Yeah, us too," said Sara. "Gotta keep going." Gatsby snored peacefully under the bench.

Mia gave a cute little wave with her cute little hand, and the two jogged away. They looked like the couple everyone wants to get together on "The Bachelor."

Ann's face flushed red again. "That was so embarrassing! Are you out of your mind?" she shouted and broke into a run—the opposite direction.

Sara wrapped a limp arm around Gatsby and whispered to him. "I might be."

೪

At 3:00 AM, Sara's shredder began to smoke, which set off her fire alarm. She moved the shredder to her back patio and then fanned the smoke detector with a ten-page paper on *Ellery Dawson* from Binti's class.

A few hours later, she texted Ann. She sighed hard, defeated. "Fine. I'll talk to Phil."

"Fine. I'll send you his number."

"Fine."

"Fine."

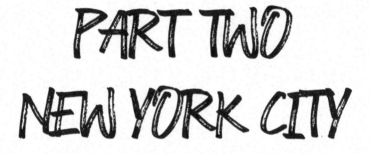

PART TWO
NEW YORK CITY

CHAPTER 14

When you can't go forward, and you can't go backward,
and you can't stay where you are without killing off what is
deep and vital in yourself, you are on the edge of creation.

SUE MONK KIDD

Phil Dvornik lived in the Theatre District on 8th Avenue in Manhattan. Sara felt certain he had never attended a Broadway musical in all his life, yet there he was living next door to all of them. What a waste of a great location. Then she realized Phil probably went to all of those heart-wrenching plays—the slow, sad ones that get rave critical reviews, but which most people only attend to look smart at dinner parties.

Sara squinted up at Phil's stodgy building from across the street. The brick was brown, like an old potato, and the ornate cornice along the roof's edge was a sorry bandage for what was clearly an expensive but cantankerous old building. "It figures he'd live in a place like that," she said aloud to no one. New York was a safe place to talk to oneself. Even the doorman muttered to himself as he wrestled with the plastic on a dry cleaning order in the muggy wind.

Sara's hair blew in her face and stuck to the ointment she'd just applied to her lip. The cold sore had magically appeared overnight, upper right lip.

She'd just stopped at Duane Reade for ointment. Now she smelled like camphor oil. She swept her hair back into a low ponytail.

"I can do this." She looked at her watch. Five to ten. She crossed the street.

Although Phil had been a prominent part of Cassandra's life since Iris published her first novel more than twenty years ago, he had always lived in New York, so Sara never spent much time with him. She remembered meeting him for the first time as a child. He said very little, and his efforts to smile looked awkward, like his face muscles weren't accustomed to that position.

Sara had asked for today's meeting with Phil via email. He wrote back three hours later: "My place, Monday at ten. We'll talk. Phil."

That was it.

Her stomach now crawled with insecurity at the thought of asking him for help. She carried her work bag, heavy with her laptop, writing notebooks, and a skittish plate of what her dad would have called humble pudding.

It had been nine years since Phil reviewed Sara's one and only novel. When she first gave him the book, she had high hopes. She'd workshopped it with some writing friends from UVA who loved it, and her mother called it "promising."

Not Phil. He complained of Sara's "tunnel vision" and an "inability to get to the heart" of her characters. Her book was "shallow," her characters "flat and incomplete." His ten-page diatribe cut into Sara's soul, and if there had been anything good or redeeming in that book, he failed to mention it.

Sara wouldn't have admitted it at the time, but she was deeply embarrassed. The hardest part was that deep down, Sara knew Phil was right. Mike made excuses for her. He said Phil probably wasn't as mentally sharp anymore and wondered if Sara would really be happy as a writer anyway. Cassandra told her the opposite—that she could write stories—that she *needed* to write stories. She said Phil was one of the toughest editors around and not to give up.

Sara was in the process of applying to grad school at the time, looking for a good fiction writing program. Three weeks after Phil's scathing review, she determined that she didn't really like fiction writing after all and applied instead to a number of rhetoric and composition programs. Sara hadn't written a speck of fiction since then.

She smoothed her hair back and introduced herself to Phil's doorman. She paused at the elevators.

"Are you getting in?" a resident asked impatiently. He held a large brown bag from Pick-A-Bagel that smelled like maple syrup and bacon. She stepped inside. The smell mixed with the camphor oil from her lip made her queasy. Her left eye started to twitch.

Sara exited the elevator on the 22nd floor, stepping out slowly, like she was scanning for possible land mines. She found his apartment, just past the elevator. She paused a moment, summoning the strength to knock. She swallowed hard, lifted her chin, and raised her hand to knock. Before her knuckles hit the wood, Phil swung the door open. It startled her.

"Um…hi?" she said. She gripped her bag tightly.

She waited for Phil to make some snarky comment like, "Finally decided I know something?" Or, "Crawling back to me now?"

Instead, Phil just looked tired. His eyes were a little red, his face thinner. His beard was scruffy, and his gray hair and eyebrows were in need of trimming. How old was he now? Seventy?

"Come in," he muttered.

"Thanks?" Sara followed him in, feeling increasingly nauseous.

The entryway opened into a living room with high ceilings and large windows. Dark cherrywood shelves lined an entire wall filled with books. The floors were a light cherry, and the tall window frames had the same rich wood. There were stacks of books in the corners of the room and more stacks next to the end tables. A large purple vase held black irises on a sofa table behind the couch.

Phil motioned for Sara to sit down on a modern looking black leather sofa. He sat across from her in a black reading chair. She sat stiffly, reminding herself to breathe.

Phil's face looked weathered, his cheeks reddish, like an old fisherman. He had a cup of coffee on an end table and a stack of history and art books on the coffee table between them.

Phil wore dress pants, a crisp gray button-down shirt, and black socks, those kind with the gold toes. Sara had never seen Phil in socks. Maybe he would have been less intimidating all these years if she'd seen him in socks. Even Mussolini was probably less menacing in socks.

"Want something to drink?"

A cup of tea sounded nice, but Phil was a strict coffee guy. "Some water, maybe?"

Phil brought back a glass of water and handed it to Sara. She cleared her throat and took a shaky sip. He leaned back, crossed his legs, and folded his arms firmly against his chest.

Just get this over with. She set her water down on the coffee table and cleared her throat again. "Well, I just wanted to talk about—"

"*Ellery Dawson,*" Phil interrupted in his deep, raspy voice. He leaned forward, his arms resting on his thighs. "Book Five. You're supposed to write it."

Sara liked him better leaning back. Farther away. "You already know?" She took another sip of water and held onto the straps of her bag propped against her knees.

"I still own Iris."

She felt foolish. "Yes, of course."

"But I knew before then. Your mother told me."

"You knew *before*?" Sara hated the thought that someone else knew and did not warn her—warn her in time to get out of this mess before it ever assumed its "dying wish" status.

Years of aggressive frowning had carved deep ridges between Phil's brows, but he didn't actually look mean that morning. Instead, there was a sort of slumped sadness about him. "Yes. I told her you shouldn't write it," he said.

"Oh. Okay." Actually, he did look mean. She studied the triangular patterns on the rug, wishing she'd never come.

Phil rubbed the back of his neck. "Look, you don't have the practice, the expertise—"

"I think I'll go now." Sara placed her water back on the coffee table. It was lousy water. It was just like Phil to serve her lousy New York City tap water. And no ice. She stood up to leave.

"Sit down, Grayson, okay? Let me finish." Sara audibly sighed. She sat back down, but stayed on the edge of the couch, ready to spring at the first opportunity.

"Look, you don't have the expertise to write this book...but you do have the talent."

Sara leaned forward. "Excuse me?" She pulled her bag onto her lap and hugged it like a flotation device.

Phil took a sip of coffee and eyed her carefully. "I never said you couldn't write or that you don't have talent. What you haven't had is persistence. You know the saying, 'Writing is easy, just open a vein.'"

Sara studied Phil's face again, not sure where he was going with this.

He set his mug down and looked at her sharply. "Why didn't you finish your novel? The one you sent me years ago."

Sara took a deep breath. Something she had buried long ago began to poke around painfully inside her. The rug was suddenly interesting again. She couldn't look up at him.

"I don't know," she whispered to the carpet.

"Sure you do," he spat out, clearly unsatisfied. "Come on. Why didn't you finish your book?"

She studied the frayed leather on her bag straps. "It's not like that. I changed my mind. I decided to teach instead."

"Like hell. Come on, Grayson. Why didn't you finish your book?"

"Look, writing fiction just didn't work out for me."

"Oh yeah?" Phil scooted forward in his seat. "So why didn't it work out for you?"

Shame washed over her, warm and sticky. What was she doing in Phil Dvornik's crummy apartment anyway? She didn't come there to be interrogated.

She stood up again. "Maybe this was a bad idea. I need to go."

"It's a simple question."

Sara shook her head. *I can't do this.* She walked straight out his door. Actually, she couldn't figure out the locks. She jimmied with the one on top and then the bottom and finally wrestled her way out. She punched the call button on the elevator and then stood completely alone in the 22nd floor hallway, reading a poorly handwritten sign about the proper use of the "garbage shoot."

She looked back at Phil's door and remembered his critique, the heat of the pages in her hands as she flipped through his searing commentary, every harsh word etched permanently on her brain.

The elevator opened. An older gentleman wearing a tweed cap like her father's stood inside. "Going down, love?" Her breath caught in her throat as she immediately detected the lilt of his English accent. She wiped a stray tear with the back of her hand as she told the man to go ahead.

She watched the elevator lights tick down as it descended without her and then she looked back at Phil's door. Was she any different than she was when Phil's critique exploded in her hands? How long would she bleed?

She took a deep breath and turned back to Phil's door. She knocked. Phil opened the door, his eyebrows raised…expectant.

She looked right into his weary eyes and said, "I gave up, okay? I quit."

"Yeah. I got that." He cocked his head to one side. "Why?"

She leaned her body against the door frame and closed her eyes. "Because I didn't think I could do it. I didn't think I was good enough."

"Hmm. Well, that's something." He took a step back and gestured for her to come back in.

She sat down in the same spot. Her glass of water was gone. Instead there was a cup of tea on a saucer. She lifted it with an unsteady hand and took a sip. Earl Grey with milk and sugar. Her mother's way. She sensed Phil watching her. She looked at him. He nodded.

She set her cup down and pressed her hands together. "Phil, I have to write this, and I need your help. I can't do it without you." If he only knew what it cost Sara to say those words.

An uneasy silence followed while Phil leaned his head back against his chair, his arms folded. She smoothed her bag straps nervously between her fingers.

Phil pointed a weathered finger at her. "You need grit, Grayson."

"What?"

"Grit. You know…persistence, determination, tenacity. I'll help you, but only if you'll see this *all the way through*."

"Grit," Sara repeated. She looked past Phil's face and out the window. She used to have something like that. Or was it just naïve overconfidence? Had she ever had grit?

Phil leaned forward again, both arms resting squarely on his thighs. "If we work together, I'm going to tell you that your writing sucks. Do you understand that? You'll be mad and sad, and then you'll need to get over it. Quickly. You'll revise. And then I'll tell you that it still sucks. But eventually you'll get it. Because that's how good writing happens: one shitty draft at a time until you've revised the hell out of it. And then you just might find that you've written yourself one decent little book." Phil pointed his finger again at her, his eyes fierce and unflinching. "And that is the only way you will ever finish this thing."

"Grit and shit," she said slowly, her chin up.

Phil turned quiet, his eyes studying hers like they were in some kind of staring contest. Her eyes shot to the floor, but she willed them back to his. "Phil, I'm not the same person who wrote that novel nine years ago."

"Well…let's hope not."

Sara bit her lower lip.

"I want everything you've written so far. Everything. I can access your contracts with Iris, but forward all your correspondence with Jane Harnois and anyone else there." Phil stood up, clearly indicating that this meeting was adjourned.

Sara stood. She swung her heavy bag across her shoulder and almost fell back into the sofa. She regained her balance. "So…you'll work with me?"

"I think we've settled the terms." Phil reached over the coffee table and shook her hand. "Lousy handshake, Grayson. Work on that. Meet me at Iris Books tomorrow morning at nine. We need to talk to Jane."

"Iris?" Sara couldn't stand the thought of going anywhere near Jane Harnois. "Um, they don't really like me there."

"That's okay. They like me. Nine AM tomorrow."

Chapter 15

Those who tell the stories rule the world.

Hopi Proverb

Iris Books occupied two floors of the Ashburn building on 7th and 68th. Tall display cases framed the lobby walls, filled with some of the best published works over the last twenty years. One case highlighted Cassandra Bond and the *Ellery Dawson* series and showcased a beautiful portrait of her mother: "In Memory of Our Beloved Friend and Author, Cassandra Bond." Sara walked up to the photo. Her mother's eyes were warm, her smile filled with gentle light.

Sara wiped her cheeks, wet with tears. She took a deep breath and walked back out to the street to wait for Phil. She needed to focus, to generate strength, but her brain felt scattered.

And Phil was late.

What if he'd changed his mind? He could have read her chapters last night and decided there was no hope. Her eye twitched again. She smoothed her ponytail back.

She finally saw Phil crossing the street with a tall cup of coffee. She heard her mother joke once that his basic requirements for survival included coffee, oxygen, and books. In that particular order. Sara wondered how the man ever slept. From the looks of him, he didn't. She waved to Phil as he approached the building. He walked past her with a quick nod and gestured for her to follow him. He nodded to the security guard at the front desk, and they entered an elevator.

Sara shifted from one foot to another. "Um. I'm not exactly sure what I'm supposed to do up there."

He shrugged his shoulders. "Well, listen carefully and then say what you think."

"Oh, okay."

A short, balding man stepped into the elevator. He smiled at Phil. "Good morning, Mr. Dvornik. How's retirement treating you?"

Phil kept his gaze fixed on the elevator doors and sipped his coffee. "It just got busier."

The elevator opened to a well-appointed reception area with the sign, "Iris Books," in large gold lettering above the front desk. A white vase held tall purple irises on a glass entry table.

An aging receptionist at the front desk wore a crocheted sweater, crocheted hoop earrings, and a crocheted flower clipped to the side of her wavy hair.

"Good morning, Mr. Dvornik."

"We'll see. I'm heading to Jane's office. She's expecting me."

The receptionist turned to Sara and raised her eyebrows, "Can I help you?" Her name plate said Gloria Knott.

"Umm. I'm with him."

Phil nodded towards her. "This is Sara Grayson."

"Oh, you dear thing. I'm so glad to finally meet you. You probably want to see Mr. Keecher. I'm afraid he's at a doctor's appointment this morning. You could wait here...although it could be a while. Let me check his schedule."

"It's okay." She turned to Phil, but he'd already been pulled into a conversation with a bearded man in a blue suit and white tennis shoes.

Gloria followed Sara's eyes. "Oh, that's Stu Clements. He's the CFO." She smiled easily. "I'm Gloria." She pointed to her name plate, "Gloria Knott—but with a K instead of an N." She adjusted the flower in her hair. She looked down a moment and then back at Sara. "I knew your mother." Tears filled her eyes, and she cleared her throat. "I'm very sorry for your loss."

There was something strangely comforting about this woman. Sara smiled.

Gloria glanced at Phil. Stu's face looked red and agitated as he handed Phil a stack of papers. Gloria stood up and leaned towards Sara. "Your mom changed my life."

"She seemed to have a knack for that."

"Your mother always liked my things." Gloria gestured towards her earrings and sweater and the crocheted pencil holder on her desk. "One day she noticed me looking online at a crochet contest—it was for the Crochet Guild of America and highly competitive. Anyway, she said, 'Gloria, you ought to enter that,' and I said, 'Oh I don't know.' And you know what she did? She took one of my Post-its and she wrote, 'Why Knott?'"

Gloria laughed hard enough to bounce her crocheted earrings, then glanced at Phil, and tried to look more serious. "'Why Knott?'" she whispered, smiling. Then she reached for a tiny paper tucked into the photo frame of a Yorkie and handed Sara the actual pink Post-it note that said, "Why Knott?" Sara traced the familiar script of her mother's hand. A warmth filled her chest.

"And you know what? I won. First place for my 'Netted Sundress in Royal Blue.' I went to the convention in San Diego and everything. 'Why Knott' is my new mantra."

She handed the paper back to Gloria. "I'm really happy for you." And she meant it. It was the most pleasant feeling she'd had in weeks. Maybe months.

"I could do all my desk accessories in crochet, but Ms. Harnois prefers a sleeker look."

Phil called for Sara as he shoved the stack of papers onto Gloria's desk. Sara caught a quick look. It was mostly numbers.

She reached for Gloria's hand and squeezed it. "Thanks for telling me."

Back in Phil's presence after Gloria's warmth felt like passing into East Berlin through Checkpoint Charlie. She followed him to Jane's office. Sara wondered again how someone as gracious and kind as her mother could even think of dating someone like Phil. Take that morning, for instance. Could he at least have started with something like, "How are you?" Sara felt like a puppy along for the ride, not sure where she was going or what she should say or do. How was she going to work with this man?

They stopped outside of Jane's office. Phil pointed to a chair just outside the door in the hallway. "Wait here." She wished she could have waited back with Gloria. Maybe learn to crochet.

Sara reluctantly sat down. Jane's door was immediately to her left. She shifted in the hard office chair while Phil walked into the devil's lair. The door was left ajar. She could hear Jane's welcoming voice and its familiar smoothness.

"Phil, wonderful to see you. Please sit down."

"Yeah. Well, it was time."

"It's been months since we've seen you around here, so I was pleasantly surprised to get your email yesterday about taking on some new work. We're thrilled, of course."

Sara could see a sliver of Phil through the door jam. He shifted around in one of Jane's retro-chic, white office chairs attempting to find a comfortable sitting position. The chairs looked curvy and strange, like something designed for a waiting room at a spaceport. He crossed a leg and leaned back.

"I've already notified senior management, and we're all elated, truly."

"Sure."

"I actually have a project we'd like to recommend to you. Something that could use your expertise."

"I won't waste your time. I'm here to work with Sara Grayson."

There was a pause. Jane coughed lightly. Sara heard a tapping on her desk. Maybe a pen or a fingernail. Or a claw.

"Sara Grayson?" Jane's voice sounded confused. Maybe she thought Phil was joking or just generally unwell. "Cassandra's daughter?"

"That's the one." Phil exhaled loudly. "She's writing the book, Jane."

Sara groaned inwardly at the awkwardness of being talked about. She stared at the prints of famous book covers lining the hallway and felt completely out of her league.

Jane spoke more slowly, like maybe Phil needed a little hand-holding. "Well, of course she's writing the book. She has our full support. We all want Sara to succeed."

Phil rested a hand behind his neck. "No, you don't. Not really."

"Excuse me?"

"It's clear to me what's been going on. You took Lucy Glen-Kelly off the project and gave her Benedict Keecher? Come on. Benedict? He edits historical non-fiction. I've reviewed his correspondence with Sara. So far he hasn't given her one ounce of helpful criticism."

"Sara's correspondence? With Benedict? How…?"

"Look, I get your strategy here, and it's clear you have no intention of supporting Sara."

"Now Phil, you, of all people, know how much is riding on this. Cassandra's daughter isn't capable of writing the finale—the denouement—to the bestselling series in the world. Surely you can anticipate the financial implications of a failed Book Five."

"Stu just gave me the numbers with multiple scenarios."

Sara felt her face turn red. She touched a hand to try and cool her cheeks, trying to suppress the urge to escape the building or live out her remaining days in a nearby janitor's closet.

Everything turned quiet, and then fingers tapped loudly on a desk again. "Choosing her daughter was an emotional choice, not an intelligent one."

"I've read Sara's work."

"Oh, you're a fan of Cutie Coupon? Or her greeting cards?" Jane's voice climbed in both pitch and disgust.

"She wrote a novel years ago," said Phil. "It needed work. A lot. But it had promise. I'm certain she can write."

"Well, isn't that thrilling." Jane's voice turned bitter, which she quickly covered with a new saccharine tone. "Phil, let's not be hasty. I know you have an *emotional* connection here. You and Cassandra were *very close*."

Phil chuckled softly to himself. "Hmm. An emotional connection isn't a bad thing in business. I wish I'd known that twenty years ago. Look, I'm not here to get your permission. I'm just letting you know that I'm Sara Grayson's new editor. Please inform Benedict."

"Wait, Phil. There's more to consider."

"I've brought Sara with me. She's waiting outside your office." He pointed to the door.

"What? Here?" She cleared her throat. "Now?"

Sara's stomach dropped. Phil reached to swing the door wide open without moving from his chair.

"Come in, Grayson."

She jumped up and straightened her jacket. The necklace she'd been fidgeting with fell to pieces, small beads rolling down the hallway. She quickly swept up what she could and shoved it in her bag. She rolled her shoulders back, took a deep breath, and walked in.

Jane stood up and forced a tight smile. She had to be mentally reviewing everything Sara might have heard.

"Hi…Jane."

"Lovely surprise, Ms. Grayson. Please sit down." She pointed to an empty chair, but kept her eyes narrowed on Phil as Sara sat down.

Sara quickly scanned the room. The entire space, designed in shades of black and white, looked more like an office display at a Pottery Barn than a genuine workspace. Sara half-expected there to be price tags still attached to the office furniture. She studied a couple of photos on a bookshelf: Jane next to a beautiful young woman at her college graduation, and Jane holding a toddler, his sweet pudgy hand reaching up to Jane's face. She caught Phil looking at the same photo. She caught a flash of pain in his eyes so quick she almost missed it. She met his eyes. He looked away.

"Well," Jane cleared her throat, "we were just discussing this *new arrangement* with you and Phil. Honestly, Ms. Grayson, if you had concerns about Benedict, you could have come directly to me."

Sara's frustration with this woman now bordered on loathing. She leaned forward in her chair. "Come *directly* to you?"

"Yes, of course."

"Jane, you have been anything but *direct* with me. Can we just agree to cut the bullshit?"

Jane placed a well-manicured hand over her heart, her eyes wide at the accusation.

Sara huffed loudly. "It's clear you don't want me to write the book. I get it. Most days I don't want to write it either, but I'm doing it. So, if you can't support me, then maybe you could at least stop acting against me?"

"*Acting against you?* I'm sure I don't know what you mean."

"She means get out of her way, Jane," said Phil without emotion.

Sara looked at Phil and back at Jane. "Yes. *That.*"

Jane clasped her hands together, resting them on her desk. She pressed her lips together in a forced smile. "The feelings I've expressed are nothing personal towards you."

"Nothing personal?"

"I'm just doing my job."

"Then let me do my job."

Jane shifted in her seat. She looked back and forth between Sara and Phil, her index finger tapping on her desk before she clenched it up in a fist and clasped her hands together again. She looked at Phil. "We can still only give her until December. A later release date would be a disaster for all the other stakeholders involved. Surely you know that. You can't forget what's at stake here."

"I read all the contracts last night," said Phil. "Your secretary sent them. And don't lecture me about what's at stake. Nobody knows this better than I do...except maybe Sara." Phil stood up to leave. Sara followed.

Jane stood quickly. "I only want what's best for the company."

"Which is why Sara's writing the book. I'll be in touch."

They walked briskly out of the office, past the reception area, where she heard Gloria Knott's voice, "It's a great day at Iris Publishing—how may I direct your call?" She waved at Sara as she passed.

Alone in the elevator, Phil stepped back and turned towards Sara. He raised his eyebrows, cocked his head to one side. "Grit and shit. Not bad today, Grayson." Then he laughed, short, but deeply. "There's a reason I left Jane's door open."

Sara felt some warmth return to her chest. She smiled at her mother's photo in the lobby and walked out with Phil. They had work to do.

Chapter 16

*Stories are so powerful, they can make
you root for your own oppressor.*

Laila Lalami

They passed at least four chic and cozy coffee shops on 55th before Phil led her into Adina's, which appeared to be a cross between a 1980s café and a Jewish deli. It had vinyl tablecloths, peach wallpaper, and dirty floors, but, according to Phil, "the very best coffee."

Phil drank a tall black while Sara sipped green tea with lemon at a cramped table too close to the restrooms. Sara brushed some lingering crumbs away with a napkin.

"The first thing you need to know," Phil said, "is that there's no magic writing pill that will make everything flow. It's damn hard work—and a lot of it."

"I know."

"And don't say, 'I know.' The only way we learn the good stuff is hearing what we already know. Again and again."

Sara nodded.

"So, no magic pill. Got that? You write and you rewrite. And rewrite."

"I know—I mean, okay."

"Last night I read everything you have so far—your outline, the first three chapters. What you've written so far is—"

Sara squeezed her eyes shut. "I know. It's crap."

"Not *all* of it. You have some good ideas in there."

Sara's eyes widened, then closed. He was probably kidding.

"Novelists generally fall into two different camps. Those who outline their books and those who fly by the seat of their pants. George R.R. Martin, you know, *Game of Thrones*? He calls the two types architects and gardeners. Architects plan it all out and know exactly where they're headed. The gardeners plant a seed and watch it grow—they let their story unfold. It's a stare-out-the-window, organic process. So, what are you? A gardener or an architect?"

"I'm in the *I-don't-know-what-the-hell-I'm-doing* camp."

Phil chuckled dryly. "No. *Every* writer is in that camp."

"Okay, then I think I'm an architect. I write better with a plan."

"Fine. We start with the outline this week."

"I have a two-page outline already."

"That's nothing. I'm talking about a fifty-page outline, chapter by chapter. One we can arrange and rearrange, write and rewrite. Are you renting an apartment at Longacre?"

"Yes, where my mom used to stay."

"I know where she stayed. Go back to your apartment and put the chapters you've written aside. Right now think in terms of *scenes*. List every scene you can imagine, even if you don't know where it fits in the book yet. If dialogue comes to you, write the dialogue. Don't think of getting sentences right. Don't worry about chapters. Write again tomorrow morning and start writing every morning in four-hour sessions. We'll meet afternoons at my place. In the evenings, I want you to read Books One through Four again. You've got to be thinking about how Cassie structures her books, and you've got to match her voice."

Sara took notes. She could feel new knots forming in her neck.

"We'll meet at my place tomorrow at one. I'll send you a reading list, the best work on fiction writing. Start with Stephen King's *On Writing.*"

"I've read it."

"Read it again."

Sara nodded and scribbled that down too while she massaged the back of her neck with her other hand. She wasn't sure where sleep fit into this schedule.

Phil stood up.

Sara capped her pen and looked at his tired face. "Hey Phil…thanks for sticking up for me today. You know, in Jane's office. You didn't have to do that."

"I know." Phil dropped a twenty-dollar bill on the café table and left.

❧

Sara arrived at Phil's the following afternoon. The cherrywood looked freshly polished, and she smelled more coffee brewing. Phil stepped into the kitchen. She stopped at the sofa table and studied the black irises. She touched one, just to see if it was real.

"Can I ask you something?" she called out.

"Depends."

"What's the deal with irises? Like Iris Books and irises in your apartment? Why *irises?*"

Phil walked back in and handed Sara a cup of tea.

"When did you learn to make tea?"

"It's just a tea bag. Not your mom's fancy stuff."

He sat down in his reading chair and motioned for Sara to sit. She put her bag down and sat on the couch. His socks were striped today, gray and black, practically whimsical for Phil.

"The iris is the national flower of Croatia," he announced, like it was something so obvious.

"The national flower of *Croatia?*"

"I lived in Croatia until I was eleven. Then I moved here with my parents."

"Oh…I didn't know that. So, you speak Croatian?"

"Not as well now. My son actually speaks it better than I do even though he was born in New York."

"Is this him?" Sara pointed to a photo on an end table, Phil with a dark-haired teen, decent looking, but stiff and awkward in the photo. It was hard to imagine Phil as a father. Poor kid.

"That's an old photo. Philip lives in Maine now."

Sara looked at another picture, Phil and his son in front of a light-house. Phil Jr. was taller, stronger, twenties maybe, with warm, dark eyes.

"Do you ever go back to Croatia—to visit?"

"I took your mother last summer." Phil's eyes softened. He looked away.

Phil took her mother to Croatia? How did she not know this?

"When she was in Paris. I met her there. It was a side trip before she came back. Let's get started."

"Oh." Sara followed him into a surprisingly large office. There were two black swivel chairs at a large worktable. One section of wall had two oversized whiteboards. Another wall had built-in bookshelves.

"Your mother and I had a storyboarding system for new novels. So unless you have a better process, I suggest we go with that."

"Okay."

They sat down, and Sara pulled out a stack of pages.

"I want you to take those scenes and use them to create your fifty-page outline. Get the story down chapter by chapter. Can you do it in three weeks?"

"Three weeks?" Sara touched a page. It felt suddenly thick.

"You've got six months to write a strong manuscript. Most experienced authors take at least a year to do that."

She sipped some tea and nodded pleasantly while her vital organs rearranged themselves.

He handed Sara a marker. "So, what are the big questions for Book Five?"

Sara sat thinking.

"Come on. Get up! Write them on the board."

Sara jumped up. "Sorry, right." She and Binti had already talked about this, but she stood nervously at the board now, feeling the weight of Phil's scrutiny. It was like solving a high school calculus problem in front of Mr. Mulaney, who threw erasers at students when they made mistakes. She was certain Phil wouldn't hesitate to throw objects. She just didn't know how heavy.

She started from the basics, "What happens to Ellery? Where's Ellery's father? Did he betray his country or his family or both? What is Brooks hiding from Ellery? Can Ellery's marriage survive their secrets? Can they finally defeat the terrorist network?"

Phil nodded. "Okay. Let's talk answers." They reviewed writing notes from Lucy and Cassandra. There were a few clear answers on certain characters, but no roadmap on how to get there. Sara felt exasperated again at the lack of information, the whiteboard taunting her with its stark emptiness. She wanted to bury her face in her arms, but she couldn't with Phil there, pacing around the whiteboards in his striped socks, adding questions and rearranging scene cards.

Sara rubbed her temples, trying to stave off another tension headache. "Come on, Phil. You edited the *first two books.* My mom had to know how all this ends. You have to know more than this."

Phil drank more coffee. "Normally, yes. It's the only way to write a suspense novel—for most writers. I pressed her on some of these questions, and we talked about a lot of different scenarios—yes, Ellery's father is evil; no, he's misunderstood." He stroked his scruffy chin. "Bottom line?

It's in *your* hands now." He tossed Sara another marker. She missed and scrambled to pick it up off the floor.

Phil turned away from her and went back to the board. She studied him with growing suspicion. What was he holding back?

"Well, I don't think her father's a traitor," she argued. "I think there's some explanation as to why he was missing for so long."

"Don't be ridiculous! You can't tell me there's no betrayal here. Everyone thinks the man died in the Moscow explosion, and *sixteen years later* Ellery senses his energy at a refugee camp?" Phil pointed an index card at her. "You can't make everything work out, Grayson. People are flawed. And they make terrible mistakes, even with people they love." She saw a flash of pain in Phil's eyes. He turned back to the board.

A silence grew between them, and Sara felt incredibly small. "Yeah—I get that. Like my mom asking me to write this book."

Phil shook his head, still looking at the board. "You know that's not what I'm talking about."

Sara walked over to the window, her discouragement building. She had hoped for *more answers* from Phil, not more questions. What wasn't he telling her? Sara tried to control the tears welling up in her eyes.

"Here, Grayson...write more questions." He tossed her another marker that hit her in the shoulder.

She picked it up. "Will you stop throwing these at me? I have markers. I'm good. Okay?" Sara's voice cracked, and she couldn't cover the edge to her voice. She needed to regroup. "Where's your bathroom?"

Phil pointed down the hall. He gazed back at the board, his arms folded.

She found the closet-sized bathroom. It contained more cherrywood paneling. Should she just have a good cry or rip out the wood paneling with her bare hands?

No. I'm in control. I have grit.

She pulled out a blend of lavender and cedarwood oil that she'd bought from Sybil Brown-Baker. She sat on the edge of the tub and massaged the oil into her wrists, breathing deeply.

Sara returned to Phil's office ten minutes later smelling like a health spa. He stood in front of the board and said nothing. He had written new material on one board, a gigantic "W" with spaces for triggers, conflicts, and turning points. Her self-doubt rose back up and smacked her in the face.

She shoved it back and picked up a blue marker. She studied the blank spots again. Pressure built against her forehead, like her brain might spontaneously explode. She dropped the marker back on the table. "Why are you helping me, Phil? I know you think this whole thing's a mistake."

His eyes remained fixed on the board. "I promised your mom I'd help if you asked."

"Did you think I would?"

"No."

"That's not a compliment."

"Not really."

Sara walked back to the window. Why did she ask him that? Did she think Phil would actually say something she wanted to hear?

It was a hot summer day below. Pedestrians moved quickly on their way, parting around slow tourists. A man in a yellow polo grilled meat and vegetables at a Halal stand. He served a hot pretzel to a woman with a baby in a stroller. A growing resentment stirred at the normalcy of it all.

"Do you still think it's a mistake?"

"Doesn't matter what I think."

Phil walked over and stood in front of the window, facing Sara and blocking her view. He folded his arms against his chest and forced her to make eye contact with him. "All writers have demons, Grayson. Nasty little guys that will chop you up and feed you to the pigeons down below. Listen to the part of you that believes and get to work."

Sara slowly nodded.

Phil tossed her a marker. She reached out a hand. She caught it.

She walked back to the whiteboard and went to work.

CHAPTER 17

*First forget inspiration. Habit is more dependable. Habit
will sustain you whether you're inspired or not.*

OCTAVIA BUTLER

It was Sunday night, and Sara had been in New York for one week. She
stood in front of the microwave heating up Foodscape's Chana Saag
with Yellow Rice. Watching her frozen dinners turn in the microwave
had become a nightly meditation ritual. She ought to suggest it to Sybil
Brown-Baker. Sara's phone broke her concentration. It was Anna-Kath,
who was anxious to know how things were going in New York.

"So any major fights between you and Phil yet?"

"Not exactly, but it's tense sometimes."

"Tense?"

"Okay, there are moments I still hate him. It's like working with
Simon Cowell, only without the charming accent or the fitted black tee.
But it's going better than I thought. He's definitely tough on me, but I
think he actually wants me to succeed."

"Why does that surprise you?"

Sara could hear water running at Ann's and could picture her loading
the dishwasher with Gerald T. Green, who was annoyingly adept at most
household tasks.

"Look, I've spent nine years thinking Phil was the devil. I sort of expected him to act that way."

Sara's food finished.

"What's that beeping?" Ann gasped. "Oh my gosh! Seriously? You're staying two blocks away from Hell's Kitchen, and you're eating a *frozen dinner*? What's wrong with you?"

"Hey, it's on the list you sent...and I'm very busy."

"Please dump that in the garbage right now and walk over to 9th Avenue to get something to eat. Or have something decent delivered."

Sara didn't respond for a minute. She smoothed a stray hair from her face and looked out the window to the bustle of people below.

"Sara?"

She sighed. "I have so many memories with Mum over there. Her favorite restaurants were on 9th. You remember that empanada place with the amazing guac and the three of us squeezing into that tiny corner booth to eat?"

Anna-Kath turned quiet. "Yeah, I do." She laughed softly. "Remember those Brazilian empanadas with the plantain chips? Yum."

"I wish Dad could have squeezed into that booth with us."

"I know."

"Do you ever think how life would be different if he hadn't died?"

"I used to. All the time. For starters, we'd probably be having this conversation in London right now." Ann turned off the faucet.

"If Dad were still alive, do you think he'd be the famous novelist and Mum would have stayed a nurse?"

"Maybe."

Sara nodded.

Ann had to get her kids to bed, and they hung up. Sara took out her dinner from the microwave, peeled back the plastic cover, and stirred it with her fork. It didn't smell right anymore. She dumped her dinner in the trash, tied off the bag, opened the front door, and threw it down the garbage chute. Then she walked over to 9th, where she ordered chicken tikka masala and flatbread from her mother's favorite Indian restaurant.

There had been an Indian place across the street from their flat in the East End. Sara remembered her father picking them up from school and walking home together. Her father's hand always felt strong and safe. On the way home, they often stopped for flatbread at the Indian restaurant. There was a tall man named Ashish who called her Miss Sara and handed her the flatbread with a bow that made her giggle.

Sara walked back to her apartment and spread the food out on her kitchen table. The sweet, earthy fragrance of coriander and ginger filled her tiny kitchen. She mixed the yellow rice with creamy spiced tomato sauce and chicken. She took her first bite, warm and rich in familiar flavor. She wiped her tears as she ate slowly, savoring each bite.

It tasted like not being alone.

CHAPTER 18

I love language because when it succeeds, for me, it doesn't just tell me something. It enacts something. It creates something. And it goes both ways. Sometimes it's violent. Sometimes it hurts you. And sometimes it saves you.

CLAUDIA RANKINE

Texts on Friday, July 5, 1:09 PM

Binti
Happy 4th! Do anything fun?

> **Sara**
> No, but I had my first Ellery dream! Mom said her writing always picked up when she started dreaming of her characters.

Binti
Great sign! Did she speak to you?

> **Sara**
> No. She caught up to me when I was running in Central Park. Then she rappelled down Belvedere Castle.

Binti
Why?

Sara
Didn't say.

Binti
Why not take the stairs?

Sara
Idk. Don't knock the dream, okay?

Binti
Fine. But scour the dream for
clues. Think like Ellery.

Sara
I think about her nonstop.

Binti
No. Think LIKE Ellery,
not just about her.

Texts on Tuesday, July 9, 9:38 PM

Binti
Any more Ellery dreams?

Sara
Make them stop! I've dreamed about
her five nights in a row. It's always in
Central Park. I'll be walking Gatsby
and I hear her call my name like she's
trying to catch up so I slow down and
then she zooms past me with a crazed
laugh. Freaks me out every time.

Binti
Does she say anything?

> **Sara**
> She calls my name and
> then it's mad laughter.

> **Binti**
> Follow her.

> **Sara**
> I'm dreaming. I can't follow her.

> **Binti**
> At least try and gather more details.

> **Sara**
> This isn't *Inception.*

On Wednesday Sara finished the first draft of her outline. She convinced Phil to meet her for dinner at an Italian restaurant on 5th Avenue to celebrate. Phil didn't see the point, but she convinced him that dinner was a good idea anyway. Plus, she was starting to notice that Phil *rarely* left his apartment.

They decided to wait for their table in the Carter Building's main floor lobby while Phil took a call from his son. Phil Jr. managed his property in Maine, and something had gone wrong with the water main on his street. He sounded animated about the issue and moved to a corner to talk privately. She could still hear him. He always talked loudly on his cell, like he was piloting a Coast Guard helicopter and shouting would save lives.

It was after eight and still light outside. Sara relaxed on a floral sofa, breathing deeply and enjoying her accomplishment: three weeks in NYC and a completed outline of her book! She and Phil would start fleshing out the first three chapters over the next week and a half, and then it was back to Bethesda.

She checked her email while Phil rambled on, red-faced, about the damn public works department.

Ann had sent pictures of Livvy and Jude at their first swim meet, all sweet and radiant and dripping wet. Livvy sent a short note that she loved and missed her auntie. It all made her a little homesick.

If Sara hadn't been so stuck in her phone, she would have noticed him sooner. She would have had a moment to prepare herself or plot an escape. But suddenly his shoes appeared before her, the Forzieri two-toned Italian dress shoes she bought him for their last Christmas and the light woodsy smell of his Armani cologne.

Sara froze instantly, her breath caught in her throat. He laughed that charming, low, chesty laugh, and she looked up to see her ex-husband smiling nonchalantly at her.

"Long time, no see, huh?"

What was he doing here? Sara thought he was in India or Bali or some-where on his *Eat, Pray, Love* journey, not standing in front of her at the Carter building in Manhattan. She hadn't seen him since he left her. She quickly stood and dropped her phone, which clattered loudly on the mar-ble floor. She snatched it up and shoved it in her purse.

"Hi…Mike," she whispered. Should she hug him? Shake his hand? *Just breathe.*

He laughed again, touched her shoulder, and kissed her on the cheek. Sara stiffened at his touch and pulled away.

"What are you doing here? I thought you were…away."

"Well, I did make it to India, which was really some God-forsaken place, and decided to go to back to Italy, which is, you know, *Italy.* Can't get better than that, right? Anyway, I met someone…and we decided to come back. So sorry about your mom. We were in the Alps. Bad internet. Didn't even know until a while back. What a shocker."

Sara's stomach tightened and twisted. She suddenly felt so unbearably small. "Yes…thank you." Did he really just refer to her mother's death as a "shocker"?

An unnaturally blonde woman, a few inches taller than Mike, appeared at his side. She was curvy and wore a white sundress—which clung in all the right places—with strappy, silver heels. "Michael, they have our table." She pronounced his name, "Mee-keh-leh," with a throaty Italian accent.

"This is Abrielle." Her spray tan was uneven, and she had dusted herself with some sort of body glitter that kept catching the light, making her look like a Christmas display...or a vampire in the sun.

Sara shook her warm, sparkly hand. She glanced at Phil, who was still on his phone. She caught his eyes. He looked over at Mike. His eyes widened, and he abruptly ended his call. He quickly walked over to Sara and nodded at Mike.

"Phil, my man." Mike gripped his hand and pumped it hard. "How the hell are you?"

"Fine," he said. No emotion.

Mike flashed a raised eyebrow at Sara, obviously surprised to see her with Phil.

"Phil's been helping me with...um...a writing project."

"Oh yeah? I've actually started writing a book myself. It's about my experiences in Italy; what it's taught me about leadership, business, how to win in life—that sort of thing—and it is *going well*. Writing a book always looked hard, but I'm finding it's actually not that big a deal, you know?"

Sara reached for her earring, twisting it between her fingers. Why were her ears so hot? "Well...good for you, Mike."

The presence of her ex-husband felt both familiar and foreign. His voice was the same, but his eyebrows looked darker. And was that a small grapevine tattooed on his neck? It had to be fake. Mike would call in sick over a paper cut.

Her whole body felt hot now. A trickle of sweat dribbled down her back.

"I figure it's good for business to get my book out there, right? Maybe Phil can hook me up with his connections, right, man?"

"I seriously doubt that," said Phil.

Mike laughed extra hard and slapped Phil on his shoulder, trying to act like Phil was just joking when they both knew he wasn't.

Abrielle leaned against Mike, playing absently with the curls on the back of his neck. "Hey," said Mike, "the two of you should join us for dinner."

Phil lowered his eyebrows at Mike in a cold stare and shook his head. "Sara, we've got that appointment." He gestured towards the door, and she said an awkward goodbye. Phil took Sara's arm and hurried her into a cab he quickly flagged himself.

Sara sat in the taxi and couldn't catch her breath. Everything was spinning. She heard Phil give directions to her apartment. She tried to slow her breathing. She did not want to hyperventilate in the back of a cab with Phil, and she did not want to get all sobby and emotional in front of him. She tried to channel her grit. But the shock of it all. And no warning.

She pictured Mike standing there grinning like they were old college friends. Six years of marriage and he treated her like she was an old buddy.

And he had a girlfriend. A beautiful glittery, shiny girlfriend.

"Are you okay?" Phil asked. The sincerity in his voice was so unexpected and so kind, Sara couldn't hold back her emotions any longer. Tears ran down her face and without thinking, she slipped an arm through Phil's and leaned against his shoulder while she shook with sobs. Phil was stiff at first, unsure how to respond. He awkwardly placed an arm around Sara. He hadn't raised a daughter. He wasn't particularly good with emotional people, or any kind of people, for that matter, but he settled his arm around Sara's, squeezed her shoulder, and just let her cry while he gave new directions to the driver.

They drove in silence for a while. Sara finally calmed down, found tissues in her purse, and wiped her eyes and nose. She looked out the window. "Where are we going?

"Another restaurant."

"Where?"

"You'll see."

Thirty minutes later, they crossed a bridge into Queens.

Sara looked at Phil. "Queens?"

"Trust me."

The cab stopped in front of a brick building on a desolate-looking block. A bright green awning said, "United Miners SC Rudar."

Sara narrowed her puffy eyes at Phil. "What is this place?"

"It's a soccer club. And my favorite restaurant."

"A soccer club?"

"There's a restaurant downstairs with great Croatian food."

Sara was skeptical but curious.

They entered an upstairs bar that felt welcoming and festive. Craggy old men drank oversized glasses of beer and spoke a language Sara didn't recognize. Some played card games while others watched soccer games on different screens. Phil waved to a few of the men and led Sara downstairs.

In contrast to the bar, the restaurant was quiet and inviting. There were only a dozen tables or so, each covered with a crisp white tablecloth. Large photos of Croatian landscapes decorated the walls with scenes of quaint ancient towns, rugged mountains, and deep blue beaches.

They sat at a small table next to a brick fireplace. Phil ordered a few different dishes so Sara could try a sampling. She sipped chamomile tea, and Phil drank a glass of red wine while they waited for their food. Her head ached from her crying episode in the cab, and she swallowed a couple of Advil.

"I'm sorry I got so emotional…I just didn't expect to see him."

"Mike never deserved you," he said quietly.

Sara shook her head. "What does that even mean? It's what everyone tells their friend after a bad breakup. Someone gets dumped, betrayed, whatever, and we say, 'Oh, he didn't deserve you.'" She slumped back in her seat, feeling weary.

Phil placed both arms on the table and leaned intently towards her. "Then allow me to be more clear. Mike was a self-centered ass, who made everything good or bad that happened in your marriage all about him. He neither appreciated nor cherished you like he should have, and he epically failed to prove worthy of you. *That* is what I mean."

Sara sat up. "Oh."

"Your mother and I spent a lot of time together over the years. I happen to know some things about you and Mike."

Sara nodded, unsure what to say.

A server brought their food, much more than two people could possibly eat. Sara smelled rosemary, garlic, and grilled meat, her hunger growing as the server placed several dishes on their table.

They started with *jota*—a minestrone with barley, beans, bits of pasta, and sauerkraut—and Sara tried a side of Swiss chard sautéed with mashed potatoes, which didn't look appealing, but was surprisingly delicious. Her favorite was the *fuzi*, a soft, pillowy pasta topped with a rich, brown veal sauce.

While they ate, Phil told Sara about how Club Rudar had opened in the '70s as a private social club for soccer-playing coal miners from Istria.

"I haven't even heard of Istria."

"Neither had Cassie. I finally took her there last summer. It's on a beautiful peninsula in the Adriatic. That's where we were when we got the email about Mike leaving."

Sara put her fork down. This seemed like something she should have known. Soft folk music played in the background, stringed instruments she didn't recognize. "I thought she was in Maine."

Phil shook his head.

Their server interrupted with dessert, setting apple strudel and crepes in front of them. Sara had no idea strudel could taste so light and buttery. The crepes were filled with walnuts and fresh apricot jam.

"My son brought me here, to Club Rudar, nine years ago. Your mother had broken off our relationship at the time. He introduced me to some of the guys upstairs. I hadn't heard Croatian spoken by that many people since I was a kid." Phil's eyes looked bluer as he spoke, his face gentle.

"Philip said I needed my roots. Strange that he should be the one to tell me this, but he was right. Started coming here once a week. It filled a void, something I didn't know was missing."

"You don't talk about your son very much."

"I was a lousy father when he was growing up. His mother and I divorced when he was twelve. I worked all the time. He became kind of a punk actually. We wondered if the kid would even graduate from high school. I didn't help the situation."

"Oh."

What could she say? That she'd always imagined Phil to be the worst sort of father and now he'd only confirmed it? Yet she was seeing a side of him she'd never known.

"So, Philip manages your property in Maine?"

"Yeah, and a few others. He works at a small liberal arts college. It's not what I had...well...he's a good man."

"I can't think of a better compliment." And she really couldn't. Mike had an Ivy League education, and no one ever described him that way. Maybe Philip Jr. had all sorts of problems from growing up with an absent father, and Phil just wanted to focus on the good.

Sara looked at the spectacular photos of Phil's homeland across her table and felt a longing begin to form inside her, something she couldn't quite name. She refolded her napkin and sipped more tea.

Phil studied her, his eyes warm. "When was the last time you went home?"

"Three weeks."

"I'm talking about London. Where you spent the first...what...seven years of your life?"

"Eight."

"So how long since you went back?"

Sara thought for a moment. "We stayed with my grandmother for two weeks up in Berkshire when I was nine."

"But when was the last time you went to London, walked in your neighborhood, tasted the food from your home?"

Sara bit her lip. "I haven't been back since my father died."

Phil pointed a spoon at her. "You need to go back."

"I have a book to write."

"I'm aware." Phil drank the rest of his coffee and signaled the server for the check. He pulled a card out of his wallet. "When this book is done, you need to go home. Spend some time there. Take Anna-Kath."

"Maryland's my home now. London is...*complicated*."

"Hmm." Phil gestured towards a photograph of Istria and looked affectionately around the restaurant. He looked back at Sara, his head tilted slightly. "Don't underestimate the power of your roots."

She sighed. "Even when it hurts?"

He met her gaze. "Especially when it hurts."

Chapter 19

Writing is hard for every last one of us…. Coal mining is harder.
Do you think miners stand around all day talking about how
hard it is to mine for coal? They do not. They simply dig.

CHERYL STRAYED

From: Gloria Knott
To: Sara Grayson
Date: Thursday, July 11, 12:30 PM
Subject: Never a dull moment!

Dear Ms. Grayson,

Things are plugging along here at Iris just swimmingly.
Never a dull moment! Mr. Asher Monroe stopped
by to meet with Jane today. Ring a bell? Jane asked
me not to mention his visit to Phil, which I will not
do. Anyway, I hope your writing is going splendidly.

Cheers,
Gloria Knott
Administrative Assistant, Iris Books

Texts on Thursday, July 11, 6:30 PM

Sara
Do you happen to know someone
named Asher Monroe? A friend
tells me he was at Iris the other day.
Sounds familiar. Google says he owns
a bunch of UK department stores.
My friend seemed to think his visit at
Iris has something to do with me.

Phil
Focus on the book. I'll look into it.

Text on Thursday, July 11, 7:03 PM

David Allman
I've got a few contract items to
discuss with you. I'll be up in NYC
this weekend. Saturday brunch?

It had rained most of Thursday, and now the warm evening air felt damp and drizzly. Sara walked Gatsby at a brisk pace in Central Park past some ballfields and Tavern on the Green just as the twinkly lights switched on. She breathed deeply, her mind weary from another intense day of *Ellery Dawson*. With the outline done, she was fleshing out the first few chapters. It was exciting to see them take shape, but all her brain cells had fizzled out for the night.

She stayed in the walking lane, steering Gatsby away from a Polish sausage truck. She decided they needed a quieter route and made a right turn past Sheep Meadow. She had barely stepped onto the new trail when she heard someone call her name. She ignored it, certain she hadn't heard quite right. Then she heard it again...louder. She glanced quickly behind her. Someone was approaching her from behind. It was a tall woman wearing a black baseball cap and an overpriced yoga outfit who looked an awful lot like…

No. She shook her head. That couldn't be right.

Sara kept walking.

The woman called her name again.

Sara walked faster, suddenly quite concerned for her own mental stability.

She quickly glanced back. The woman was gaining on her.

Sara's heart pounded. Perhaps she was dreaming.

But it didn't feel like a dream. Was she hallucinating? Her head ached. She needed to get more sleep. Maybe take a day off from *Ellery*.

"Sara! Sara Grayson!"

Her insides froze. She had heard of complete mental breakdowns starting like this—with some sort of grand hallucination. She would have to call the after-hours number for Sybil Brown-Baker. What would she say? *I think that Ellery Dawson is chasing me in Central Park?*

Sara's rising panic and fear propelled her forward. She tore off into a run, but Gatsby didn't pick up his pace fast enough, and Sara's foot caught on his leash. She came down hard, catching herself on her hands and knees.

Sara waited for Ellery to pass by with her maniacal laugh like she did in all of her dreams. Instead she crouched down next to her. "Sorry, mate. Are you okay?"

Sara squeezed her eyes shut. Ellery Dawson did not have an Australian accent.

But Char Fox did.

Sara opened her eyes.

Char's lovely, flawless face looked at her, quite concerned. "Sorry. I didn't mean to startle you. I'm Char Fox. Do you remember me? We met at the premiere?"

Did she actually think Sara would forget?

"Yes. Sorry. Of course." Sara tried to hop up but tripped on Gatsby's leash again. She untangled herself and stood up, feeling her face flush warm with embarrassment. She brushed some dirt off her scraped knees and tried to smile like it was no big deal. "I just didn't recognize you at first."

"There's a bench right over there. Maybe you should sit down for a minute." Char handed Sara Gatsby's leash and walked them to a bench with peeling green paint.

Sara picked more dirt off her scraped palms. "Umm, is it safe for you to be out like this, you know, alone in public?"

"Oh, I'm not alone." Char pointed to a serious looking man standing ten feet behind them on the trail. "I've got Crowe with me."

Of course she had a bodyguard named Crowe. He was built like a short Dwayne Johnson. He hung back near a sign, offering free handwriting analysis.

"I actually have more freedom here in New York. I can put on a hat, run in the park, or just blend in on the street—there's way more interesting people here than me."

Sara's knees began to sting. She wondered if Char had an herbal compound ready to apply. Perhaps an emergency poultice? Maybe Crowe kept those sorts of things for her in a fanny pack. She looked over at Crowe. No fanny pack.

Char squatted by Gatsby, scratching his head. "So who's this handsome guy?" Gatsby's ears pricked with interest. He sniffed Char and licked her perfectly manicured hands.

"This is Gatsby."

"Oooh, Gatsby, you handsome boy."

She glanced at Char a moment and then rubbed her eyes. Maybe this actually was a dream.

"Anyway, sorry to startle you. I just wanted to say hello and…" She wiped at her eyes quickly with her sleeve. She sniffed a little and then turned to Sara. "I'm really sorry about your mum. She was quite special to me."

Sara saw the tears in Char's eyes. She liked how she said "mum." Suddenly she felt less awkward. "Thank you."

Char nodded slowly. "My own mum died just a few years ago, actually."

"I'm sorry."

"Thanks. Can't say I know exactly what you're going through, but I know more than the usual lot, right?" Char squeezed Sara's arm. Sara closed her eyes and nodded.

A couple approached the path arguing loudly about someone named Monique as they pushed a jogging stroller past their bench. It was nearly dark, but lamplights kept the path well-lit. Attempting to keep a low profile, Char lowered her hat and made a funny look towards Sara after they passed.

Sara laughed.

Char faced forward again and smiled.

"Well, I'll let you and Gatsby get on with your walk." Char stood up to leave.

"Wait, Char. I have a question."

She sat back down.

Sara chewed her bottom lip, trying to figure out what to say. "The first time we met, you asked me if I knew what happens to Ellery's father? You were dying to know what happens in Book Five."

"I still am."

"Well, if you were writing the last book…what would happen to him?"

Char's eye grew wide. "So, you know who's writing the book?"

"Umm, I guess I'm…well, yes, I do know, and I've been sort of helping this person," Sara stammered. "We're just trying to get it right."

Char narrowed her eyes slightly, like she was harnessing Ellery's powers. Sara reminded herself that Char didn't have any actual powers and that Sara didn't need to tell her anything. So, she waited.

Char nodded slowly. "Okay. Well, I've felt for a long time that there are no simple answers regarding Peter Dawson. The truth is complicated."

"But is he a traitor?"

She laughed gently. "I don't know. The new author obviously has some big decisions to make, and I don't envy her...or him. When I was preparing to play Ellery, I visited your mum up in Maine."

"You did?" Cassandra had spent summers in Maine, but Sara had never been there. It felt strange now that she'd never gone. She invited her every year. Why hadn't she gone up there?

"It was pure heaven. And since that's where your mum wrote most of the *Ellery* books, there was this energy with the three of us together—your mum, me, and Ellery." Char's hands started flying again as she spoke. "Your mum told me that to make Ellery come alive, she had to become Ellery. She had to see the world as Ellery saw it, which meant she had to become fine-tuned to the smallest details, just like Ellery—and she challenged me to do the same."

Sara exhaled slowly, turning the words carefully in her mind.

"I've been trying to think like Ellery ever since. For example, did you notice you're leaning against a dedication plaque on this bench?"

Sara shook her head.

"From Theo to Martha. It says, 'Fly Home,' and there's a seagull."

Sara turned around and saw the plaque just as Char described.

"Did you get a glimpse of the baby in the stroller that just passed by?"

"Not really."

"It wasn't a baby. It was a dog. A white Westie. Quite darling, actually." Char laughed. "Anyway, your mum told me we shared a common bond as we tried to feel and see what Ellery did. Your mum called it Ellery's awareness. She said we had to develop new antennae."

Sara studied the oak tree across the path, its leaves half-lit by the glowing park lamp.

Char stood up. "So that's my message...for the author."

"Thanks. I'll pass that along."

"Sure. We're headed back to Columbus Circle. Want to join us?"

"I think I'll sit a while longer."

Char had only walked a few steps away when she turned back. "Hey Sara?"

She looked up.

"After your mum was sick, we talked a bit. She never told me who would write Book Five. But she did say I wouldn't be disappointed. Just thought you should know that."

Sara smiled. "Thanks, Char."

⟲

Later that night Sara lay on her bed reading Book Four. Gatsby slept near her feet, his ears occasionally twitching. It was 11:00 PM, and she couldn't stop thinking about her conversation with Char. She walked to her window and opened the blinds, trying to tap into Ellery's awareness. The rain had stopped. Crowds of people were exiting the Gershwin Theatre onto 51st Street, their legs stretching over pools of dirty water near the crosswalks. *Wicked* must have just wrapped up. An old man with a dirty white apron hauled bags of wine bottles that crashed noisily together as he left them on the curb for pickup. Did he do that every night? And how many times had she walked past that Chinese restaurant without noticing the sign for the psychic upstairs?

Sara started thinking about her family, about Anna-Kath, about Mike. She wondered what Ellery would see in her own life that Sara couldn't. She thought of the walk she'd taken with Ann before she came to New York. She'd brought up questions about that Meredith woman who had sued her mother. Sara had been completely dismissive about the whole thing. In fact, she hadn't given their conversation a second thought since that day in the park.

You have to see what Ellery would see...create new antennae.

When Sara first arrived in New York, management had given her a box of some items her mother had left. She had taken only a brief look and then pushed the box out of the way. She pulled it off a closet shelf and opened it again with new eyes. There was a bag of cough drops, postcards, a sweater, and a couple of books. Sara was ready to dismiss it all. But had she really *looked*?

Sara went through the box again and studied each of the books. That's when she noticed the title and author: *Silence in Stepney* by Meredith Lamb.

She stopped. *Meredith Lamb?*

But this was the woman David mentioned. Her mother left her a trust fund.

This was also the woman who had sued her mother—the one who accused her of plagiarism in a major lawsuit.

Why would her mother keep her book?

She flipped through the pages. It was set in the East End, and something felt vaguely familiar about it.

Sara ran to her workbag and found the worn-out book she'd discovered wrapped up in her mother's comfort drawer, the one with no front or back cover. The title and copyright pages were torn out. She compared the books.

She gasped. They were the same book.

What? Why?

A new sense of alertness filled Sara. She pulled out the undamaged book. *Silence in Stepney.* Publication: 1995.

Sara turned to the back. There was only a short bio:

Meredith Lamb lives outside of London with her husband and two dogs. This is her first novel.

Sara tried to Google more information. There was a short bio on Wikipedia with no personal information. *Silence in Stepney* was well-received and even won an Edgar award, but was now out of print. She had written a second book, a sequel to *Stepney*, but it received poor reviews, and Sara could find no additional books by Lamb.

Sara called Anna-Kath. "Are you awake?"

"What's wrong? Are you okay?"

"Remember when you told me how Meredith Lamb sued Mum? Well it turns out Mum kept a copy of her book in her comfort drawer."

"What?"

"Did you ever see an old book without covers in Mum's comfort drawer?"

"Yeah. She fell asleep holding it one night when she was sick."

"It's Meredith's."

"What?"

"She kept a copy of the book at her apartment here. Management had boxed a few personal items she'd left behind. I just barely put it together."

Sara heard Ann typing on her computer.

"I looked her up again too," said Sara. "There's not much information."

"Why would Mum leave a trust to someone who tried to destroy her career and then keep a copy of her book in her *comfort drawer*?"

"It makes no sense, Ann. I'm sorry I didn't pay attention to this earlier."

"You've had some distractions."

"I bet we could get more information from David," said Sara.

"I already tried, and it gets even weirder. Apparently, the details of the lawsuit are sealed, including any contact information. So we have nothing on Meredith or her dependent, who is now an adult, by the way. No contact information. Nothing."

"Why is it sealed?"

"According to David, the lawsuit settlement included a nondisclosure agreement for both parties with stiff penalties if either party violates it."

"But Mum's not alive."

"Meredith is."

"Well, then couldn't we access her info through Mum's will? She left her a trust. We'll get the info from that."

"That's sealed too. David said some people keep details of their wills private. It's not uncommon."

"Then why would he ask us about Meredith Lamb to begin with?"

"I asked David the same thing, and he got really odd and evasive about it. Turns out he was never supposed to mention Meredith at all. He screwed up. Mum never meant for us to know anything about Meredith."

"But why?"

"I don't know. We need to learn more about the lawsuit, but every article I've found basically says the same thing. It was settled quickly and quietly. No details. Anyway, I can't believe you have a copy of Meredith's book there. I've been waiting for a copy from a used bookseller, but you've had one all along?"

"I didn't realize what I had."

"So, what's in the book?"

"Well, there's only a brief bio." Sara explained her recent research online, but it wasn't anything new for Anna-Kath who had scoured the internet for information weeks ago.

"Well, what else is in the book? Inscriptions, papers, a bookmark? Come on."

"Right. Let me check."

Sara flipped through the book. "Oh my gosh! There's a whole secret code written in the back!"

"Are you serious?"

"No."

"Get serious. What about the dedication? Acknowledgments? What's there?"

Sara flipped to the first pages of the book and read aloud, "For Jack Grayson: I love you anyway."

"'For Jack Grayson: I love you anyway'?"

"That's kind of odd. Maybe it's another Jack Grayson."

"Another Jack Grayson?"

"You never know," said Sara.

"When was it published?"

"A year after Dad died. 1995," said Sara.

"Why would Meredith dedicate a book to Dad?"

"Maybe she's a cousin?"

"Maybe."

"A good friend?"

"Could be."

"Or not," Sara whispered. She suddenly experienced a profound sinking feeling, like her heart just dropped to her toes. There was a long, uncomfortable silence.

Ann slowly exhaled. "Some woman writes a book and dedicates it to Dad with 'I love you anyway'? Sara, you don't think Dad and this woman had some kind of—"

"Don't even go there. It may not even be her real name. It could be a pseudonym. She could be anyone. She could be a *he*."

"It's not a pseudonym—I checked with the London publisher. But there's something else I found. Another bio of Meredith mentioned that she volunteered at Tilney Preparatory Academy."

"Well, there you go. Dad's school. They worked together."

"Sara, do you tell your colleagues you love them?"

Sara crumpled onto a kitchen chair. "Well, he wanted to be a writer, and she was obviously a writer and like…maybe they were in the same writing group and what if…"

Sara and Ann both sat in silence. Neither knew how to finish the sentence. Sara felt sick. She held Meredith's book tightly in her hands, a book dedicated to her father by some woman who said she loved him "anyway." What did that even mean?

"Well, if they were really good friends outside of work, you could say 'I love you,'" said Ann. "I bet you tell Binti you love her."

Sara nodded vigorously. "Absolutely. Close friends say 'I love you' all the time."

Ann grew quiet again. "But from what David told us, Meredith has a grown child. And Mum had given them money—not just the money from the will's trust. He said she'd given money to this woman before." She sighed painfully. "That would be just like Mum to be so generous even if—"

"But it's *not* like Dad to betray anyone. He adored Mum. She adored him. Mum told us all those stories about how they fell in love. Remember how Mum was dating that older TA and Dad swept in that winter and stole her heart over Keats and candles and soup? They had the *perfect* love story."

"I thought so too."

"Thought?"

"I don't want to believe Dad had an affair, but it's not like we can really know that he did or he didn't. I know we always felt safe and loved, but that doesn't mean he couldn't have had an affair. Plus, why would Mum keep it a secret if there's nothing to hide?"

Sara walked back and forth from the kitchen to her bedroom window. She wished she'd never started thinking about Meredith, wished she'd kept her head down, lost in her own world. It was safer there. "It's just a dedication. We don't know anything."

"You're right. We need more information."

"Well, David is in New York this weekend, and we're meeting up. Maybe I can coax more information out of him."

"If anyone can get info from him, you can."

"What's that supposed to mean?"

"He's always had a thing for you."

"That isn't true."

Sara thought about it for a moment. Was it a little bit true?

She shook her head. "He has a girlfriend now anyway." Sara sat back on the bed next to Gatsby and stroked her fingers across his warm back. "I'll talk to him. See what I can find out."

"Good idea." Ann's voice trembled.

Sara straightened her back. "I know this doesn't look good, but we can't jump to some crazy conclusion just because of a random dedication."

Anna-Kath said her kids needed her and hung up. Sara could tell she was crying. It was disconcerting to hear her this unglued. There had to be a reasonable explanation for everything. She would push David for it.

CHAPTER 20

Write to please just one person. If you open a window and make love to the world, so to speak, your story will get pneumonia.

KURT VONNEGUT

Sara met David for Saturday brunch at a French bistro near Lincoln Center. He wore a navy sports jacket, a freshly pressed shirt, and khakis—a typical Saturday uniform for a DC attorney. He really had grown more handsome with age. She wondered about Ann's comment, that David had always liked her. It couldn't be true. They were so different from each other—he was so cerebral, practical.

David passed on the bread plate and ordered a green smoothie, an arugula salad, and an egg-white omelet. He was definitely still dating the Canadian backpacker. Sara ordered the quiche Lorraine. And the bread plate. Since Sara had rediscovered her taste for good food, she hadn't touched a frozen meal in two weeks.

David asked about her writing, and they talked about his recent hiking trip. Sara thought about how much she actually enjoyed his company. There was comfort in being with an old friend. David applied some dressing sparingly to his salad. "I actually have some good news," he said, "before all this contract stuff."

"I love good news." Sara spread hazelnut butter on a crusty piece of sourdough and took a bite.

"Mia and I are engaged. We're getting married this spring."

Sara's stomach dropped. She put the bread back on her plate. She wiped her hands on her napkin. "David, that's wonderful. I'm so happy for you. Mia seems really…great."

He was more confident, more settled than she'd ever seen him. "She's here in New York, actually. We just went to morning services together—for Shabbat."

Sara nodded. "Yes, of course." *Shabbat.*

David smiled brightly. "I never thought I could be this happy." He took a big bite of salad.

An unexpected heaviness crept into her heart. Why? She was happy for her friend…wasn't she?

The server set her quiche in front of her. It didn't look so good anymore. She smiled at David, taking a deep breath. "Doesn't this food look amazing?" She forced a few bites down.

David ate his food quickly while he talked about the kayaking trip they were taking next week and how he was never into the outdoors before, but now he just couldn't get enough. His eyes looked lively as he spoke, his arms and hands tan from all that time in the sun, probably taking Mia's hand as they hiked and sharing his water bottle when they stopped to rest. She wondered if Mike had ever talked about her the way David talked about Mia. Did he ever have that brightness in his eyes?

Her mom always lit up like that when she talked about her father: how they met at Georgetown, how it was wintertime and a harsh one and Mum won him over with her white cheddar and broccoli soup, but Dad always said she "beguiled him" with her eyes and her smile. He said he was "completely besotted."

When Sara married Mike, she thought she'd have what her parents had. It never occurred to her that she wouldn't. You fall in love, and everything falls into place. Like magic. She soon realized it wasn't like that. She loved Mike. He swept her off her feet with grand gestures like a helicopter ride over the Potomac, private rooftop dinners at his father's law firm, and surprise trips to his family's beach home in St. John's. In fact, he swept her off her feet so fully and completely that when it came time to build a real life together, there wasn't much to stand on. Expensive gifts and trips became Mike's attempts at bypassing the real work of a meaningful relationship. At the end, even those were gone.

Sara took small bites of her quiche and then ordered a green tea while David pulled out his laptop and files to discuss with her. She needed to shake off this melancholy and focus on their meeting. David and Mia's engagement was something to celebrate. Plus she had to find a way to persuade David to give her more info on Meredith Lamb.

Sara listened patiently to David's translation of the revised contracts, determined to earn most pleasant client of the year. She stuffed her sadness down by her toes, and after they'd reviewed the contracts, Sara signed in all the right places and David ordered more coffee—decaf, of course.

Sara casually tried to bring up Meredith like she was talking about an old neighborhood friend. "So, David, I actually have heard of Meredith Lamb—you know, the woman you mentioned at your office last month? She's a writer, of course, and Mom actually had her book at home. I'd like to send her a letter. Could I grab her contact info from you real quick?"

David froze up. A server brought him his coffee, but he didn't touch it. He took a nervous sip of his water, and Sara could tell he was trying to play it cool.

"Actually, that information is sealed. It's not uncommon for a large estate like your mother's."

Sara laughed gently, drawing on her middle school acting skills as Nana in *Peter Pan*. She was better at this than David—he had only been a tree trunk. "Oh, of course, David, I wouldn't want to push it, but I already know about Meredith anyway, and what would it hurt for me to know a little more?"

David looked at Sara. She knew him well enough to tell when he was just pretending to be relaxed. Unfortunately, he probably knew the same about her. He adjusted his glasses again and sipped more water while his coffee sat untouched. "I'll be honest. Mentioning Meredith Lamb was a complete misstep on my part. I apologize."

"No worries." She shrugged her shoulders and smiled again. *I am accommodating, cheerful, pleasant.*

"No. It was a mistake. I should have known better. The Meredith Lamb provisions were something my dad originally handled. I wasn't clear on the confidentiality of certain pieces."

There were Meredith Lamb *provisions?* Sara tried to hide her mounting frustration. She looked at him more seriously. "I think this whole thing with Meredith may have a really personal connection to my family. Like something about my dad." She wasn't sure why she whispered the last sentence.

"Whether I think you should know or not, I can't discuss it."

"So, you think we should know?"

"I didn't say that. It's not my call."

"So, if it was your call, you'd tell us more?" asked Sara, her voice now pleading.

David stirred creamer in his coffee but still didn't drink any. He rubbed the back of his neck as he stretched it to one side. "Do you really not know anything about this woman?"

"Ohhh...so she's a woman?"

David rolled his eyes and gave her a pointed look.

She cleared her throat. "Actually, I think we do know who she is." Her voice caught in her throat at the end, and Sara took a deep breath, determined not to get emotional about this.

David nodded. He straightened his neck and looked disappointingly resolute. "Then, there's nothing to discuss."

Sara reached across the table and grabbed his hands. They were warm, but stiff. "David, please."

He pulled his hands back and typed into his laptop. He looked back at Sara. "Look, I can't say anything else." David turned all business-like again. "Okay, so it looks like we've covered everything with the revised contracts."

Sara slumped in her chair and stared out the window. David made a few quick notes on his computer. He paused. He stared at the screen another moment. "Okay then."

Sara looked back at David. He pulled on his top button, like he was suddenly flustered. He sipped his water and announced that he had to go make a quick call. "Watch my stuff?"

"Sure."

As David stood up, he closed his laptop only partway. He locked eyes with Sara and walked away. Sara jolted up in her chair. Was that a signal? She waited 'til he left her view and slid over to his chair. She opened the laptop to find a word doc. Right in front of her was the contact information for Meredith Lamb. She grabbed her phone and snapped a picture of it. Then she half-shut the laptop like it was before and moved quickly back to her seat. She looked at her phone.

Meredith Lamb
Carwyn's Lodge
Woolton Lane, Wraxall
Bristol BS65 1BJ

Carolee Grayson
725 Albert Court
Bristol BS50 1BJ

David was back in two minutes. He glanced at Sara, his eyes a little guilty. He gathered his laptop and papers.

Sara stood and touched his arm. He placed a hand gently over hers, nodded and left.

Sara quickly walked two blocks to Central Park and sat on a bench near Strawberry Fields. *Carolee Grayson. Carolee Grayson.* She repeated the name again and again in her head. Who was she?

She called Ann right away. Her voice breathless. "I have contact info on Meredith. She lives in Bristol, England, and there's a Carolee Grayson also living in Bristol. Different addresses."

Ann was quiet. Her breathing came in short, quick breaths. She said she was driving and needed to pull over. She was quiet for a minute before whispering, "She could be our sister."

"Or a random cousin."

"Then why hide it? And why give her money? You don't normally hide relatives. I think we need to seriously consider that she could be Dad's illegitimate child."

"Don't say it like that." Sara watched runners jog past. Pigeons hopped about. Finally Sara said, "It's possible." The words stung the inside of her cheeks.

"I don't know what to think. All these years. Seems like we should have known this. I can see why Mum didn't tell us as kids, but as adults, how could she keep something like this from us?" Ann's voice broke with emotion.

Sara's body felt heavy on the bench. She watched a grandfather pull two kids along in a red wagon. He stopped and dabbed at his forehead with a handkerchief and kept going.

"Are you there, Sara?"

"I'm just...sad."

Ann cried softly. "Me too. Sad for Mum. Sad for Dad. I wish I didn't know."

"I'm not sure what to think or feel."

"Are you sitting down, Sara?"

"Why?"

"There's more. And we might as well talk about it now. I found an old newspaper article in the *London Times*. It was just a short one, but it gave a little more info about the lawsuit. Turns out Meredith claimed to have some early writings that matched part of Mum's first book, *Cache Carter*. Mum didn't even try to fight the claims. They settled it quickly, and there's a quote that Ms. Lamb was completely happy with the settlement. Like she won."

"Well, we know Mum's no plagiarist, so why didn't she fight it? And how would Meredith have gotten Mum's early drafts in order to make a claim like that?"

"I don't know. Mum was getting a lot of attention when her book skyrocketed to number one. Maybe she settled quickly because she didn't want the press. Plus the illegitimate child and all of that."

"Do you have to keep using that word?"

"Do you have a better one?" Ann blew her nose. "Sara, you don't think…" She paused. She started and stopped a few more times. Sara sat frozen on the bench. Birds could have mistaken her for a statue.

Finally, Ann's voice spilled out, "You don't think Mum actually borrowed anything from her, do you? I mean, Meredith's attorney claimed to have handwritten pages of Meredith's own writing that matched content in Mum's *Cache Carter*."

"So?"

"So, Mum's husband is unfaithful, and then she loses him to cancer—maybe in her anger and grief she felt justified. I mean her later books are quite different from *Cache Carter*. No one disputes that."

Sara shot off the bench. "Stop this, Ann! When did we become these daughters who think the worst of their parents? This is our *mother*. I know this is heartbreaking enough about Dad, but we spent our entire lives with Mum. There's no way. Use your gray matter!"

"Okay. I'm sorry. I'm just trying to look at all possibilities."

Sara sank back on the bench. "I wish we'd never asked anything about this woman. Can we just put this all away for now? Let's *not* ask any more questions, okay? We know Mum wrote all her books. Herself."

"We can't just close our eyes to this. We may have a sister."

Sara wrapped an arm around her stomach. "I feel sick."

"Me too."

"I thought Mum and Dad had the greatest love story ever."

"I know," said Ann.

"Do you think we should meet Carolee?"

"Probably."

"When?"

"I don't know."

"I need some time," said Sara. "I can't think about all of this right now. I have a book to write."

"Of course, you have to focus on that. We'll figure all this out one step at a time. When are you coming home?"

"In a week."

"Okay, well, maybe we just keep all this to ourselves right now."

"That reporter from the *Times*...do you think he knows more? Should we talk to him?"

"Focus on the book, Sara. That's what Mum would want."

They said goodbye, and Sara slowly stood up. She needed to walk, to process. She started walking towards Sheep Meadow. She walked faster and faster until she was in a slow jog and then a full run. She kept going, her heart pounding, her limbs tingling. She used to run all the time. She made it a mile without stopping and kept going. Her body didn't like it, but she couldn't stop. She ran in her t-shirt dress and white Converse, her bag bouncing to the side. She moved the strap across her chest and kept running. It was warm out, and her tears quickly mixed with her sweat. She made it a mile and a half and then swept her hair back in a messy bun.

She hailed a cab at Central Park West and rode back to her apartment in Midtown.

She walked in and hugged Gatsby and splashed water on her face and neck before she collapsed on the couch and began to tell him the whole story. She had to tell someone, but he wasn't up for listening. He just wanted to get out.

"Okay, okay," she said. She grabbed his leash and took the elevator down to the lobby.

She walked out and stopped cold.

Mike was sitting on a lobby sofa in a golf shirt and shorts, a leg crossed on one knee, looking at his phone. His head shot up when he saw her.

"Hey, Sare! How's it going?"

Her breath caught in her throat. Gatsby bolted towards him, clearly enjoying their reunion. Poor, confused dog.

Sara stood a little straighter and tried to reach inside for that spark she'd been kindling these past weeks. She found the edges of it and hung on tight.

"How did you get in here?"

"Told the doorman I was your husband."

"Ex-husband."

"Yeah, I left that part out." Mike chuckled like he'd made such a funny joke. "Hey, you guys headed out? I'll come with." He knelt by Gatsby, his face close to his. "You'd like that buddy, wouldn't you?" Gatsby hopped around happily.

She noticed Mike's sandy hair, his hazel eyes. She remembered how comfortably she once fit into his solid chest when he hugged her. Sara smoothed some wet strands of her hair back, her skin still damp with sweat. "Why are you here?"

"Thought we could walk. Or I could come up. Make you waffles. You always loved my waffles."

"I'm not hungry."

Mike took a deep breath and gave her a sweet smile, like he was auditioning for the role of a sincere human being. "You sure?"

Sara leaned against the sofa. She watched a couple chatting happily together outside the front entrance. Something made them laugh and then the man wrapped the woman in his arms and hugged her so tightly that her feet lifted right off the sidewalk. She turned back to Mike. "Why didn't we ever go to Maine?"

"Maine? Where did that come from?"

"My mother invited us every summer for the last six years. She loved it there. Called it her piece of heaven. We never went. Not once."

"Well, you love my parent's place in St. John. It's paradise, babe. Who the hell loves a cold beach? Right?" Mike forced a laugh.

Sara didn't smile. She pointed a finger at him. "*You* love St. John."

"Hey, you wanna go to Maine? I can take you to Maine. Let's go to Maine. Right now."

He locked his pinky finger playfully around hers. His hand felt warm. She looked into Mike's eyes. She'd believed all the things he'd told her for so many years. A part of her wished she could believe him one more time.

Sara shook her head and dropped his hand. "That's not what I'm getting at."

Mike's voice turned soft. "Well, here's what I'm getting at." He tilted his head slightly and looked searchingly in her eyes. It looked suspiciously like a smolder. "I still think we have something. And I think you feel that too."

He reached for her arm, but Sara pulled away. She lifted her chin and drew Gatsby back to her. "Actually, I do feel something."

Mike closed his eyes and nodded, like he knew he was *so* right.

Sara straightened her back. "What I feel is disappointment. Disappointment that I've wasted so many years on you."

Mike's eyebrows shot up. He stepped back. "Come on. What are you talking about? We had a lot of good years…and there can be more ahead."

He moved closer. He was using a different aftershave. It smelled earthy and expensive.

"I think Gabrielle would be sad to hear that."

"It's Abrielle...and," he shook his head sadly, "I don't think it's meant to be."

"Oh." Sara noticed the tattoo on his neck was gone. So it wasn't real, after all.

And neither was any of this.

She reached for that spark, that hum building inside her again, cocked her head to one side, and said, "Your feelings don't have anything to do with the fact that I just inherited a major portion of my mother's estate, right?"

Mike's mouth opened a little too wide, and he pressed a hand to his chest. "Come on. You know me better than that."

"Yeah. Actually, I think I finally do." She saw the flash of anger cross his face and his quick switch to hurt and misunderstanding. She shook her head. "I know your rich daddy cut you off five years ago. I know you've blown through your grandfather's trust in record time."

"Come on, babe. You aren't seeing this clearly at all."

"No, Mike. For the first time I think I actually am. I only wish I could have seen it sooner."

He took a step back. "You're making a big mistake."

Sara looked at Mike, squared her shoulders, and took a step forward. "No. I already did that."

His face hardened, and he clenched his fists against his side. "I am the best man you will ever find."

"The best man for me would never need to say that."

"Well, then, get ready to spend the rest of your sorry life alone. I'm outta here," he muttered and walked away.

Sara watched him hurry out the door. He really was a sad shell of a man. Sara sank into the sofa. Gatsby hopped anxiously around her and dropped his leash into her lap. He still needed to get out. She exhaled slowly. She didn't want to risk running into Mike again and took Gatsby to the building's inner courtyard instead of the street. They made a few loops inside after Gatsby did his business. Sara sniffed and wiped her eyes against her arm as they walked. Then they sat next to a pot of trailing red petunias. Gatsby looked up at her puffy face. His gentle eyes told her what she already knew.

It's time to move on.

CHAPTER 21

Some of the story is taken from my real life, but all of the story is taken from my real heart. I have experienced every emotion that I put onto these pages.

TAYARI JONES

Monday afternoon Sara was irritable and unfocused in her session with Phil. She studied the whiteboard again and announced that she was sure Ellery's father had betrayed them *all*. "It's perfectly clear to me now."

"Wait a minute," said Phil. "I thought we were taking a more complex approach here. Now her father's gone from boy scout to full-blown traitor?"

"Well, I didn't say there wasn't good in him," said Sara, "but it's obvious the guy betrayed his family. He let down his wife, his kids. I mean Peter Dawson had *everything*, and then he just threw it all away. He acts like he's father of the year when Ellery's young and then abandons them all. He should be put in prison. Or stoned in Pakistan."

Phil looked at Sara, confused. He hadn't seen her since Friday afternoon. "What the hell happened this weekend? You seem rather *unhinged*."

"Nothing."

"Nothing?"

"Well, Mike did show up at my building Saturday night."

"And...?"

"He thinks we still have something. I basically told him to get lost."

Phil closed his eyes and nodded. "Well done."

Then Sara couldn't keep it in any longer. "There's more."

Phil's eyes widened at the explosion of information suddenly spewing out of Sara. She told him everything—how her dad cheated on her mom and how he had an illegitimate child that her mother tried to keep secret and that this woman, Meredith Lamb, was the one her father cheated with and she sued her mother for plagiarism and what if it was true? What if her mother did borrow some work from this Other Woman as she dealt with her own grief? Sara was practically hyperventilating as it all tumbled out.

Phil sat quietly in his chair at the worktable, his arms folded in front of him. His face unreadable. "Are you finished?"

Sara nodded, out of breath. She sank back in her chair, staring blankly at the wood floor.

Phil tapped a marker on his thigh. "So you're finding out that your perfect little family isn't so perfect, and it hurts like hell." He tossed the marker back on the table. "You know, I never liked Jack Grayson."

Sara's head shot up. "You never met my father."

"You so sure about that?"

Sara closed her eyes and rubbed her temples. Phil could be so annoying. Of course he didn't know her father.

Phil cleared his throat. "Georgetown. '79. I was a grad student and the TA for his fiction writing class. He was a talented but arrogant son-of-a-bitch."

Sara opened her eyes wide. Her hands dropped to her lap. "You knew my father? Like actually *knew* my father?" How did she not know this? Her eyes turned moist at the thought. Other than Ann, she didn't know anyone who knew her father.

"Don't get all soft about it. I don't have nice family stories to make you feel all warm inside. We entered the same writing contests, and he always won. In fact, he won every competition. Then he married your mother, moved back to England, and I never saw him again."

Sara's mouth hung open. "Wait. But then…did you meet my mother at Georgetown, too? She was there at the same time."

"When I said your father won every competition, I meant *every* competition."

"Oh."

A painful sadness crept into Phil's eyes. He shoved his hands back into his hair, pressing his head against his hands. "I don't believe your father ever betrayed your mom, but who the hell knows what a person will or won't do? As for your mother, I worked with her on eleven novels. She didn't take anything from this Meredith woman. Can we move on?"

Phil didn't wait for an answer. He said he was getting more coffee and left the room.

Sara just sat there. Didn't move. Didn't fidget. She hardly breathed. *Phil knew her father.*

He walked back in and set a cup of tea down in front of Sara. He sat next to her with his coffee.

"Were you friends?" Sara asked, her eyes earnest.

Phil huffed. "Now there you go, thinking I've got heartwarming tales about your father's college days."

"Do you?"

"We weren't buddies."

Sara nodded. Phil probably never had buddies.

She walked over to the window. She gazed out a moment and then turned back towards Phil. "Look, there are a lot of big questions that have come up for me and Ann. We just want to know the truth."

Phil's eyes peered at Sara over his coffee mug as he drank and then set it down. "Truth," he repeated, sounding skeptical. "Then I'm sure you'll find it…or at least some version of it." He held up Sara's latest chapter with his editing notes. "But finish the book *first*. This thing has a deadline. A big one."

"The *Times* is working on another story, Phil, about the lawsuit."

"Let PR handle it. All inquiries go—"

"To Thea. I know." Sara knew Phil was right, that she needed to focus on the book, but she couldn't help feeling that there was more he could tell her—but that he was *choosing* not to.

"Look, Cassandra's level of success will always come with its critics and those ready to pounce. I don't know what the hell this stuff with your family means, but can you focus on your book and play Ellery with it later? It's your last week in New York. If we can get through chapter six before you go home to Maryland, you'll be in a strong position going forward. Can you do that?"

Sara exhaled slowly. "Yes…but I'm not going home."

"What do you mean? You're staying here?"

"I'm going to Maine."

Phil raised his eyebrows. "Maine."

"Maine." Sara repeated, her arms folded across her chest.

He leaned back in his chair. His lips curved up, almost smiling. "You know that's where your mom wrote most of *Ellery*."

Sara nodded. "I'm renting a place near—"

"You'll stay at my cottage."

"I'm fine, Phil, I already have—"

"My cottage is free—"

"I'm fine."

He exhaled slowly. "Please. Stay at my place. It's empty right now. I can't—" Phil's voice cracked just a little on the last word. "She would want you there." He quickly wiped at his eyes and drained the rest of his coffee.

Sara's eyes softened. "Okay. Sure."

Phil stood up and went to get more coffee.

And a cup of tea.

PART THREE
MAINE

CHAPTER 22

Reading is my inhale and writing is my exhale.

GLENNON DOYLE

The first thing Sara noticed was the air. It smelled different. And it felt different. Cleaner. Fresher. Even a high school gym would smell good after Manhattan in July, but it wasn't just leaving New York. There was this heady mix of forest and ocean—of pines mixed with salty sea air.

The stress of the past three weeks breezed past her as she wound her way farther north into Maine. In Wiscasset, she rolled her windows down all the way, turned off her music, and just *breathed deeply*. The blue water sparkled, and Sara's heart skipped every time a coastal view emerged along Route One. Rivers, lakes, inlets—water was everywhere.

Phil's place was in a quaint little neighborhood just blocks away from the Village Green in Bar Harbor. Sara followed her GPS to Phil's address, but on seeing his cottage knew there must be some mistake. She parked in front of the home and slowly got out. Gatsby was thrilled to be out of the car. He circled around the house, sniffed the porch, and barked at a few squirrels. Sara leaned back against the car, folded her arms, and studied the place. It was a white, two-story, New England clapboard home with red shutters, a cheery red door, and red geraniums in window boxes—nothing "Phil" about it.

She was double-checking the address when a pickup truck pulled into the driveway. A dark-haired man with a trimmed beard hopped out, smiled warmly, and greeted Sara. "Hey, looks like you made it."

Gatsby bounded back to the front yard. He barked happily and tried to jump up on the man's legs.

"Gatsby, get down. Sorry. He's excited to be out of the car."

The man knelt down by Gatsby and rustled his fur affectionately. "Good to meet you, Gatsby. I think I read a book about you once."

"You must be Phillip—Phil's son?"

He stood up and smiled. "My friends call me Nik." He reached out and shook her hand. He'd been younger in most of Phil's photos and the beard was new, but she recognized his eyes. "In high school my friends shortened Dvornik to Nik, and it just sort of stuck. Although, not for my father. I'll always be Phillip to him. Anyway, welcome to Maine. It's nice to see you again."

Sara looked at the house and back at Nik, still processing. "I'm sorry. We've met before?"

"It was at a Christmas party in New York at Iris. It was—I don't know—maybe five years ago? You were there with your sister?"

Sara had no memory of this. "Sure...of course. Sorry. It was a while ago."

"Right." He paused a moment, looked down, and quickly cleared his throat. He looked back up at her. "I'm sorry about your mom."

Sara half-smiled and wondered if this ache would ever get any easier. She met Nik's eyes. There was a kindness in them so unexpected that she almost looked away. She nodded. "Thank you."

"You know, she came up here a lot. We'd spend time together on occasion. She was a wonderful person." Nik's voice got a little shaky as he spoke about her. He reached down to scratch Gatsby's neck, who kept sniffing around his legs. "Anyway, if you need anything, I'm in the blue house, just down a piece. I watch my dad's property and some other homes in the summer."

"Blue house, great." Sara turned towards the cottage again, still analyzing it.

"Phil says you're here to write. The college has a decent library, great coffee, some quiet spots to work. Bernadette's café is a local favorite."

Sara noticed "College of the Atlantic" written on the side of his truck. "So you work at the college?"

"Seven years now. I do a bit of everything there, I guess."

She gazed back at the house. "That's nice."

"You okay?"

"Oh, sorry. I'm fine." She gestured towards the home. "It's just...not how I pictured Phil's place." Her eyes scanned the wraparound porch, the red rockers. "It's just so *charming*."

Nik looked up. "It's a favorite around here. Of course, you know the story about this place. A small monument to love, right?"

Sara nodded. She had no idea what he was talking about.

"Listen, are you hungry?"

What was a polite way to turn him down? He seemed like a nice guy, but she wasn't really here to make new friends.

"I brought you a sandwich from Bernadette's," said Nik. "It's in your fridge. For when you're hungry."

"Oh...that's thoughtful—thank you." She wondered how much longer she'd need to be polite.

Nik offered to help Sara bring in her things, which she refused. He ignored her. He popped the trunk from the driver's side and started bringing in her luggage. She grabbed her backpack from the front seat and followed Nik inside.

The cottage was filled with natural light and had a cozy, coastal feel. Upstairs, Sara found an office with floor-to-ceiling windows. Just over a few rooftops and trees, the blue sea sliced through the top of the view, and Sara felt her pulse quicken as she took in the spectacular scenery.

After they'd brought everything in, Nik gave Sara his cell number and then left to check on some properties.

There were fresh hydrangeas on the kitchen table with a welcome note from Bernadette and directions to a café called "The Lieberry." Was she a friend of her mother's?

She walked through the two bedrooms and bathrooms upstairs, each with its own skylight. There were photos of Phil and Cassandra together in Maine, landscapes of Croatian coastlines, and a painting of an East London church that seemed softly familiar.

The office had a small walk-in closet with file cabinets and bins labeled in Cassandra's handwriting. As Sara took in each room, she was overwhelmed with the sense that this was not Phil's space at all. The home was relatively small, not more than 1,500 square feet, but every inch of it felt like her mother's.

She walked back out to the porch with Gatsby and sat in one of the red rockers. She stared pensively at the woods across the street.

Sara had thought she was going to Phil's cottage. And he might have built it. He might own it. But this place was all her mother's. Every bit of it. The touch of red in every room. The flowers, the chairs, the paintings, the furniture. The tea kettle on the stove. The familiar pain of loss turned suddenly sharp against her chest, and tears filled her eyes.

She knew her mother had been seeing Phil again.

But this?

He'd built her a home?

Pieces of conversations with her mother came to mind now. Moments when Cassandra tried to talk with her about loving Phil again and times when Sara had simply been unwilling to listen, too wrapped up in her own unhappy marriage and blinded by her bitterness towards Phil.

After a while, her mother stopped trying. She would make references to Phil, but she shared very little about him or their relationship. Cassandra and Phil mostly spent time together when her mother was in New York or when they were together in Maine. Sara chose to believe Phil and Cassandra were simply "seeing each other." It was a more palatable perspective and required little empathy on her part.

The pain of her mother's death washed over her once again, now laced with an agonizing layer of regret. Regret that she didn't share her mother's joy the last years of her life—and regret that perhaps she had denied some of Phil's happiness too.

Her breathing came in rapid, short breaths, and she struggled to slow it.

Is it possible that she didn't know her mother as well as she thought? But how could that be? They talked all the time.

Or did Sara mostly do the talking?

She grabbed her phone and dialed Phil's number.

"Yeah," said Phil.

Sara thought that people only answered their phones like that in the movies, but she was wrong. Phil did. Every time. "It's Sara."

"I know."

"I thought you were sending me to *your* house in Maine." Tears filled her eyes. It was hard to speak.

"You there, Grayson?"

"Yeah." She wiped her eyes with her sleeve. "It's just...Phil...this place...it feels more like my mum's."

"Of course it does. I built it for her."

"But why didn't you tell me?"

Phil paused. She could picture him setting his reading glasses down next to his coffee. He cleared his throat. "Maybe the question is why didn't *she* tell you?" He could have said it accusingly, but the words came with a note of gentleness she might have overlooked before.

"Look," said Phil, "there's a lot of pain I've caused other people. Some serious rewriting of my life I wish I could do, but I can't. If your mom taught me anything, it's this: Own your shit. Know when you've been a jackass and move on."

Sara rested her head against her hand. "Is that a direct quote?"

"My spin."

She closed her eyes. "When did you build this place?"

"About six months before Cassie's mom died."

"But…isn't that *before* you got back together?"

"An act of faith."

"So you were really close?"

"Yeah."

"It's beautiful here."

"I know."

After Sara hung up with Phil, she walked to a closet in the master bedroom. A thick, plum-colored cardigan lay folded on a shelf. She held the familiar sweater close to her face and inhaled the fading scent of her mother. She put the sweater on and wrapped it close around her body. She curled up on her mother's bed, hugged a pillow, and wept so deeply she could feel its waves down to her toes. Though it was barely sunset, Sara fell deeply asleep and didn't move until morning.

CHAPTER 23

Nice people with common sense do not make interesting characters. They only make good former spouses.

ISABEL ALLENDE

Sara slept until 7:00 AM when Gatsby woke her up. She felt groggy, and her head ached. She took him out front and leaned against the porch railing while he did his business. The chilly morning air was a pleasant surprise. Cool summer mornings were unusual in Maryland.

She realized she never ate dinner last night and felt incredibly hungry. She grabbed a bag of potato chips from her backpack and stood on the porch letting Gatsby explore the front yard some more. A truck gave her a friendly honk as it passed her house. Sara looked up and saw Nik give her a neighborly wave as he passed. She crumpled the bag of chips closed. She clutched her shirt and her hair thinking how terrific she must look in yesterday's rumpled clothes and smeared mascara, eating barbecue chips for breakfast. She wiped her orange hands on her jeans and tried to smooth her hair back. She wished she didn't know anybody here. It was already a burden to have one acquaintance she was supposed to smile at.

ço

That evening, Sara took Gatsby on a walk to the Shore Path, just a few blocks away. The view overwhelmed her. Piles of boulders lined the shore, and the sea stretched out calmly to the horizon, the water a grayish blue. The path itself was shaded, but the setting sun lit up the nearby islands in golden light. She could see an old schooner out with tourists for an evening sail. As she rounded the Shore Path to the bay, the sunset filled the sky with streaks of orange and pink, the ocean turning a brilliant blue.

Sara walked past the Bar Harbor Inn and stretched out on the grass at Agamont Park with Gatsby. The park nestled onto a hill with beautiful views of the harbor. There was something calming about the bay. She closed her eyes a moment and breathed deeply. Maine was a good idea.

కు

Sara settled into a routine her first two weeks in Maine. She'd walk the Shore Path first thing in the morning with Gatsby and then write for four to five hours. It was the beginning of August, and Sara had until December 15th, to produce a 400-page manuscript.

One morning, Sara found a bright red bike on her front porch with a note from Nik. It had belonged to her mother, and he'd tuned it up for her. She hadn't spoken to him since she first arrived and had only seen him in passing since then.

After writing for a few hours, Sara rode the bike a few blocks into town looking for a café called "The Lieberry" where she hoped to meet the Bernadette who left her the flowers. She found The Lieberry close to the Village Green in a gray and white renovated craftsman cottage. She stepped inside and smelled buttery pastries, coffee, and French fries. Bookshelves made of distressed, gray wood framed a large back corner next to cozy chairs and plump sofas. Tables, comfy booths, and more bookshelves filled the main dining area.

A cashier named Gina worked up front. She wore duck boots, cut-off shorts, and a t-shirt that said, "Crustacean Nation."

"Excuse me, does Bernadette work here?" Sara asked.

"You mean Bernie? Yep, this is her place. She'll be back in thirty or so."

The place had an artsy, homey feel that made Sara want to stay awhile. She wandered through the shelves and then looked through the colorful assortment of flyers on the community board. A small stack of neon green flyers caught her eye:

> WRITERS GROUP: Community members are invited to workshop their writing with students at the College of the Atlantic. A great opportunity to give and receive feedback by fellow writers and COA faculty. Tuesday nights at 7:00, beginning September 7th, Thorndike Library Seminar Room, COA Main Campus.

Sara read it carefully, thinking how much her writers group helped her with her first novel years ago. Writing could feel so isolating at times. She took a flyer with her and found an empty seat next to a window. She ordered a blueberry scone with tea and then opened her laptop to review Phil's edits for the week. She sipped her Earl Grey while she worked.

Thirty minutes later she noticed Nik's truck pull up to the front of the café. A sixty-something, heavyset woman with carefully coiffed brown hair hoisted herself out of the passenger side. Her floral button-down shirt hung loosely, and her too-tight, polyester pants seemed to stretch with her as she walked around the back of Nik's truck. Was this Bernadette? Nik helped the woman heft some boxes out of the truck bed, and then they disappeared to the side of the café. A few minutes later, Sara watched the woman talking to Nik outside again. She patted his bearded cheek in a maternal sort of way and hugged him. He kissed her cheek. There was something in his affection towards her that suddenly heightened what was, admittedly, a very handsome face.

Sara quickly looked down and went back to Phil's notes. She had a hard time concentrating. She found herself trying to remember what Phil had told her about his son. They'd been so focused on the book, and it's not like Phil was a great conversationalist. She knew Nik spent time in Croatia and that he worked at the college. Phil mentioned he was divorced but said nothing about when or why.

Sara remembered that every time she would ask a follow-up question about his son, Phil would answer it in the briefest possible sentence followed simply with, "Phillip's a good man." Nothing else. Most proud fathers loved to brag about their sons. Why didn't he? Then she remembered Phil saying his son was kind of a rebel in high school, had lots of problems—maybe drugs and alcohol—and she got the impression that Phil felt guilty for not being there for his kid.

Sara took a bite of scone with satisfaction. Her new Ellery Dawson antennae felt stronger than ever, helping her make connections she might have missed before. Well, at least Nik had a steady job now. She imagined Phil having high hopes for his son, probably ready to send him to the best universities. Maybe he was supposed to be a lawyer or an investment banker or whatever Phil deemed important, and instead he spent Nik's college savings at expensive rehabs. Well, living in a small, safe little town here was probably a great place to practice sobriety. At least he seemed to be a productive, contributing member of society. "A good man," like Phil said.

"I was wondering when you were going to stop by here, Miss Sara-girl." She looked up to see the woman she'd just watched out the window smiling widely at her. She had a low, gravelly voice and that clear Mainer accent that said "heah" instead of "here."

"I'm Bernadette Corrigan, but you can call me Bernie."

Sara stood up and reached to shake her hand, but Bernadette pulled her close and hugged her warmly. The affection was unexpected, but somehow it didn't feel awkward.

"Looks like you're writing away, just like your mother. She'd write here many days. Sat right over in that corner table by the window and drank away all my tea. Earl Grey with milk and sugar?"

Sara smiled.

"I'll bring you more. Nik, come on over and keep Miss Sara company while you wait for your lunch."

Sara turned around, her eyes surprised to meet Nik's. Living close by, she thought she would have seen him more. He'd wave whenever she saw him, but sometimes it felt like he was actually making an effort to avoid her which felt rather odd since he was her only real acquaintance in town. Sara remembered telling Ann she hoped Nik wasn't expecting anything. Well, clearly he wasn't.

Nik smiled and walked over to Sara's table. She closed her laptop and quickly swept some crumbs off the table.

"Mind if I sit down?"

"Sure. I mean yes…please." Sara felt suddenly awkward. And a little nervous. She didn't know why. She noticed how he always wore the same brown work boots, jeans, and an open flannel shirt with a black tee, like he was answering a casting call for the next Croatian Eddie Bauer. Yes, he was handsome, but the man clearly had no imagination.

"Thanks for the bike."

"No problem."

"So…it must be a busy time to manage properties around here, I guess?" she asked.

"I only look after a few homes."

"Oh, right."

"Busy at the college, though. We try to hit a lot of projects in the summer months."

"Right, of course. So, you enjoy your work?" She thought how important it must be for Nik to stay busy. She heard that was key to sobriety.

"Sure. My dad told you what I do here…at the college, right?"

"Yeah. Well, he told me you managed some properties, but I didn't know until we met that you actually worked at the college too, you know, doing maintenance."

Nik smiled to himself, as if there was something he found a little funny in their conversation, but Sara couldn't place what it was. He cocked his head to one side, cleared his throat and said, "I know it's not as prestigious as maintenance work at a *major* university." Again, that easy smile.

"No, I wouldn't say that. It must be very satisfying to work with your hands." Sara winced as she spoke. It felt so "elite Washingtonian."

"Sure, but actually, I use my mind quite a lot there too."

"Oh, of course. Yes, I'm sure it's really, um, *stimulating*." She could still detect the slight condescension in her voice, like smelling her own sweat. She tried to compensate. "I'm sure there's a lot of problem solving."

Nik nodded and smiled and didn't say anything for a moment. Then he said he better check on his order, which meant she certainly had said the wrong thing. Sara thought that for someone trying to write a book, she apparently had no talent with words.

He seemed to know all the servers up front and the cooks in the kitchen and had this quiet, relaxed way with people. Someone in the back had shouted something funny that made them all laugh. She found his easy manner almost unnerving. No pretense. He seemed completely comfortable with his work and his life.

Phil mentioned Nik was divorced, and Sara wondered if he'd been married long and what happened, and she wondered what she'd do if he ever asked her out.

Not that he would.

Why would he?

Except that their families were friends and maybe that would be just a normal, friendly thing to do even if he didn't find her attractive. Right?

Did Nik have children? No, of course not. Phil would have said something if he had grandchildren. And Phil as a grandfather? Now that would be fascinating. And maybe a little scary.

If he did ask her out, you know, just as friends, that would be fine, but what if he wanted to go out again? She didn't know. She just knew she kind of liked his company.

Sara opened her laptop again and tried to go for "relaxed busy."

Nik sat back down with a cup of coffee. "Not sure why it's taking so long."

He stirred some cream into his coffee. A lot, actually. Sara watched the white swirls lighten his coffee to a creamy, sensible tan.

He sipped his coffee and then gestured to her computer. "So, how's the writing coming along?"

She quickly closed it. "Oh, well. Bit by bit. I'm getting there. I heard you do a little writing as well. Anna-Kath told me you play guitar and write some of your own songs."

"Yeah, something like that."

"It's great to have a creative outlet."

Nik laughed more heartily. "Absolutely."

"Why are you laughing?" Sara had the niggling discomfort that she was missing something.

"It's nothing, really. I just find you, incredibly...*validating.*"

Sara bit her bottom lip, not sure what he meant by that, but then Bernie interrupted, holding his to-go sack in one hand and an empty plate in the other.

"Don't mind me," she said as she set another cup of tea in front of Sara and then casually began unpacking Nik's grilled chicken sandwich to-go and his waffle fries onto a real plate directly in front of him. She handed him a bottle of ketchup and walked away, leaving the two of them together.

"Well, that was subtle," he said, popping a waffle fry in his mouth.

"You don't have to stay. I'm sure you're busy."

He took Sara's cue and started to stand. "I don't want to hold you up."

She held up a hand. "It's okay. Really. Please sit down."

"Okay." He shrugged his shoulders and sat back down. He squeezed ketchup on his plate and offered her a waffle fry.

Sara tasted it. It was crispy on the outside and soft on the inside, seasoned with some kind of pepper and paprika mix. "Wow. That's really *good*."

"Tell me that's not your first waffle fry."

"Hey, I'm new around here."

He pushed his plate towards her. "Have all you want."

She ate a few more.

"So tell me about your writing project," Nik said. "I know you're here to write. But that's all Phil told me."

"Do you always refer to your dad as Phil?"

"Do you always avoid the question?"

Sara smiled as she mixed sugar into her tea. "I'm working on a creative project."

"Well that's descriptive. Fiction, nonfiction, poetry?"

"Oh my gosh—not poetry. I'm terrible at poetry. I don't get poetry."

"Sara Grayson, how did you get a graduate degree in English without an appreciation of poetry?"

"How did you know I have a degree in—"

"Your mom."

"Right. Well, it's not that I don't *appreciate* poetry, I just don't always get it. It's not my thing."

Nik laughed.

"What's so funny?" She ate another waffle fry.

"Well, according to my father, poetry is the ballet of writing."

"The ballet of writing?"

"Yep. That's what my father told me after I failed my ninth-grade poetry exam." He deepened his voice and imitated Phil's tough-guy-lecture voice. "It's the barre work for all your other writing, son, and you need to learn the freakin' dance—only he didn't say freakin'."

She laughed at his spot-on imitation of his father.

"Then I failed English twice, and he signed me up for military summer school in Pennsylvania. That was fun." Nik dipped his sandwich in ketchup and took a big bite.

Sara stirred her tea.

Nik tapped her closed laptop. "So, what are you writing, really?"

"It's a little fiction piece. Still in…development."

"Hmm. Purposefully vague. Interesting."

She picked up an empty sugar packet and rolled it between her fingers. "It's not that interesting." She dropped the packet and clasped her hands together. Like she'd completed her report and it was time to move on.

"Must be fun to write then." Nik chuckled to himself. He ate another waffle fry and seemed to finish his sandwich in a matter of five bites.

Sara wrapped her fingers around her warm teacup. They both sat quietly for a moment. Then she said, "You know, you're welcome to stop by my place sometime, or, I mean, your dad's place. We *are* neighbors, besides the fact that our parents worked together and…you know…liked each other."

Nik laughed softly. "That's one way to put it."

There was another pause in the conversation. He was done eating. Sara wondered if he needed to get going. He looked out the window across the street, like he was thinking something over. He rubbed his hands on his jeans and quickly exhaled. "Look, Sara, Phil told me you have a lot of work to do and a looming deadline. I've just been wanting to give you some space. He told me you'd need that."

Understanding dawned, and Sara smiled. So that's why he'd kept such a firm distance. "Well, yeah, I do have a lot of work to do, but you don't have to be a total stranger."

"So I could be a…mild stranger?"

"Of course. That's exactly what I meant. Every girl needs a mild stranger."

"I can be that," said Nik as he stood up. "But for now I need to head back to work." Then he pointed to the green flyer on the table, the one about the writing group. "You might want to give that a try. I've heard great things."

Sara nodded. "Thanks."

Nik smiled and left. Sara went back to her editing. She glanced out the window again and watched him get into his truck. She saw him turn back at her and smile. *Blast.* He caught her looking at him. Her face felt warm. She looked back at her computer and tried to go back to Phil's notes, but she kept thinking of how Nik's eyes matched his dark lashes. *Ugh,* she thought, *I'm noticing his lashes.* She squeezed her hands together in her lap and looked at her screen. "Focus, Grayson," Phil's voice rang in her head. She ordered more waffle fries.

CHAPTER 24

Love words, agonize over sentences.
And pay attention to the world.

SUSAN SONTAG

From: Anna-Katherine Green
To: Sara Grayson
Date: Sunday, July 28, 11:43 AM
Subject: Times reporter

Sara,

The *Times* reporter showed up at my house yesterday.
I didn't let him in, but I talked to him on my porch.
I know it's not protocol, but I was curious. He said
he talked to a former secretary at Thornton Books
in London, the publisher of *Silence in Stepney,* you
know, Meredith Lamb's book? The secretary claims
she knows both Meredith Lamb and Dad's sister, Mary
Grayson. Apparently the three were close friends.
The woman insists Mum's first book was plagiarized.
She says she can prove it. Meredith is bound by the
nondisclosure clause when she settled with Mum,

but I don't think Mary is. We could try and find her. Maybe she would answer some questions.

Cartwright wants to go public with the new claims, but I think he's looking for more solid evidence before he does that.

Don't you find it strange that we hardly know Dad's sister? Mum always said that Mary wanted nothing to do with the family and that she moved to Australia right after Dad died. I have vague memories—picking up fall leaves with her when we were little and her bringing us Pixy Stix.

Anna-Kath

Texts on Sunday, July 28, 3:22 PM

Sara
I remember the leaves and the Pixy Stix.

Ann
I overheard an argument between Mum and Grandma Charlotte after we moved to Bethesda. It was about our trip to visit her and Mum said there's no way we were coming to England if Aunt Mary was going to be there. Mum was really upset. And remember, we didn't go that summer?

Sara
And we didn't go to Grandma's
funeral a few years later.

Ann
I think it's because of Aunt Mary.
It's like Mum felt this need
to protect us from her. I wish
we knew what happened.

Sara
Where's Aunt Mary now?

Ann
I'll see what I can learn. We
could try to contact Meredith.

Sara
"Hey, you slept with my father and
sued my mother and she still gave
you millions. Want to have tea? Oh,
and bring our little sister along?"

Ann
Wasn't the approach I was going for.
Don't you want to know the truth?

Sara
I liked the old truth better.

Ann
There is no old truth.

Sara
Okay. The stories formerly known as
the truth. Can't I stay in that world?

Ann
Said half of society. That's
why Sybil Brown-Baker drives
a brand-new BMW.

Sara
It's a Lexus. Her seventeen-
year-old drives the BMW.

❧

Nik stopped by Sunday evening. Sara sat on the porch editing pages on her laptop. She wore cut-off shorts and a t-shirt, her bare legs stretched out on a wicker ottoman.

Nik walked up to the porch, and Gatsby hopped around him happily. He wore dress pants, a light blue button-down shirt, and freshly-shined dress shoes.

"You look nice," said Sara. "What's the occasion?"

"Church with Bernie at St. Andrews."

Sara nodded her head thoughtfully. She had heard how important faith can be in addiction recovery.

Nik sat down in a chair next to Sara and gently scratched the base of Gatsby's ears. "So my dad's helping you write?"

"Yeah. Quite a bit, actually."

"Well, I hope you get through this without wanting to kill your editor."

"Too late for that. He basically took the first novel I ever wrote and bludgeoned it to death. Despised him for years."

Nik squeezed one eye shut.

Sara realized how insensitive that sounded. "That didn't come out right. I mean Phil's *very talented.*" She felt her face turn red and stopped talking. She took a breath. "I'm sorry, I shouldn't have said that."

He shrugged his shoulders and stretched his legs out in front of him. "All I can say is…welcome to the club. I hated him for half my life, so I think I've got you beat."

He gave Sara a sweet half-smile, and she felt relieved she hadn't offended him, but sad for his situation. She closed her laptop. "So, not a great relationship with your dad?"

"Come on. Are you surprised?"

"I guess not."

"We're good now. Actually, I have your mom to thank for that."

"Really?"

"Yeah. When my dad first started dating your mom years ago and she found out how rocky things were with us, she put serious pressure on him to patch things up. She pretty much told Phil to man up and be a father."

"That sounds like her."

"He'd bought a home up here—where I live now—and invited me to work on it with him. Maine became this thing that connected us like nothing ever had. I owe that to your mom."

Sara smiled.

"So what about you? I heard your dad passed away when you were young?"

"Yeah. He died of colon cancer when I was seven."

A gentle breeze moved through the trees.

"I'm sorry."

"It was a long time ago."

The evening was cooling down. Sara slipped her mom's sweater around her and tucked her legs beneath her. She felt Nik's eyes gently watching her.

"Do you remember much about him?"

"Quite a bit, although a lot of my memories feel more like snapshots. He used to tell me and Ann these amazing stories about a crime-solving girl named Billie Donovan. She was the daughter of a famous East End detective, Brandt Donovan. We would hang on *every single word*." Sara smiled at the memory. "He loved to write. He's the one who dreamed of being the famous writer, not my mom." Sara looked up at the sky. "Funny how life turns out."

"Did he ever publish?"

"Writing journals, mostly. He won a few awards in college. He was working on a novel before he died, I think about Brandt Donovan—Mum said it was really great, actually. There was this fire at his school, and he lost his work. Everything was at his office."

Nik placed a fist to his heart and groaned. "Oh, that's painful."

"I know. Can you imagine? He was really sick by that point, though, and writing just sort of faded in importance."

Nik nodded.

"He seemed basically perfect to me." Sara exhaled slowly and turned back to Nik. "But, of course, no one is, right?"

Nik scratched Gatsby behind his ears. "This guy might be."

Sara smiled at Gatsby. "Now that is true."

They watched the first fireflies of the night flash among the trees while all the unanswered questions about her father poked around inside her. She tried to change the subject. "Tell me about Croatia. Phil says you've spent a lot of time there."

"My baka—grandma—made me go when I was sixteen, and we spent the entire summer in this tiny village with cousins I'd never met. That's where I learned to build and fix things, an education you don't get at a private Manhattan prep school. I'd felt so alone in New York, and all of a sudden, I had this place where I *belonged*. I can't explain it, but when I got back, I felt different. I still hated my father, but I decided to live my own life. I went back to Croatia again the next summer. It changed everything for me."

She liked the way Nik talked with his hands to emphasize a point and the way his eyes smiled before his mouth did. He told her more about his cousins in Croatia and the farm and the food his aunt would make. She told him more about London and found out they loved the same Indian restaurant on 9th Avenue in New York. He began to tell her about a Croatian place in Queens.

"Club Rudar? Phil took me there."

Nik raised an eyebrow. "He didn't."

"He did! And I loved it! It was exactly what I needed."

"The strudel or the crepes?"

"Everything."

Nik grinned and leaned his head back against the rocker.

Gatsby had fallen asleep next to Nik's feet and began to snore a little, which made both of them laugh. Nik's cell phone rang. He apologized for having to pick up. He touched her arm as he left to talk over by his truck, leaning his back against the car door. It sounded like something was wrong at one of his properties.

Sara thought how Nik never mentioned his college years. Maybe he went to trade school or just started working. Is that when his life got derailed again? But he seemed happy now. Actually, it was more than that. He had this sense of living in the present that Sara envied.

Was it a Maine thing? A Nik thing? A recovering addict thing?

She looked back at Nik, still leaning against his truck. She liked the way she felt when she was with him. His eyes met hers for a moment, and he smiled. Her face felt warm, and she quickly looked away. Instead of enjoying that gentle exchange and the warmth of just being with him, she felt suddenly seized with a bumbling sense of her own insecurity.

Nik walked back to Sara's porch. "Listen, I've got a hot water heater that's leaking. I've gotta go check it out."

"Sure. No problem."

He paused before he left the porch and looked at Sara. He tugged on his collar a moment and cleared his throat. "Do you want to have dinner tomorrow night?"

Sara paused with her mouth open, painfully unsure of herself. "Dinner? Tomorrow night?"

Why was she hesitating? Of course she wanted to go. How could she not?

He was personable, someone she liked talking to. Handsome. Someone who could be a really good friend, but she felt completely gripped with the utter ridiculousness of the whole thing, like she was watching herself in a reality show and shouting to her character that she was acting like a fool. She had a book to write. A big book. She didn't have time to start something here. She didn't have time to like someone and wonder if he liked her back and wonder if he'd ask her out again. She didn't have time to worry if she offended him or said the wrong thing.

No. All this was bad timing. Even Anna-Kath would completely agree with her on this point. Phil certainly would.

"Sara?"

"Dinner, um, right...well, I have this writing project." Sara hated how her voice sounded timid and unsure. Mike complained about that, told her to say what she meant, but then he shut her down whenever she finally said what she meant.

"It's just dinner."

"Right. It's just...there's a lot going on for me...and..."

Nik nodded. "It's okay, Sara. I understand." His response was so kind, so sincere—it felt like new territory for her.

"I mean, it's not you," she said, stumbling over her words. Did she really just use that line? "I just can't really go there right now. I'm sorry."

Nik squatted down and stroked Gatsby's back. "It's okay. Really. You just need a 'mild stranger.' I get that." Then he smiled—like, genuinely smiled. Not put off or bugged or offended that Sara had turned him down. Not hurling choice words at her to blame her for his discomfort. He just smiled and wished her a good night and drove home.

She walked into the house and collapsed face first in the couch. She groaned. "I am so stupid, Gatsby." She turned over on her back and pressed her palms against her eyes until she saw stars. "And what the hell is a mild stranger?" Gatsby lay his chin and paws on the edge of the sofa, looking at her expectantly. She looked at his perfect brown eyes for a response.

She smiled. "You don't know either."

Sara found the love letter she'd saved from her father to her mother in her purse. She curled up on the couch with a soft afghan that smelled like her mom. She traced the familiar script on the envelope with her finger. She opened it up. "My Lovely Cass," it began. She held it in her hand and wondered if anyone would ever write words like that to her.

But if a love like her parents' was betrayed so easily, maybe it didn't matter anyway.

CHAPTER 25

*You must be unintimidated by your
own thoughts because if you write with someone
looking over your shoulder, you'll never write.*

NIKKI GIOVANNI

S ara didn't sleep well. She kept dreaming about Ellery, who shouted relationship advice while they rode the streets of Brussels on a Vespa. She woke up troubled and just needed to get lost in her writing. She checked her email mid-morning:

> **From:** Gloria Knott
> **To:** Sara Grayson
> **Date:** Monday, July 29, 9:55 AM
> **Subject:** My latest creation
>
> Dear Sara,
>
> I hope your writing is going well. I crocheted a new bracelet. It's a lovely, lacey pattern. I just wanted

to share it with you, since your mother was such a splendid inspiration. Please enjoy the attached photo.

Cheers,
Gloria Knott
Iris Book Publishing

Sara brought up the photo and looked at the bracelet. It was quite lovely, but she found the whole email a little odd. Then again, so was Gloria. Maybe she just needed some encouragement. Yes, that was probably it. Sara began a new email complimenting Gloria on her work.

She stopped.

She opened the photo again and looked more closely. Gloria's wrist sat on a document. Sara enlarged the photo. There, just below Gloria's wrist, was a check from Iris Books to Asher Monroe for $35,000. She gasped as she read the notes on the lower half, "Advance for *Ellery Dawson*, Book Five."

Book Five? Asher Monroe? She remembered Gloria emailing her about a private meeting between him and Jane earlier in the summer, but when Sara had Googled the man, she had found no connection to herself, just a UK department store owner. Phil said not to worry about it.

She Googled him again, now adding the words *Ellery Dawson,* and leaned back in her chair, breathless, as Asher Monroe's credits unfolded before her. She leaned her head back, shoving her hands into her hair with a moan. How had she missed this? Monroe was the screenwriter for the first *Ellery Dawson* movie, and Jane had just cut him an advance for Book Five.

She texted Phil. Then called. She tapped her foot, her fingers, waiting for Phil to pick up. She got his voicemail. She called again, pacing the room, her neck and back tensing up. Voicemail again. Finally she got a text:

Texts on Monday, July 29, 10:27 AM

Phil

I'm at Iris right now. I can't talk. I
know about the advance. I voted
against it, but the board overruled
me. They want Monroe to write
a detailed outline, like what we
did in New York. Jane is making
preparations—just in case.

Sara
In case I fail?

Phil
Yes.

Sara
Did anyone else on the
board vote with you?

Phil
No.

Sara sank back into her chair.

Phil
Ignore it. Keep writing.

Sara
How? Jane can't really do this,
right? We have a contract. You
own Iris. Do something!

Phil
I'll email you after our meeting.

Sara scoured both bathtubs waiting for Phil to respond. Finally she heard back.

From: Phil Dvornik
To: Sara Grayson
Date: Monday, July 29, 12:01 PM
Subject: Update

Grayson,

Iris is legally bound to honor Cassandra's contract rider as long as you have a solid draft by December 15th. Should your book fail to sell more than 100,000 copies, Iris has the right to re-publish another *Ellery* Book Five with a different author. Right now Jane is anticipating your failure on either count. If you don't meet the deadline, she'll use Monroe. If you meet the deadline, but your sales are poor, she'll use Monroe. You also need to know that Jane controls how much marketing they do for your book. Jane could simply refuse to funnel resources into your book with the hope that it's a tiny blip that comes and goes in the book world and then put resources into what she really wants.

Yes, I still own Iris, but Jane has convinced the board to side with her on securing Monroe and when I "retired," I gave up my veto power.

Phil

Texts on Monday, July 29, 12:03 PM

Sara
Can't you just fire her?

Phil
Not without the board's support.
She's a good editor. She's
just scared that our biggest
book is about to flop.

Sara
Something Jane and I can agree on. It's
your company. Aren't you scared too?

Phil
Oddly, no.

Okay. That was sort of an expression of confidence. Kind of.

She stood up, her arms stiff and her hands clenched. She felt so completely outgunned against that woman. Sara could do everything right, create the best work of her life, and Jane's carefully placed land mines could blow it all apart.

She threw on her running shoes and sprinted towards the bay. She could only run a mile comfortably, but her anger fueled her run and at two miles she kept going. Her heart pounded through her chest. Her legs burned. At three miles she slowed down, her breathing heavy and her throat dry. She drank from a water fountain and then sat on a park bench in the Village Green with her head between her legs, trying to catch her breath, still angry, but too tired to go any farther.

"Out for a run, Sara-girl?" asked Bernie, who had appeared in front of Sara in her usual polyester pants and Keds, holding a paper bag. "You okay? Saw you out here from the Lieberry."

"I'm fine," Sara muttered.

"Good to know."

Bernie sat down next to Sara. She pulled a carton out of the bag and took the lid off. Something smelled heavenly inside. She put a spoon inside and handed it to Sara.

"Glad you're fine. You need my lobster chowder anyway."

Sara took a bite. It was creamy and smooth, and the bits of potato and lobster were so tender they seemed to melt on her tongue. It was the most comforting food she had eaten in days, and Bernadette grinned knowingly, like she knew exactly what she was delivering.

Bernie sipped a cup of coffee and ate a blueberry muffin while Sara ate her chowder.

"I'm a good listener, if you feel like talking."

"I'm stressed about a book I'm writing," Sara admitted.

"Ayuh…that wouldn't be Book Five, now, would it?"

Sara's head popped up, her mouth full of chowder. She quickly swallowed. "What did you say?"

Bernie laughed and patted Sara's knee. "I figured as much." She looked out towards the bay and sighed. "Your mama was the finest kind. I sure do miss her."

Bernie spoke with so much love that Sara began crying—ugly, sweaty, red-faced crying. Bernie handed her some stiff napkins from the café to wipe her nose and eyes and arms—it was that bad. Then Sara found herself opening up about her frustrations to Bernie. She told her about Jane's scheming, her father's betrayal, her mother's secrets, the relentless pressure of the book.

"Sweet Moses, you're carrying a lot on those shoulders," Bernie quietly exclaimed, patting her back.

"I miss my mother so deeply. And then sometimes—like today—I'm so angry that she forced me into this situation. How do I stop being angry at her?"

Bernie finished her muffin and swept the crumbs off her lap. "Well, Lord knows the past is a complicated thing and I'm fairly certain you didn't tell your mama everything about your own life."

"Well, I don't know if—"

Bernie held up her two palms to stop her. "As for the present," she said, turning to Sara and looking directly in her eyes, "what if you stopped worrying about yourself and just wrote the damn book?"

"Excuse me?"

"Maybe this isn't about you."

"My mother asked me to write the book. Of course it's about me."

"That's one conclusion. I'm suggesting another. What if your mama just wanted a good book?"

"I don't get it."

Bernie smiled. She took Sara's hand. "Put everything else aside. Maybe she just wanted a good book, and the writer happens to be you?"

"My feelings are very real, Bernie, and they are telling me something entirely different." Sara was firm on this point. She knew she was right.

"I have no doubt your feelings are real, but that doesn't mean they're telling you the truth."

Sara squinted her eyes at Bernie. "I don't think you understand what's going on here."

"Maybe so. But with all due respect, maybe you don't either."

Sara dropped her hands in her lap. She stared at the grass, unsure how to respond.

Bernie squeezed Sara's arm. "You're drawing all these big conclusions—making all this new meaning for yourself—what your mama meant or didn't mean and blah, blah, blah."

Sara pulled her legs to her chest and hugged them. She said nothing.

"Your mama asked you to write the book. You said yes. Stop making up stories about what your mom was trying to do or not trying to do and just write it. Make it work. And you don't have time to worry about what

Miss Smarty-Pants Publisher is doing because you are busy writing your own hell of a book. You got that?"

Bernie gave her a hug. In spite of all her straight talk, her eyes were full of warmth. Sara nodded. She wiped her eyes, took a deep breath. Bernie headed back to work.

Sara began her walk home. She held her head a little higher. What if her mom really did just want a good book, and she believed Sara could do it?

Well, the reality was that right now she was doing it. She was writing the book. And she was making progress every day. She just had to keep showing up.

So, how would she get through this with her own publisher scheming against her?

That night, Sara decided that Asher Monroe may have more experience, but she would work harder. She'd get up earlier. Write longer hours. Listen to Phil. And keep revising her book until she had it right. Again and again and again.

She would do whatever it takes.

A week later Binti sent her a doormat with the face of Asher Monroe and a chair pillow with the face of Jane Harnois. "Every day you can wipe your feet on Asher's nose, and when it's time to write, you can sit your ass down on Jane's sorry face and show her what you've got."

It was all about perspective.

෨

Over the next month, Sara wrote with more energy than ever. It was now Labor Day, and she'd made it through eighteen chapters—about a third of the way through the book. By all accounts, this was progress. She felt good about her momentum, but here was her problem:

Her writing was just *okay.*

The best she got from Phil was: *This will do. Good enough. Okay. Fine. Move on.*

He was merciless in his criticism, picking everything apart, but after repeated drafts, she'd get the "okay" comments, and they'd move on. How could she make her writing better than just okay? Asher Monroe's writing was going to be better than okay.

Phil would visit Sara in three weeks when she was halfway through her draft. She'd circled September 20th on her calendar in bright red ink. It began to feel like an evil eye. She took the calendar off the wall and shoved it in a drawer.

❧

Labor Day evening, Sara ordered a sandwich and iced tea at The Lieberry and then sat at the Village Green. She thought she saw Nik's truck down the road, and her chest tightened up.

It wasn't him.

She still felt foolish about turning him down a month ago. She was the one who smiled at lunch and told him not to be a total stranger, and then he came over and they had this great conversation and he asked her out…and she totally choked. She had seen him a few times since then. He repaired her dishwasher. They got talking about a favorite park on the Upper West Side. She almost asked him to stay for dinner, but didn't. She'd hardly seen him after that. Bernie said it was a busy time at the college with all the students coming back. Then she smiled like Sara should totally understand Nik because they both worked at colleges.

She sipped some of her iced tea. A couple lay on the lawn ahead of her, the woman's head nestled into her partner's chest. The man stroked the woman's hair away from her face. She imagined what it would feel like to lean into Nik's broad chest and to feel his breath in sync with her own.

Sara shook her head. The most likely scenario would be a repeat of Mike, who left her drained instead of filled—like a leaky air mattress you patch up and refill, and no matter the effort, you're on the floor by morning.

She was in line for her Almond Joy ice cream at CJ's when she saw that writing group announcement again—the one at the college that invited community members to join in. It started the next day, and, after six weeks in Maine, she felt desperate for something—anything—to help bring her writing up another notch.

Phil would kill me. She had asked him if she could work with a writers group in New York, but he shot it down. "Too risky," he said. "We need complete anonymity." He was right, but maybe there was a way to minimize those risks.

Binti FaceTimed Sara that night and they talked it over. "Just do it," said Binti. "If it's a good writing group, it can make a huge difference in your writing."

"And no one there would even know who I am," Sara added.

"Exactly."

"I'll just be an amateur writer, practicing fan fiction…as a hobby."

Which was almost the truth.

CHAPTER 26

Most people know what a story is until
they sit down to write one.

FLANNERY O'CONNOR

The College of the Atlantic was a tiny liberal arts school situated on thirty-eight acres of picturesque coastal property in Bar Harbor. Sara parked early so she could explore campus before writing group. She wandered through the student center and over to the pier. The college might have been small, but there was an energy about the place she sensed immediately, and the views of Frenchman Bay were breathtaking.

This was a good decision.

She found the seminar room in the library just before seven. There were only five students there—no one looked older than twenty. She was clearly the only "community member" until a wiry old man with a full, gray beard walked in. He looked like someone straight out of a Jack London novel, someone who could survive inside a tree for winter and talk to wolves for emotional support. Maybe this was the professor. Sara smiled and said hello. He ignored her, grabbed a couple of chairs, and walked out. Maybe the chairs would be firewood to cook his dinner.

A few students began moving some chairs around.

"Hey, come on over—we always sit around the main table in a circle," said one girl with buff arms. She reached over and lifted a couple of chairs over to their new location with ease. "I'm Miriam."

"I'm Sara, a community member." Her voice was shaky. Did she really just introduce herself as "a community member"? Like she was attending an HOA meeting at her retirement village?

"Yeah. I figured." Miriam sat next to her and began chatting about how she'd been a river guide down in West Virginia for the summer. It made sense, since she looked like she arrived on campus via canoe in her khaki shorts, Tevas, and tie-dyed tank top.

"Was that old man the professor?" Sara asked.

"Holy Shamoka—no! Dr. D. teaches this one." She leaned in. "You know the chili pepper icon on *Rate My Professor*? He has more than anyone."

"That's nice." Sara looked at her watch.

"Don't get me wrong. He's brilliant too. He actually gave up a tenure track position at Columbia to work here…*with us…at COA*." She applied coconut lip balm. "Who does that?"

Sara had no idea. Maine was beautiful, peaceful, but who would give up Columbia for a tiny liberal arts college in the middle of nowhere?

"Everyone takes his poetry class here—it's not required, but it's like a rite of passage. He says everyone's a poet, and it's his job to help us see that. Sounds crazy, but everyone leaves his class feeling like one. So what are you writing?"

Sara didn't get a chance to answer because he walked in. *The professor.*

Her back went stiff, her neck rigid. She didn't breathe for several seconds.

He wore a tie with that familiar blue button-down shirt and, though his hair was still too long, it looked recently trimmed and combed back. He placed his leather satchel on the teacher's desk at the front of the room and pulled out a few files and books.

No work boots, flannel shirt, or tool belt.

He smiled at the group, and his eyes stopped abruptly on Sara. He raised his eyebrows and smiled again as he welcomed everyone to the writing group.

She set her hand around the base of her throat. *Just breathe.*

A professor? Nik was a professor? And a poet?

She reached for her water bottle and took small sips while Nik introduced himself to the group. She glanced at the door a few times, thinking of her best options for escape.

She missed the first five minutes of his opening spiel while she ran her own postmortem on all their past conversations. He did say he worked at the college. And now that she thought about it, he did tell her he wrote.

But he drove that work truck. He did maintenance.

She remembered a conversation when she told Nik it must be "rewarding to work with his hands" and actually congratulated him for having a "creative outlet."

She groaned inside.

Nik explained the structure of the workshop. They would critique the work of three class members each week with work submitted digitally at least two days in advance. Then Nik took a seat in the circle and asked everyone to introduce themselves and their writing projects.

Regret pulsed through her body. Why did she ever think this would be a good idea?

Then again, maybe this wasn't entirely her fault. She may have been hasty in her conclusions, but Nik could have corrected her. Yes, he *should* have corrected her and he didn't. She narrowed her eyes at him, her resentment growing.

Introductions started with Tembi and Ty, twins from Boston. They were writing a graphic novel together. Tembi talked energetically. Ty said little and yawned excessively. Nashid cracked his neck when he spoke, and a kid named Heath was obsessed with Jason Bourne. Someone named

Beale looked like he was fourteen and was so pale Sara wanted to yell at him to eat more spinach and to stop wearing so much black.

Why was she so annoyed at everyone? She narrowed her eyes at Nik and then back at the class. "Displacement of anger," Sybil Brown-Baker whispered in her ear. She ignored that.

Miriam seemed to be the only sane person in class. She was from Augusta and working on a poetry collection clustered around local rivers.

Nik leaned back casually in his chair and gestured toward Sara. "Glad to have a guest from the community joining us." He pressed his lips together in an effort not to smile too much. It wasn't a good look for him. "Please, introduce yourself."

She clenched her hands tightly in her lap and breathed through a wave of nausea. "I'm Sara and I'm from Bethesda, Maryland. Just here in Maine for a few months, you know, getting away, doing some writing. So, uh-yeah. That's me." She sounded like one of her anxiety-ridden freshmen she would refer to the counseling center by the second day of class.

"So...tell us about your writing project," said Nik.

"Um-right. So I'm writing some-uh-fan fiction." She stopped there. No need for details. Surely they could just move on.

"*Fan fiction*? Really?" asked Nik. "Tell us more about that." He did that cute thing where he smiled and raised one eyebrow. Why did she ever mistake that as charming?

"It's...uh...*Ellery Dawson*."

"Really? Now that is *interesting*," Nik said. "Like picking up where the last book left off?" Why was he asking her so many follow-up questions and putting her on the spot like this? He looked way too comfortable.

"Something like that." She looked at her hands, refusing to look at him. Why had she ever liked his eyes?

"Oh, like your own *Ellery Dawson* Book Five!" said Miriam. "You know, *Ellery Dawson* is what turned me into a reader. I wrote to Cassandra

Bond once, and she actually wrote me back. Like a real, hand-written note. Seriously. I cried. I still have the note."

Sara looked at Miriam. She felt a familiar pang in her heart.

"I heard the publisher's going to have a contest," said Nashid, "to find a writer to finish the series." He cracked his wrists against the table.

"No, I heard they already have an author working on it," said Tembi.

"Well, if there's a contest, you should totally enter that. Plus, what's the point of fan fiction if you can't get it out there?" said Miriam.

"Fan fiction is a legitimate genre," said Heath. "You should check out some of the stuff on Jason Bourne. It's awesome."

"Yeah, but as good as it may be, you can't *do anything* with it," said Tembi.

"Have you even been to any fan fiction sites? Some fanfickers have thousands of readers," said Heath.

Sara hoped to blend into the butter colored walls while the class argued on.

"Good discussion here," Nik jumped in. "So, what's your take on all this, Sara?"

She sighed, unable to hide her annoyance. "Well, *Doctor* Dvornik—"

"Please, call me Dr. D or *Nik*." He smiled again. "Nik is fine." He was clearly enjoying this whole awkward scenario.

"Okay, *Nik*," said Sara. "Well, fan fiction is definitely motivating for me."

"Are you writing on *Ellery World*?" asked Beale. "What's your handle?"

Sara exhaled. "Sorry. No."

"Well, Sara, glad you're here."

"Thanks *so much, Doctor Nik*." Sara couldn't suppress the sarcasm that crept into her words.

Miriam looked at Nik and back at Sara, like she was evaluating some undercurrent she couldn't quite place. "Wait a minute...do you two already know each other?"

Sara looked at Nik and then back at Miriam. She cleared her throat. "Our families are friends."

Nik gazed at Sara. "Yes, old friends."

Tembi was impressed. "Really? So have you met Dr. D's father? He's, like, one of the most famous editors in the country. He spoke on campus last year."

"Uh, Phil Dvornik? Yes, actually, I have. He's a very nice man."

Nashid whispered to Miriam, "I don't think he's known for being *nice*."

"All right," said Nik, "I can see we've got a lot of good discussions ahead." He stood and brought up a list of guidelines for writing feedback on PowerPoint and then had everyone share contact information while he set up a schedule for sharing work.

After the workshop was over, Sara gathered her things. Should she say something? Demand an apology? Apologize herself? Jump out the window? She stood up to leave.

"Sara, will you wait for me?" Nik asked.

She nodded and sat back down.

An awkward silence hung in the air while Nik talked with a few students and then packed his bag to leave. Although, if Sara was being honest, there was never anything awkward about Nik, only her. Even now, he seemed at ease. What was wrong with him?

She walked over to him. "Why didn't you tell me?"

He slung his bag over his shoulder. "I've got to stop at my office. Walk with me?"

"Sure." She followed him past a cluttered bulletin board and out the door where the night was already dark and turning chilly. Sara wished she had brought her sweater.

"You look cold. Want to borrow my jacket?"

"No. I'm fine." Sara didn't believe in borrowing jackets from professors.

"So, what did you think of the writing group?"

"Are you avoiding my question?"

"Sorry, what was your question?" Nik said with a faint smile.

She rolled her eyes.

Nik shrugged his shoulders. "I told you I worked at the university. You're the one who assumed it was strictly maintenance, which I like doing in the summer. It's good to get out of my head, and COA doesn't hold a regular summer term for students."

"C'mon, Nik. You weren't up-front with me."

"And you were?"

She swallowed hard. He had a point.

Nik led her to a beautiful stone building that looked more like a French chateau.

"Your office is in here?"

"It's called the Turrets. Yeah. It's one of the old mansions from the gilded age. The building is magnificent, though my office is rather ordinary." They wound their way up through some side stairs and into a narrow hallway where Nick unlocked a door and held it open for her.

He flipped on a desk lamp, lighting the small office in a soft golden light. Bookshelves lined the wall behind his desk, and the space smelled of old print, coffee, and a stale cinnamon roll she spotted in the trash. He moved a mound of student papers from a padded chair opposite his desk.

"Have a seat."

She sat stiffly, holding her bag on her lap. She chewed her bottom lip as she studied a bookshelf with poetry collections by David Whyte, Ada Limón, and Elizabeth Alexander. There were three collections by Filip Dvornik. She didn't know he used that spelling. She could have found all this out on Google if she'd known that.

He sat down at his desk and leaned forward, his weight on his elbows. He tried to hide it, but she caught it anyway. A smirk. And then an outright smile.

She cocked her head to one side. "You find this amusing, don't you?"

"Slightly." He bit his lower lip in an attempt to minimize his smile.

Sara dropped her bag straps. "You could have just told me you were a professor."

"And you could have told me what you're writing."

She rubbed her forehead. "Okay. So we left out a few details."

Nik's face turned softer. "I'm sorry. I could have been more up-front with you. To be honest, I thought we'd have more opportunities to talk... but it's okay."

Sara shifted in her seat. "No. I'm sorry. This whole thing was a bad idea anyway."

"Hey, these kids are great readers. I'd give them a shot. Writing can be some pretty lonely work."

She sighed. "I know."

"And that's why you need to come back. Although, let me warn you: these kids do not hold any punches."

"If I can handle your father, I can handle your workshop."

"Agreed. And I'm glad to finally know the truth—that Phil sent you to Maine to write *fan fiction*. I guess that's the new big thing at Iris, right? So, are you going to enter that contest to write the last *Ellery* book?" He leaned back in his chair and chuckled at his own joke.

Sara finally laughed a little. "How else can I explain what I'm doing in your class?"

"I know. It's a good cover. And I like imagining my father as an editor of fan fiction. It's a nice image for the great Phil Dvornik."

Sara smiled, feeling more relaxed.

"So, apparently you won the *Ellery Dawson* contest." He loosened his tie and leaned on his arms again. "Tell me about your book."

Sara cleared her throat. "Well, it's my *mother's* book. And believe me, I didn't *win* anything."

"When did she tell you?"

"She didn't. Her attorney told me three weeks after she died." Sara's voice cracked a little, her eyes grew moist. "He gave me a note she'd written to me. Told me the book was mine, that I had words, that she wanted me to write it."

"But didn't you always want to be a writer? I thought your mom said something about that."

"Oh I'm sure she mentioned it more than once." She tucked some loose strands of hair behind her ear. "Look, she's right. I did want to be a writer. I used to write stories next to my dad whenever he'd write…but all that changed." Sara closed her eyes. "Now here I am trying to write this massive book…" She laughed. "I really wish it was fan fiction." She studied her hands. "Writing this is the hardest thing I've ever done. I feel like I have to fight for every single word."

He watched her thoughtfully, his thumb moving absently along his jawline. "You know, I can't think of a single writer who doesn't feel that way at some point. Writing is an incredibly vulnerable act."

She glanced up. "Well, you're looking at the poster child."

"So are you."

"I doubt that."

"Days when your writing's a complete mess and you wonder if it will ever make sense to anyone else and you should really do the world a favor and just quit right now?"

Sara smiled softly and nodded.

A janitor began vacuuming outside the door.

Nik stood up. He picked up his satchel. "Can I walk you to your car?"

They walked outside, where students still milled about campus. It was a clear, bright night, the smell of dried leaves and smoky wood in the air.

They stopped at her car. Sara found herself a little disappointed to say goodbye already. "I'm sorry I assumed all the wrong things about you." She shook her head. "And I guess you're not a recovering addict either." She laughed out loud as she opened her back door and tossed her bag on the seat.

"What?" Nik shifted the weight on his feet. He looked uncertain how to respond.

"Oh, it's nothing." She laughed again, quite amused with herself. "Sorry. You would think it's hilarious now."

He stood quiet.

She chuckled again. "I just sort of thought that…well, you mentioned how you were kind of a high school rebel, and got into trouble a lot, and I know you go to St. Andrews where they have support groups for addiction recovery, and I just thought…well, never mind. I assume way too much. And we all know the root word of assume. And believe me, I am no Ellery Dawson." Sara laughed again and then finally caught on to Nik's quiet, uncertain gaze. She stopped.

He took a deep breath. He kicked some gravel on the parking lot. He looked up at the night sky and back at Sara. "Actually, you got that part right." He smiled tightly, his jaw tense. "I'm six years clean."

"Oh." Sara felt so foolish. She didn't mean to throw him into some kind of uncomfortable confession. "Well, six years—that's really great."

He stuffed his hands in his pockets and looked past her. "I hit a rough patch before I came here. Something happened…and…I didn't handle it like I should have…."

Sara touched his arm. "You don't owe me an explanation. I'm sorry I brought it up." At what point would she stop tasting her own foot in her mouth?

Nik leaned against the driver door. Both were quiet.

"You don't need to apologize," he said. "My life is good—really good."

He opened her door. She stepped forward to get in her car and stopped. "Can I ask you something?"

"Sure."

"Miriam said you left a tenure-track position at Columbia for this place." She gestured towards the campus. "Why here? Why small-town Maine?"

Nik threw back his head and laughed openly, freely. The awkwardness of the earlier moment evaporated. "Why? Look around. What have you seen during your stay?"

"Oh, it's beautiful. I walk the Shore Path every day."

Nik folded his arms and squinted his eyes at Sara. "You haven't gotten out much, have you?"

She laughed. "Well, I have a lot of fan fiction to write."

"Meet me at the main dock by the Bar Harbor Inn on Saturday. Ten AM?"

She opened her mouth to protest, then closed it.

"It's not a date. We're old family friends."

"Old family friends?"

"It's a *writing* field trip, okay? Bring your laptop or notebook. I'll take you somewhere inspiring, and we'll both write."

"Okay."

CHAPTER 27

Not only is your story worth telling, but it can be told in
words so painstakingly eloquent that it becomes a song.

GLORIA NAYLOR

S aturday morning, Sara rode her bike to the dock under a cloudless, blue September sky. Nik smiled when he saw her and waved her over. He wore jeans and a navy COA jacket, his usual flannel plaid shirt sticking out underneath. He walked her down to a thirty-foot, converted lobster boat named "Miss Theresa." It was low tide, and the clean ocean air held the pungent scent of fish and salt.

"So, where are we going?"

"Baker Island. About nine miles offshore."

"Baker *Island?*"

A young park ranger hopped out of the boat. Nik introduced her to Ted Babin, who lifted his hat and said hello, but little else.

"Ted's our ticket to the island today—it's Park Service land and you can't get on without a ranger or a permit."

Ted kept a pack of corn nuts sticking out of his front shirt pocket that he'd snack on between tasks and that spilled out now and then as he readied the boat.

Sara and Nik helped load a few boxes. "So, what is this place... this island?"

"Baker's one of the Cranberry Islands. Tours go out every day in the summer, but it's closed this weekend." Nik heaved the last heavy box and stacked it next to the others. "Ted has some work to do before the fall tourists arrive. We'll ride in with him, and then you and I can explore."

Sara had spent the morning reviewing Phil's notes, and her brain was already tired. She welcomed the escape.

Ted started the motor and slowly guided "Miss Theresa" out of Frenchman Bay. Sara and Nik sat on a couple of hard seats in the back, the wind whipping their hair as they picked up speed. The air definitely felt colder on the water. Nik covered them with a plaid wool blanket as the boat sped past Sand Beach and Otter Cliffs. He sat close, his arm and leg touching hers. She liked feeling his warmth. She wondered more about his past, his work, and his life here.

Nik leaned back against his seat and told Sara more about Baker Island, how it had a lighthouse and only a few temporary residents, mostly researchers they were re-supplying today. The island was settled in 1806 by William and Hannah Gilley and their three children—they eventually had twelve. Nik's voice was animated as he spoke of the Gilleys. When the government built a lighthouse in 1828, William became the lighthouse keeper, and the Gilley family members lived on the island until 1930. It was clear Nik envied something about them.

Sara loved the forty-five-minute boat ride, the cold, invigorating wind in her face. Nik pointed out some harbor porpoises on the way, and they even saw a few seals. The boat docked on a small rock beach at Baker Island. After they helped Ted load some boxes onto carts for the researchers to pick up, they walked up a grass covered hill towards an old, red schoolhouse and a couple of white, clapboard homes. The grass was long—just the type Anne Shirley would run through at Green Gables or stretch herself out upon to think and dream. As they made the climb, they turned back to enjoy the spectacular view. Nik pointed out the closest neighboring island, Little Cranberry, or Isleford.

"At low tide, there's a bar between Baker and Isleford," he explained. "Legend has it that when Hannah Gilley needed to deliver a baby, she'd walk across the bar at low tide, deliver her baby on Isleford, and walk back with a babe in arms by dinnertime."

"Incredible." Sara looked around, taking in the rugged beauty of the place. "How did they survive out here?"

"They farmed, fished, cultivated livestock. A tough existence, really. Maybe that's what I love most here, this feeling of utter determination, you know, against a harsh existence."

"But a breathtaking one. I can't imagine waking up every day to this kind of beautiful."

They stopped at the lighthouse, steady and majestic. The wind rippled through the long grass like ocean waves, and the blue sea glistened in the sun. They hiked through some forest down to the other side of the island. About a quarter mile later, the forest opened up to the ocean again. Massive boulders and slabs of granite lined this side of the coast.

"They call this 'The Dance Floor.'"

The waves crashed loudly against the rocks, and the wind ripped fiercely through Sara's jacket. And yet the place felt surprisingly peaceful.

"Did the Gilleys actually dance here?"

"I like to think so."

Sara and Nik sat on a wide table of granite and wrote for a while. She imagined Ellery out on these rocks seeing her life through fresh eyes, making peace with her father, her husband, herself. She wrote another page and then set her pen down and sat up straight, her legs crossed. She inhaled deeply, feeling her breath swirl all the way up inside her brain, clearing and creating space. She smelled the briny air and watched the waves moving in and out, the shooting spray of the ocean as it crashed against the rocks.

The wind chilled her hands, and she placed them under her thighs to warm, feeling the granite's gentle heat beneath her hands. The air's cool dampness settled on her cheeks, her neck and hair. She lay back on the rock, stretching her body out and resting her head back against her palms.

She imagined Hannah Gilley alive on this island with all its perilous beauty. It occurred to her that maybe the island's magic couldn't be separated from that struggle for survival—that maybe life was all the more beautiful *because* of that struggle.

Sara started to cry light tears that slid down her temples and into her ears, making her face wet and cold. Why was she crying? And why was she suddenly envious of Hannah Gilley? She wasn't ready to move to Baker Island or walk across a sandbar to birth her children.

"Come on. There's more to see." Nik reached for her hand and pulled her up. She quickly wiped her eyes with her fingers. They hopped from rock to rock, climbing tall boulders for different views of the coastline and the sea.

They found another spot to sit, and Nik pulled out a lunch he'd picked up from a deli in town: turkey-bacon-avocado on focaccia with parmesan chips and a thermos of hot chocolate. Nik stretched out his legs next to hers and leaned back on his hands, his foot occasionally touching hers.

She sipped her cocoa. "When did you become a poet?"

Nik leaned his head back a moment and closed his eyes, soaking in the warmth of the sun. "You know that first summer I told you about? In Croatia? There were these hills around the farm and a small creek that ran through my cousin's property. After a long day's work, I'd sit on those hills and watch the sun go down. I was a city boy—I'd never been immersed in a landscape like that—and I wrestled to find words to describe it. And for the first time, I *really longed* for the words to describe it."

Sara noticed a softness in his eyes whenever he spoke about Croatia.

"I finally bought a notebook, and I started playing with words and… *they came.* New words, new emotions filled my mind. I felt compelled to write what I was seeing and feeling. For a fifteen-year-old, obsessed with looking cool, this was completely foreign to me."

"So, is that when you first felt like a poet?"

Nik looked out at the ocean, the tops of his cheeks and nose pink from the wind. "Not quite. I didn't even realize I was writing poetry at first. Why would I write poetry? I didn't even like poetry. When I went back to New York, I stopped writing, and so the words gave up on me and left, like they got tired of waiting for me to do something. They packed up their suitcases and walked away.

"When I went back to Croatia the next summer, the words came back. I think they wondered if I'd take them seriously—they didn't know if I'd give them a real home. When the words returned, I promised I'd take care of them, and they've been with me ever since."

Sara scrunched up her lips in thought for a moment and then pushed Nik's shoulder. "You poets are weird."

"Agreed."

"Really?"

"We're also incredibly sensitive. So thanks a lot." He pushed her back, both laughing. "What about you? When did words come to you?"

She shifted uncomfortably on the granite slab and pulled her knees up to her chest. "I don't really consider myself a true writer. I mean, greeting cards, coupon writing? It's not like I have words."

"But you've taught writing for years—and you're writing a novel. Maybe it's time to see yourself as a writer—you know, not just something you do, but maybe a part of *who you are?*"

"It's complicated."

"Maybe. Maybe not."

She shook her head. "You sound like my mother."

"Wise, funny, interesting. I'll take that as a compliment."

"Is there an opening at your cousin's farm in Croatia?"

Nik smiled. "How are you at milking goats?"

Sara laughed. "I'll work on that."

Nik began packing away their lunch.

Sara wrapped the leftover chips and handed them to Nik. "Will you share a poem with me?"

"Because poets are always dying to share poems, right?"

"Uh-oh. Is that a misconception about poets?"

He scratched the side of his face. "No. That one's true."

She tightened the lid on the thermos and handed it to Nik. "I'm ready." She sat up expectantly, pulled her legs up, crisscrossed. She gave an exaggerated hand gesture for him to proceed.

He packed the thermos in his backpack, zipped it up, and narrowed his eyes at Sara. "You want a poem."

She threw her hands up, "Come on, Dr. D. Before winter sets in!"

Nik leaned back on his arms, one hand almost touching hers. He thought for a moment, glanced at the sky and then at Sara. His eyes were a much deeper brown than she'd noticed before. Nearly black. He held her gaze a moment and smiled softly. Then he turned back to the ocean.

> *Words arrive at my doorstep.*
> *Raw. Awake. Alive.*
> *What can I offer to make them stay?*
> *A clean room, plush towels—a soft bed?*
> *No, they whisper. You are the room we want.*
> *Weave us into your soul.*
> *Let us become your breath, blood, bones.*
> *Conjured, infused, enmeshed.*

Sara studied Nik's face as he continued. The soft arch of his right eyebrow. His laugh lines. The open space of skin between his beard and his lips. Nik closed his eyes, as if each word was something to be savored.

I close the door, unsure. The space I hold
Is clumsy,
Awkward and unsteady. Afraid to share.
To be misunderstood. Best to keep words
Out on the stoop, not entangled, not confused.
Yet I feel the longing, a stretching.
The scent of possibility.
If I crack myself open, if I let them in

It was unexpected. This stirring she felt. This resonance to his words from the beginning to the end. She couldn't look away from him.

Will they sink into my blood,
Spread warmth upon my skin?
Will they give me voice
For the ways I ache and question?
I want to feel them on my tongue,
need to swirl them in my mouth,
taste them, test them,
swallow them whole.
I open the door.

They sat quietly in the space of the words. Listened to the rhythm of the ocean waves hitting the rocky coast. When Nik began, she had prepared something witty to say about poets at the end, maybe even a little snarky. Now she was blinking her eyes rapidly to stop her tears.

She closed her eyes a moment and took a deep breath. "Is that one of yours?"

"Yes."

"That's why you love this place." She brushed her hand against the coarse stone. "You feel words here."

Nik looked at the sky and said nothing.

Sara wiped her eyes and felt that sensation again, that blend of the island's raw beauty with its rugged demands for survival.

Nik stood up. "Come on. I have another favorite spot to show you."

They hiked away from the The Dance Floor. Grass and shrubs began to fill the space between the granite slabs until the woods emerged again.

"Would you ever live on an island?" Sara asked.

"I kind of do, I mean, Bar Harbor's on Mount Desert Island."

"Yeah, but an island—*like this?*"

"Some days I think I would. But then I wonder if it would become too hard to ever leave."

She nodded. The climb back up the hill towards the lighthouse was rocky, and Nik pressed his hand against the small of her back to steady her. The warmth of his touch lingered there.

They found a spot to spread a blanket in the woods beneath the lighthouse. In one direction, the lighthouse rose up protectively through the trees and the other side boasted ribbons of blue ocean between leafy branches. They wrote, they talked, and then Sara drifted asleep in the forest shade on Nik's jacket that smelled like the sun and his soap and the woods. When she woke up, she lay on her side, her face away from Nik and the sound of waves in the distance. His hand rested on her shoulder. She closed her eyes again, hesitant to move. He brushed her hair back, away from her eyes.

"I have a son," said Nik. His voice was quiet.

The words were so unexpected. Had she missed something he said before? His words filled every ounce of air around them. She began to sit up.

"Don't move. It's easier this way." Sara lay back down on her side, still not able to see Nik's face. He smoothed her hair back again. How did she not know he had a son? Surely Phil would have said something.

"I *had* a son," he corrected himself.

Oh.

"He was two. He slipped in the bathtub. Hit his head. Should have been no big deal. Kids slip in the tub all the time."

"I'm sorry. I didn't know," she whispered.

"It's easier not to talk about it. Corinne and I had been married a few years. I was busy trying to get tenure at Columbia, and she was doing the same at NYU. It was a crazy life, way too fast, too full, but we both just sort of went with it.

"We had a nanny for our son, Liam. He slipped when he was with her. Hit his head on the faucet. He cried a lot, but she thought he was okay. Then he didn't wake up from his nap. She found him blue and not breathing. The paramedics resuscitated him. They tried to control the brain swelling and bleeding, but after two days, he had no brain activity. We turned off life support three days later. The shock, the grief of it all, it exposed every crack in our marriage. And every crack in myself. Cracks I didn't even know were there. And made new ones."

Sara sat up now. She needed to see his face. She looked at him. He looked past her, a shadow of pain she hadn't seen before.

"I blamed myself for Liam's death. I still do—like I could have stopped it if I'd been there. I know it's not logical. I've been over this a dozen times with a dozen therapists. I understand *intellectually* that it's not my fault, but I can't seem to shake the weight of it. Corinne and I divorced a year later. I left Columbia the next year and moved to Maine. I've found a peace for myself here. See, everyone worked so hard to convince me it wasn't my fault, to let go, but acceptance of my culpability and forgiving myself has been more healing for me."

"But you believe something that isn't true."

"That's the human condition, isn't it?" Nik chuckled softly. "For me, I've found more peace accepting my burden in this and moving forward, rather than convincing myself otherwise. Or trying to numb my way out of it. That didn't work either. Serenity, I suppose. Accepting the things I cannot change and courage to change the things I can. The wisdom to know the difference."

"I'm still working on that last part."

"Aren't we all?" Nik picked up a fallen leaf, slightly orange, and rubbed its sides between his fingers.

"Where's Corinne?"

"New York. She remarried. I'm told she's happy."

He said it so sincerely. No hard feelings or judgment. She looked at Nik, studied his dark brown eyes more deeply. There was a depth there, a sense of peace that she envied. How could she get that? So much was crashing in her head these days—the loss of her mother, the truth about her parents, her divorce, writing *Ellery*.

She thought of this island. All the heartache, peril, and sorrow that created something so beautiful. She reached past the edge of the blanket and raked the rich, black soil with her fingers. Nik ran his fingers in the soil next to hers. She placed her hand over his, the softness of the cool soil on both their hands. "I'm sorry about your son. And Corinne."

"I'm in a good place now."

She smiled. Her hand lingered over his another moment, and then Nik stood and packed up their things. He took Sara by the hand and didn't let go as they walked quietly back to the boat.

The two sat close together on the way home, their feet stretched out, propped on a storage container in front of them. Nik wrapped an arm around Sara. She leaned in close enough to feel his breathing, her head pressed comfortably against his shoulder just beneath the softness of his bearded chin. She closed her eyes, sensing something she hadn't felt in years, something missing for so long she had almost forgotten the feeling.

She felt *safe*.

CHAPTER 28

I know my stuff looks like it was rattled off in twenty-eight seconds, but every word is a struggle and every sentence is like the pangs of birth.

DR. SEUSS

Sara reviewed one of her favorite scenes with Phil Sunday night via Skype. It was chapter three, when Ellery and Brooks were in Brussels for Christmas and she felt strong traces of her father's energy in a market with a Syrian refugee. The scene was tense and dramatic, and Sara thought it was going really well, but when she discussed it with Phil, he kept harping on her about its emotional depth.

"You have to make me feel this, Grayson. If your readers can't connect here, they won't care what happens next."

"I get that, but if I overplay it, then Ellery looks weak and indecisive—and that's not Ellery either."

"But that's exactly why you've got to deepen this. Look, her father's been missing for sixteen years. What's she going to feel? You have to go there yourself. How would you feel if you sensed your father could possibly be alive right now—that after all this time he'd actually been alive and you didn't know it?"

A sad feeling crept in. "This isn't about my father. It's about Ellery's father."

"And that's where you're wrong. Your connection to your father is Ellery's path to hers. I'm not saying they're the same. But that's the current you must ride in order to get to Ellery's truth. If you aren't willing to go there, your book will be hollow."

"You're the one who told me to focus on my book, Phil, and not all these questions about my family."

"I'm talking about going places emotionally."

Sara wrapped her arms around her stomach. "Can we talk about this later?"

He folded his arms across his chest. "Do you think I haven't noticed your father's writing journal you keep in that God-forsaken bag you haul everywhere?"

"How do you know about that?"

"The leather one with the compass?"

"But how would you know…?"

"He had it in college."

"Oh."

"Look, maybe you and Ellery are looking for the same thing."

Sara rubbed her eyes. "I don't understand."

"*The truth*, Grayson. You're both looking for the truth, okay? It's tapping into whatever it is you feel towards your father and connecting it back to Ellery. You have to go to some hard places, and so far I don't think you've been willing to go there."

"Okay. I'll try."

"And Sara?"

"Yeah?"

"Jack and Coke."

"What?"

"Your father's favorite drink in college. Jack Daniels and Coke."

❧

Sara decided not to change anything yet in the scene. She wanted to see what her writing group thought on Tuesday night. She felt certain that they would *get* what she was trying to do with her chapter.

They didn't.

Just like Phil said. He wasn't feeling it. And they weren't feeling it.

Oh, they liked the setup and the suspense, and pasty-white Beale assured her that she could make the all-star page on the *Ellery World* fan fiction site "for the very best fanfickers." And then they all got sidetracked on the value of fanfickers again. She wanted to scream.

Sara met Nik in his office afterwards. Her feet felt fidgety, and she kept waiting for Nik to say something, anything. He loaded up his satchel with student papers. Finally, she blurted out, "I don't get why everyone got so hung up on fan fiction *again*. What's the big deal?"

"That's not where they were hung up."

"What do you mean? They couldn't get off it."

"They'll get off it when you write with more heart."

"You too?" She bit her lower lip. "So, my writing's as shallow as everyone says?"

"What's Phil telling you?"

She shifted in her seat. "The same."

He gazed at her, his eyes kind. "Do you want an honest response from me or an ego boost?"

Sara half-smiled. "Do I have to choose?"

Nik stood up and offered his hand. "Come on. It's a beautiful night. Let's walk over to the pier."

"I think I have an appointment to go open a vein tonight and bleed all over my manuscript."

"Let's go for a walk."

The cool air felt good against her face, and she felt herself relax as they walked along the shoreline toward the pier. She smelled something spicy grilling from the dining hall. They passed a group of students gathered under an outdoor pavilion making signs for a "green dorm" competition.

They walked to the edge of the pier and sat down on a bench. They watched the moon's reflection ripple out across the water. Sara slipped an arm through Nik's, leaning her head against his shoulder, enjoying his warmth.

"Okay," she whispered. "I want your honest feedback."

Nik leaned his head against hers and exhaled slowly. "All right then. It's about yearning."

She lifted her head and looked at him. "What?"

"That's what you're missing."

Sara eyed him skeptically. "*Yearning.*"

"Come on, think about it. All stories—the good ones, the best ones—they're really about yearning, right?"

"I guess."

"So, what does Ellery yearn for in your book? What does she want more than anything—even if she doesn't recognize it at first? As a writer, you have to make that yearning undeniable. And it doesn't matter if she's yearning for the right thing or the wrong thing or if she even recognizes what her yearning means. Your job is to make your readers *feel* that. If you fail, your book will have the emotional depth of a tide pool."

Ocean waves lapped gently over the rocks while Sara thought about Nik's words. She felt him watching her and turned to meet his gaze. He brushed a few strands of hair away from her face and studied her eyes a moment. "What do you yearn for, Sara?"

She quickly looked away, her back turning stiff. "Well…I don't…"

He took her hand, and she felt the warmth of it instantly. She looked at him again.

"You don't have to answer that now," Nik reassured her. "I haven't even earned the right to know, but…you should probably be able to answer that for yourself."

Sara watched the lights of a small boat in the distance. She sat up a little straighter. "Nik, are you sure you don't have your poet hat screwed on a little tight here? I mean, poetry and fiction are a lot different."

He shrugged his shoulders. "Honestly, I don't see as much difference between what you write and what I write."

"There's a vast difference."

"Not as wide as you think."

Sara eyed him warily.

"Aren't we both trying to express a truth?" asked Nik.

"But hardly the same way."

He scratched the side of his face and half-smiled. "Hmm. I think my father might not be the most difficult one in your working relationship."

Sara laughed drily. "Depends on the day."

"Look, some people write using only their intellect, their mind—they're all analysis and reason. They focus on the mechanics of plot and pacing. But the great ones use mind and *soul*. They tap into *both*." Nik touched his heart. He opened her hand and stroked the inside of her palm with his thumb. "Go deeper, Sara, inside yourself. Good writing—and I mean the great stuff—it's all poetry to me."

Then Nik leaned in toward her face, close enough for Sara to feel the warmth of his breath. He reached for the side of her face while his lips and his soft beard brushed gently against her cheek. He pulled back for a moment, gazing into her eyes, and brought her mouth to his, pressing his lips to hers softly, harder, and then slow. She slipped her arm around his back, drawing him closer to her. As she leaned back and looked into the richness of his deep brown eyes, she felt for a moment that she just might know the answer to his question.

CHAPTER 29

At its best, the sensation of writing is that of any unmerited
grace. It is handed to you, but only if you look for it.
You search, you break your heart, your back, your brain,
and then—and only then—it is handed to you.

ANNIE DILLARD

Sara woke up Saturday morning at 4:30 AM. Nik had invited her up to Cadillac Mountain for the sunrise, and she was suddenly questioning the whole idea once again.

"Are you sure this is worth it?" she asked when he picked her up at five.

"It's the first point of sunlight for the US, so we'll be first to soak in all that inspiration."

She raised one highly skeptical eyebrow but got in his truck.

They arrived at morning twilight when early light was starting to fill the sky but the sunrise was still thirty minutes away. Nik grabbed a few blankets and a thermos for each of them. It was cold and windy. Sara shivered and leaned close to him as they made the short walk up to the expansive viewing area.

They stopped at the peak. She didn't breathe at first. The 360-degree view was unlike anything she had seen before. Through the growing light, Sara could make out the darker shapes of the Porcupine Islands and

Frenchman Bay in the distance. The Schoodic Peninsula stretched out across the bay to the east. Sara sighed deeply. It was the most perfect blend of ocean, forest, mountain, and sky. Though the wind whipped through them and the temperatures felt frigid, Sara couldn't stop smiling.

"All right," said Nik. "Here's a blanket and your thermos. Go stake out a spot for yourself."

Sara looked confused. "For myself?"

"Your first sunrise here is best alone."

She shifted her weight on her feet and screwed up her lips to one side. "Alone?" Sara had imagined sharing a blanket with Nik, sitting close to his warmth, taking it all in together. Not freezing alone on a slab of cold granite.

Nik reached over and pulled the hoodie of her sweatshirt up and over her head. He cinched the strings up a bit and then placed a hand on each of her shoulders. "Trust me. I'll find another place to sit. I'll be back here in forty-five minutes. Meet me when you're ready."

Nik walked away with a blanket slung over his shoulders, his thermos swinging as he left to find his own place.

Sara rolled her eyes and headed the opposite direction, watching her step, and trying not to feel like she'd just been stood up. She found a stretch of pink granite, away from some other tourists. She sat down and wrapped her blanket around her shoulders. She looked around and couldn't see Nik anywhere.

"It's fine." She sipped hot English breakfast from her thermos and pulled the blanket close around her. It smelled like Nik's soap. She thought of their first kiss and their moments together in the few days since then and how all the red warning flags and caution signs should be going up. This is when she would normally feel worried and insecure and doubting herself.

But she didn't feel that way with Nik. She just felt...happy.

She faced the horizon ahead, waiting for her first glimpse of the sun to emerge so she could check it off her list and head back to Nik's warm truck.

Time slowed as she waited in the quiet stillness.

She stared blankly at the horizon and rubbed her hands together to keep them warm. The sky was the lightest baby blue with hints of orange lining the horizon's edge, like an artist used her thumb to smudge its color along the farthest edge.

She had to admit, it was lovely.

The trees below, now touched by fall, were a blend of shiny gold, vibrant orange, and fiery red all mixed with green spruces and pitch pine.

She gazed back to the east. Almost imperceptibly, the first rounded, burning arc of sun moved up onto the horizon. Sara forgot about the cold wind and the cold rock and being alone.

She sat utterly transfixed.

In that moment she realized she had never actually witnessed a sunrise before. She thought that she had, but she hadn't. Not like this. Not fully engaged. Fully present. And to think this happened every day. Everywhere. While people mixed creamer into coffee and ate their corn-flakes and checked their email.

It was like seeing the expanse of the world for the first time, and she felt something new. What was it? She thought of her tendency to live life close-up, wrapped tightly and inflexibly in her world, not stepping back to see more, mistakenly believing her narrow view was reality, when maybe it wasn't.

She felt incredibly small, like a tiny speck, and yet this sense of her own smallness in this wide world was actually *liberating*.

She listened now. The wind. A few birds. Insects.

How could something that happened every day feel this holy? It seemed like watching the sun rise should be prerequisite to becoming an adult.

The sun was fully visible now. Sara glanced quickly around her. There were people huddled in various spots throughout the sprawling peak. What did they see? What did they feel? Wouldn't each one have their own unique perspective? And in a wave of perfect clarity, she could envision her characters' different perspectives in ways she hadn't seen before and pictured a way to capture those viewpoints as a writer. She breathed slowly as ideas unfolded in her mind.

She shook off her blanket and pulled out her thick notebook. She wrote down her feelings, her thoughts, and visualized a new way to tell her story—a vision that was bold and transformative. But could she actually pull it off? And would Phil ever agree to it?

She opened a new section of her notebook and poured out everything she saw. Her pen could hardly keep up and her pulse raced with her soul's need to write and write. She hardly noticed the tourists leaving and the light growing brighter and brighter as she wrote. She knew Nik joined her again at some point. She locked eyes with him for just a moment and he seemed to recognize the feverish need she had to create in that space.

Sometime mid-morning, she gathered her blanket, grabbed her thermos, and found Nik writing nearby.

He looked into her intense eyes. "Are you okay?"

She smiled. "Better than okay. Mind if we go back now? I need to get to my computer."

"Yeah. Of course." They hurried back to his truck.

Nik studied Sara's face as he opened her door. He touched her arm. "Words came?"

Sara nodded quickly. He seemed to sense her need for quiet on the way back and said little. She continued to write all the way home.

Back in her mother's office, she read, rewrote, and deleted pages. Soon the emotional walls between Sara and her characters began to crumble and she felt their deepest yearnings for the very first time.

CHAPTER 30

I am not lucky. You know what I am? I am smart, I am talented,
I take advantage of the opportunities that come my way and I
work really, really hard. Don't call me lucky. Call me a badass.

SHONDA RHIMES

Sara wrote all day Saturday, Sunday, and Monday, finally closing her laptop that evening at 6:00 PM. She breathed deeply. Her back and neck ached, her brain was tired, but her soul felt content, like it had finally expressed something it had been aching to get out. She pulled on a clean sweatshirt and sat on her porch with Gatsby.

She texted Nik: "I've come up for air."

He replied: "Leaving my office. I'll stop by."

Fifteen minutes later, he stood on her porch and smiled. "So you're alive."

"I think so."

"That was quite a run."

Sara grinned. "I'm exhausted, but that was so much…*fun*." She shook her head. "I didn't know it could be like that."

"What changed for you up there?"

"I don't know. Something happened to me on Cadillac. I felt like I was seeing things differently, and I felt free to write from a new place." She took another breath. "I've made changes to *Ellery*. Big ones. Can you read them before Phil gets here on Friday?"

"Absolutely. But come over to my house. I'll cook you dinner, and then I can read. Besides, you probably haven't eaten a good meal all weekend."

"You sound like Anna-Kath."

"Good. I like Anna-Kath."

ॐ

Sara showered, slipped on a t-shirt dress and a jean jacket, and walked over to Nik's. He kissed her at the door and led her inside. It was her first time in his home, and she was curious. There was a small office to the left with messy, overstuffed bookshelves, and a living room to the right with a black leather sofa and a couple of odd reading chairs that looked pieced together from Scottish kilts. She followed Nik back to the kitchen. He had changed into a Columbia sweatshirt and jeans and carried a dish towel over his shoulder while he washed bell peppers.

"Do you like to cook?" she asked.

"I don't mind, but my skills are limited. I make three meals—with variations on a theme: pasta, tacos, and steak sandwiches. Tonight, it's steak sandwiches."

She looked at the artwork in the dining area. There were beautiful prints of Acadia, but her eye was drawn to several framed collages made of cut and folded paper scraps. She studied them closely, feeling Nik watch her, like he was gauging her response. They weren't scraps. Each collage was made almost entirely of tickets: concert tickets, theatre tickets, boarding passes, subway passes, and snippets of photographs mixed in. Each collage of tickets and pics created an overall shape for each piece: a mountain, a dragonfly, a star, an ocean wave, each one full of texture and life.

"What are these, Nik? Who made them?"

"They're mine."

"You made these?" Sara's eyes widened. She studied them again.

Nik began chopping peppers and onions. "I like tickets."

"I've seen collages, but not like this—these are *incredible*."

Nick wiped his hands on a towel and walked over. He studied one with her. "I think I've saved every ticket I've ever had."

Sara raised her eyebrows. "*Every* ticket?"

"The way I see it, there's…*possibility* in a ticket. It's a hopeful sort of thing. I mean, who doesn't love to keep a good boarding pass?"

"Me. It's functional. Use it and toss it."

Nik held up an index finger. "Ah, but a boarding pass is pure possibility." He went to the stove and pulled out a large frying pan. "Didn't you ever save any tickets or programs, playbills, even when you were younger?"

"Maybe as a teenager."

Nik drizzled olive oil into the pan and turned the gas on. "After my grandfather died, they found three shoeboxes full of tickets. He even saved his boarding pass from a ship he took from Croatia to New York in 1956. My grandma wanted to throw it all away, but I convinced her to let me keep it. The first collage I made was his."

Nik paused. He switched the heat off. "Come with me. I want to show you something."

He took her hand and led her to his office. Sara's eye immediately went to a photo on his desk of a smiling little boy. She touched it. "He's beautiful." There was something familiar about his sweet face. His hair was much lighter than Nik's, but he definitely had his father's eyes.

He stopped and touched the photo. "It's my favorite."

He went behind his desk and pulled out another collage. "I just finished this one." He held it up.

Her breath stopped. "Wait…is that a…"

"Gardenia."

"My mother's favorite."

"It's hers. She gave me a box of tickets last summer and asked me to do something with it. She didn't know what shape it should take. Phil suggested the gardenia. I didn't finish it…*before*…I was saving it for you and Anna-Kath."

They sat on the sofa as Sara studied some of the pieces up close. She smiled when she'd spot something familiar, like tickets to Elton John or a White House tour at Christmas. Nik smiled as she rediscovered cherished memories.

Then she stopped. "Twelfth Night?" Sara's eyes filled with tears. "That's one of my parents' first dates." Sara covered her face with her hands. "It's a really happy story," she said, miserably.

Nik touched her back. "You okay?"

Sara wiped her eyes. Then she leaned her head against his shoulder and explained what she and Ann had recently discovered about their parents.

He tucked some loose strands of hair behind her ear. "I'm sorry. That's a lot of unanswered questions."

Sara exhaled slowly. "Were your parents happy—at least at first?"

"They got along, I guess, but I never got the feeling that they were ever, I don't know—passionate about each other. Not like yours. I wonder if it was more of a marriage of convenience. I mean they cared about each other, but more as companions. When I was eleven, I overheard a really heated argument. My dad had gotten involved with another woman. He swore to her it was a one-time thing, but they divorced a year later. It only gave me reason to hate him more."

"I'm sorry, Nik."

"I've had years to process it. This is all fresh for you."

"It just doesn't make sense. My parents were so happy, so in love with each other."

"You were seven when he died. Can you really know that?"

"True. Maybe my rosy view is more from my mom's stories than from reality."

"Betrayal hurts no matter what."

Sara gazed longingly out the window. "My parents got in this really big argument when they were students at Georgetown, and they didn't speak to each other for, like, a whole week. So my mom goes back to Philadelphia over spring break to house-sit for her parents, and my dad just shows up at her door one day with a bag of groceries, and my mom is all feisty and says, 'What are you doing here?' And my dad doesn't say anything. He walks into the kitchen. Finds a frying pan and sits it on the stove. My mom is still trying to fight, but he calmly starts taking out eggs, cheese, mushrooms, ham, whatever. Finally my mom quiets down and sits at the table and watches. My dad makes her an omelet and sets it down in front of her with a glass of orange juice. And he just says, 'I'm sorry.'

"She tastes the omelet, and she says it's the most amazing omelet she's ever tasted. And she starts to cry, and she says she's sorry too, and three weeks later my dad asks her to marry him. When Dad used to say, 'Cass, how did I ever get a woman like you to marry me?' She'd shrug her shoulders and say, 'It was the omelet.' And he'd pull her close and give her a kiss that would make me and Ann laugh and squirm."

Nik laughed gently. "That's quite an omelet."

"I know, right?" She studied the collage again. All these tiny fragments reflecting moments of her mother's life—happy, painful, joyful moments—pieces that now made something whole and beautiful. "It's strange how quickly we reduce ourselves—and others—to one shred, one sliver of a life's performance when our lives are so much bigger than that." She traced her finger along the edges of the gardenia petals and took a deep breath. "Thank you for this. I love it."

They went out to Nik's patio after dinner and turned on a string of soft lights. They sat on a wicker love seat, and she handed him the new pages a little nervously. It was nearly dark outside and turning colder. Maine didn't seem to have warm Septembers like Maryland. She noticed the outdoor fireplace and the stacks of wood in the corner.

"Can I build a fire while you read?" she asked.

Nik's face looked skeptical. "City girl knows how to build a fire?"

Sara looked indignant. "I went to summer camp. I know how to build a fire."

He handed her the matches, and she went to work while Nik started reading quietly.

"Will you read it aloud? I want to hear it."

He nodded and began reading aloud while she crumpled some newspaper, arched some kindling above it, and lit a match.

He read the first few paragraphs and stopped. He glanced over the second and third pages. He looked at Sara. "Wait a second. This is in first person."

"I know."

"You were writing in third."

Sara added more kindling and stoked the fire with a metal poker. "Yes."

"But all the other *Ellery* books are in third person, right?"

She closed her eyes. "Yeah." A wave of nerves rolled through her, and she shivered. She held her hands up to the fire and slowed her breathing.

Nik half-smiled. He was obviously intrigued. "Okay then."

She bit her lower lip. "Just keep reading." The wood cracked and popped as the bigger pieces caught fire.

Cassandra had written the series in third person omniscient—a narrator who basically knows everything and can tell the reader things Ellery doesn't know. When Sara returned from the sunrise, she could hear the main characters' voices telling their own stories from their own perspectives, and something just felt alive and right about it. She told chapter one from Ellery's point of view, and then chapter two switched to her husband, Joshua Brooks, and later she added her daughter Lydia's point of view. She had cranked out a draft of the first 200 pages with the new narration over the weekend in a breathless speed she'd never achieved before. There was something in the shift that had liberated her voice and unleashed a force of creativity.

She stoked the fire again while Nik continued reading. She listened uncomfortably. She stood up. "Keep reading. I'm going to make some tea."

She came back ten minutes later with cups of tea for both of them. He stopped reading and looked up at her. "It's good. It's really good."

Sara took a deep breath and found a blanket to spread over them. She leaned into Nik's warm shoulder while he read. Sara knew there were books like this—told by different narrators. It wasn't unusual by any stretch—but switching narration in the final book of a series? She knew it was risky.

Nik finished the chapter from Brooks's point of view. He stopped. His hand reached for her leg under the blanket. He squeezed her thigh gently, kept his warm hand there and continued reading.

She breathed in the cool air. Listening was painful at times, hearing all the things she needed to fix, especially the stuff she didn't know how to fix yet. Nik stopped occasionally to circle or underline something, share a note or ask a question, but mostly he just read.

Exhausted from her intense weekend, Sara fell asleep and woke up on Nik's couch in the front room sometime later. She sat up, feeling disoriented, wondering how she got there.

Nik sat across from her. He looked pensive, rubbing the front of his beard with his thumb.

Sara stretched her arms. "What time is it?"

"About eleven."

"Sorry I crashed."

"You hardly slept over the weekend. Your office light never seemed to turn off."

She rolled her neck forward and back trying to work the kinks out. "Have you been stalking me?"

"Only mild stalking."

He set the thick stack of pages in front of her on the coffee table next to an illustrated book of Croatian folk tales. She saw his name on the front, "Translated and edited by Filip Dvornik." She scratched the back of her head and sighed. She was really more accustomed to dating underachievers.

"How far did you read?"

"All of it."

"All?"

"I've been reading for three hours."

"Oh."

Nik pointed to her. "*You* are finally in there." He lifted the stack again for emphasis and set it back down. "*This* is what I've been talking about. It's powerful."

"It's still really messy."

"Of course. But the emotion, the yearning, it's in there." He picked up the stack again and fanned through the pages. He shook his head.

"So it's good, but you're shaking your head." She chewed her bottom lip.

"Most series don't shift point of view in the final volume."

"I know." She wrapped her arms around her shoulders. "So…what will Phil think?"

Nik laughed. "I gave up that kind of speculation years ago. He gets here Friday so I guess we'll find out soon enough. When will you send the changes to him?"

"I don't know. Soon."

"Send the first three chapters to the writing group tonight. Let's get their feedback on this."

CHAPTER 31

You can't use up creativity. The more you use, the more you have.

MAYA ANGELOU

The writing group critiqued Sara's revisions on Tuesday night. No one said anything about writing with more heart or more feeling. And no one said a word about fan fiction.

"There's something different here. It feels much more...*real*," said Miriam.

Most didn't even notice the narration change until she started shifting to the other characters' perspectives.

Nashid called the switch badass. "When does the real Book Five come out?" he asked.

"No one knows," said Miriam. "After reading Sara's version, I might be disappointed with the real one. Can I buy yours instead?"

"Yeah," said Beale. "This is all-star material on *Ellery World*."

Phil arrived at Nik's place, Friday night at six-thirty. It had rained for two days straight. Everything was cold and muddy, and wispy clouds of low fog still lingered about. Sara had sent him the new draft the night before, hoping that if he hated it, he'd at least sleep on it and let things settle while he drove up.

Nik took Phil's suitcase upstairs and got him something to drink. Phil actually seemed rather relaxed, even pleasant when he arrived, but he greeted Sara with a look that said, *we-have-things-to-talk-about*.

Sara and Phil sat at the kitchen table while Nik mixed sauce into the pasta and then brought it over on a large platter. She saw that they needed a serving spoon and jumped up to get one, knowing exactly where Nik kept them. She noticed Phil's eyes follow her. He looked at Nik and back at Sara as they started to dish up their food.

"Well, it's good for you two to finally meet."

Sara and Nik nodded in agreement.

"So, Phillip, you should tell Sara about your work at the college." He turned to her. "You know he's a professor over there."

"And does maintenance too, I've heard," said Sara. She nervously twirled her fettucine but decided to cut it instead.

"Yeah, my son definitely has some skills I never developed."

Nik glanced at Sara, smiled quickly, and kept eating.

"Any salt, son?"

"Oh sorry, I'll grab it."

"No bother." Phil walked over to a cabinet near the stove and picked up a saltshaker. A box of Earl Grey tea sat nearby. "Drinking a little tea these days?"

Phil and Nik locked eyes a moment. "I make some now and then."

Phil moved the pasta around on his plate without taking any bites.

"So, how was the drive up, Dad? Hope the fog wasn't too bad."

"A little traffic out of Hartford."

Gatsby wandered in from the front room and settled by Nik's feet while they ate, looking quite comfortable there. Phil raised one eyebrow. "So, you and Sara have gotten to know each other."

Sara's face turned warm. She focused on her salad and stabbed some lettuce and cucumber with her fork.

"Well, she's been here for several weeks now." Nik handed Phil the basket of breadsticks.

They ate quietly for another few minutes.

Gatsby started whining to go out. "I better go with him," said Sara. "He may try to run back to the cottage."

"I got it," said Nik. He grabbed Gatsby's leash and took him out the back door.

"I'll join you," said Phil.

Sara and Nik exchanged glances. He opened the glass door and walked out.

Phil and Nik talked on the patio while Gatsby did his business. A kitchen window was open, and Sara could hear their conversation.

"What the hell?" said Phil.

"What?"

"You and Sara Grayson? Are you kidding me? What about giving her space?"

"We started with space...and then...not so much."

"She cannot have this kind of distraction right now. I take it you know what she's writing. This book will sell out faster than *Mockingjay*. There hasn't been this much riding on a book since *The Deathly Hallows*."

"She's a grown woman, Dad."

Sara rolled her eyes and stood up. She popped her head out the back door. "Why don't you talk about me inside? It's warmer, and I can hear you better."

Nik gave his father a pointed look. He brought Gatsby in, and Phil trudged back inside.

They all sat at the table again. There was a lot of food shifting around on plates and little actual eating or talking.

"Coffee anyone?" said Nik. He stood and poured some coffee and tea while the quiet still hung heavy in the room.

Finally, Sara put her fork down. "Phil, I appreciate your concern, but we're taking this slow." She looked at Nik and smiled. "I'm a much better writer with Nik around."

Phil wiped his face with his napkin, studied the two skeptically, and pushed his plate away. "Okay then. Let's talk about this writing."

This wasn't the transition she'd imagined.

Nik handed Phil a coffee mug and a cup of tea to Sara.

"I know the changes are big," she said.

Phil slowed his breathing and looked at her, like he was measuring his words carefully. It was very un-Phil-like. "The chapters you sent...they're good, solid chapters, as far as the writing goes. But..." He paused again, like attempting to use a filter was exhausting work. He leaned forward on his elbows. "You can't do it. You can't change the narration—not that drastically."

"So it's good writing, but I can't do it?"

"No. You can't." Phil's voice grew more intense with each word. "You can't change the entire narration for the final volume in the world's most popular series. It's completely out of the question. It's too, um..." He searched for the right word.

"Audacious?" said Sara.

"Foolish."

Nik gripped his napkin tightly.

Sara set her cup down. "But you said yourself that this is good writing. I know it's a big change—but this is what my mom asked me to do when she gave the book to me. She told me to be audacious. This change, it just *feels* right."

"The answer is no." Phil's face looked resolved, stone-like. She wondered if he was still breathing. She looked at Nik. His breaths rose quickly in his chest, and his napkin was a tight ball in his fist.

She turned back to Phil. "What about grit? You said I needed grit."

"This isn't grit. It's insanity. Try it on your next book. Not this one."

Nik made no attempt to hide his irritation. "Dad, you know her writing is stronger with the changes."

"What Sara had before is good enough for this book."

"Good enough?" said Sara. "So that's the standard we're going for?" She rubbed her forehead. "I want this to be great, Phil, not good enough. Is that really what you want? Is that all you expect from me?"

"Dad, Sara shared several chapters with a small writing group I lead at the college."

Sara tried to catch Nik's eye, to call him off, but he didn't notice and kept talking.

"Granted, it's a small focus group, but the responses were incredibly positive, and these are *Ellery's* readers, real readers. These changes could be the difference between a good series finale and a great one."

Phil slammed his coffee down, spilling it on his hands and the table. "What the hell?" He turned to Sara. "A writing group?" He stood up, throwing his napkin on his plate.

Nik looked at Phil and back at Sara, trying to understand his father's strong reaction. Sara gripped both hands tightly around the table's edge.

Phil pointed his finger hard at her. "You are writing one of the most anticipated finales to a series—*ever*. You're the one who wanted to keep your authorship a secret. You're willing to blow that? You know Jane's already hired Asher Monroe. Your situation is precarious enough. And do you even comprehend the risk of leaked pages? This isn't just about you, Grayson. There are a lot of people depending on the successful conclusion of this series. I've gone to bat for you. And you risk all this because you need kudos from a bunch of amateur writers?"

"Phil, it's a small group, and no one even knows who I am."

"Because you used a different name?"

"No…but my name is different than Cassandra's."

"Oh great."

Worry began to wash through Sara. Why hadn't she used a different name? A few Google searches and maybe someone could link her to her mother. And what about leaked pages? Why hadn't she thought more about that? She looked at Nik. She saw the flash of concern in his eyes, even as he tried to assuage Phil.

"Dad, sit down. Let's talk through this. Nobody in the writing group has any idea of Sara's connection to Cassandra. They think she's writing fan fiction."

Phil sat back down. His face pinched, his neck red and splotchy. "You need to get all the pages back. And please tell me you used hard copies. You didn't share digital copies, right?"

Nik pressed both hands against his forehead. Sara groaned and covered her face with her hands. "That would have been a good idea," she mumbled.

"No, a good idea would have been to listen to me, to trust me as your editor, and to never have gone to this writing group in the first place. Do you even comprehend the risks? The last Harry Potter—all 759 pages—leaked online a week before its release date. *Game of Thrones*, five episodes leaked." Phil took his coffee cup and dumped it in the sink, slamming the cup on the counter. He pointed a finger towards the two of them like he was trying to control an unsteady cursor with a jumpy mouse. He looked hard at Nik. "Get the pages back. Make the students sign a confidentiality agreement." He narrowed his eyes at Sara, "And don't go back."

"I'm sorry. You were right," she whispered.

Phil exhaled slowly. He looked suddenly weary, his mouth drawn, his eyes jaded. He leaned forward against the counter, like he needed it for support. The tension hovered in the room like the low-hanging fog outside. No one said anything for a few minutes.

"I'm going for a drive to cool off. I'll see you in the morning." Phil grabbed his jacket and walked out.

Sara and Nik sat at the table, both uncertain what to say.

Nik started. "I'm so sorry. The writing group. I didn't realize…"

"It's my fault. Phil told me not to do it." She shook her head. "I just didn't think through all the risks. I thought he was overprotective." She slumped back in her chair. "So what do we do now? We can't get the pages back. They're out there."

"I'll tell everyone there's a confidentiality contract required for class now and hope it doesn't make anyone too suspicious. They don't need to know it's to protect you."

Sara leaned her head back against her chair and stared at the ceiling. "What if we're too late?"

"We'll trust the group. In the meantime, you keep writing."

CHAPTER 32

When you write, try to leave out all the parts readers skip.

ELMORE LEONARD

Sara was sitting on the front porch with Gatsby when Phil arrived the next morning for their work session. He said a tense hello and sat next to her in one of the rockers. His fingers rubbed back and forth against the smooth edges of the armrests, and he closed his eyes. She wondered if he was still angry.

"About last night, Phil…"

"I've said all I needed to say."

"But I haven't." She looked down at her bare feet, her red toenail polish chipped and faded. "I'm sorry about the writing group. You were right, and I won't go back." She cleared her throat. "But the point of view changes—isn't there some way—"

"I can't budge on that one, Grayson."

"It's my strongest writing. Don't you want my best work?"

He exhaled and rubbed the ever-present stubble on his chin. "Let me tell you something about being an editor. You've got one foot deep in the creative process—trying to help your writer generate the best work they can do. Then you've got one foot deep in the commercial business of selling books. A good editor has to balance both. Even if I did think this was worth the risk, I could never convince Jane Harnois."

Sara leaned towards Phil, her eyes earnest. "If you could convince Jane, would you take the risk?"

"I'd never convince her."

"But would you take the risk if you could?"

"Jane's got Asher Monroe. Why would she take the risk when she can get the book she wants from him?"

Sara dropped her head back and sighed aloud in frustration.

Phil's lips stretched into a smile. "Your mother used to do that. That *throw-your-head-back-and-sigh* thing."

"Yeah? Apparently you have that effect on women."

He shrugged his shoulders. "We should get started."

Sara called Gatsby and opened the door for Phil. He paused a moment before he stepped inside.

❧

They spent the rest of the weekend trying to incorporate Sara's new soulful writing back into Cassandra's third person voice and style. It worked on a functional level, but it definitely wasn't as strong—only "good enough." She told herself she needed to accept it and move forward, but it wasn't easy.

They wrapped up late Sunday afternoon with a plan to finish the first full draft in six weeks. This meant that she needed to complete the second half of the book *in only six weeks*, when it had taken her three months just to write the first half. This plan would leave them six weeks before the deadline for rewriting. It was hardly enough time to get the manuscript right, with many writers spending at least six months for revisions alone. Every time Sara looked at her calendar, the next three months and its twelve measly weeks seemed to shrink before her eyes and her entire chest cavity clenched up.

"Stop looking at the calendar, Grayson. You have to keep going. Just keep showing up, okay?"

❧

Sara went to Nik's early Sunday evening and overheard him and Phil arguing loudly before she even knocked. Nik didn't answer, and she let herself in. They were in the kitchen talking about a position at Yale that Nik had apparently turned down. Sara paused in the entryway, not sure what to do. She walked back out on the porch and sat on the steps with Gatsby. She could still hear the conversation and was far too curious to step away entirely.

Nik's voice was strained and lower-pitched. "Dad, we are not having this discussion. You know my feelings on this. I'm happy here. My work is strong. Better than ever."

"I know it's good. That's what's killing me. Do something more with it. Look, I'm glad you're happy, but you're playing it small, son. It's time to reenter the real world. You've had offers at Harvard, Notre Dame, NYU… but you choose to stay here at this little college with little influence in the real world."

"The *real* world? Why is the real world always in a bigger city at some prestigious college or holding some big shot faculty chair?"

"Okay. Let's say you stay here. The school doesn't hold summer classes. None. And yet you turn down every summer workshop position, even Bread Loaf and Iowa, in order to manage properties and help out the maintenance department? Do you realize how crazy that sounds?"

"How crazy it *sounds*? Or how crazy it actually is?"

"Is there a difference?"

"Oh, there is. We've been through this. You know we *live* for summers in Maine. Why would I leave then? And you know I feel differently about my property work. It helps me feel grounded. My writing is better *because* of my summer work."

"Facilities management is fueling your creativity? Fine. Stay summers here, but move your career forward somewhere else. Or earn summer fellowships that allow you to write here in the summer instead of doing maintenance. It's been seven years since…"

It was quiet a moment. Sara could feel the weight of the silence even from the front porch.

Then she heard Phil's voice again. "It's okay to experience some success. You're not doing your boy any favors by living a stagnant life here."

"My life isn't stagnant. I'm happier here than I've ever been."

"I can't argue that your writing is better than ever and you're publishing more widely than most poets dream of."

"Then what's your problem with my life here, Dad?"

"No risks. You're playing it too safe. Too small. Widen your circle of influence."

"My circle of influence? Why do you insist that breadth transcends depth?" She'd never heard Nik this frustrated.

Phil finally said, "Look, I'm only asking if you're playing it small for the right reasons and not because you're too scared to move forward with your life, because I think you're playing it too damn safe."

"Safely, Dad. An adverb."

She heard a coffee cup slam down. Probably Phil's.

"I've gotta go. Just think about it, okay?"

Phil walked out onto the porch with his overnight bag and a sports jacket slung over his arm. He looked surprised to see Sara there. "Did you catch all that?"

"I think so."

"Good. Maybe you can talk some sense into my son." He set his bag to the side and squatted down to say bye to Gatsby. Phil ruffled the hair around Gatsby's face, Gatsby licking his hands. Phil's face looked instantly more relaxed.

"I think you need a dog, Phil."

He stood up and brushed a little hair off his pants. "Yeah. Maybe."

"Admit it. You love Gatsby."

"Well, he's certainly better grounded than his namesake."

They stood up together on the porch a moment, neither one saying anything. Phil touched Sara's shoulder. "Fifty pages, end of the week. Keep the story moving forward and watch for…"

"She's got it, Dad," said Nik as he walked out onto the porch. "Better get going."

"Right. We'll talk." Phil left, and the two of them sat on the porch steps. Gatsby settled in next to Sara. Nik looked a little disheveled, his shirt untucked and his hair a bit messed up.

"What are you looking at?" he teased.

"You look like you had a good wrestle today." She reached over and smoothed some crazy strands of hair.

"Okay…what did you hear?"

"Offers from Harvard, Notre Dame, NYU?"

"Yeah."

"Are you playing it small, Nik?"

He leaned back on his arms. "Why does small mean something bad? Why don't we ever congratulate each other for playing it small? Shouldn't it be about what fits—about what's right for a life?"

"Sorry. Poor word choice."

A flock of geese flew noisily above them, maybe arguing about where to eat and where to stop for the night.

The sun peeked out through the gray clouds. Nik closed his eyes and turned his face toward the light, breathing gently. As she studied his face, a thought passed through her mind with sudden clarity. "You don't really know anymore, do you?"

He looked at Sara. "What do you mean?"

"These past years, you've had the right fit. You've been exactly where you need to be, your writing and teaching flourishing. Everything's been right in your corner of the world. But now…you don't know."

Nik screwed his lips to the side and began tapping his fingers against the porch step. "I'm happy here."

"I know. But it doesn't mean there aren't new possibilities. If we always stayed where we're happy—or safe—we wouldn't..." Sara paused, sifting through the thoughts in her head.

"Wouldn't what? Say it."

"I don't know....*Be alive?* I mean fully alive, not just *existing*. Look, I'm an expert on playing it safe, and I'm learning a little late that maybe *safe* isn't actually safe at all. That maybe it's actually more...dangerous?"

Nik leaned back on his elbows and looked up at the sky, all gray again.

Sara touched her nose, her cheeks. They felt cold. She smelled the comforting scent of burning wood in the fall air. She leaned into Nik's shoulder, felt his warmth, and slipped her arm through his. "You're the most alive person I've ever known, Nik. So I guess it's deciding what keeps you that way. But maybe there are new possibilities for you."

"I know I like this one." He drew her into his chest and wrapped his arms around her.

Sara closed her eyes. "Me too."

CHAPTER 33

*You better make them care about what you think. It had better
be quirky or perverse or thoughtful enough so that you hit
some chord in them. Otherwise it doesn't work. I mean we've
all read pieces where we thought, 'Oh, who gives a damn.'*

NORA EPHRON

She first noticed the sporty black Nissan in the parking lot of
Hannaford's Grocery Store on Tuesday morning. She'd woken up with
a sore throat, a runny nose, and a bad case of writer's block. She walked
back to her car with Sudafed, cough drops, and a can of chicken noodle
soup. She sneezed three times walking back to her car and almost bumped
into an abandoned shopping cart. The black Nissan was in the farthest
row with New York plates, and the engine was left idling even though she
couldn't see anyone in the car. "Global warming, anyone?" she said aloud
and sneezed again.

She saw the same car drive slowly past her house the next morning.

The next Monday, the worst of her cold was over, and she took Binti's advice to write somewhere new. She walked to Camille's, a sandwich shop famous for its smoothies.

Miriam was working in the front and looked happy to see her. Her hair was tied up in a bandana, and she wore a black apron that said, "Stressed, Blessed, and Smoothie Obsessed."

"Hey, Sara! When are you coming back to writer's group? Don't you need us anymore?"

She smiled. "Oh, it's not that. I've been sick, and my project is changing anyway. Maybe I'll get back at some point."

Miriam talked as she scooped fresh berries, bananas, orange wedges, and flax seeds into a blender. "Look, you should know, you're really good." She tightened up her bandana with a hard yank at the top of her head. "I'd buy your work."

"I appreciate that."

"Just telling the truth." Miriam punched on the blender like it was her exclamation point.

Sara found a table near a window and pulled out her latest draft and a pack of Kleenex. She sipped her smoothie while she read through the pages she'd written early that morning. She was supposed to have fifty pages to Phil two days ago. Instead, she'd sent him ten pages on Saturday and blamed her cold. She felt an incessant pull to write *Ellery* in first person, and every day she had to ignore it and try and write in third.

She reread her most recent chapter. Her eyes kept shifting to the window on her right. It was turning blustery outside. Intermittent gusts swept and swirled up piles of red and gold leaves. When the latest Acadia park shuttle pulled out, she saw the black Nissan again, parked by the movie theater, same blue New York plates.

A few tables over, a fifty-something man with droopy eyes had just entered and began working on his laptop. He wore a velvet green jacket with khaki pants and bright blue running shoes. There was something familiar about him. She looked back at her computer and noticed the man occasionally casually glance at her.

She couldn't put her finger on it, but something about him felt *off*—something Sara would have preferred to ignore, but that Ellery wouldn't. It was then that she noticed a man standing outside next to the Nissan snap a photo of her. Or maybe it was a photo of the shop. She didn't know, but she quickly packed up her computer and left.

Sara zipped up her jacket and pulled up her hood against the cold wind. She hadn't walked more than fifty yards when Miriam caught up with her, winded.

"Sara, there's a guy in Camille's—the one in the green jacket. He took pictures of you as you walked out. He told my manager he was from a Boston newspaper, but then he told me he's from LA. He asked about you. I just thought you should know."

Sara pulled her hood lower over her head, her heart pounding. "Thanks, Miriam. I better get home." She gave her a fast hug and took off.

The wind made her eyes watery. She picked up her pace.

What did that man know?

And what about the other man who also snapped a photo?

But why would anyone care anything about her? She was a complete nobody.

But her mother wasn't.

She broke into a run with her shoulder bag jostling awkwardly on her side. She was two blocks from home when Nik pulled up in his truck alongside her. He rolled down the window.

"Sara, I need to talk to you. Did you get my text?"

She shook her head. She could hear the worry in his voice. She got in the truck, her face hot and her hands clammy. "Nik, there was a reporter at Camille's asking questions about me. I think he knows."

He nodded. "You can't go home yet. The story's out. I just saw it on the morning news. There are several cars parked in front of your place. A few more keep circling the block."

Sara felt like she'd been kicked in the stomach. "This isn't happening. This isn't happening," she whispered to herself again and again like a spell she could reverse if she tried hard enough.

"I'm sorry, Sara. It's out there."

"Define *out there?*"

"The major news networks have it. I'll take you to my place for now, okay?"

"This cannot be happening." Her breath was fast and short.

"Stay calm. We'll work this out." They pulled into Nik's place and hurried inside. He turned on his TV and cued his DVR to *The Today Show.*

Sara immediately saw a picture of herself and her mother side-by-side at the last movie premiere while Savannah Guthrie reported: "Like mother, like daughter? The secret is finally out. A source close to the Bond family reports that Cassandra Bond's own daughter, thirty-two-year-old Sara Grayson, will be writing the final *Ellery Dawson* book, scheduled for release next year. Sara Grayson, a lecturer at the University of Maryland, has *never* published *any* fiction, but fans of Cassandra Bond are hoping this apple does not fall far from the tree. Iris Books, Bond's long-time publisher, has been unavailable for comment."

Sara felt something heavy press against her chest. Her hands trembled, but she couldn't seem to move the rest of her body.

"You better sit down. I'll get you something to drink."

She sat on Nik's couch. She felt suddenly nauseous and lowered her head. The patterns in the rug began to swirl. She closed her eyes.

Nik brought her some cold water and sat next to her. "Just breathe, okay?'

"The other networks? Cable news? Are they running the story too?"

"I did a quick scan on my news app. Yeah. And it's trending on social media already."

Sara's head hurt from trying not to cry, from trying to maintain control. Why did it feel so hard to breathe? Why was it so *hot* in Nik's house? The room began to spin again.

Nik took both of her hands in his. "Hey, look at me. Sara?"

She couldn't look at him and stared blankly past him. "I was barely making it," she choked on her words. "I don't know how to write the rest of this book with the whole world watching...waiting...for *me*." Her voice broke, and she couldn't stop the tears. He leaned forward and kissed her forehead, drawing her into his chest.

"We'll get through this. The initial interest is going to die down, and you'll be able to get back to work."

"Damn right!" Bernadette stood in the doorway with drinks and a large brown bag from the café. Sara looked up at her and smiled weakly. There was something comforting about her imposing presence. "Want me to go scare those reporters away or cook them something to eat with a side of salmonella? Like we needed anymore flatlandahs around here?"

"City folk," Nik whispered.

She set the food and drinks down on the coffee table. "Come here, Sara-girl." She stood up, and Bernie wrapped her plump, strong arms around her. "We've got your back, hon. Let's get our game plan on, okay?"

The three sat together at Nik's kitchen table. Bernie dished up blueberry pancakes, scrambled eggs, and sausage, though Sara had no appetite. Nik made her a cup of tea.

What she really wanted was to know who tipped the press. She thought of that reporter at Miriam's café and that black Nissan she kept noticing the past week. "How did the press even know where to find me?"

"Well, whoever leaked it knew your location. The press clearly had an advance tip," said Nik.

Sara blew her nose and wiped her eyes. She reached for the glands on her throat. Were they swelling up again? She sipped some tea. "You should be at work," she told Nik. "Not here working out this mess."

"I don't have class for a couple of hours. Let me help."

They started with Sara's voicemail and texts. Her agent, Elaine Chang, was already on her way to Maine and bringing Cassandra's publicist with her. Phil wanted a video call ASAP. Jane Harnois wanted one too. David Allman had called twice. Iris Books was sending a cybersecurity expert from New York to modify and protect Sara's phone, internet connection, and her computer from hackers. Anna-Kath just wanted to know if Sara was okay. Binti didn't know yet. She was in New York and texted a photo of herself and the back of someone's head she claimed was from *Hamilton* in line at Shake Shack last night. "So awesome!"

First video call was with Phil. He was already shaking his head the moment he appeared, a deep furrow between his brows. "What the hell did I tell you?" He pulled at his collar and pointed his finger repeatedly, hitting his own screen with it several times.

"I'm sorry, Phil. You know I never intended…" She couldn't finish her sentence and rubbed her eyes with the heels of her palms like her mother used to do.

His face softened, and he suddenly looked more tired than angry. "Look, we move into damage control, and we try and swing this to our advantage. Cassandra's publicist, Thea Marshall, knows what she's doing, okay? Call me when she and Elaine get there. I'll handle Jane for now. She thinks you leaked it."

Sara clutched her throat. "Me? That's ridiculous. How would this help me?"

"That's what I told her." Then Phil was quiet a moment. He looked away from the computer. He rubbed the back of his neck. "Hmm…well, maybe it could." He downed the rest of his coffee in a quick swig. "Don't panic, Grayson."

§

Thea Marshall arrived from New York that afternoon with calm and control. She wore a short pixie cut, a tight turtleneck sweater, and big hoop earrings that pulled on her ear lobes. She had new press releases ready, and her company took control of Sara's social media presence that afternoon, establishing separate "Sara Grayson, Author" accounts on Facebook, Instagram, and Twitter.

There were vigorous discussions about whether Sara should give interviews or not. Some felt that keeping a low profile created more mystery and hype, but as Elaine fielded interview requests from media outlets, such as *People*, *Ellen*, CNN, and *Sixty Minutes*, it was obvious that this was a wave they'd be crazy not to ride.

"Yeah...I get that," said Phil, "but we're not gonna have a Book Five if Sara's off doing photo shoots and interviews instead of writing. December 15th is still the deadline. I'd better come up there."

Thea had the kind of silky, reassuring voice you'd hire for meditation apps. "Phil, we know how to handle this—let us do our job. You manage things in New York, and we'll take care of things here." She convinced everyone that instead of a bunch of lengthy interviews, Sara should do a day's press junket at a hotel in Portland, Maine. "We'll invite reputable news organizations to send a rep, and they'll each get ten minutes with Sara. The interest should taper off after that, especially since there isn't much more to the story at this point. I can set it up for this Saturday."

The thought of doing a series of interviews made Sara's stomach crawl. Perhaps she might drop dead by that point, and then *Dateline* could take over her story. They loved to cover young, tragic, and mysterious deaths. Add a beloved unfinished novel, and Lester Holt would be weeping by the end.

No, he wouldn't. That man was a rock. Maybe they could get Kate Snow?

Bernie invited Sara to stay with her the rest of the week so she could keep her distance from all the reporters in her neighborhood. She set Sara up in a small bedroom with mauve and blue wallpaper, circa 1984. Sara couldn't sleep, although Gatsby snored peacefully curled up at the end of her bed.

Sara finally switched on a lamp and grabbed her phone. Another twenty new texts appeared from Binti, including another photo from New York. Her eyes were wide and goofy, and she was about to eat a big slice of pizza she held up to her mouth. "At Luigi's! A boring conference without you!"

Sara texted back, "Check. Your. Newsfeed."

There were seventeen texts from Binti the next morning. The first five said nothing but, "OMG, OMG, OMG, OMG, OMG." The next five: "CALL ME. CALL ME. CALL ME. CALL ME. CALL ME."

Then: "Sara, this is crazy? Who the hell leaked it? I'll go after them. Did you know I keep a baseball bat under my bed?"

CHAPTER 34

*Writing is like sausage making in my view; you'll all be
happier in the end if you just eat the final product
without knowing what's gone into it.*

GEORGE R. R. MARTIN

CNN Newsroom
Washington Post Book Critic: "It's a publicity stunt. Fans loved not only Bond's books, but they loved Bond herself. This is the publisher's attempt to transfer that affection to her daughter."
CNN Host: "Will it work?"
Critic: "Personally, I think it's publishing suicide to go with an untested author. I think they'll push pre-orders big time in case it flops."

PBS News Hour
PBS Host: "For those who don't know the *Ellery Dawson* books, how big a deal is this and is there a precedent?"
Panelist from *The Nation*: "This is huge, no question. In terms of precedent, Brandon Sanderson, a relative unknown, was chosen to finish the late Robert Jordan's *Wheel of Time* series."

Panelist from *NYT*: "Sure, but Sanderson had published a couple of novels by then, while Sara Grayson has published nothing. It's a nice idea, but I'm just not seeing it."

NPR: 1A
Live Callers

"Yeah, Ethan from Baltimore here. I had Grayson for freshman English last year. I think she was more bored than we were. I met her for office hours once, and she was asleep at her desk with her hand in a bag of barbecue chips. I don't think she's a well person."

"This is Zoe from Rockville, Maryland, and I'm in upper management at Cutie Coupon where Sara was our superstar coupon writer. She and I were very close. She was like a sister to me, and I just want to say that I think she'll do an amazing job."

Texts on Tuesday, Oct 1, 11:30 PM

Binti
I just read chapter four. It's fabulous!

Sara
I never sent you chapter four.

Binti
Crap. I thought you knew.
It's online. Multiple sites. My
students showed me.

Sara? Are you there? Do you
know who leaked it?

Texts on Wednesday, Oct 2, 1:02 AM

Binti
Hot damn! Just saw the
Char Fox interview with
Fallon where she shut
down the other *Ellery*
cast members who dissed
you and threw her full
support behind you. Epic!

From: Phil Dvornik
To: Sara Grayson
Date: Wednesday, Oct 2, 3:50 PM
Subject: Not bad

Grayson,

So chapter four has gone viral. Looks like it was
first posted on a fanfiction site by some kid in
your writing group who Nik says didn't know what
kind of shit he was getting you into. Thought he
was doing you a favor. Look, water under the
bridge. Can't get it back. Here's the crazy thing:

Ellery Dawson sales are up 35% across the board.
We're expecting the first four *Ellery* books to take
spots one through four on the best-sellers list by
this weekend. In short, the public loves the idea
of Cassandra's daughter writing Book Five.

This is nothing short of a win. This also means that
Asher Monroe is out of the picture. The board voted

last night to put their full support behind you. Jane still proposed a joint authorship with you and Asher but had no support. The numbers speak loudly enough.

Good luck at the press junket Saturday. I need you back at your computer Monday morning.

Full focus.
Phil

AP News Release, Thursday, Oct 3, 9:30 AM

Iris Books has released the title of *Ellery Dawson* Book Five: *Resurrection.*

Cassandra Bond's daughter, a relative unknown, will be authoring the book, scheduled to be released this summer.

Texts on Thursday, Oct 3, 10:03 AM

Sara
Resurrection? Who released this? I thought you said the title was negotiable.

Phil
Sorry. We had to get it out there.

Sara
I don't even know what that title means. Who gets resurrected?

Phil
You could start with yourself. You don't look so good. Is that

toothpaste on your sweatshirt?
You know Thea has a stylist for the
press junket. You two should talk.

Sara
I'm hanging up now, Phil.

The Portland Harbor Hotel sat comfortably in the Old Port district, within walking distance of the waterfront. Sara and Thea worked on Friday in a blue conference room decorated with rustic lighthouses. Thea pressed her with difficult questions, instructing her on effective ways to respond and certain phrases to avoid.

Milo, a bald stylist with a peppery goatee, met her at the hotel Saturday morning. After a short consult, he ordered her hair cut to the shoulders with layers to frame her face and colored her hair a deeper brown. The new cut and color looked perfect. She was so used to seeing her hair pulled back in a ponytail or messy bun, she'd forgotten what it felt like to feel this beautiful.

She spent Saturday in a director's chair across from a rotating circle of journalists who interviewed her in ten-minute increments next to an imposing *Ellery Dawson* poster. It was the same one she'd paid a Barnes and Noble employee to knock down only four months ago. So karma was real—even for movie posters.

She'd seen her mother do dozens of these junkets. It was harder than it looked, but most of the questions were the same, and Thea had prepared her well.

Sara returned to Bar Harbor Sunday morning and back to the cottage. Most of the journalists had left, and things seemed to be settling down. They had a final meeting before Thea's flight home that evening. Her team was managing the story, and Sara was ready to return to her writing the next morning.

Sara FaceTimed with Ann that night.

Ann
Livvy scored all four goals at her
soccer game this morning

    Sara
    All four? That's amazing!

Ann
Yeah. The score was 2-2.

    Sara
    I wish I could have been there.

Ann
I've already seen some of your
interviews—you look amazing!

    Sara
    Could you tell how nervous I was?

Ann
Yes—but I'm your sister. I
think you did great.

    Sara
    Thanks.

Ann
You okay?

Sara

I'm just trying not to let it
mess with my head.

Ann

In what way?

Sara

Millions of people waiting for me to
write this book. Being talked, tweeted,
memed, blogged, posted about.
It kind of gets under your skin.

Ann

But Asher Monroe is gone.
That's a plus.

Sara

Yeah—the leak was good that
way. I just need to get my head
to where it was before. Pretend
like no one is waiting for me.

Gatsby is barking. Someone's at
the door. Let me check it out.

Sara was surprised to see Thea standing there. "I thought your flight left tonight."

"Something's come up. Can we talk?"

"Sure. I'm talking to Anna-Kath. Let me—"

"Keep her on. This involves her too."

Thea sat with Sara at her kitchen table and Ann on Sara's phone. She briefed them on a cluster of new tabloid stories. *National Enquirer* and two others were reporting some variation of Cassandra Bond, the plagiarist. One claimed that she tried to cover up her own hidden love child with a plaintiff in a plagiarism lawsuit. Another reported a lesbian affair with Meredith Lamb; another suggested a love triangle with Meredith Lamb and Bond's husband. Some were more outlandish than others, but they all pointed to Bond plagiarizing her first series, and each referenced the huge settlement costs of the lawsuit. The *Star* reported that Bond made payments of hush money to Lamb throughout her life and titled the story, "Empire of Lies."

The tabloids had written about her mother before, but all of this felt different. There were too many kernels of possible truths.

Thea rubbed the back of her neck. "We've ignored stories in the past, but these are connected to some legitimate inquiries."

"You're talking about Gibbs Cartwright," said Ann.

Thea nodded. "This isn't going away."

Sara and Ann exchanged worried looks. Thea noticed.

"Your mother hired me ten years ago to represent her, and her story about the lawsuit never changed: Meredith Lamb accused her of plagiarism, but Cassandra insisted she never stole a word from anyone, and she settled the lawsuit early so she could put it quickly behind her. I'm going to be frank with you. There are pieces to the story that don't add up. Your mother and Phil signed a nondisclosure that prevents them discussing the settlement. Until now, I've been able to get by with inadequate information. I just got off the phone with Phil, pleading for anything else he can tell us. I'm baffled as to why he won't give us something more—even under the table to clear her name and help us out. There's something more going on, and I don't know what. At this point, I need you to tell me anything you know."

"Did Mom ever mention our father's relationship to Meredith?" asked Sara.

"I didn't know he knew her."

Sara slowly exhaled. They told Thea everything they knew about Meredith Lamb: her book, the dedication to her father, and how Meredith worked at his school. Sara talked about the trust fund for Meredith and her daughter and how everything pointed to her father having an affair with Meredith. Ann told Thea about her recent conversation with Cartwright and his new sources.

"Cartwright told me the same thing," said Thea. "I think the moment he confirms his new evidence, he'll run his story. But, ladies, what do you believe? Do you think your mother borrowed anything from Lamb? We have two sources who say they have proof."

Sara looked at Ann. She swirled the tea in her cup.

"It wouldn't make any sense," said Sara, "but I don't think we *know* anything anymore."

Thea pulled out a thick black notebook and set it in the middle of the table. "Ladies, this is my crisis management bible. It's my guide for getting any person or organization through a PR crisis. We aren't there—yet. But I will tell you right now that one of the golden rules of crisis management is to get ahead of the story."

Sara shoved her fingers in her hair. "How bad could this get? Like, if Cartwright gains credible evidence that our mother plagiarized and runs his story, what could that mean for her legacy—and for me—for Book Five?"

"Look, it's hard for a…a deceased person to defend herself, to make a comeback. In my line of work, *trust* is the single hardest thing to rebuild. I'm not saying it's impossible in this situation—I'm good at what I do—but we'd be looking at a potential collapse of…" Thea paused and shook her head.

Sara whispered, "Of everything?"

"Maybe."

"And this book I'm writing—the world of *Ellery Dawson*? What happens?"

"I don't know. It would certainly rock everything she's touched."

Sara nodded.

Thea pointed to her bible. "We need to get ahead of the story so we can shape it. Let's hire a private investigator to go to London, to find Lamb and her daughter."

"Why would Meredith or her daughter even talk to some investigator—after years of keeping that nondisclosure agreement?" asked Sara.

"It's our best shot," said Thea. "And we can find other sources, maybe, once we're there."

"I'll go," said Ann.

"What?"

"Well, Sara has a book to finish, and Thea is right. We have to stay ahead of the story. I'll come to Maine next weekend as planned, and then I'll head straight to London. I have to work it out with Gerald—" She paused. "We haven't seen eye-to-eye lately, but I'm sure he'll understand."

What did that mean? Did they disagree on whether to use a trifold or bifold on the kitchen towels?

"We'll work it out," said Ann.

"It's a good idea," said Thea. "If Carolee is your sister, you or Ann may be the only ones who can get her talking."

୬

Monday morning Sara was back at her computer, determined to keep writing.

By Wednesday night, the book was worse than horrible. It was mediocre.

In three days she had spiraled into a severe case of writer's block, producing only two pages when she planned to have fifty.

It didn't help that she'd hardly seen Nik. He was at a conference that week in Augusta. With Sara managing the leak last week and Nik at his conference this week, they'd hardly had a moment together in ten days.

He called and texted her every day, but she wasn't as responsive as she could have been. It felt like all she had to give right now were leftovers of herself. What if Nik grew tired of her before she had something more to give? Anna-Kath would arrive on Friday. She clung to this. Ann would know how to help Sara sort out the craziness in her mind.

Bernie showed up Wednesday evening with lobster chowder and hot popovers. Sara's body relaxed while she ate at the table and Bernie rinsed out a kettle for tea.

"You're working too hard, Sara-girl. You don't look good at all." She finished filling the kettle and turned up the gas on the stove.

"I know." Sara had noticed her own baggy eyes and lack of color in her face. "I keep picturing all those fans wanting this book, waiting for me to finish. I don't know if I'll be able to pull this off."

Bernie sat next to Sara and wrapped an arm around her shoulder. "You know, your momma wasn't always brimming with confidence. She struggled too."

"But at least she knew she could do it. The jury's still out with me. I'm a total maybe."

"Oh no, honey. At this point you are a *confirmed* maybe."

Sara pulled away and looked skeptically at Bernie. "A confirmed maybe?"

"Look, I'm no writer. My food, my café—I guess that's my art. But I do believe that creative courage means staring down that chasm of self-doubt and making the chowder anyway. There's no guarantee of an outcome. You do it because there's something in your soul itching to get out."

"So what makes me a *confirmed* maybe?"

"You being willing to try—in spite of all that fear."

Sara nodded.

Bernie walked to the stove to pour the tea. "I remember your momma talking about Book Five last spring. 'What if this is the year of my epic fail?' she said."

Sara shot up. "Book Five?"

"I think so. Hard to remember exactly. Anyway—"

Sara grabbed her arm. "Book Five is what I'm writing. You mean *Book Four*?"

Bernie laughed. "Right. I get them mixed up."

"Please tell me you're *sure* it was Book Four."

"Now why would your momma put you through this if she'd already written it? Of course it was Book Four. I just misspoke. Don't get your nets in a twist."

"Okay, you're right. Of course, you're right."

CHAPTER 35

*Fiction was invented the day Jonah arrived home
and told his wife that he was three days late
because he had been swallowed by a whale.*

GABRIEL GARCÍA MÁRQUEZ

Sara slept fitfully that night and woke before dawn to the sound of rain. She kept replaying what Bernie said about her mother writing Book Five. It had to be a slip-up. An easy mistake.

But what if it wasn't? What if her mother really had been working on Book Five?

She shook it off. Sara had already searched for days and found nothing. *In Bethesda.*

Sara jumped out of bed and went to her mother's office closet. She turned on a light, her sleepy eyes squinting against the brightness.

What if…?

What if her mother did write it? Bernie mentioned that Nik would sometimes help her mom out. Did she ever talk about Book Five with him? No. He would have told her. He would never keep that from her.

She walked inside the closet. There were many boxes she hadn't opened. With all the loose threads she'd discovered so far, she hadn't been ready to look for more.

She shook her head.

No. There's no Book Five.

She turned off the light and climbed back into bed.

But she couldn't sleep. If her mother did write the book, wouldn't it make sense to keep it here? Sara covered her face with her hands. What if it had been at the cottage all along?

Sara got up and went back to the office closet. She pulled out the first box and began going through every file, every speck of paper she could find. It was mostly personal stuff: memorabilia from Sara and Ann's childhood, old birthday cards, artwork, and report cards. Phil told her she'd brought boxes up a few summers ago with plans to organize it all.

Sara unpacked a thousand stories with no time to feel nostalgic. Papers, photos, files of early *Ellery Dawson* chapters, and fan mail began piling up in the office. Still no sign of Book Five. Sara went to her mother's computer, sifting through copies of files she had already seen at home.

Her mother had plenty of time to write this book before she ever got sick. And after she got sick and decided to have Sara write the book, she certainly would have made provisions in case Sara didn't come through. Wouldn't she have tucked the book away *somewhere*? She had to have some sort of contingency plan.

Sara sorted through another box. Still nothing.

A surge of anxious energy pushed her forward. If she found the book, it would mean instant relief from this nightmare, right? The escape hatch. A way out.

And yet Sara had worked so hard. Is that really what she wanted? She continued to search, her heart a confused mix of both fear and longing.

It was late afternoon when Sara emptied the last box. She lay on the floor staring at the ceiling. There was no sign of Book Five—not a Post-it or index card or legal pad. She'd wasted an entire day. She was tired, frustrated, and angry at her mother and herself. She didn't know if she should cry or scream or both. She had also ignored her phone all day, so when she heard the knock at the door, she covered her eyes with her arm and decided to ignore it, but Gatsby barked excitedly.

She heard the knock again, louder. "Sara? It's Nik."

She shot up. Nik? He wasn't coming back until tomorrow. She felt suddenly embarrassed about her appearance and the total disarray of the cottage. Had she even brushed her teeth?

Maybe she could ignore him. Call him later. Say she was in the shower. Gatsby was barking and scratching at the door now. Then he looked at her and whimpered.

She smoothed her hair back, took a deep breath, and opened the door.

Nik's face was bright and happy to see her. He hugged her, practically lifting her off her feet, but Sara felt stiff and dirty, like she'd been camping for a week.

"So you're alive? When you stopped answering my texts, I was thinking you must be in the zone again." His eyes were wide, his smile easy. He reached for Gatsby and ruffled the hair around his neck. "So... good writing?"

She closed her eyes and bit her bottom lip. "Not exactly."

She invited him in. He quickly surveyed the piles of papers and boxes everywhere. "Whoa. What happened here?"

She should feel happier to see him. And she was happy to see him. But she was so frustrated at the lost day, the lost book. And she'd hardly slept last night. She could feel him taking the whole room in, and the place felt stifling. "You could have called first."

"I did."

"Oh." She wasn't sure where her phone was. She plopped down on the couch. Some papers crunched beneath her.

Nik moved a stack of files off an armchair and sat down, Gatsby sidling next to his feet. "So, some cleaning out?" He still sounded cheerful, happy to see her. Why was that so irritating?

This would be a good point to excuse herself. Maybe take a shower. Make some tea. Approach all of this calmly. But her anger at herself and her mother suddenly veered off course, and her words flew at him. "Why didn't you tell me that you'd helped my mom with *Ellery Dawson*?"

He shifted back in his seat. "It's no secret. I'd read some chapters on occasion. I helped her with some poetry for Book Three."

"Anything else?"

Nik shrugged his shoulders. "Not really." He looked around again. "What's this all about?" He leaned back in his chair and brought an ankle to rest on his knee. She could see his socks now. They had an imprint of Bob Dylan's face with sunglasses. He wore that blue button-down shirt she liked. He loosened his tie. He was calm. Freakishly calm. And it annoyed her. So did the socks.

Her throat felt dry. Her eyes darted around, looking for her water bottle. She moved some stacks around the coffee table, looking for her water bottle. It was the overpriced blue one she'd bought at L.L. Bean on the way up. *Where was that thing?* She got on her knees and looked under the couch. Nothing.

"Could you move your feet?" She looked under Nik's chair. Nothing. She stuck her hand along the back of the couch.

"Sara, you haven't answered my texts or calls for two days. Are you okay?"

She sat up on her knees. "Can't find my water bottle." She scratched her nose.

Nik looked around. "Your water bottle?"

She exhaled loudly and pulled her legs in front, her back resting against the couch. "I'm looking for the book."

"What book?"

"My mom's Book Five."

Nik leaned forward, his arms resting on his thighs. "What?"

Sara retied her ponytail and rubbed her eyes. They were irritated from all the dust she'd kicked up. She sat back down on the sofa. More papers crumpled beneath her.

"Mum had a system. Four months research; two months on an outline; four to write; two to edit. Slam bam, thank you ma'am. She'd have a book in twelve months. According to the system, she'd have written it by *last September*, months before she got sick. So, where's the book? It isn't in Bethesda. Her editors and agents don't have it. I realized this morning: it has to be here."

Nik rubbed the back of his neck. "Sara, this makes no sense. Why would your mom ask you to write a book she'd already written?"

"*To make me write.* Brilliant, when you think about it. And terribly passive-aggressive, don't you think?" The sound of her own voice, all cynical and full of snark, made her feel a little sad, but she clung to her anger.

Nik pulled the rest of his tie loose. "So she's done stuff like this before?"

"Well, no. But this is. This is—"

"*Writer's block.*" He moved next to Sara on the couch and put an arm around her. "You'll get past it. Why don't we get out…get something to eat? I've been excited to see you."

She wriggled away and sat on the floor next to an open box. She grabbed a file and flipped through it a little too vigorously. She felt Nik studying her. Analyzing her. She shoved the file off to the side and hugged her knees to her chest. Where was that water bottle? She'd paid thirty-six dollars for that thing. She looked between a few more boxes. Nothing. She sat back on the floor.

This is where Nik should say something funny or unexpected and help Sara snap out of it. Instead he stood up and walked to the window, staring out pensively. It was raining again, the sky a chalky gray.

"How long did you say she'd take to write an *Ellery* book?"

"Twelve months. So if she was on schedule, it would have been done last September—before she got sick. See? Doesn't this make sense?"

"If she was on schedule." He pressed a hand against his beard, thoughtfully.

"Nik?"

"Huh? Sorry. I was just thinking."

"Well, you can see where I'm coming from? Right?"

Nik's eyes looked distant. He refocused them on Sara. "No...I mean, yes." He dropped his arms and exhaled loudly. "I didn't know Cassandra's writing process, her schedule, you know. So I was just thinking—"

"That this makes logical sense?"

Nik sat back down. "No...I get your mom's time frame, but this..." he pointed to the boxes, "isn't logical." He leaned forward on his elbows and rubbed the back of his neck with both hands.

"You okay, Nik?"

He sat up and put his hands down. "I'm fine."

But he was clearly distracted. He rubbed the space between his lower lip and his beard with his index finger, something she saw him do when he was thinking deeply.

"Nik?" She paused. "Wait..." Sara moved a stack of files and sat across from him on the coffee table. "Do you know something? About Book Five?"

Nik's eyes widened, and he sat up. "No. Absolutely not." He pressed his palms against his thighs. "I'm just...processing...everything."

Sara tilted her head as she met his eyes for a moment, but he looked past her again.

He gave a quick shake of his head and looked back at her. "When did you say the book would have been written?"

"A year ago last month. She was here at least part of that time. What was she doing, Nik? Do you know what she was working on?"

He closed his eyes a moment and then slowly shook his head. "Your mom was always working on something, but it's not like I saw her all the time. We'd talk about her writing. It's not like she'd give me status updates." Nik ran his fingers quickly through his hair. "No. If Phil says it isn't written, it isn't written. You've gotta go with that."

She stood up. "You're acting strange."

"And you're not? Let's clean this up. Get you something to eat, okay?" He picked up a stack of files next to an empty box on the sofa. "Do these go here?"

"But she was working on *Ellery* when she was here last? Right?" She grabbed his arm. "Was it Book Five?"

He dropped the files in the empty box with a crash. It woke up Gatsby. He sniffed around some boxes.

"Is there something you're not telling me?"

"I already told you. I don't know." Nik pushed a box out of his way. He saw a flash of blue poking out. "Here's your water bottle."

She took it. Empty. She looked back at Nik, feeling guilty now for taking her frustration out on him. For trying to read something into nothing.

She closed her eyes a moment and took a deep breath. "I'm sorry, Nik. I'm not thinking clearly. Let me get you something. You want anything to drink?"

He reached for his jacket. "I think I'll head back to my place. I've got work to catch up on. Looks like you do too."

Gatsby walked past them and into the kitchen. She could hear him lapping water out of his bowl. Outside the sky had turned darker.

Nik surveyed the room again as he put on his jacket. Then he kissed Sara on top of her head. "Look, Sara, I think that..." He shook his head. "Never mind."

"*Never mind?* What? Tell me."

He placed a hand on her shoulder, studying her face. "Stop looking for a rescue."

She huffed. "This isn't about a rescue. It's about finding the truth."

He shook his head. "No. You've told me you're stronger than ever. You don't need a life preserver so...stop looking for one. Finish this thing."

Sara stepped back and pointed a finger at him. "You have no idea what I'm going through."

"I think I do."

"Really? Have you ever had fifteen million people waiting for your work, counting on it to be something amazing? My mom's dead, my father's a cheat, my mom might be a plagiarist. Everything I'm doing could go down in flames. All of this struggle could mean *nothing*."

"Welcome to the creative process."

"What's that supposed to mean?"

"Who gave you the idea that this was supposed to be easy? Or that the rest of your life should be nice and tidy so you can be at liberty to create? Stop resenting, stop blaming the very pieces of your life that give you something to write from."

Sara looked away.

"You'll get past this block." His voice turned hopeful. "I could take you somewhere to write."

She squeezed her eyes shut. "I want to go home, Nik. I want to be done with all this and just go home." But in that moment, Sara had never felt more uncertain about where "home" actually was.

Sara looked at him, her eyes pleading. "You would tell me if you knew something, right?"

"I just did."

Chapter 36

Abandon the idea that you are ever going to finish.

John Steinbeck

Sara woke up early the next morning and showered, trying to wash away all the sickly grime of her discouragement and self-pity. She was embarrassed about her meltdown with Nik the night before, and she desperately needed a new start. She texted him first thing.

Texts on Thursday, October 11, 7:32 AM

Sara
I owe you an apology about last night.
You were trying to help and I was
self-absorbed. I'm really, really sorry.

Nik
It's okay. I know you're under a lot
of pressure. And you're right. I don't
get what it's like to have millions
of people waiting for my work.

Sara

I shouldn't have said that.

Nik

It's true.

Sara

No excuse. Sometimes I wish I could have met you at a different time. When I wasn't so burdened and distracted by this book.

Nik

The book brought you here.

Sara

I know. And I'm glad. I'm not looking for the book anymore. I'm going to finish it.

Nik

Good. It's your book.

Sara

And you're right. Phil would know if my mom wrote it. Ann flies in tonight. Join us for dinner?

Nik

Going to Isleford for the weekend. Staying with some friends.

Sara

Oh. I thought you were around this weekend.

Nik
Came up last minute.

Sara
Want to stop here before work? Or
I could meet you at The Lieberry.

Nik
I'm already at my office.
Tell Anna-Kath hi.

～

Sara tried to shake off the disappointment of not seeing Nik that weekend. She knew last night had created some distance between them, and she wasn't sure what to do.

She drove to the top of Cadillac that morning for a fresh start and actually made some decent progress on her writing. She went home at lunchtime to clean up the disaster of boxes and papers before Anna-Kath arrived, but when she pulled up to the cottage, there was a car parked out front and Ann was sitting in a rocker on the porch.

"Ann, what are you doing here already? I thought I was picking you up tonight."

"I got an earlier flight and then just rented a car. Thought I'd surprise you."

Sara hugged her sister fiercely. "I'm so glad to see you. I've had the worst writing week and a total meltdown last night. I'm better now, but anyway…I'm just glad you're here."

Ann smiled back at Sara, but her eyes looked a little red, and she looked unusually weary. Must have been the early flight.

They walked inside the cottage. Boxes, files, and papers were still strewn throughout the front room.

"What's all this stuff?" asked Anna-Kath.

"I'd meant to get this cleaned up before you got here. Sorry! I'm just so glad you're here. You can help piece me back together again."

Ann looked unsettled. She wasn't wearing any makeup, which seemed odd. Ann was one of those people who actually looked good when she travelled. Sara wore leggings and a sweatshirt.

"Mind if I take a shower, Sara? Then I can help you out with all this."

"Oh yeah, of course." She took Ann's suitcase upstairs and got her settled in their mother's room. Ann seemed unusually quiet. Normally she'd be instructing Sara on the best way to tackle the mess in the cottage and the mess in her life.

With Ann in the shower, Sara cleaned things up as quickly as possible. She moved swiftly, placing files back in bins and moving bins back into the office. Ann would come out of her shower, smile, and see that Sara took care of things herself. Then Ann would make tea, and Sara could vent.

Ann was in the shower a *long* time. At least an hour. Then the shower was off, but the bathroom door was still closed

"Are you okay in there?"

She didn't respond.

Sara finished cleaning the front room. Then the office.

When the bathroom door finally swung open, hot steam spread out like a sauna.

Ann found Sara in the office. "Sorry I took so long. Just felt good to relax in there."

She looked like she'd been crying. Maybe it was just the long shower. Ann forced a smile and said, "Let's talk. I'll make us some tea."

Ann filled a kettle. "What was all that mess about?"

"Stupidity. I hit a low point with my writing and suddenly believed that maybe Mum really did write Book Five and that she'd hidden it somewhere in the cottage."

Ann opened some tea canisters. "And how did that work out?"

"What do you think?"

Ann smiled weakly at Sara—her lips tight, her eyes tired. Sara sat at the table while Ann made a blend of apple, clove, and black tea. It smelled like their mother's kitchen in the fall. Sara told Ann all about her writing stress and Nik coming over last night.

Ann brought her a cup of tea and sat down across from her. She kept glancing at the red maple out the kitchen window, lines of worry furrowed deeply on her forehead.

Sara paused. Is this what she would have missed before? She put her teacup down. "Ann?"

She was looking out the window again. "Oh sorry. What were you saying?"

Sara reached for her hand. "What's wrong?"

Ann flicked her wrist in the air. "Oh, this and that. It will all be fine."

Sara leaned forward. "No. I want to know. Something's really bothering you."

Ann brought her cup to her mouth, but her lips began to tremble and her hand started to shake. She opened her mouth to say something, but she couldn't speak.

"Ann?"

She set her cup down. "Gerald left." Her lips hardly moved when she said it. Like the words had been waiting so long they simply tumbled out when her lips opened. Then a great sob burst out, a deep, guttural sound. She buried her head in her arms. Sara sat frozen at first, having never seen her sister cry like this. She'd seen Ann get teary or a little sad, but she was a dust-yourself-off and go-to-work-with-a-smile sort of person. She didn't have time for sadness. She had too much to do.

Sara scooted her chair next to Ann's. "That's impossible. Gerald T. Green would never leave you."

"He isn't leaving me. He says he just needs some time. We had a big fight last night. He says I'm difficult to please. That it's too stressful for him always trying to get it right…to live up to my high expectations."

"But he does get it right. He's, like, the perfect husband."

Ann brought her head up, her eyes swollen and her face flushed. "I know that, but apparently I haven't been letting him know that. He said I'm a perfectionist, and he's right, and I don't know how to change that, and he said he doesn't want me to change, but could I soften my expectations a little? He stayed at his mom's last night and came back this morning to be with the kids while I'm gone and packed me a lunch for my trip. Can you believe that? The man's nice even when he's leaving me."

Sara handed her some tissues. "He's not leaving you. It sounds like he wants to work things out and I'm sure you do too."

Ann began to cry again. "But what if this is it, the beginning of the end?"

Sara reached for Ann's hands. "I don't think this is how it ends. I think it might be how it lasts."

Ann nodded and slowly exhaled. She rested her head on Sara's shoulder for a moment before she managed to sip some more tea.

Sara hugged her and refilled Ann's teacup.

"I'll make you tomato soup and grilled cheese, okay?" said Sara. "You and Gerald are going to be all right."

Ann wiped her tears. "Thanks for that."

"For what?"

"For calling Gerald, 'Gerald.' You always call him Gerald T. Green, like he's a congressman. Like a brand instead of a person."

Sara's heart slipped. She was right. Why did she do that? Was it her way of minimizing him, of minimizing Ann's perfect marriage, perfect everything? "I was wrong. I won't do that anymore. I promise. And Ann?"

"Yeah."

"You can't go to London on Tuesday."

"I have to go. We can't wait on this. Thea said so."

"You need to get back to Gerald. We'll hire a PI like Thea suggested. Or I'll go after the book is done. We'll work it out."

Gerald called Ann by dinner time on Friday and apologized. They both agreed to counseling. Ann seemed more peaceful, hopeful.

Ann insisted that Sara still write that weekend. She did—she had to, but she felt different when she wrote. For the first time since Sara read her mother's dying wish, the book wasn't the most important thing in her life right now. And her writing was better for it. Sara finished the rewrite of the first half of the book on Saturday. They invited Bernie and Nik over to celebrate Sunday night. Nik wasn't back yet. But Bernie came.

"Nik's not back?" Bernie seemed surprised. "But he talked to you before he left, right?"

"We texted a few times," said Sara. "Why?"

Bernie waved her off. "Oh, nothing. Let's cut into that cheesecake."

"Right," said Ann. She lifted her glass to Sara. "Here's to making it halfway!"

Before Sara went to bed, she looked out her office window, down the street towards Nik's home.

It was still dark.

CHAPTER 37

Talent is insignificant. I know a lot of talented ruins.
Beyond talent lie all the usual words: discipline,
love, luck, but most of all, endurance.

JAMES BALDWIN

Nik found Sara Monday morning writing on a bench in Agamont Park. It was a brilliant fall day. Clear blue skies and the perfect degree of autumn chill. It was low tide, and the bar between Bar Harbor and Bar Island was exposed in the distance. Tourists were busy crossing the narrow stretch of land before ocean covered it again in a few hours.

Sara looked up, happy to see him. He hugged her, more intensely than she expected. She kissed him freely, wanting to close whatever distance she'd wedged between them since he left her place Thursday night. He kissed her back with an unexpected urgency. Sara sighed in relief. Maybe things would be okay.

"Ann told me you were here. I missed you." Nik sat beside her and drew her close.

"Something amazing happened this morning," she said. "I went running, and this completely new story came to me—one that's from my soul—one that I can't wait to tell. I feel like all these stories are alive in me again. Like the words have come back to me. I just have to find a way to make them stay."

Nik took Sara's hand. He kissed it. "You'll find a way." He studied her face. "There's something different about you."

"I feel different. The book is still Mount Everest, but all I can do is keep writing." Sara smiled. "I know I can do it." A cold breeze stirred the leaves up around them. "How was Isleford? That's the one Hannah Gilley would walk to, right? To have her babies?"

"Yes. That's the one."

Sara kissed Nik happily on the cheek. She felt his body stiffen. It was slight, almost imperceptible. If she hadn't been worried earlier, she might have missed it. But then she noticed that when he smiled, it didn't quite reach his eyes. "Are you okay, Nik? I know I've been swinging a little wide emotionally. I'm sorry."

He looked out at the bay. Nik brought her hand up to his chest and kissed it. He looked back at her, his eyes troubled.

"Why are you looking at me that way? What's wrong?"

He placed her hand back in her lap and exhaled slowly. "Your mom was a great friend to me. I felt very loyal to her."

Sara felt suddenly queasy. "What are you trying to say?"

"During your mom's last visit here, she asked me to keep something for you and Anna-Kath."

Sara's heart began to race. It was difficult to swallow.

He stared at his leather satchel beside his feet. "I didn't realize what she gave me at first."

"When?"

"Last November."

She closed her eyes tightly.

"I was supposed to keep it for a certain time and then give it to you."

Her body froze in disbelief. She fought for breath, but then it came in short gasps.

She gripped his arm fiercely. "You have the book."

"No…I don't know. Maybe." Nik dropped his head into his hands. "She gave me a key to a safe deposit box."

"Here?"

"In Portland. She didn't say what it was. All I know is it's something for you and Anna-Kath, and I was supposed to give it to you in two years."

"Two years? Why *two years*? And why you? Why not David Allman?" Her hands began to tremble. "This makes no sense."

"I asked her the same thing. She said she wanted someone to keep it who wasn't connected to her daughters."

Sara pressed her fingers against her eyes. "But what else could it be? I guess I'd never have a reason to ask Nik Dvornik about the book, right?" Sara's face suddenly turned hard; her eyes narrowed at Nik. He reached for her hand, but she moved away. "How could you not tell me this? All this time we've spent together. Everything I've been going through, and you never said a word?"

"I'm so sorry. Believe me. I never imagined it could be the book. Not until Thursday when you described your mom's writing schedule."

Sara's eyes widened. "When I was looking for the book."

"That's when I put it together. When you explained her time frame. The possibility started to make sense. It's been almost a year since she gave it to me. I haven't thought about the key in months."

Sara covered her face in her hands. She pressed on her eyes until swirly stars appeared in the blackness, and she wished she could disappear into all that nothingness.

"Cassandra was my friend, Sara. She trusted me. And except for my father, I am—or *was*—entirely unconnected to her life in Bethesda. I don't think she planned on me meeting you like this. Of me falling for you the moment I saw you. Of me thinking of you constantly, wanting to be with you every moment I can."

She looked up at him. "Nik, I asked you directly if you knew something. You saw how miserable I was. You knew something, and you didn't say anything. That was *four* days ago."

"I was trying to do the right thing. You have to understand that."

Sara was crying now. "I need to go. I need to be alone." She reached for her bag and stood up.

Nik grabbed her arm. "Sara, I just had to work it out in my head."

She stopped. She sank down on the bench again. She wiped her tears with her hands and then wiped them onto her jeans.

He reached into his satchel and pulled out a large goldenrod envelope. "Here. Your signature and Ann's are already on file with the bank."

He placed it in her hands. A simple envelope had never felt heavier. She set it on her lap and looked down at it. She saw her mother's familiar script: "For Anna-Katherine and Sara."

"It could be something else," said Nik.

Sara stared at it. Her heart heavy. She nodded. "Could be."

Nik turned to her. "Listen to me." His eyes were intense, pleading. "You don't need this. Writing this book has been a new start. A new life for you. Don't...don't walk away. Finish this. Your way."

Sara's head shot up. "Do you even realize your own hypocrisy?"

"What?"

"A new start. A new life. Don't walk away. You tell me all this while you hide here on your island, avoiding risks and staying safe."

"That's incredibly unfair."

"Phil told me you haven't left Maine in five years. He says you give away all of your travel funding to colleagues."

Nik looked back at the harbor. He said nothing.

"What about all those offers piling up in your office, summers spent in your work truck instead of reaching out to the world with your writing?

A series of summer flings that go nowhere? Is there even a single leap of faith you have taken in the last five years?"

Nik looked into Sara's eyes. "You."

Sara dropped her head in her hands. Her words had injured him. She didn't know what to say.

He sighed. "Maybe this isn't working. Maybe we just need to step back."

Sara winced. "Don't say it...."

Nik looked at his hands. "Maybe we should give each other some space."

Sara huffed. "*Space.* Is that the best breakup line you've got? You're a poet, Nik. You can't be more original than that?" The words stung her own mouth.

Nik locked his hands behind his neck and stared at the ground. Sara watched tourists walking towards the dock with disposable cups of coffee and little brown bags of breakfast to-go. Seagulls trolled for crumbs in the park.

"I can drive you back," he said.

She wiped her eyes. She'd felt such lightness earlier. Such hope. Now she hadn't felt this depth of sorrow since her mother died. She should walk. That would be good for her, but she didn't feel like she could move yet. "I'll stay here."

Nik walked away behind her, up towards the Village Green. She wondered if he ever looked back.

CHAPTER 38

Art hurts. Art urges voyages...and it is easier to stay at home.

GWENDOLYN BROOKS

S ara walked into the cottage an hour later, overwhelmed with a sorrow that throbbed deep in her bones. She sank on the sofa next to Ann. She closed her laptop.

"You okay?"

It was hard to speak. She gave the envelope to Ann. "Nik had this and...and he wants," she sniffed, "he wants to give us *space*."

Ann recognized their mother's handwriting. "Oh." Then she gasped when she opened the envelope and saw the key. Neither of them moved.

"Nik was supposed to give this to us next year."

The key sat in Ann's open palm. It was small and copper and attached to an orange keychain with CNB, Coastal National Bank, engraved on the front. Just a little key, like something you'd use to lock up your bike while you went for ice cream. All innocent-looking. So unaware of its own painful little wake.

Sara leaned her head on Ann's shoulder. "It has to be the book."

"It could be something else."

"Do you think it's something else?"

"Oh, Sara." Ann wrapped an arm around her. "It always made sense to me that Mum would have already written it, but it never made sense to me that Mum would ask you to do it if she already had." Ann slipped the key back in the envelope. "I don't know." She sighed. "But I think you're right."

Sara closed her eyes and leaned her head back against the sofa. Had she found the book months ago, she would have rejoiced. Now she felt only loss. But loss of what? She thought of all that searching in Bethesda in desperate hopes of finding the book. She realized now, five months later, that all her searching last week in the cottage had really been in hopes that she *wouldn't find it*.

Anna-Kath reached for her hand. "Don't open it, Sara," she pleaded. "Finish the book. You've come so far. Your writing is good. It's really good."

Sara looked ahead blankly and slowly shook her head. "It will never be as good as Mum's."

"You don't know that. Think about it, Sara. Mum *trusted* you to write her book."

"That's the thing that's killing me. She didn't. She didn't trust me. *Ellery* is in that safe deposit box as a fail-safe for when I didn't come through. If she trusted me, there would be no book. She would have just *trusted* me."

"So you've been wanting the book all this time, and now that there is one, you're hurt? You can't have it both ways, Sara: all of Mum's trust, but a safety net for you whenever it suits you."

Sara hugged her knees to her chest. "Nik said maybe the book isn't even there."

"With or without the book, Mum believed in you. Maybe you should too."

Sara wiped her face with her sleeve and rested her head on her knees.

"Does Phil know about the book?" said Ann. "Do you think he's known this whole time?"

"I don't know. I haven't told him. Maybe Nik has. I think I'm afraid he'll want Mum's book. Want it more than mine. And how could he not?"

Sara noticed a tiny ant on the floor. Looking for something to shoulder home. It kept randomly switching directions.

Ann put her hand on Sara's shoulder. "Maybe you should finish the book first. Finish what you started. Then open the box."

Sara looked up at Ann, her shoulders slumped, her eyes red. "I just can't stand not knowing."

"Then go. See what's there. But you have to see this all the way through to publication—your book, Mum's, or a hybrid."

"If Mum's book is there, mine is over."

Ann stood up. She reached down and gripped Sara's hand firmly to help her stand. Sara stood up, feeling like an old woman with stiff, creaky joints.

"Have you tried my cranberry apple tea blend? Just a hint of coconut? I'll make you some. We'll watch Food Truck Wars on Netflix."

Sara hugged Ann. "You should work at the state department and broker peace deals with your tea. Can they cure cancer?"

Ann smiled. "Not yet."

୬

Sara decided to drive Ann to the airport in Portland the next morning for her flight home. The final decision was to stop at Coastal National Bank and open the safe deposit box together. Then Sara would fly directly to New York and take the book to Phil, where the two of them would figure out what to do next.

She hadn't spoken to Nik since yesterday morning.

The rain was persistent. Clouds of gray fog rolled across the road, and Sara couldn't stop thinking about Book Five. She wondered how her mother's book would differ from her own. She hoped her mom didn't kill off Ellery's husband or her father or the dog. And what if her mom didn't help Ellery heal her marriage? She wouldn't break them up, right? She felt a sudden surge of protection for her people. And she would be doubly furious if her mother didn't clear up the questions about Ellery's father. What if her mom got all artsy with it and decided to leave things ambiguous about her father? Her mother did that once at the end of an earlier book series. Critics loved it, but Sara hated it. Her mother wouldn't try that stunt again, would she?

It's just a book. Ellery Dawson is not real. Her husband is not real. Her father is not real.

And yet they were real to her. Quite real, in fact.

Sara thought of so many good days she had spent alone with her characters the past five months.

Her characters. She shook her head. *No. My mother's characters. That's what I meant. They're not mine.*

Why was she getting so worked up about this? *I'm just tired.*

But she couldn't deny a sense of purpose seeping slowly out of her life the closer she got to Portland. What would she do now? What was next for her? She had cursed the book again and again, but it had become her reason for getting up in the morning. She finally had work that made her feel alive. Words had come back into her life, just like Nik had described, sinking into her blood, giving her skin warmth, swirling inside her mouth and soul. If she didn't give them a place to stay, would they leave and never come back?

Don't be so dramatic. Writing isn't everything.

Ann slept in the passenger seat. She had so many reasons to get up in the morning. Sara could find purpose in other areas of her life. She thought about her teaching at the university. Maybe if she put more heart into it, she would develop more passion for her work. She could apply again for senior lecturer.

Then she thought about that idea she had for a new book. She had felt such excitement about it. If she went back to teaching, would she ever write it?

And what would she and Ann do about London and all the unanswered questions about their parents? She wished they could hire Ellery Dawson. Give her a map of their East End neighborhood and let her social map all their connections. She'd find Meredith and Carolee and give Sara a full report while they sipped one of Anna-Kath's herbal tea blends.

So what would happen to Ellery?

Sara gripped the steering wheel firmly with both hands. *I'll be happy with whatever Mum wrote for Ellery—*

As long as she doesn't mess things up with Ellery's husband and...

Stop it! Everything is going to be fine.

Sara probably needed to hire one of those life coaches.

Maybe I could become a life coach.

That made her laugh so hard she snorted out loud and woke up Ann. "Sorry. Go back to sleep!"

Ann dozed off again.

Sara turned on the radio. Why did every song make her think of Nik? She switched it off.

❧

Sara's GPS finally guided her to Coastal National Bank, a modern, steel-and-glass structure in downtown Portland. She began looking for a place to park and could find nothing within a mile of the bank.

"This is ridiculous. We're not in DC. How hard can it be to find parking?"

But it was. All the lots were full, and the whole ordeal was taking too much time.

Finally Ann said, "Look, I'll drop you off. I'll keep circling around and pick you up in twenty minutes. It shouldn't take longer than that, right?"

"But I need you with me."

"I'll miss my flight if we keep looking for a spot."

"I can't do this myself."

"Of-course-you-can," said Ann, stringing it together like a happy Welsh phrase. Sara felt sick to her stomach as she pulled up to the bank. She got out, and Ann switched to the driver's seat.

Sara looked at Ann with painful uncertainty.

"Just go, Sara. Don't think about it. Go!"

She walked towards the bank. The rain had stopped, but it was still dark and overcast and easy to see the interior through the glass windows, a glowing fishbowl of gray cubicles, overgrown office plants, and posters of happy people whose lives had been transformed by banking services. She stepped into a small courtyard with a water fountain. A bench circled the fountain where perfectly calm people sat eating pretzels and potato chips and Cheez-Its out of perky little bags from vending machines and swigging back cold Maine Moxie without a care in the world.

Her feet felt heavy and hot as she walked. Each step slow and arduous until she stood in front of the large front door.

She stopped.

She stepped back several paces. She sat on the edge of the fountain. She wrapped her arms around her purse, clutching it to her stomach like a life preserver. She slowed her breathing.

She watched people walk in and out of the bank. They walked with purpose, like they knew where they were going and who to love and how to create so that the core of themselves wouldn't die off leaving them hollow and empty.

Sara opened her purse and pulled out the envelope and took out the key. She rolled it between her fingers. She remembered the moment David Allman handed her the "dying wish" and her mother's use of the word "audacity." It really was a great word. And she knew in that moment that there was not a shred of audacity in opening that box. Nothing bold or risky. Nothing fearless, creative or inventive.

She closed her fingers tightly around the key.

She pictured the look on her mother's face after she read Sara's first chapter of her novel nine years ago. How she took off her reading glasses and held Sara's hands and said, "You have words, my dear." She could see her dad's face in their London flat, how she kissed him good night as he sat at his desk tapping his dreams into his computer. After she would climb into her bed, she would fall asleep to the tap-tap-click of his fingers like music on his keyboard. She pictured stacks of his first drafts written on yellow legal pads poking out of the worn leather satchel he always carried with him to school.

She thought of her mother's last premiere when Char Fox asked her, "Are you a writer too?"

Sara looked at her wavy reflection in the bank doors.

She looked back at the key in her hand.

Mum trusted me to write this book.

Can I trust her?

Can I trust myself?

In one swift motion, Sara shoved the key back in the envelope and into her purse. She stood up, turned her back on the building, and walked away.

She called Ann. She pulled up a few minutes later.

Ann looked at her with wide eyes. "That was fast."

Sara nodded.

"Well, do you have it?"

Sara shook her head. "I didn't open it. I couldn't." Her voice filled with new conviction. "I can't stop now. I have to write this book. And I'm not going to New York. I'm going to London. Tonight."

"Tonight?"

"I've spent five months trying to help Ellery Dawson find the truth about her father, and I realized I'll never find him if I don't know the truth about my own. I need to know about Dad. I need to know about Mum. I'm going to complete this book. I have to finish what I started. I have my own words now, and I'm determined to keep them."

PART FOUR
LONDON

CHAPTER 39

My illustrious lordship, I'll show you what a woman can do.

ARTEMISIA GENTILESCHI

Sara stood in London's Heathrow airport in front of an aging passport control officer with wildly overgrown eyebrows. His eyes looked permanently suspicious, half-closed and squinty.

"State the purpose of your visit."

"Business...I guess."

"You guess?" He looked at Sara's passport and then back at her. "What do you do?"

Sara looked down at the dingy, gray countertop and back at the officer. She straightened her back and said, "I'm a writer." It tumbled out naturally, unexpectedly, without thinking. Sara's arms felt tingly. "I'm a writer."

She didn't know why she said it again. Maybe just to make sure she meant it.

The officer stamped her passport. "Welcome to the UK."

She'd spent her seven-hour flight to London in a window seat next to a motivational speaker named Lois who had spikey hair and wore several pieces of "intention statement" jewelry. Sara could make out the words "Ignite" and "Fire-Up" on Lois's wrist. An hour into the flight, Lois asked Sara what her own intention was. Sara unwrapped the thin airplane blanket, pulled out her eye mask, and said, "Sleep?" Lois looked extremely disappointed in her and gave Sara a free bookmark on making more courageous choices.

Sara was surprisingly calm when she first made her decision to go to London. Now she felt jittery and nervous as she tried to rest. It was 11:00 PM, and her mind kept going back to Nik and that awful morning. How did he really feel about her? Did he mean what he said? Did she mean what she said?

Phil didn't know she'd left yet—only Anna-Kath. She knew leaving like this was crazy and too close to her deadline, but she had never felt more compelled to act on anything and was quite certain about two things: 1) She would write this book, and 2) In order to do that, she needed to know the truth about her parents, about Meredith Lamb and Carolee Grayson.

She would give herself three days. Three days to turn up information. Then she'd finish the book.

Sara gave up trying to sleep and finally pulled out Meredith Lamb's *Silence in Stepney*. It was about an East End police detective named Shad Colton who had a penchant for detecting truth tellers and liars. She wanted to hate the book, really. After all, the author was a homewrecker and sued her mother.

But the book was actually good. Like *really good*. And there was something about it that made her feel like she was back in her old neighborhood in London with people she knew and loved.

She finally fell asleep for the last few hours of the flight. When she woke up, Lois was snacking on dried edamame and reading *Ellery Dawson* Book Four. In fact, she was so engrossed in the book, she hardly spoke the rest of the flight.

Sara sipped tea with her breakfast and looked out her window. Her plan was to go straight to Bristol when they landed. She had addresses for Meredith Lamb and Carolee Grayson, but she had no way to call or email them first. She tried searching local directories before her flight but came up with nothing. She was just going to have to show up, which made her stomach turn inside out.

As the plane began its descent into London, she found the view mesmerizing. It was late morning, and the skies were unusually clear, dotted with only a few wispy clouds. She saw the Thames, brown and wide and majestic, winding its way through the city. She could make out Canary Wharf in the East End and London Tower and the Tower Bridge, and suddenly she was crying. What was this feeling? As her eyes rested on her birthplace for the first time in twenty-four years, her mind suddenly felt light and clear, and her chest filled with warmth. A sense of love and security washed gently over her, and her plans changed in an instant. She knew she needed to go home first.

It was an emotional decision, but also an Ellery decision. While Sara was void of any special powers, she felt certain that if she started back at her home base and worked through her old neighborhood in the East End like Ellery would, maybe she would actually discover dots she could begin to connect and then be ready for Bristol.

After her flight, Sara stopped in an airport pub and emailed Phil. It was 10:00 AM in London, so 5:00 AM in New York, and he'd probably be asleep—which was good. He was expecting her at his place in just a few hours.

To: Phil Dvornik
From: Sara Grayson
Date: Wednesday, Oct 16, 10:03 AM
Subject: My Café Rudar

Phil,

Remember when you took me to Club Rudar and you told me I needed my roots? I'm taking your advice. I just arrived in London. I've spent five months helping Ellery search for her father and I realized I've got to connect to my own roots, just like you said. Plus, if I don't protect my mother's legacy, then what I write won't matter anyway.

I'm going to find Meredith Lamb and her daughter and try to get answers. I'll be here for three days, tops, and then I'll finish the book. Did Nik tell you about the safe deposit box? I didn't open it. It doesn't matter now anyway. I'll be in touch.

Sara

Unfortunately, Phil was not asleep.

From: Phil Dvornik
To: Sara Grayson
Date: Wednesday, Oct 16, 10:14 AM
Subject: RE: My Café Rudar

What the hell? I thought Anna-Kath was going. Where are you now? When I said to find your roots, I didn't mean during the LAST EIGHT WEEKS OF WRITING THIS BOOK. Do you know how reckless this is? Focus, Grayson. I'm calling you right now. Answer your damn phone.

To: Phil Dvornik
From: Sara Grayson
Date: Wednesday, Oct 16, 10:18 AM
Subject: RE: My Café Rudar

Phil,

I'm not picking up. You want a good book. I do too. My gut tells me I've got to do this. Trust me on this. Grit. It's what you wanted, right?

I'll have the book done by December 15th, as promised.

Phil began texting her.

Texts on Wednesday, Oct 16, 10:22 AM

Phil
This is the most shit-awful idea I've heard from you all year. Are you still at the airport? If you're at Heathrow, there's a returning flight that leaves for NYC in one hour. Get on it. I'll meet you at JFK. Write the book first. Explore your family tree later.

Sara
Gibbs Cartwright isn't going to wait around. I can't either. If we don't get ahead of this story it may not matter what I write. Thea agrees. I'll be back in three days. I'm going

home to the East End today and then
I'll find Meredith Lamb tomorrow.

Phil
Do NOT go near that woman.

Sara
Why? Care to explain? Look Phil, if
you've got answers, send them my
way, but since you haven't been
much help in that department,
I'm obviously on my own.

Phil
You know I'm legally bound.
Let the past be the past. Move
on. Your mother did.

Sara
I'm going. And I want to find
her daughter too. If she's my
sister, I need to know.

Phil
You won't find what
you're looking for.

Sara
You don't know that.

Phil
Jane Harnois is heading
to London this week for a
publishing conference. If you
aren't on a plane in three days,
I'm sending her after you.

Sara
Is that a threat or a promise?

Phil
Both.

Sara left the pub. She would not allow Phil's ranting to diminish her resolve. Her phone buzzed again at baggage claim.

Texts on Wednesday, Oct 16, 10:44 AM

Phil
I'm worried about you.

Sara
Why, Phil—you do care.

Phil
Of course, I care. Does Nik know about this?

Sara
Nik wants some "space." So you can rest easy now.

Phil
What's that supposed to mean? My problem was never about the two of you. It was the timing. It was about your focus.

Sara
I really can't talk about Nik right now.

Okay? And you never answered my
question about the safe deposit box.

Phil

He told me. Do you think that I'd
leave my comfortable retirement
and help you through this
hell of a mess if she'd already
written the damn book?

Sara

I have to go now. Would you
tell Nik where I am?

Phil

You tell him.

Sara

I can't right now.

Phil

Yes, you can.

It was a chilly October day, and Sara inhaled the familiar, damp air before she stepped into her cab for the hour-long ride to the East End. She'd booked a room from the airport at the Donovan Hotel, near Spitalfields Market just blocks away from her family's old flat. She clutched an old bank envelope that Anna-Kath had used at the airport to write down every place she remembered going as a child in their London neighborhood.

Once off the expressway, they drove through narrow roads lined with pubs, shops, and rowhouses as they made their way to the East End. At a stoplight, Sara rolled down the window, breathing in more of that cool, humid air, soaking in everything British around her. Pubs with their unique names like "Flogger and Jam," hanging baskets overflowing with flowers, red double-deckers, and eclectic street art, the modern mixed with old English charm. She couldn't stop smiling.

After she dropped off her luggage at the hotel, she headed straight for her family's old flat. She wandered a bit and then let her GPS guide her. The architecture and the feel of these streets were all familiar to her, but there was nothing she recognized with certainty until she turned onto Phelps Street. Her pulse quickened as she saw the sign for Tilney Preparatory Academy, where her father had been headmaster.

Sara stood in front of the brown-brick building and the high, wrought-iron fence and watched students in blue blazers milling about, talking and eating lunch. When their mother had a shift at the hospital, she and Anna-Kath would walk from their primary school to wait for their father to finish work here, and then they would all walk home together. Sometimes they would read or do homework at a small, wooden table in the main office waiting for him to finish, where a plump secretary who wore wide, floral dresses and smelled like sausage gave them biscuits to eat on Fridays.

The gate looked exactly the same, although the lettering of the school's sign looked modernized. She wondered who sat in her father's office now. Were any teachers or office staff still the same? She touched the gate and leaned her forehead gently against it. The iron felt warm from the sun. The light from the trees turning a golden pink from the colored leaves.

She knew the way to her family's flat now, though this section of town had never looked quite like this. Rather than being the somewhat seedy place it was twenty years ago, the effects of gentrification were everywhere. As she turned on Allerton Road, all the same buildings were there, but many had new storefronts. Other places had been completely gutted and repurposed as upscale cafés, art galleries, and chic clothing shops. In spite of some shiny new store fronts and new businesses, the character, the grittiness, the determination of the East End still felt like home to her. And oh, how the street art still sang. It was more vibrant, more beautiful than ever. She stopped in front of a woman's face painted on a garage, her expression full of surety and hope. Shades of blue sprayed out in a halo around her curly, black hair. Her eyes knew something important, but they weren't saying what.

A block down the road, Sara found her family's favorite Indian restaurant, Chaakoo. She wondered how that little place had survived all the redevelopment. She walked in and breathed the heady mix of saffron, cumin, and curry. She ordered lamb biryani and sat next to a window, watching people walk by. Her food came with the garlic naan her father often bought. She still felt the ache of his betrayal. Wondered why she still carried his love letter to her mother.

She held tightly to the fact that she and Ann were loved and cherished at home. That was something worth holding onto, even if there were things about her parents that she may never understand. She ate and cried and ate some more, trying to gather the courage to walk to her old home, just four blocks down the road. She ordered tea and sipped it slowly, trying to calm her jumble of emotions.

She paid her bill and slowly walked down the street. That's when she saw a refurbished building across the street with a big sign: "Flats for Let." Something inexplicable drew her inside. She asked to see one of the flats, and then found herself reading through a short-term lease on a furnished one-bedroom flat.

What if she stayed for a couple of months? She needed a place to finish her book. She was yards from where her own story began. And they had a flat available in two days. The idea held a strange sort of right-ness.

She picked up a pen and signed the lease.

Too impulsive?

Maybe.

Phil would tell her to go home and finish her book.

But wait…maybe she *was* home.

She knew she could do it. She knew she could finish *Ellery* right there in the East End, free from distractions and only steps away from where her father wrote.

But Phil was going to kill her.

Well, he didn't need to know just yet.

She sat in the lobby of her new building and texted Nik.

Texts on Wednesday, Oct 16, 1:45 PM

Sara
I didn't open it.

Nik
You what?

Sara
I walked right up to the bank
and decided I couldn't do it.
I'm going to finish the book.

Nik
Where are you?

Sara
I'm sitting one block away from
my family's flat in the East End.

Nik
You went home.

Sara
Yes. I thought I would stay for a few
days, but I've decided to finish the
book here. I don't know if it makes
any sense, but it feels right.

Nik
I know we talked about space, but an
entire ocean feels like a lot right now.

Sara
I know.

Nik
I have Gatsby. Bernie had to
leave town for the weekend. I
can take care of him for now.

Sara
Thank you.

Nik
Are you ready for what you'll find?

Sara
That's not a requirement anymore.

Nik
Remember your mum's collage.

Sara
?

Nik
We're never just one piece.

She tightened her grip on her phone. She missed him already. She tried to shake it off. She drank some water and then began her walk down the street. Finally, she stopped in front of a red brick building still named The Aston. She recognized the old, carved, wooden doors and the large, brass handles. It was home.

She stepped inside.

CHAPTER 40

Deliver me from writers who say the way they live doesn't matter. I'm not sure a bad person can write a good book. If art doesn't make us better, then what on earth is it for?

ALICE WALKER

Sara's old building was now a mix of residential flats and small businesses. The first level contained a modern art gallery, and the other side housed a small, organic grocery store that smelled of citrus and coffee. She slowly walked up the stairs to her family's second-story flat. She thought of her family holding the same banister as they walked up and down the stairs each day, skipping steps and counting steps and later her father's slow, labored steps.

She stopped at her family's door, number 208. She touched the numbers and wondered who lived there now. Maybe it wouldn't hurt to knock. Maybe they'd let her take a look inside.

She knocked a few times, but no one answered.

A door swung open across the hall.

"Hello, deary. I don't think they're home." A petite, elderly woman stood in her doorway holding an obese, orange cat. She wore a powder blue dress suit with pearls and a diamond flower brooch near her shoulder.

She looked prepared to go somewhere important, except for the purple house slippers on her feet.

"It's okay," said Sara. "I don't even know them. I used to live here as a child and was just…you know…*remembering*." She looked back at number 208 and then turned back to the woman. "You look familiar. Have you lived here long? Maybe you'd remember my family. Jack and Cassandra Grayson?" Sara showed the woman an old picture of her family on her phone.

"Oh dear. He's the one that was sick…yes." She clicked her tongue. "Oh. So sad. Come in, come in. We'll chat. I'll make tea."

She remembered the woman now. Yes…Mrs. Clegg. She'd sit with Sara and Anna-Kath on occasion and serve them Scottish treats called Lucky Tatties. She remembered trying to find them at a store after they moved back to the States, and no one knew what they were talking about, and Sara cried and told her mother she wanted to go home to London.

Sara walked in her flat and felt like she'd gone back in time. The place was a holy sanctum to the late Margaret Thatcher. There were framed photos of the former prime minister, decorative plates, political buttons, a bronze bust, and a ceramic handbell with her image.

"She's my fourth cousin, twice removed. Practically a sister," said Mrs. Clegg with pride. "We almost met at a wedding once, but she was detained—that mess in the Falkland Islands. I've never forgiven Argentina for that."

Sara sat on a pink, velvet sofa next to a glass coffee table with a crack in the middle while Mrs. Clegg prepared tea in the kitchen.

The large cat moved uncomfortably close to Sara on the couch. She saw a tag on her collar: Maggie. Sara scooted away.

Mrs. Clegg returned and began pouring the tea. Sara asked, "I know it was a long time ago, but did you know my parents very well?"

"Oh yes. Lovely couple." She placed a powdered cookie on Sara's plate. "My neighbors for eight or nine years, I'd say, until the sad thing with your father...." Mrs. Clegg looked down into her tea. "Much too young. I'd watch you and your sister sometimes. Of course I may not look it, but I'm eighty-five now and still quite sharp." She tapped her temple for emphasis, leaving a dab of powdered sugar in its place.

"Mrs. Clegg, do you happen to know a Meredith Lamb—did she live around here or come to my family's home?"

"Doesn't ring a bell, dear." She stirred more sugar in her tea.

"Maybe you knew my father's sister, Mary Grayson?" Sara sipped her tea. It was hot, but bitter. She wondered if it was reheated.

"Oh dear, yes—I mean, no. Well, she used to come around more, but then she got married and moved away. Pretty thing and so sweet, but not right in the head, that one. Your mum and Mary were quite a comfort to me after the IRA tried to kill Cousin Margaret with the bomb at the hotel. Quite trammeled me, that one." Mrs. Clegg sipped some tea and added more sugar. "Of course, that was before the burglary. Awful time, don't you know."

Sara raised her eyebrows. "Burglary? What burglary?"

"Oh, the one at your flat, of course. All that commotion and your dear mum crying, and the police there rootling for evidence—"

"What?" Sara had no memory of this, and she wasn't quite sure she could count on Mrs. Clegg's. "When was this?"

"Hmm. Let's see. It was just before Margaret's second volume of her memoir came out, *Path to Power*. Perhaps 1994? Have you read Margaret?"

"I'm sorry. No."

Mrs. Clegg dabbed her eyes with a lavender handkerchief. "Ousted by her *own party.*"

"Can you tell me more about the burglary?" Sara's father had died in 1994. She was seven.

"Oh...well...your parents came home one day, and the whole place had been ransacked. It was something terrible, just terrible. More tea, dear?"

"But I'm sure I would have remembered something like that. And I don't remember anything missing from our home."

"It was during the school day, and apparently not much was actually taken from your flat, though it was a wreck. Mostly your father's computer and his writings were gone and some cash, of course. Police suspected it was some of those punk druggies."

"Are you sure about this?"

"Well, it might have been Margaret's first memoir. She was so accomplished—it's a lot to remember."

"My parents always said my father lost his writing in a small fire at the school."

"Well I don't know about that. Maybe. I just know it shook everyone up on the floor, and your mother acted like she knew exactly who was responsible, and I said, "You can't go around blaming everything on Margaret, you know." She looked sternly at Sara. "Crime actually went down during her first term.""

Sara left Mrs. Clegg's more confused than when she had arrived. Why had her parents never told her about the burglary? It made sense to keep it from them when they were young, but certainly it would have come up later. Was the story about the fire at her father's school just a cover for the burglary?

Perhaps there was someone at her dad's school who remembered him.

&

Classes had already dismissed, and only a few students lingered around the courtyard. Sara went to the main office, where a tired looking admin intently stirred a bowl of Asian noodles in a Styrofoam cup. He wore a knit tie, like something made by Molly Weasley, with a crumpled shirt in need of pressing.

"Excuse me?" said Sara.

He answered in a jaded tone, his eyes still fixed on his noodles. "The complaint cards regarding the Lady Gaga song at the boys' choir concert are on the counter." He blew on his noodles and stirred some more.

"Um, sorry, no…." She cleared her throat. "My father was the headmaster here more than twenty years ago, and I just wondered if there was anyone here who might have known him. Jack Grayson—or John Grayson?"

His face relaxed. "Hmm, I can check with Mr. Trodding. I do know the name though. We have a bench in memory of him. It's in the inner courtyard if you'd like to take a look." He took a bite of noodles and pointed with his fork to the double doors outside the office.

Sara walked into a spacious courtyard, filled with birch trees, leafy shrubs, and chrysanthemums in bloom. She found her father's bench under a droopy cherry tree, its leaves a pinkish-orange. A plaque on the bench read, "In memory of a beloved teacher, Headmaster John Charles Grayson III"

She traced her father's name with her fingers, wishing she knew more about him. She had her own memories, stories from her mother, and his writing notebook, but it felt like so little.

"Can I help you, miss?"

Sara looked up to see an older gentleman in a brown. tweed suit walking toward her. He had sparse hair on top, but a full moustache, and he held a brown hat. "Bertie said you were asking about John Grayson."

"I'm his daughter, Sara."

"Of course, you are, dearie. I see you have his eyes." He smiled. "Matthew Trodding." He reached for her hand and motioned for her to sit down.

Sara sat on her father's bench and ran her fingers along the curved iron armrest.

"A great fellow, your dad. We worked together for several years here." He turned his hat around his finger as he spoke. "You and I have met

before, of course, but you were a little tike, and I was much better looking." He wheezed a bit as he laughed.

Sara held the edges of the bench with both hands and tightened them
against the smooth wood as she listened, wishing to create a conduit to
her father.

"You know, some folks like your dad arrive here all puffed up with
their pedigree and fancy education—all mouth and no trousers—but not
your dad. He came here to work, to make a difference. Always thought
we'd lose him when he became a famous writer, he was such a good one,
you know." He stopped twirling his hat and looked pensive. "Never
thought we'd lose him the other way. He was a good friend."

Sara nodded. Her throat felt tight, and she swallowed hard. She had
arrived fueled with questions, but now a deep melancholy settled in her
chest, and she found it hard to speak. She looked at the oldest trees in the
courtyard and envied their time with her father—envied whatever knowledge they had that she didn't.

She turned to Mr. Trodding. "What did he like to talk about?"

"What's that?"

"Like at lunch or at tea—when it wasn't about work and you were just
chatting. What did he *talk* about?" Sara couldn't explain it—this sudden
longing to know her father as an adult, to have a relationship with him as
a grown woman. To speak to him if she could, face-to-face, sitting under
this cherry tree.

Mr. Trodding smoothed his moustache thoughtfully with his fingers.
"Well…you, of course, and your mum and sister. You were his world."

Sara nodded.

"And the Labour Party."

"The *Labour Party*?"

Mr. Trodding began chuckling a deep laugh that rose up and out
of him into full blown wheezing laughter. "It was well-known among
Jack's friends that if Jesus himself had been on the Conservative ticket,

Jack Grayson would have still voted Labour." Mr. Trodding exploded in laughter again.

Sara couldn't help laughing along with him. This small gift of knowledge felt like an enormous treasure, and her heart felt lighter than it had in weeks.

Mr. Trodding sighed and placed his hat back on his head. "Of course, it was the same with Meredith."

Sara felt a sudden jab straight to her chest, and her breath caught short. "Meredith?"

He chuckled. "Those two had a lot in common, and when Meredith worked here, they were inseparable. She volunteered here most afternoons."

Sara swallowed hard. "Right." She already knew this basic fact, but the word "inseparable" made her feel queasy.

"Yes, quite a good teacher's assistant. Your father helped her get the job, of course."

"Meredith Lamb?"

"Ah, yes, that was her married name."

Sara's heart sank further. So, it really was a work romance, only worse—Meredith was married too. She closed her eyes. "Did they know each other a long time?"

Mr. Trodding laughed heartily. "Well, a lifetime, I'd say."

"Oh. Old friends then." Sara began to scratch her arms uncomfortably. Facing the truth was more painful than she anticipated. Why did she think she could do this alone?

Maybe it was time to go now.

Don't be ridiculous. She had come this far. She had to ask.

"Mr. Trodding, this is a delicate subject, but I really do need to know, how *close* were Meredith and my father?"

"Well, I always admired his devotion to her, no question—"

"I'm sorry, you 'admired' his devotion?"

"Well, as you know, things were never easy for your Aunt Mary, and he wanted her to succeed here."

Sara shook her head. "What? I'm confused. Do you mean my Aunt Mary worked here as well? I'm told she and Meredith were friends, but I didn't know they worked together."

"They are the very same, Ms. Grayson. Meredith went by Meri. M-e-r-i. Everyone called her Meri. She struggled with a mental illness...though I don't recall the name. She wouldn't always take her meds, and sometimes she became quite manic. Had to hospitalize her at one point. She got a little better, but then she'd repeat the whole cycle. Quite difficult. Well, there I go prattling on. I'm sure you know the rest of the story anyway."

Sara sat in stunned silence. Meredith, Mary, *Meri.* The same person? Her aunt? How did she not know?

"How's she managing now?" Mr. Trodding asked. "Lovely woman."

"We lost contact, actually." Sara's mind was whirring through a deluge of questions and answers. There was sheer relief in knowing that her father didn't betray her mother, a light giddiness working its way through her heart.

And then utter confusion.

If Aunt Mary was actually Meredith, then why would she sue Sara's mother, her dead brother's wife? Who does that sort of thing? Something must have happened between her mother and Meri? Did her mother plagiarize Meri, or did Meri plagiarize her mother? Whose work belonged to whom?

Mr. Trodding said that Meri had been mentally ill. How was she doing now? If Sara could get to the bottom of this, maybe she could officially end the recurring questions about her mother's integrity.

Or face some uncomfortable truths.

"Thank you, Mr. Trodding. I have to go now. I'm hoping to find my aunt while I'm here. Soon...I hope."

She hurried across the courtyard but stopped and turned back. "Mr. Trodding, was there ever a fire here, a small one perhaps, that damaged my father's office?"

"Indeed there was, but it was contained to the dining hall, thank goodness. No damage elsewhere."

Sara quickly left the school and flagged down a taxi. She called Ann on the way back to her hotel, filling her in on everything. They cried with relief about their parents, but all of this plagued them with more questions.

"Then who is Carolee Grayson?" asked Ann.

"Maybe she's Aunt Meri's daughter."

"But then why is she named Grayson instead of Lamb?"

"I need to get to Bristol and try and meet them face-to-face."

"Sara, be careful. Aunt Meri may not want to talk to you at all. Maybe there's a good reason Mum always kept us apart. Do you even know what to say?"

"I have no idea."

CHAPTER 41

Creativity is a crushing chore and a glorious mystery. The work wants to be made, and it wants to be made through you.

ELIZABETH GILBERT

The morning drive to Bristol took more than two hours. She had tried calling Phil several times the night before. She left him messages about what she'd learned that day, but he never called back. She really needed to talk to him about Meredith. Did Phil know her or just about her? Would he tell her anything more at this point?

The concierge arranged for a driver named Kalechi. He wore a dark suit, drove a black car, and looked more like a secret service agent than a hired driver, except that he smiled a lot and played the Beach Boys on a continuous loop for the entire drive.

They arrived at Meredith's at 10:00 AM. Sara studied the sign for Carwyn's Lodge and rechecked the address. "Are you sure this is right?" she asked Kalechi.

"Yes ma'am."

Sara had expected a large home or a set of apartment buildings. Instead she was staring at a residential nursing care facility in a modern brick complex. A rush of anxiety filled her chest.

"Want me to walk you in, ma'am?"

Her stomach churned. She took a deep breath. "I'm okay."

She walked inside a spacious lobby filled with sofas, chairs, and overgrown house plants. An old woman in a flowery hat shuffled along in her wellies, spritzing the plants with a spray bottle.

Mrs. Clegg had said Meri wasn't quite "right in her head," and Mr. Trodding mentioned some kind of serious mental illness. What condition would Sara find her in? Would she even talk to her? When Sara was growing up and asked about her father's sister, her mother always said Aunt "Mary" chose to estrange herself from the family, that she'd cut off all contact and moved to Australia and that she hadn't been well. Sara desperately wished Anna-Kath was with her now.

There was an office in the corner of the lobby. She ignored the pounding in her chest and walked over.

A sixty-something woman in SpongeBob scrubs sat behind a counter and wore a nametag that said, "How can Vera assist you today?"

"Hello, I'm here to see Meredith Lamb."

"Just light spritzes, Beadie," she shouted at the woman spraying the plants.

She turned back to Sara and scratched her head with a pencil. "Meredith Lamb, did you say?"

"Yes."

"Only immediate family allowed, dear." She went back to watching a show on her TV, occasionally rolling around in her chair to return patient files to the correct drawers.

"Could you make an exception, please? Meredith is my aunt, and I've come a very long way to see her."

Vera looked up, somewhat annoyed. "Immediate family only, unless you're on the list. Are you on the list?"

Sara sighed. "I doubt that."

"We have strict policies here, *because we care*."

"Could you at least tell me how she's doing? Her current condition?"

"I can't comment on that *because we care*. Have a butter mint on your way out, dear."

Sara took one just to be polite, but when Vera turned away, she grabbed a handful, which made her feel slightly better. She walked slowly to the car, her disappointment settling deep inside.

Kalechi rocked his head to his music. He turned the volume down. "All good, Ms. Sara?"

"Let's try this one." She gave him the address for Carolee Grayson and several mints. GPS showed a fifteen-minute drive. She tapped her feet nervously as they drove, anxiously eating stolen butter mints. What if Carolee wasn't there? What would she say if she *was* there?

They drove into a neighborhood of small rowhouses, with small patches of green grass and an inordinate number of gnomes, ceramic toadstools, and other lawn ornaments. They pulled up to Carolee Grayson's home, number 725 Albert Court. It looked innocent enough, a tan brick house with a pretty stone bench and a bright green front door.

Sara stepped out. Her heart beat faster, and she was ready to throw up the butter mints on the friendly gnome family next door.

Maybe this was a terrible idea. Thea was ready to hire a whole team of investigators. She didn't have to do this. She could drive back to London and send someone else.

She shook out her shoulders. Kalechi leaned out the window. "You look pale, ma'am. Do you want some Coca-Cola? Coke makes everything better."

"I'm fine, thanks," she stammered. The window rolled back up.

I can do this. She pulled her purse up tight against her shoulder and looked up and down the street. That's when she noticed a black sedan idling across the street.

The door opened, and Phil Dvornik stepped out of the car.

CHAPTER 42

*There was another life that I might have
had, but I am having this one.*

KAZUO ISHIGURO

She blinked a few times and then squinted her eyes. "Phil?" She shook her head, trying to make sense of this. He crossed the street. "Phil?"

"Hey, Grayson."

She grasped the front of her shirt, trying to make sense of his being there. "What...what are you doing here? I told you I could handle this and...wait." She pressed her fingers against her mouth. "How did you get this address? Did Anna-Kath talk to you? I don't understand."

Phil scratched the side of his cheek. He took a deep breath. "Carolee lives here—"

"Yeah. But...wait...how do you know that? And how do you know her name? How did you even get here this quickly? And how did you know I'd be here at this time?"

"Your message last night? And if you'd let me get a word in, I can explain."

They stood in front of Sara's car. The window rolled down again as Kalechi leaned over, music wafting out the window. "You need some help, Ms. Sara? You know this man?"

"It's fine. He's okay." The window rolled back up.

"He's my security detail," she joked, but Phil wasn't laughing. He placed a hand on the hood of the car, as if to steady himself. Something was up with Phil. She noticed his V-neck sweater off center, his unruly hair, and red eyes. "Are you okay?"

Phil closed his eyes a moment. All the color drained from his tired, unshaved face. He gestured to the home.

"Carolee—" He cleared his throat. "She goes by Cree. And she's not your father's daughter. Or your mother's." He took another breath as he pulled at his shirt collar. "She's mine. She's my daughter."

Sara's mouth hung open. Her eyes wide, her mind racing and confused. "I don't understand. How…? You? You and my Aunt Meri…?"

"Had a brief relationship. I'd met Cree before, with your mother, but I never knew she was my daughter until six months ago. Meredith *never* told me."

"What? But all this time—*you* could have told me. You let me think my father betrayed my mother—"

"No. I told you from the beginning that your father was no adulterer."

"But gave me no alternative explanation."

Phil looked down. "I couldn't."

"Well, you can now. Please. Explain this one to me."

"Look, there are things I can't explain—"

"No, Phil. I did not come this far to get half-answers." She looked at the house. "Maybe someone in this family will tell me the truth." Sara headed straight for the front door. She knocked firmly. She heard footsteps and then nothing.

"No one's home," Phil called out.

She knocked again. Waited. Nothing.

Phil walked to the porch and tugged on Sara's arm. She wriggled away and knocked again.

"Let's go, Grayson."

Just then the door swung open. A dark-haired, twenty-something woman with heavily tattooed arms opened the door. A swift sense of surprise crossed her face, which she masked immediately. She looked right at Phil, folded her arms, and scrunched her nose up. "Really, Phil? I don't think so." Then she slammed the door.

Sara turned to Phil with wide eyes.

"I told you this was a bad idea," said Phil.

Sara shook her head. "I don't get it."

Phil pulled on his shirt collar. His face looked flushed now. Sara had never seen him look so uncomfortable. "We had a…a disagreement."

The door swung open again. "Is that what you'd call it, Phil?"

He exhaled. "I'm sorry. You were right."

"Yes, I am." Then Cree looked Sara up and down with one hand on her hip.

"Cree," said Phil, "this is Sara Grayson."

"I know who you are." Cree had black, short-cropped hair, a beautiful face, and familiar dark eyes.

Sara looked at Phil and back at Cree. What had she just stepped into?

"She can come in," said Cree, "but not you."

Phil shoved a hand into his thinning hair. "Come on, Cree. Can we talk about this?"

She pressed her lips together, eyeing Phil narrowly. "Fine. Come in… but I'm not ready to talk to you yet."

Sara gripped the strap of her purse tightly as she followed Cree inside.

They walked into a bright front room with turquoise-painted walls. Two faded, yellow chairs faced a vintage, fuchsia love seat on a black and white striped area rug. An array of photography equipment sat in one corner of the room.

Sara felt tingly and weak. She sat on the love seat. She noticed a worn leather satchel on the floor next to her with a tripod poking out. The bag looked somehow familiar. Sara brushed the top of it with her hand.

Cree briskly scooted the bag off to the side along with a stack of art books.

Phil sat across from Sara and turned to Cree. "Could you give us a minute?"

"No. Mum has kept this family from me long enough. I'm not leaving this room." She sat on the edge of the love seat, her colorful arms folded tightly against her white tank-top. She wore ripped boyfriend jeans and—with a few less body piercings—she could model for Abercrombie and Fitch.

Sara's mind raced with questions. She studied the photographs on a nearby bookshelf—pics of her grandmother Charlotte and photos of Cree and a woman together. "Is this your mum?"

"Haven't you seen her before? I've seen pics of you."

"I don't remember her. I don't know why we don't have photos." Sara pressed her fingers against her forehead. "I'm so confused."

"Five minutes, Cree?" Phil asked again.

"Fine." She left the room.

Sara's eyes settled on a framed snapshot leaning against a book. She picked it up and stared intently at it: a college pic of her parents with another man and woman. She'd seen a copy before in her mother's things, but never knew who the others were. As she looked up at Phil and back at the picture, she finally put it together.

She held it up. "This is you, isn't it? Standing next to my mum."

Phil gently swept a finger across the photo. The wrinkles around his eyes etched with pain. "I loved her first. And I loved her last."

Phil touched the photo again and shook his head slowly. "I was a grad student at Georgetown when your mother took my creative writing class. She was beautiful. Brilliant. I asked her to go out with me. She refused, but we started meeting for coffee to talk about her writing. She had talent. I tried to convince her to drop nursing and focus on writing. She said she was too practical for that.

"Jack Grayson was a friend and colleague—same grad program. One night, Jack and I were having a drink at The Tombs, and your mother walked in, and I made the biggest mistake of my life." He handed the photo back to Sara. "I introduced her to Jack." He laughed with his lips pressed tightly, his eyes distant.

"Your mother chose him. Easily. Meri came to visit over spring break. That's her in the photo next to me. Jack set me up with her. We talked, laughed. Nothing more. She was a lot younger than me, and I really wasn't interested. I finished that June and took an editing job in New York. Two years later, Cassie married Jack and moved to London. I married Mira, a nice Croatian-American girl."

Sara rubbed her temples. "But Cree…Meri? That would have been years later. What happened?"

Phil studied his hands. "It's complicated."

"I can handle complicated."

"No. I mean, there are pieces of this related to the settlement. I can't explain all of this to you. I mean *legally* I can't."

Sara shot out of her seat. "Do you see any attorneys around here, Phil? Do you think the place is bugged? What is your insistence in keeping so many secrets? What are you trying to hide?"

"Let's ask my mum." Cree stood in the doorway between the front room in the kitchen, holding her car keys.

"Would she talk to me?" asked Sara.

"I don't know, but we can try. I'll take you there." Her eyes narrowed at Phil, like she was helping Sara just to annoy him.

He held up a hand. "Bad idea."

"She only has months left," said Cree. "What harm can she do now?"

"Ask her lawyers."

"She can't afford lawyers," Cree snapped.

"They'll sue Iris and Cassandra's estate for free. Happily."

"I don't understand," said Sara.

Phil explained, "Part of the nondisclosure agreement of Meredith's lawsuit was her insistence that there be zero contact between her and Cassie or between their children. It's why you and Cree have never met."

"Why would my own aunt want something like that?"

Phil pinched the space between his eyebrows. "Look, I've already told you too much. If Meredith talks, that's one thing, but I still have to be careful."

"I have to see her, Phil. You understand that, don't you?"

"You have no idea what you're getting into, Grayson."

"And who can we blame for that, Phil?" said Cree. Phil shook his head slowly and walked alone into the kitchen.

Sara let her driver know she could meet him later and followed Cree to her red Peugeot. They drove in silence at first. Cree focused on the road, her face stony and difficult to read. She glanced quickly at Sara and back to the road, her hands gripping the steering wheel tightly.

"Why are you a secret, Cree?"

"Funny. I could ask you the same thing." She pulled a visor down with a Slade Art School sticker. "Honestly, I'm so sick of secrets."

"Me too."

"I want to know my brother," said Cree. "That's what the big fight's about. Phil keeps saying to wait."

"Nik?"

"You know him?"

Sara closed her eyes and nodded. "He's worth knowing."

"Phil's too scared to tell him. Says he needs more time."

Sara nodded, pulling her sweater closely around her. "I could try talking to Phil about it. Maybe I can help."

Cree laughed, hollow and sad. "Not holding out hope." They drove another mile in silence. "So, what did Phil tell you about him and my mum?"

"Very little."

"Look, I'll tell you what I know. You can tell me stuff you know. Together, maybe we can come up with, like, twenty percent of what the hell happened to our families."

"That's reaching."

"Ten? Five?"

Sara exhaled slowly. "Cree, what happened to your mum?"

She chewed on her lower lip, her black eyebrows gathered in. "The hallucinations started at university. Schizophrenia, they said. Then later they said it was borderline personality disorder. Who knows? Then the girl went and got mixed up with drugs and alcohol. Made her mental illness impossible to manage. She's been in and out of rehabs for most of her life. On her meds, off her meds. When she's sober she's pretty cool—likes to have fun—kind of a kid at heart. We had some good years in Australia, just the two of us. When she isn't sober, well…" Cree's eyes turned hard. "I didn't have a great childhood. She's hard to live with. She doesn't think straight. They found the brain tumor last year. It's inoperable. Now and then she has a good day."

"I'm sorry."

"For what?'

"Everything."

"Your mum saved me. Your parents and my mum had some kind of falling out years ago, before I was born, and my mum always said how horrible Cassandra Bond was. I knew she was famous. I'd see her on the telly sometimes. She always seemed nice. When I was fourteen and we were about to get the boot again, I found your mum at a book signing in Melbourne and told her who I was. She helped us, even after Mum had burned through the money from the settlement. Mum hated her, but she helped. Found a way to get money to us without my mum knowing who it was from. She tracked down my mum's Aunt Evie who stepped in to help care for me. Then Aunt Cass paid for art school. Photography. I have my first real show next month in Dover."

Cree reached into her bag and pulled out a card about the show. She handed it to Sara. She realized she'd seen her photography before. Her mother had some postcards with some of her pieces. Cree did street photography and was clearly quite talented.

"Once I was an adult and had my own place, your mum would come to visit me. She even came to my degree show in London at the Slade. That's when I met Phil. She started bringing him along on visits when they were in town. I had no idea he was my father. He didn't know. Aunt Cass didn't know. All my mum ever told me about my father was that he was an American, a friend of my Uncle Jack's that lived in NYC, and that it was a one-off. No name on the birth certificate. Nothing."

Cree turned onto a quieter road past golden farmland and stone fences.

"So how did you find out?" asked Sara.

"So, Mum's dementia—from the brain tumor—it's strange. There's things she's open about now that she wasn't before, but the truth and fiction are hard to sort out. After Aunt Cass died, she started talking about my father and told me he was a powerful editor in New York and his name was Phil, and I'm thinking she must really be out of her mind. She couldn't possibly mean the Phil I knew. I didn't know they'd ever met. Then she showed me that college picture you saw at the house, pointed to Phil, and told me that he's my father.

"I sat there thinking she is really, truly mad. I had Phil's email address, and so I just decided to tell him everything and said, 'Crazy, right?' But Phil didn't say anything back at first. Then when he replied he just asked, 'When's your birthday?' That's when I was like, holy shit, this could be real.

"Phil came here a week later. Blood test proved it. He told me that in '94 my mum showed up in his office with a manuscript she wanted to sell his new publishing company. They went out for drinks, and one thing led to another. Phil was married and felt really guilty, plus he says he read one chapter the next day—just one—and refused to publish the book. Mum was furious about it and threatened to tell Phil's wife if he didn't publish the book, but Phil wouldn't budge. He told me it would have been 'impossible' to publish but he wouldn't tell me why. He confessed to his wife himself. They divorced a year later. Phil wouldn't admit it, but he also lost a major contract for his new company because *Silence in Stepney* went on to do incredibly well. Mum never told him she was pregnant. 'Phil's big loss,' she said, only she wasn't talking about me. She was talking about the book."

Cree tightened her hands on the steering wheel again and increased her speed by ten kilometers. She took the next three curves too fast and nearly took out a roaming peacock. She said little more the rest of the drive.

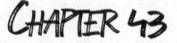

CHAPTER 43

*Writing a novel is like driving a car at night. You can only see as
far as your headlights, but you can make the whole trip that way.*

E. L. DOCTOROW

When they walked to the front office, Vera was watching *The East
Enders* while sharpening a basket of tiny pencils.

She glanced at Cree. "Sign, please." She pushed a clipboard towards
her. Cree signed her name, but for Sara she signed "Billie Donovan."

"Best not to use your own name, right?" whispered Cree.

"Your mum's in the atrium, love," said Vera. She popped another pencil in the sharpener as they walked away.

"But how do you know that name?"

"My mum would tell me stories about—"

"A crime fighting girl with a dog named Honey?"

"Yeah."

"My dad told me the same stories."

Their eyes locked for a brief moment.

They stopped at the entrance of a grassy courtyard with patio tables
and benches. A small water fountain trickled water around a chubby angel
statue with a missing nose.

A few residents sorted colors on pegboards. Another worked on a simple puzzle. Ten yards away, a woman sat alone on a bench with her eyes half-closed. Cree pointed to her. "That's Mum."

Sara stared with fascination—and a little fear. She had long, curly, auburn hair with a few inches of gray roots. She wore a long, green cardigan with gray sweatpants and black Crocs.

"How old is she?"

"Fifty-eight. But you'd never guess it, right? Doesn't look a day younger than seventy-five."

It was true. Her weathered face looked hard and weary, her eyes vacant.

Here was her father's *sister*. Someone who grew up with him, who had memories and stories about him somewhere behind those distant eyes.

"Some days I have to remind her who I am. Other times, she's more lucid."

They pulled up some plastic chairs. She tapped her shoulder. "Mum, it's me, Cree."

Meredith didn't respond.

"Mum?"

She opened her eyes. One shot open wider than the other. "Oh poppet, what have you done to your arms?"

Cree whispered, "She fixates on my tattoos, like every time."

"Mum, this is Jack's daughter, Sara. Your niece." Meri stared past them. "Hey, Mum?" She reached for her arm, trying to get Meri to meet her eyes. "This is Sara. Right here."

Sara's heart raced. She had so many questions and emotions. She cleared her throat. "Hi Aunt Meri." She pulled out some leaves she'd collected that morning. "My sister said you used to take us on walks to collect leaves."

Sara set a few in her lap. Meri ran her fingers along the veins of the leaves. She looked at Sara. She scrunched her eyebrows together. "Jack's eyes."

"Yes. I have his eyes."

"Chestnut. Jack had a horse named Chestnut."

"Yes. He did." She pressed a hand against her heart, hoping she might remember more. "He told me stories about Chestnut."

"Chestnut was a good horse." Meri began sorting through the leaves. She cast a few aside and kept others. "Jack loved Chestnut. And Honey. Silly dog."

Sara smiled. She knew about Honey too.

"Jack's a good writer. But I'm better." Meredith began ripping the leaves in little pieces.

"Mum, stop ripping those up. Sara brought those."

"It's okay." She sighed and turned back to Meri. "Anna-Kath told me about the leaves and said our mum would buy you Pixy Stix from the US and we'd eat them together." Sara reached in her purse. "I found some here." She opened a bag and handed several to Meri.

She took them and clutched several in each hand. She didn't look up. Then she dropped them in her lap and began opening a few in the middle, letting the colored powder spill out.

Suddenly she began aggressively tearing them open, the colorful sugar spilling onto her sweater, her lap, and the grass. She stared at all the torn pieces. "Jack stole my book. He stole my stories."

Sara looked at Cree.

Cree shrugged her shoulders. "What do you mean, Mum?"

"They were *mine*. Jack took them." Meri's voice grew louder, more animated. "Chestnut was good. Jack was bad. He stole my book. So, I took it back."

Cree leaned towards Sara. "Sorry. She rambles like she's smashed."

Sara scooted her chair closer to Meri, trying to make eye contact. "My dad stole your book?"

"Jack died."

"Aunt Meri, what about my mum? Did she take any of your book? Your stories?"

"Who's your mum?"

"Cassandra. Jack's wife."

"Oh. So pretty. She was nice to me." Her fingers played absently with the bits of paper on her lap. "Jack took my book. I took it back. Aldrich helped me." Then she slapped at her thighs in agitation. Powder stuck to her hands. She stopped suddenly and then studied her hands. She licked the powder off one of her fingers.

Sara whispered to Cree, "Who's Aldrich?"

"Aldrich Lamb. Her ex. Total wanker. Died of a drug overdose. She only kept his name 'cause she published her book with it."

Sara pressed her hands to her forehead. She thought of the burglary Mrs. Clegg described, how the thieves only took her father's computer, his writing, some cash. How her mother seemed to know exactly who did it. But did her father actually take something of Meri's? Whose work belonged to which writer?

Meri was licking all her fingers now, pieces of ripped leaves sticking to her hands, which she spit out. Sara handed her another Pixy Stick. "Aunt Meri, do you have Jack's book?"

She ripped the stick and threw it down, her eyes fiery. "It's *my* book!" Everyone in the atrium turned to look at them.

Then Meri's face turned blank again. She saw the Pixy dust on her sweater, like she was discovering it for the first time, and licked more of it off her fingers. "Chestnut. We'd ride fast. Jack died."

Sara handed her more sticks. Meri smiled, her lips and teeth bright blue. Sara took a deep breath. "Okay then Meri...where's *your* book? The one Jack took? Do you know where it is?"

She ripped the new Pixy Stick in her lap. She licked more off her palms and smiled. "*Everywhere.*"

Sara exhaled and rested her head in her hands.

"Sorry," said Cree as she started picking up Pixy Stix wrappers off the grass. She tried to sweep the powder off her sweater, but Meri slapped her hand away.

"It's mine. Go away," she yelled. She began rocking back and forth, her face now red and agitated. "It's my book," she screamed. "My book!"

A large nurse in too-tight scrubs came over and patted Meri's hand. "Going off 'bout that book again, Miss Meri? How 'bout some telly in your room?" She helped Meri stand up. "Think I'll take her back now." She shook the powder off Meri's cardigan and walked her back inside the building.

The two sat there. Neither saying anything. Sara's head hurt. How could she possibly defend her parents' integrity with two dead parents, one insane aunt, a web of three writers, and a slew of secrets no one could explain? She had no idea where to go from here. She sat unmoving in the orange, plastic chair, staring at the green film floating in the fountain.

She looked at Cree, whose eyes looked just as weary. There was everything to talk about and nothing to say. "I'm not sure what to do next."

Cree pointed to a large facility schedule hanging next to the double doors. "Looks like Tai Chi at three. Or we could work on one of those pegboards."

Sara smiled weakly. "I was kind of holding out for bingo at five."

"I kill at bingo. Won a heating pad here once—with *three* heat settings."

Both stared aimlessly at the little fountain cherub with the missing nose.

"I won a Spice Girls poster at church bingo," said Sara.

"Your church gave away a Spice Girls poster?"

"It was supposed to be Jesus and the apostles."

"Which one was your favorite?"

"Apostle?"

"Spice Girl."

"Scary Spice."

"Really?"

"No. I didn't know them. Anna-Kath told me to say Scary Spice."

"That's sad."

"I know."

"Peter's cool."

"Who's Peter?"

"The apostle."

"Not a Spice Girl?"

"Didn't make it."

They finally got up, moving slowly through the lobby, past Vera who yelled at the television, "Be a real man, you bloody tosser!"

They sat in Cree's car. She put the key in the ignition but didn't start it. She stared pensively across the parking lot. "I need a cigarette. You have one?"

"Sorry. I don't smoke."

"Of course, you don't."

"Pixy Stick?"

Cree rolled her eyes but took one. They each opened the end of their sticks and shook the tangy powder into their mouths.

Cree shrugged. "Not bad."

Sara opened more sticks. And another bag. They went through dozens, like two druggies getting doped up on flavored sugar.

Sara opened her last one.

Cree looked in the rearview and stuck her tongue out. Bright purple.

"Hey, you have a tongue piercing," said Sara. "Did it hurt?"

"Like bloody hell."

Sara stuck her tongue out in her mirror. "I'm more purple than you." Maybe it was the jet lag or the sugar rush, but Sara started laughing and couldn't stop...and Cree started laughing too.

"You didn't know a single Spice Girl?"

"I read *Publisher's Weekly* and *Writer's Digest*. I went to writing conferences with my mum."

"I didn't know my cousin was such a plonker."

"What the hell is a plonker?" They started laughing again. Sara's stomach hurt, her eyes wet from laughing. A security guard rapped on Cree's window with her knuckle. They both jumped and started laughing again.

"No loitering around here. Private facility."

"Yes ma'am," said Cree, with a remarkably straight face. Then they both busted out laughing again. They wiped their eyes as Cree pulled out of the parking lot. Sara gathered their wrappers and stuffed them back in the empty bag.

She sighed and leaned her head back into her seat. Day two in the UK, and Sara had more questions now than she did twenty-four hours ago.

CHAPTER 44

*The greater the artist, the greater the doubt. Perfect confidence
is granted to the less talented as a consolation prize.*

ROBERT HUGHES

Sara's stomach felt unsettled on the drive back to Cree's. All that sugar
didn't help her tired, jet-lagged body. Quiet crept back into the car as
Sara replayed the conversation with Meredith in her mind.

"Cree, do you know much about the lawsuit—your mum accusing
my mum of plagiarism?"

"I grew up believing it was true. That your mum stole from my mum.
It's what she told me. She said it's why she got so much money from the
settlement."

"And now?"

"Once I finally met your mum, I couldn't believe it anymore. She's
just not like that."

"And she never said anything about it today—she only talked about
my dad stealing her book and her taking it back."

"She's not in her right mind."

"The thing is...there was a burglary at my parents' flat, years ago
when my dad was sick, and all of his writing was stolen. Everything. My

parents always said Dad lost his work in a fire at his school, but it was all a cover." Cree took a turn too quickly, and Sara clutched the car door.

"All his writing was taken?"

"Yeah. And your mom just said she and Aldrich took *her* writing back. What if the lawsuit, the burglary, the settlement—what if that was really about my father? Do you think he took something from your mum? I mean, maybe my mum was protecting my father when she settled. Maybe that's why she settled for so much money."

Cree gripped the steering wheel with both hands, her eyes focused on the road. "I don't know what to think anymore. Sometimes my mum speaks the truth, but so many times it's her twisted version of it—"

"Does your mum keep her old writing somewhere—anything in storage?"

"She's kept some file cabinets and a few boxes at my place."

"Can I take a look?"

"I don't think you'll find anything, but yeah. It's mostly her attempt to write her second great novel. *Stepney* won all these awards, and she never could replicate it."

When they got to Cree's place, Phil was gone. Cree took Sara to a tiny back room with even more photography equipment and stacks of prints. Floral wallpaper was stripped from the walls, like a renovation in progress. She pulled a few boxes out of a closet and pointed to an old, metal, four-drawer filing cabinet in the corner.

"I'm taking my camera out for some street work. I'll leave you to it."

Sara stood alone in the tiny room. What was she looking for, exactly? She wasn't sure. Something that could prove her mother took nothing from Meri? Meri claimed Jack stole something from her, but she told Sara outright that she "took it back." And Mrs. Clegg told her that Cassandra seemed certain who had burglarized their apartment. What kind of thief only steals files, a satchel full of writing, and her father's computer? It had to be Meri.

She froze.

She pictured her father's worn leather satchel. The one he carried with him everywhere.

She went back to the front room and stopped at the familiar brown leather bag leaning against the bookshelf in the front room. She knelt down next to it. Could it be? She ran her finger across the top. She looked for the deep scratch on the back side. It was there—exactly where she remembered. She emptied a tripod, a few lenses, and folders and found the second deep scratch on an inner pocket.

"A small Scottish dragon got hold of this one," her father had told her and Anna-Kath. "See the scratch from its young claws?" She smiled at the memory and lifted the bag onto her lap. She lifted the satchel to her face and breathed in that worn leather smell. She could see the strap clearly across her father's chest, the bag bouncing on his back as they walked home, Sara's hand securely in her father's warm hand.

She came back to the present and stood up sharply.

If Cree unknowingly had this, what else did she have?

Sara returned to the file cabinet boxes and began emptying them in earnest.

She sorted through drafts of writing she didn't recognize. She discovered full manuscripts of Meredith's *Silence in Stepney*. She moved to the filing cabinets. She found stories with Jack and Meri's names on them as co-authors, dating back to when Jack would have been in prep school. She set these aside. She found legal pads of notes and handwriting she didn't recognize. Some work had Meri's name with Aldrich Lamb. It was dated after her father's death.

Some files were labeled, but mostly the drawers were a hodgepodge of writing notes and stories. She found bits of research, articles about crime scenes and police work. Meredith even tried to write some fantasy. There were press clippings about *Silence in Stepney* and copies of critical reviews in one file. Stashed in the back of the bottom drawer, Sara pulled out a rectangular box, like something designed for a birthday cake. It was wrapped tightly in an old plastic Hewett's grocery bag.

She remembered the small Hewett's market by their East End flat where they bought groceries. She ripped open the tightly knotted bag and opened up a stack of faded yellow legal pads with hundreds of hand-written pages, all heavily marked up. There was no title, but she instantly recognized the tiny, messy handwriting. Sara's heart raced as she went to her purse and pulled out her father's letter to her mother and compared the handwriting to the legal pads. It was the same.

She started reading chapter one about an East End police detective named Brandt Donovan. As she moved through the first chapter, familiar details leapt from the pages. She jumped to another section and found the same familiar story. Though the character's names were different, every-thing else was the same. On her father's pages the main character was Brandt Donovan, but he was the same detective from *Silence in Stepney*, and the pages were nearly identical to *Stepney*. On the fifth legal pad, she saw editing notes in the margin in her mother's handwriting. She flipped through more pages and saw hearts and leaves scribbled in the margins. Sara's own scribbles—her early attempts at "'lustrations" that she loved to do as a child. This draft also had a different title: *The Shallows of Shoreditch*.

In that moment, Sara knew with complete certainty that *Silence in Stepney* was not Meredith's and not her mother's.

It was her father's book.

His words.

The pages she held felt so undeniably filled with him that she began to cry. She clutched the pages to her face. She smelled them, held the paper against her cheek, anxious to feel what he touched, what he created. She ran her fingers along his sentences and felt like he was suddenly alive and real and with her.

It was his. All along. No wonder Mum kept it close to her. She found more of her little drawings in the margins and sometimes a note for grocery items like marmalade and Earl Grey and "I love you, Jack" written at the top of a page.

At the bottom of the stack was the beginning of another book. An outline and maybe a hundred pages of text. She read the first several pages and flipped quickly through the rest. She gasped, her fingers clutching the legal pad, her breathing fast and shallow. She dropped it on the floor, as if it had suddenly burned her fingers.

Cache Carter. Her mother's first book. Her first series.

But in her father's hand.

She took a deep breath and picked it up again. The pages read just like her mother's book, but after a hundred pages, there was nothing. She turned back to the prologue. It was the same, almost word-for-word, as her mother's. There were notes for the book's sequels—some of them with details that had appeared later in the *Cache Carter* series. Other ideas were completely different, including characters she'd never heard of.

Then she found another legal pad. It picked up where the last hundred pages had stopped. It had only ten more pages, but everything was reversed—the prose was *in her mother's hand,* and the notes and corrections were her father's. His notes were shaky. His handwriting less certain. There was a medication note at the top.

He was sick. Her mom was clearly writing *Cache Carter* now, but not dictating what her father said. Her father's editing notes were about her mother's writing. She was the author now. That much was clear.

Then it stopped. There was nothing else of *Cache Carter* or any writing.

Sara held the pages close to her heart. "Oh Mum…*Cache* was Dad's book…but *you* finished it?"

She closed her eyes, trying to make sense of it all. She pictured her father writing late on his computer in their bedroom at his old mahogany desk, wearing a knit beanie after all his hair was gone.

She remembered her mother writing in their new apartment in the States, and Sara stomping in one evening. "Dad's the writer, not you,

Mum." Her mum looked at her, a permanent grief in her tired, baggy eyes. "I couldn't agree more, sweet-pea." Then she wrapped her in her arms and whispered, "And you'll be the best writer of us all." Then she went back to her computer. Sara winced at the memory, knowing now that, at the time, her mum only did it for him.

Sara could understand that better than anyone now. She imagined her mother trying to trust her husband, trying to fulfill his own dying wish, and she suddenly felt a closeness to her parents fill her soul in a new depth of understanding.

Sara heard Cree walk in the front door with Phil. She saw it was getting dark outside. She listened to their steps in the hall, heard running water in the kitchen, the clank of plates and glasses. She sat on the floor, her back against peeling wallpaper, embracing old legal pads and a worn-out leather bag.

Phil opened the door to the room and flipped on a light. Sara wiped her eyes and squinted against the light.

"What the hell, Grayson? You look terrible." He pointed his bent finger at her. "I warned you not to go see her. That woman lives in an alternate reality."

Sara wiped her eyes against her shoulder, her arms full of her father's work—and her mother's. "No, Phil. I..." Her legs felt weak, her head woozy. "Want to sit?"

Phil pulled up a short stool next to Sara. He studied the leather satchel she held. "Wait, that's not...?"

"It's my dad's. And all of this. Well...most of it." Sara sat up and gestured to the stacks of legal pads, handing one to Phil.

Sara opened a box and unloaded more piles of legal pads onto the floor. Then she handed him the stack that contained *Stepney*.

He fumbled for his reading glasses in his shirt pocket and clumsily put them on as he looked at the legal pads below. He raised his eyebrows and then furrowed them as he saw *Shoreditch*—or *Stepney*—on top with her father's name clearly on the front.

He flipped through the pages, stacking the legal pads on a card table beside him. She saw the recognition of the *Stepney* pages spread across his widening eyes, then a quick intake of breath. He quickly wiped the beads of sweat off his forehead with the back of his hand. His mouth open, his own breathing labored now.

"How?" He shook his head. "How?" He pressed his hands into his forehead. "Where did you find all this?"

"This file drawer belongs to Meredith."

He looked away, his eyes lost. He took off his reading glasses and rubbed his eyes. "Then you know."

Cree knocked on the door and popped in. "Hey, I picked up Indian… oh…" She stopped. She looked around. "Whatever. I'll go."

"Cree, stop," said Phil. "Come back." Sara gestured for her to come in. She sat stiffly on the floor next to Sara, carefully eyeing the stacks of paper.

Sara pointed to her father's first manuscript and then looked at Phil. "*Silence in Stepney* was my father's book, wasn't it? I'd know my dad's handwriting anywhere—"

He put his hand up to stop her. "I know it too, and I know he drafted longhand before he typed. And I know this book. He started *Stepney* at Georgetown with me. I helped him revise the first three chapters…which is why they're so damn good."

He looked at the pages of Jack Grayson piled on the floor and picked up a stack. "It's also how I knew this wasn't Meri's book when she showed up at my office with it, claiming it was her own and wanting me to publish it." He turned to Cree. "That's why I refused to publish it. I knew she was trying to sell Jack's work as her own."

Cree stared past Phil, her arms folded and her lips screwed up tightly to one side. "So, Aldrich Lamb helped her pass it off as her own work."

Sara nodded. "I think so. They changed some names and the title, but everything else is basically the same."

Cree's fingers played absently with the line of earrings that snaked up the edges of her ears. "It's not surprising. Just shitty."

"So why does Meri still believe my father stole that book from her?"

"*Stepney* was based on stories he used to tell Meri as a kid. Cassie told me that when Meri got sick, the truth got all twisted up in her head, and she believed the stories belonged to only her. She became obsessed with it, with her own reality, and her addictions created a downward spiral."

Sara handed Phil the stack of *Cache Carter* pages. "And this is what you couldn't explain. What Mum could never tell me." Sara took a deep breath. "She finished my father's book, didn't she?"

Phil didn't move. Didn't even touch the pages.

"Phil?"

He set one hand slowly on the pages.

"How, Phil? How did she manage it after Meri stole these pages?"

He slowly exhaled. "It was you."

"Me?"

"Your parents had started typing up *Cache*—you had apparently taken that copy from your father's satchel before the burglary. They found it a week later in your sock drawer. You said it needed pictures."

"I remember that. My mother found it and started crying, and I didn't understand why."

"Jack begged Cassie to finish the book for him. She thought the idea was insane. Told him she was a nurse, not a writer. But he pleaded with her until she relented. He insisted she use only her name—not even Grayson. He wanted the book to have no connection to Meri. I think Jack was crazy enough to dream that *Cache Carter* could be a new start for her. He died a few months later."

Sara brushed some tears from her cheeks. She picked up the original *Cache Carter* pages and ran her fingers across the worn grooves of pen and ink in the paper.

"Cassie showed up in my office a full year after Meri did. She handed me a completed manuscript for a book called *Cache Carter*...with her name on it. She told me right from the start. 'It's half Jack's.'

"I agreed to publish the book under Cassie's name. Once *Cache Carter* made it to the bestseller list, Meri sued Cassandra with these stolen first hundred pages as proof that Cassie plagiarized *her*. It could have been a vicious court battle, with Meredith holding those pages as proof of plagiarism and Cassandra countersuing for Meri's theft of *Stepney*, but Cassandra's career was so new and promising that if the lawsuit went to trial it would have permanently damaged her reputation and her future—and I knew she had talent, more than she realized. Kind of like you, Grayson.

"Both parties had the power to bring the other down. So, we settled. I think your mother was angry enough at Meri that she was willing to fight it out—she didn't know the incredible career she had ahead of herself. But she found out Meri had a child, just a couple years old at the time. She accidentally met the dark-haired little toddler in an empty office waiting with her grandmother during the negotiations. Cass backed down. Gave her a million dollars and the rights to Jack's book for twenty-five years, including all profits from the book during that period. She couldn't envision any other way for Meri to support her child."

Cree's lower lip quivered. She chewed at it to keep control and focused her eyes on the window, away from Phil and Sara.

"Other terms came up. Meredith was bitter and demanded a clause of no contact between the two families, and both parties agreed to the twenty-five-year nondisclosure agreement."

"I'm sorry," said Cree, her face staring blankly ahead. "I'm sorry my mum caused so much pain."

Phil and Sara turned to Cree. He leaned forward and looked her in the eye. "You owe no one an apology for your mother. She had her own struggles. You hold no responsibility for that or for her choices. Do you understand that?"

A tiny tear slid down Cree's steel-like face, like some sort of anomaly she refused to acknowledge.

Sara reached for her arm. "Phil's right."

Cree stared past them, twisting a thick, silver bracelet on her wrist. She nodded.

Sara turned to Phil. "Cree needs to meet Nik."

"I know."

"What are you waiting for?"

"I'm not sure Nik will forgive me...but...Cree's right." His chin trembled. He covered his mouth, an effort to mask his emotions, and in that moment, Sara thought how alike Cree and Phil really were.

Sara reached for Phil's hand. He took her hand in both of his.

"Phil, Nik already knows...about the affair."

"What?"

"He told me once. He overheard a conversation years ago between you and your wife. He did feel betrayed. It was hard. But I think you have to tell him the truth. Nik would really want to know his sister." She looked over at Cree and met her eyes. "She's worth knowing."

Cree looked at Sara and then at Phil, his eyes weary. He nodded. "I'll talk to him."

❧

They stayed the rest of the evening at Cree's, talking late, looking at Cree's portfolio. They talked about her photography, her upcoming show, about *Ellery Dawson*, Anna-Kath, and Nik. Sara fell asleep after midnight on the couch, and Phil went to a hotel. Sara overslept the next morning and woke up hearing Phil and Cree talking over a late breakfast in the kitchen.

Sara opened her eyes, thinking how so much in her life had shifted in the last ten months, the last six months, the last six weeks, the past *two days*. She took a deep breath and knew it was time to go to work. Time to finish her book. It was no longer a ridiculous dying wish. She was meant to do it. She needed to do it.

Like her father and her mother—Sara was a writer.

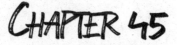

CHAPTER 45

It's like my whole world is coming undone, but
when I write, my pencil is a needle and thread,
and I'm stitching the scraps back together.

JULIA ALVAREZ

Phil drove Sara back to London that afternoon. She opened her laptop as Phil merged onto the M4 and read through where she had last written, stepping back into the world of *Ellery Dawson*. She and Phil had already talked last week about the end of the book, but now Sara had new ideas about where to take the conclusion and how to tackle the questions about Ellery's father.

Sara called Anna-Kath right before lunch and updated her on a long FaceTime call in which she met their cousin for the very first time. Ann planned to call Thea that afternoon with an update so she could generate a new PR plan.

As they got closer to Sara's hotel, Phil mentioned he had delayed his flight home.

"Why?"

"Jane wants to meet up tomorrow. She's in London at that publishing conference. Been texting me since last night. Says it's urgent."

"Did she say what it's about?"

"Take a wild guess."

Sara sighed. "She knows I'm out here—and she's freaking out about the book."

Phil chuckled. "She termed it a 'matter of the most exigent nature.' I told her I'd be back in London tonight. Look, Sara, I know all this has been a lot to process, but—"

"I know. I've got to work like hell."

Phil locked eyes with Sara and nodded. He pulled in front of Sara's hotel and waited for the valet.

She could tell he was worried. It had taken six months to get through the first half of the book, and now she had less than eight weeks to complete the last half. But she felt a new fire inside.

"Phil, I feel ready for this. I can do it." She took a deep breath. "I've rented a flat here, a few blocks away. I'm going to finish the book here. No distractions."

"You what?"

"I've already signed a lease. I want to stay here and write."

Phil looked at Sara, something softening in his eyes. Was it trust? Understanding? Jet lag? Or really excellent eye drops?

"Not a bad idea, Grayson."

She felt unaccustomed to his confidence in her.

"Let's go inside," he said, "and talk details before I drive back to my hotel tonight."

He handed his keys to the valet. They stepped out of the car, and Phil grabbed her bag from the back seat. "Does Nik know you're staying?"

"I texted him when I signed the lease. He's taking care of Gatsby."

Phil gave her a quick nod.

She reached for his arm. "Don't worry, Phil. I keep thinking about my mom, and if she could finish my dad's book, I sure as hell can finish hers."

The hotel lobby was lined with carved wood-paneling and hosted a cozy gathering space of deep blue sofas and velvet armchairs next to a cultured stone fireplace where a real honest-to-goodness fire crackled in the hearth. Hotel staff had just set out trays of warm scones and biscuits for afternoon tea service. Sara walked with Phil straight towards the tea and inhaled the fragrance of buttery shortbread and chocolate croissants. London was good.

Just then a well-dressed woman sitting across the lobby in a Queen Anne chair rose and glided purposefully towards Sara.

Her hair did not move.

Sara held an empty teacup and froze in place.

"Ms. Grayson. I'm thrilled to see you here. Phil—always a pleasure."

Phil scratched his stubbly chin. "I'm heading your way tonight, Jane. You didn't need to come out here."

Sara located her breath caught somewhere near the back of her spine—once she remembered she had one. She took a breath and shook Jane's hand. "Um, nice to see you, Jane."

Sara hadn't seen Jane in person since New York. She still felt small in her presence.

Jane always looked the same. *Crisp.* Like she just walked out of an Ann Taylor photo shoot in her tailored, white shirt, jacket, and pencil skirt.

Crisp words. Crisp brows. Crisp kitten heels.

"How did you know I was staying here?" asked Sara.

"Oh that. Well, we need to talk." She turned to a nearby employee carrying a hot water dispenser and a pitcher of cream. She eyed his nametag, "Mr. Grigsby, might we use that empty sitting room next to the restaurant?"

"That room needs to be reserved in advance, ma'am."

She waved him off. "I appreciate you making an exception. A short meeting. And of course some tea and coffee would be lovely. Thank you, Mr. Grigsby."

Sara watched in fascination as the man set down his items, pushed his glasses up, and said, "My pleasure."

They followed Mr. Grigsby into a small sitting room with Victorian floral couches and end tables with floor-length coverings. Small lamps with green shades lit the room in a soft light while the sounds of Bach played gently through a sound system.

Phil and Sara sat on a sofa while Jane sat across in a tall wing-back armchair, like she was the host of *Masterpiece Theater*. Jane sat upright, knees close together, ankles crossed.

Sara felt anxious, like she'd been called to the principal's office for poor behavior. What was this about, anyway? Was it a last-ditch effort to get Sara to quit? Was Asher Monroe ready to jump out from behind one of the heavy curtains?

Phil rubbed the back of his neck. "Jane, I told you I'd meet you at the conference tomorrow. I'm heading back there tonight."

"If you're worried about the book," said Sara, "I can assure you I will meet the deadline."

Jane clasped her hands in her lap. "What I need to say involves both of you and, as you know, time is of the essence."

Sara felt nauseous. She opened her purse to look for her Tums. Pixy Stix bags and wrappers exploded out. She quickly shoved them back in. Phil eyed Sara quizzically. She gave him a pained smile, her lips pressed tightly together.

A server brought tea and coffee on a tray and placed it on the table between them.

"Well," Jane said, "I was at home two nights ago reading manuscripts, when my former son-in-law shows up at my apartment with a rather large but handsome dog named Gatsby. It was way too late, mind you, but he asks to speak with me."

"Gatsby—what?" Sara squinted at Phil. He crossed a leg, resting his ankle on his knee, not appearing remotely surprised. She looked back at Jane in confusion.

Then Sara dropped her hands in her lap as pieces came together in her mind.

"Well, I'm sure you're aware that my daughter, Corinne, and Phil's son Nik were married some years ago, but I haven't talked to Nik in ages." She huffed. "I was actually more interested in the dog, but I invited Nik inside to talk anyway."

Sara's mouth hung open. She reached for Phil's arm. He looked at her nonplussed. "I thought you knew," he whispered.

She turned back to Jane, Sara nervously chewing her bottom lip with no idea where any of this was going. She pressed her hand to her mouth as she distinctly recalled a photo of a sweet toddler in Jane's office.

Nik's son.

Sara felt the room quiet in her mind as she tried to absorb this new information and still try to follow Jane.

"So, Nik introduces me to Gatsby, tells me he's your dog. He knows I have a soft spot for labs—poets can be annoyingly observant."

There was a moment when Sara thought she might be in the middle of a very odd dream. She did pick up a chocolate cupcake at a petrol station on the way back. Maybe there *was* something extra in it. It was a *really good* cupcake.

"So, we visit a bit, and I quite like him—the dog, not necessarily the other. Then Nik brings up your book, and he insists that I haven't read your best work. He hands me a manuscript of the first half, one I haven't seen before. I start scanning through the pages and immediately see the narration changes. I say, 'Those are impossible' and hand it back to Nik. He gives it back to me.

"'Read it tonight,' he says. 'I'll be by your office first thing in the morning.' 'Fine,' I say. 'But only if you bring the dog.'

"So, I read the manuscript. Not only do you shift to first person narration, but you shift to four different characters' perspectives in the book. It's not done, I tell myself. Oh, sure, it's fine for other books, but not for the *fin de serie*." She flicked both her wrists with the added French. "But I keep reading, and I put it down and think about how it's actually good—surprisingly, shockingly...*good*. Nik already tells me Phil read it and deemed it too risky. And I agree. It's best—most prudent—to play it safe with this one, and I plan to tell Nik that in the morning.

"But then I can't sleep. I keep thinking of how we used to take more risks in our business. Do you remember that, Phil? Smart risks, of course, but risks, nonetheless."

She paused and smoothed out her skirt. Even brushed some lint off even though there was no lint. Jane Harnois was immune to lint. Her eyes drifted past them for a moment, and her voice softened. "Remember how that was part of the thrill? To discover powerful writing and give it a home, a voice?" She looked directly at Phil.

She waited for him to return eye contact. "Isn't that why you left your big firm and started Iris?"

Phil looked away.

Then a strange thing happened. The tightness around Jane's eyes and lips softened, her shoulders relaxed. She sighed softly. And she smiled.

Phil's ankle still rested on his knee. He picked at his sensible, brown socks, avoiding Jane's eyes.

Sara had never seen Jane look so...sincere. And she wasn't sure how to respond.

Jane closed her eyes a moment. She leaned her head back against her chair and took a deep breath. "I was thinking about our grandson, Phil. Oh, he was a beautiful boy." She looked at her hands, now relaxed in her lap. She took another breath. "Liam would be eight, you know." Her eyes seemed to light up with both pain and sadness at his memory. "Do you remember how fearless he was?"

"All toddlers are fearless," Phil mumbled, eyes still on his socks.

"Not like Liam."

Phil finally looked up and met Jane's misty eyes. "I know."

Jane moved to the edge of her seat, her face hopeful. "Let's be a little more fearless." She reached in her leather tote bag and pulled out Sara's manuscript. She handed it to her and then turned to Phil. "This is exceptional writing. Let's give Sara the green light. Let's take a risk and let her write the book with the narration changes."

Sara clutched the manuscript to her chest, her heart racing, her mind daring to believe. This was the work that felt the most real to her, the most authentic. And she wanted to be more fearless too.

Phil's eyes were red. He wiped at them and sniffed a little. He studied his fingernails. He opened his mouth to speak, but then stopped. He was suddenly still and the room so quiet that Sara could hear only her breathing and her pulse thumping steadily in her brain.

Phil met Jane's gaze. "I think Liam would like that."

Sara looked back and forth between the two of them, waiting for one of them to call it off, say it was just a prank and have a good laugh at her expense. Or maybe she would suddenly wake up from a strange dream about Jane, Gatsby, and a really good cupcake.

"Sara, what are your thoughts on this?" asked Jane. "You have to be on board, of course."

Sara looked at her manuscript and back at Jane. "When my mom asked me to write this book, she wasn't asking me to play it safe." Sara's eyes were moist. She quickly wiped them. She looked at Phil and then at Jane. She straightened her back. "I'm all in."

"Well, then, that's settled." Jane smiled her usual tight-lipped smile, but it actually seemed warm this time instead of the usual cue to assume a tactical position. "Coffee anyone? Oh look, they brought sandwiches. Lovely place."

Sara still clung to her manuscript, feeling like the world had just opened. She shook her head in wonder.

Jane poured Sara a cup of tea. "Oh, and Gatsby just adores the Blue Buffalo Health Bars for dogs. I hope you don't mind I gave him some. All natural. Very healthy. I'll send you a link." She handed Sara her tea. "By the way, I think he quite likes you."

"Gatsby?"

"Nik."

She felt her face warm slightly and tried to look natural.

"Of course, he's always had excellent taste, like his father."

It sounded suspiciously like a compliment, but it was still hard to be sure with Jane. At this point it didn't really matter.

ॐ

Phil agreed to drive Jane back to their hotel in the West End. While Jane stopped in the restroom, they waited for her in the lobby.

Sara looked at Phil thoughtfully. "I can't believe Nik went to New York. When was the last time Nik actually *left* Maine?"

He nodded slowly. "It's been a long time."

Sara hugged her manuscript. She was still surprised at the turn of events and moved by what Nik did for her. Leaving Maine. Pitching her book to Jane. She couldn't recall the last time she felt more warmth in her heart.

And she suddenly missed Nik. No. It was more than that. She already knew she missed him. Now she *longed* for him.

Phil looked gently at her. "Your father would say he's 'besotted' with you."

She smiled. "I've always liked that word."

He turned away, his expression wistful. "So did Jack—and all these wonderfully British words that I could never get away with using the way he did. I actually liked him, you know. Your father. Despised him later. But I liked him. I suppose it's how most men feel about George Clooney."

Sara raised her eyebrows. "George Clooney?"

Phil shrugged. "Most men both like and despise George Clooney. Handsome, intelligent, always gets the girl—or the guy. But poor taste in coffee."

Sara laughed.

Jane emerged from the restroom, pushing the door open with her foot to avoid touching the handle. She shook Sara's hand firmly. Jane told Phil she'd take care of their bill with the concierge and then meet up at the valet desk.

Sara looked at Phil. He had flecks of blue in his gray eyes that she'd never noticed before.

&

Sara slept restlessly for a few hours and then woke up at 2:00 AM, 9:00 PM on the East Coast. She sat up and texted Nik.

Text on Saturday, October 19, 2:00 AM

Sara
I don't know what to say. Jane and
Phil signed off on the changes.
Thank you doesn't seem enough.

Her phone remained stubbornly silent for an hour before it buzzed back. Her heart jumped.

Nik

They signed off? It's a go?

> **Sara**
>
> Yes. I'm cleared for takeoff.

Nik

That's incredible. Congratulations.

> **Sara**
>
> I don't know how you pulled this off.

Nik

I didn't. You did.

> **Sara**
>
> You went to New York. You went to
> Jane. You pitched my work to her.

Nik

When you told me you didn't open
the box—that you walked right
up to the bank—and then walked
away and went to London—I
don't know. I kept thinking about
what you said to me before you
left. I wanted to do something.

> **Sara**
>
> Why didn't you ever tell me about
> your relationship with Jane?

Nik

Well, she and I never clicked
as lovers. She only wanted
to make love indoors.

Sara
That's not funny.

Okay a little bit.

Nik
Never really came up.

Sara
Come on. You avoided it.

You don't like to talk about that time.

Nik
It's hard. Still.

Sara
It's hard to admit this—I keep shoving the thought away, but here it is:

I need you.

Nik
I know

Sara
I know? Like who are you? Han Solo after Leia says I love you just before Jabba the Hut freeze-dries him? I'd rather not know you're a poet. It creates unrealistic expectations.

Nik
I accidentally hit the send button before I finished what I wanted to say.

Sara

Oh.

Nik

I know you need me, because I
feel it too. Deeply. And I'm worried
that what you said that morning
in the park could be right.

I need some time to figure some
things out about myself. And you
need to put everything you have
into this book. Everything.

Sara

Where does that leave us?

Nik

Let's wait and see.

Sara exhaled slowly. She feebly typed "Okay" back, misspelling it twice, and tapped "send" as a languid sadness crept into her chest. What else could she say? There was no snappy response to "Let's wait and see." It wasn't a terminal phrase. It wasn't an encouraging phrase. Just a waiting phrase. The hardest kind.

She stared at her phone and then set it on her nightstand. She got back in bed and pulled the duvet close up around her chin. What could she do with a longing she both wanted to feel and hold, and a longing she wished she didn't feel—at least not this deeply? She decided that longing could be the best part of loving someone and the worst part—a feeling that sparks energy and joy or summons the murkiest sort of sadness.

She dreamed of him that night. They sat in the long grass at the top of Baker Island, and he was tracing answers with his finger onto her open palm. Low tide had exposed the sand bar between Baker Island and Isleford. She leaned her head into Nik, finding that comfortable spot where she fit perfectly between his head and his shoulder. She straightened up as her parents appeared far across the bar, but a fog rolled in and she couldn't be sure. Then the mist began to evaporate, and she could see them there so clearly. They smiled like they had been there all along, just waiting for her to notice.

She woke up thinking of her mother and what she might have felt finishing her father's book. What kind of painful longing did she feel for him then? Did the writing make her feel closer to him? Did it make her miss him more? Sara imagined her mother tapping into all her mixed-up emotions, using up all that grief and loss and turning it into her book, her story.

Sara got out of bed that morning, determined to do the same.

CHAPTER 46

How can I explain to anyone that stories are like air to me,
I breathe them in and let them out over and over again.

JACQUELINE WOODSON

Sara moved into her furnished flat the next morning. It was a small one-bedroom on the seventh floor of the Westley Building, two blocks from her family's old place. There had to be good energy here. She put on a pair of her most serious writing clothes—yoga pants and her UVA sweatshirt. She slipped on her mother's socks and her dad's beanie. She moved a desk from the bedroom to the front room and placed it next to the main window. If she leaned in towards the glass, she could see her old flat just down the road.

She opened her computer. She breathed deeply and began to type. It was a slow first hour, but her mind and heart started kicking in with words to match her vision, and she found her rhythm and flow faster than she expected.

She settled into a writing routine that week, working at her computer in two four-hour stretches during the day. Evenings were for revisions and conferencing with Phil.

Jane provided one more surprise. She gave her Lucy back as a second editor. She and Phil were now reading everything she wrote each week, and then the three would conference together every weekend. Jane joined in on occasional video conferences, and Sara learned there was a reason Jane was at the top of her game. Years of experience made her a keen, insightful editor.

Thea had called off Gibbs Cartwright with the explanation that Meredith Lamb and Mary Grayson were the same person, a fact that immediately discredited his source at Thornton Books. Thea also promised him an exclusive story when the nondisclosure agreement expired. If any other questions from legitimate journalists arose, they would lean on the manuscripts Sara found at Cree's. Phil was shipping copies to Iris Books and David Allman.

Sara's work was exhausting but exhilarating. This creative process she started six months ago awakened aspects of Sara's soul she didn't know had slept, and she felt more alive than she had in years. She felt like she was seeing the world and herself through new eyes. For years she had blamed much of her lifeless existence on her unhappy marriage and then her divorce. She realized now that her loss of self was so much more than that: she understood now that the moment she stopped creating was the moment she stopped living. This realization stopped her cold in her tracks at Robin's Park one morning. Understanding spilled over her and left her breathless. She braced herself on a damp wooden bench, vowing to never stop creating, to never deny that part of herself ever again.

Four weeks after she arrived in London, Phil showed up at Sara's flat for an intensive editing visit with a surprise guest: Gatsby. Sara felt like she jumped and hopped around as much as Gatsby did, hugging him close to her, nestling her face in his soft fur, and getting practically licked to death with the joy of their reunion.

Over the last final weeks, the streets of her beloved London sparked forgotten memories—moments with her father, her mother, Anna-Kath.

There was still a street she avoided: the one that led to the cemetery. She wasn't quite ready to go there. Not yet.

There were still days she wrestled and struggled to get the story right and times she could feel a scene but grappled with words to convey what was so clear in her mind. Binti sent her writing quotes from famous authors, snapchat pep talks, and funny *Ellery Dawson* memes. Anna-Kath sent her links to local restaurant delivery services so she would keep eating "like a decent human being," and they made plans for Ann's family to join Sara for Christmas after the book was done so she could finally meet Cree.

ఇ

She wrote to the end of the book in four weeks, and then they spent the next two weeks in rewriting and revisions. Phil came to London again the week of the deadline, and on December 15th, they made the final edits. Sara made Phil take a picture of her as she hit the "send" button to Jane Harnois.

It was *done*. Finished. Complete.

"Can we print the book, Phil, the whole thing? I just want to hold it. I want to see every page printed up."

Phil smiled and nodded, but he wouldn't trust a copy shop to do it. He found an office supply store on Linslade and bought a brand-new printer and two reams of paper. After he set it up that night, the two of them sat on her sofa and shared a bottle of wine, leaning back with their feet up on the coffee table while they listened to the pages print and print and print. It was the most beautiful sound she'd ever heard, and she fell asleep on her couch, lulled to sleep by its rhythm. When she woke up in the morning, Phil had left, and there were two copies of her book bound in three-ring binders sitting on her kitchen counter. She picked one up and hugged it to her chest and rocked back and forth while she cried happy tears.

She knew what was next. She showered and changed and found *Silence in Stepney* in her carry-on bag. She opened it up and used a big, black marker to cross out Meredith's name and replaced it with Jack Grayson. She grabbed a tote bag and put *Stepney* inside with her own book. Now she just needed a copy of the first *Cache Carter*. She purchased one at a nearby bookstore. The cashier gave the book a firm pat and told Sara, "Did you know this was Cassandra Bond's very first? *Ellery's* still my favorite, but there's always something special about the first, don't you think?"

Sara smiled. "I couldn't agree more." She placed *Cache Carter* in her bag with the others and then took a cab to East London Cemetery.

It was a gray December day with scattered clusters of brown and orange leaves still hanging onto a few trees. The cab dropped her off at the west entrance. She felt tears welling up in her eyes the moment she stepped inside the gate. She found the coordinates the cemetery office had emailed her and slowly approached the black granite headstone until she stood before it:

John Charles Grayson III

Beloved husband of Cassandra
Loving father to Anna-Katherine and Sara Beth

Her throat tightened up, her chest ached, and oh, how she missed him! They laid him to rest twenty-five years ago, and somehow she would *never* be at rest with that. He was good and kind and believed in her.

Sara knelt at his grave, the grass icy and crunchy beneath her. She took a glove off and traced his name and all the words with her fingers. She pulled a worn, green blanket out of her bag and spread it on the grass next to his marker. She knelt again, her hands clasped in her lap, remembering when her family was all together. A warmth soon filled her heart, and a sense that no matter what happened, her family would always be her people, that there was an inextricable link binding them together—impossible to break.

She opened her bag and pulled out the books. She placed *Silence in Stepney* in front of her father's headstone first. Then she set *Cache Carter*, by Cassandra Bond, down beside it. Finally, she placed her own book, *Ellery Dawson: Resurrection*, next to the other two.

She looked at the three novels sitting there together. "I did it," she whispered. She opened the binder of her book just to see "Sara Grayson" written there on the title page—to remind herself that this moment was real. A cold breeze fanned the pages up, another gust turning them over, flapping the pages in the wind. She placed her fingers again on her father's name, cold against the smooth granite, and closed her eyes. "Thank you, Dad, for making writers out of all of us."

The December wind picked up again, turning colder. Light snowflakes began to swirl with bits of dry leaves and grass sweeping up from the ground. Sara gathered the books, the blanket, and stuffed them in her bag. She began walking the narrow pathway back to the west entrance when she saw a dark-haired man watching her, maybe fifty yards away. She ignored him at first. Then glanced over again. She stopped. She stared. She moved closer, and he walked closer to her, and then he was standing right in front of her. She dropped her bag, her arms suddenly weak at the sight of him. He wrapped his arms around her and pulled her close to him.

"Nik," she whispered, every ounce of her soaking in his presence, his smell, his hair, the way his broad chest felt pressed against her own.

He removed his gloves and wiped her tears, his fingers warm. Then he cupped her face between his two hands and kissed her lips. Her entire body clung to him, feeling his warm breath on her neck and his hands and arms squeezed tightly against her back.

"Phil told me you finished the book," he whispered, "and that you were coming here. I couldn't wait any longer." He pulled back from her and looked into her eyes. "I needed to see you. It was all I could do not to call or write the last eight weeks. I had to step back, let you do what I knew you could do."

Sara reached for his hands, interlocking her fingers in his. "I did it. It's done." She inhaled deeply and slowly exhaled, her breath smoky in the cold air.

"You did it."

She loved the way his smile reached his eyes before his lips. She leaned close into his chest, her arms now hanging limp with exhaustion, and he wrapped his arms around her again.

"I have a car," he said. "Let me drive you back."

Sara got in Nik's rental. There was a brown sack in the seat behind her. "What's in the bag?"

"You'll see."

Sara gave Nik directions to her flat and led him up to her place. He brought the grocery sack with him and set it on the counter in the kitchen while Gatsby barked and jumped and fell all over him.

Nik knelt beside him and scratched his neck. "Good to see you too, buddy."

He stood up and pulled Sara close and kissed her again while Gatsby still hopped around them.

He touched her face and smiled at her.

Nik stepped back in the kitchen and started opening up cupboards and drawers, looking for items he needed: bowls, knives, and pans.

She eyed him curiously. "What are you doing?"

He leaned towards her and placed a finger over her lips. "It's a surprise. Go sit down." He turned her toward the sitting room and gave her a gentle push forward. Then he went back to the kitchen. He pulled out ham, bell peppers, mushrooms, and onions and began chopping them up. Then he opened a carton of eggs and whipped up six of them until smooth.

This caught her attention. She stood up and walked to the counter, her heart swelling, her throat aching with happiness as she watched him work. After sautéing the ham and vegetables in a small separate pan, Nik poured the egg mixture in a large frying pan, letting it cook several minutes before adding the ham and vegetables and folding the omelet in half. He divided the large omelet in two and dished the two pieces onto plates. He poured them orange juice, and they sat down together at the little kitchen table.

Her eyes filled with tears. "How did you remember this?" Every breath filled her with warmth, and she felt a heightened sensitivity to his closeness—to everything he said or did.

He smoothed her hair back and ran his fingers down the side of her neck. "You said it was one of your favorite stories about your parents."

She nodded and wiped a tear away. She cut into her omelet and tasted her first bite. She closed her eyes, savoring the flavor. She exhaled slowly. "It's really good."

"I practiced."

"You practiced."

"Gordon Ramsey on the Food Network."

"Gordon Ramsey?"

"I needed to win the girl."

"You did that a long time ago."

And then Nik was kissing her lips, her cheeks, her nose, her forehead, her neck, his arms and hands reaching around her. They fell onto the too-small couch, their arms and legs clinging to each other. She reached up into his hair and drew him back to her lips, feeling the soft scratchiness of his beard against her face and mouth and feeling the sense of creating a new, inseverable bond.

৯

She woke up alone on the couch with a blanket over her. It was already getting dark outside. She sat up. Nik was at the table, working on his laptop.

"How long have I been asleep?"

"Three hours." He smiled at her, his fingers brushing against his cheek as he studied her.

She smoothed her hair back and wiped under her eyes, which had to be black with mascara. "My mom used to sleep for days after she finished a book. 'Like there was nothing left,' she told me. I get that now." She pulled her knees up to her chest and leaned her head against the back of the sofa, studying Nik, thinking how complete she felt having him there with her. "What are you doing?"

"It's December 16th. We need a Christmas tree. Just looking up some lots."

"A Christmas tree?"

"Anna-Kath is still coming with her family for Christmas, right?"

"Of course…" She rubbed her eyes again. "Rather behind on holiday sorts of things."

Nik started laughing. "Can you hear that in yourself?"

"What?"

He repeated her phrase with a London accent. "You're sounding like a Brit. I like it."

"Hmm. I hadn't realized—"

Nik punched a few more keys on his laptop. "Let's try the Christmas market at Spitalfields. We could find a tree tonight."

❦

Sara hadn't been out after dark in weeks. Hadn't seen all the lights, the wreaths on the lampposts, the long strands of white lights stretched like canopies across Hamish Street. She and Nik walked through the stalls of Christmas trees for sale, taking in the crisp, invigorating smell of pine, and picked one out for delivery tomorrow.

They wandered through a glorious variety of street food vendors and sampled sizzling duck-meat burgers dripping with cheese and onions and cranberry confit. As the night turned colder, they bought mulled cider that smelled like Cassandra's kitchen on Christmas Eve and sat on an outdoor table away from the crowds near a tall heat lamp.

There was so much she wanted to tell Nik and yet she was also simply basking in his presence. She loved sitting next to him, touching him, looking at him. They talked more about the past weeks, about her parents and finishing her mother's book.

"So, when will you open the safe deposit box?" asked Nik.

"Next year, like my mom asked. I'm trusting her on this."

"Think you can wait that long?"

"I left the key with Anna-Kath, so that helps."

"I have something for you," said Nik with a half-smile. He reached inside his coat pocket and slid a boarding pass over to her.

She picked it up and read the top. "It's your boarding pass to London." She looked at the dates. "You've been here for three days already?"

"I wanted to be here when you finished…and…I met my sister."

Sara reached for Nik's arms. "You met Cree? When? How did it go?"

His eyes were bright and hopeful. "It was a little awkward…and strange…and kind of amazing. She's definitely a lot like Phil." He paused and rubbed his hand across his beard. "But I have a sister. I keep telling that to myself over and over. It's a lot to take in." He looked down a moment. "I worry about my mom and how she'll feel about all this, but I like Cree. She knows nothing about Croatia, and I can't stand her smoking. But she's also an artist. That's something we can build on."

"I like her too."

Then Nik slid another paper to her, this one in a trifold. "It's my return itinerary."

She opened it up and read it. She looked at him, her eyes puzzled. "I don't understand." She checked it again. "The return date says May 3rd."

"I accepted a visiting professorship at University College London. Starts in January. I'm keeping my position at College of the Atlantic for now, but…" he exhaled slowly, "I thought a lot about what you said to me in the park that morning about avoiding risks. At first I thought it was incredibly unfair, but when you walked away from the safe deposit box and got on that plane to London, I suddenly knew you were right. I was still angry, but this time I was angry because I knew you were right. I had gotten a little stuck. A little too safe. A little too comfortable."

"But how did COA let you go? You've already got classes scheduled next semester."

"I offered them a visiting professor—someone they couldn't refuse."

"Who?"

"Phil. They loved the idea."

Sara's eyes widened. She gently pressed her hand against Nik's cheek. He covered her hand with his own and closed his eyes. Something in Nik's love was rewriting and revising pieces of herself. She felt renewal...a healing in her heart she didn't know was possible.

"I love Maine," he said. "It's where I want to live, but I'm not William Gilley on Baker Island. I love islands...but I don't want to be one."

He took her hand and brushed it against his lips, then held it close against his chest.

"Sara, the past eight weeks have reminded me how much I need you. I don't want to live without you in my life...I don't think I can live without you." He closed his eyes as he exhaled slowly. He paused. "Will you stay here with me?"

"What are you saying?"

"Just for the semester. And then we can make a home together back in the States. I'd choose Maine, but I choose you first. It can be Maryland. It can be Alaska. I don't know what the future holds for us, I just need to be wherever you are. Would you even—"

He never got the chance to finish. Sara leaned into Nik and kissed him slow and long and completely.

Words had arrived. Raw, awake, alive.

She opened the door.

THE END

ACKNOWLEDGMENTS

Deepest appreciation goes first to my husband, Mark Elliott, who read every page I ever wrote of Sara Grayson. His unfailing belief in me and his loving partnership has made this book a reality. He is brave enough to tell me when something isn't working and makes me feel heroic when I get it right. And he makes excellent omelets. I'm very grateful to my daughter Alexa Elliott. She was a fifteen-year-old with braces when I started this journey and is now a college junior, a grown woman and talented writer who has become one of my most trusted readers. Thank you to my sweet daughter Grace who loves so freely and helps me keep all of this book nonsense in perspective.

Thank you to my brilliant agent, Jennifer Weis. She has been an extraordinary champion for me and my book and I feel unbelievably blessed to have her represent me. Special thanks to her outstanding literary assistant, Sarah French, for becoming my unsung hero. She provided insightful editing, ideas, and moral support throughout this process.

Much gratitude to my team at Post Hill Press. Many thanks to my talented and dedicated managing editor Kate Monahan, who has kept so many plates spinning expertly in the air.

Thanks to my acquiring editor, Linda Marrow, for believing in my book and giving us a home at Post Hill. Thank you to Heather Breed Steadham for her insightful editing skills and encouragement. Special thanks to Cody Corcoran, Alex Sturgeon, and Rachel Hoge whose talent and skill helped guide this book to publication.

A million thanks to Melissa and Jason Howell who read Sara Grayson as an outline until she became a full, finished novel. Their insight and feedback has proven to be invaluable. On top of that, their love and encouragement in this process has been a tremendous gift.

Thank you to my amazing mother, Pennie Scadlock, who told me, "You have words, my dear," and encourages me to fight for them. She has nurtured and believed in me and my talents my entire life. No words are enough to thank this exceptional woman. Thank you to my loving dad, Charles Scadlock, who believes in me and keeps cheering me on.

One of life's gifts has been the blessing of extraordinary siblings. Thank you to my six sisters and two brothers who ensure that my life is never lonely: Jennifer Skoubye, Duaine Scadlock, Shelly Eddington, Sara Graff, Ryan Scadlock, Amanda Layton, Susie Scadlock, and Katie Gardiner.

I owe a debt of gratitude to my incredible Maryland writing group. I have often referred to these women as my Writing Midwives because they truly helped me labor and deliver the story of Sara Grayson. These women saw my manuscript from beginning to end—twice over two years, offering honest feedback, encouragement, friendship, and a lot of laughter. These exceptional writers—Jenny Greer, Jen Stover, and Ann Jex—helped transform my book, and I owe them my deepest gratitude. I also want to acknowledge Amelia Pinegar, Debbie Neuenschwander, and Mary Ellen Rose, who stepped into this group at various seasons to provide thoughtful feedback to my work as well. My profound thanks!

Thank you to my Writing Sisters! I met this phenomenal group of women at the New York Pitch Conference in September 2019 and I never could have imagined walking away with the friendship of such remarkable, talented, and diverse women. We cheer for each other on the good days and build each other back up on the hard days. I express my gratitude to these wonderful ladies for believing in me and my work: Alicia Blando, Melissa deSa, Robyn Fisher, Kate Jackson, Geneva Kachman, Pia Kealey, Delphine Ledesma, Angelina Madison, Laura Malin, Marti Mattia, Lisa Rayner, Victoria Sams, Grishma Shah, and Maria Skytta. Special thanks to Marti and Geneva for their gracious help in editing Nik's poetry. Much gratitude to our inspiring workshop leader, author Susan Breen.

Deepest gratitude to all my dear friends in Maryland and Utah. Our walks, our lunches, your listening, your encouragement have meant the world. You filled me with belief.

Special thanks to my Muses: Angie Anderson, Jenn Trinidad Batchelor, Julie Thomson, LeeAnn Loader, Michelle Jones, Mindy Steadman, Trina McGowan. Ours is the thirty-year sisterhood without the traveling pants—one of the extraordinary gifts of my life (you, not the pants-thing). I love you with my whole heart.

I never planned on or dreamed of becoming an author in my early life. For me, this path began in graduate school with a creative writing workshop that I took on a whim in 2001, taught by YA author Louise Plummer. That's where, at age twenty-eight, I made my first attempt at fiction writing. Louise was the first person to make me feel like becoming an author could even be a possibility for me. So Louise, wherever you are—I remember you. I thank you.

ABOUT THE AUTHOR

J oani Elliott believes in the magic of stories, a good cup of tea, and the power of living a creative life. She has taught writing at the University of Maryland and Brigham Young University. She lives with her husband and two daughters near Salt Lake City, Utah. For book club resources, virtual author chats, and more, visit joanielliott.com.